TRAP

About the Author

Martin Sketchley grew up in Staffordshire. Following a brief but passionate affair with music, he began writing behind a market stall in Burton upon Trent at the beginning of the 1990s, and sold his first short story to a small press magazine in 1994. Having worked in retail and then catalogue publishing, he is now a freelance writer and editor. He lives in Birmingham with his wife, Rosaleen, and their two children.

For more information, visit Martin's website:

www.msketchley.pwp.blueyonder.co.uk

THE AFFINITY TRAP

Martin Sketchley

SIMON &
SCHUSTER

London • New York • Sydney • Tokyo • Singapore • Toronto

First published in Great Britain by Simon & Schuster, 2004
A Viacom company

Copyright © Martin Sketchley, 2004

1 3 5 7 9 10 8 6 4 2

Simon & Schuster UK Ltd
Africa House
64–78 Kingsway
London WC2B 6AH

www.simonsays.co.uk

Simon & Schuster Australia
Sydney

A CIP catalogue record for this book is available from the British Library

ISBN 0-7432-5734-0

This book is a work of fiction. Names, characters, places and incidents are either
a product of the author's imagination or are used fictitiously. Any resemblance to
actual people living or dead, events or locales is entirely coincidental.

Typeset by SX Composing DTP, Rayleigh, Essex
Printed and bound in Great Britain by
Mackays of Chatham plc, Chatham, Kent

Acknowledgements

I'd like to say a huge thank you to:

John Jarrold, for making The Decision – I always knew it would be you.

John Parker of MBA Literary Agents, for immeasurable patience and wisdom.

Darren Nash and everyone else at Simon & Schuster, for being gentle with me.

Joshua Bilmes, for valuable input.

David Garnett, for ensuring that I went to more than one SF convention.

Stephen and Rita Copestake, for publishing that first short story.

Radiohead, for inspirational music.

Emma Gibbs, may she rest in peace, for setting me on a new course.

Tom Game, whom no one will know.

Mr Turner, English teacher at Rawlett High School.

And to Mom and Dad for all those things parents should be thanked for, but so rarely are.

Very special thanks to Christopher Priest, for help, advice and inspiration in equal measure – plus a good swift kick up the arse whenever I really needed one . . .

. . . and to Daniel and Orla, for showing me what life's really all about.

To Rosaleen, for love, support, and two beautiful children.

There are places I remember . . .

One

a satyr's berceuse

The cold air was sharp in Delgado's lungs as he walked up the slope, his hard, bony face passing through clouds of breath. The previous night's frost had turned footprints formed in the mud the day before to small, hard-ridged craters. He looked towards a tree to his left; coated in a thin layer of ice by freezing rain, its branches creaked like leather in the breeze.

As he continued to climb, a black and white spaniel scampered past him. The animal looked at Delgado and chewed on the moss-covered stick it had discovered in the depths of a hedge. Delgado considered calling the dog, but knew there was little point: it would not allow him to take the stick, and if he did somehow manage to get hold of it, the animal would refuse to fetch it once thrown. Maybe it was time for a change. A retriever, perhaps. Or a collie. Something less independent, at any rate. He would check the options list next time.

Delgado reached the top of the slope and paused, looking across the fields of frosted grass in the valley before him. The sky was filled with grim cloud, fat plumes and extrusions at different altitudes. A band of early morning sunlight penetrating a cleft in the cloud to the east gave some of the lowest layers a brilliant golden luminescence, while that at higher altitudes remained dark and foreboding, colours ranging from ash to slate. On a hill in the distance a church spire and a water tower were prominent geometric shapes that contrasted starkly with the chaos of the pregnant sky.

Alexander Delgado enjoyed such solitude, experiencing a time even he was too young to remember, when limitless open space and fresh air could be enjoyed by all; now, despite the scale of the gigantic habitat towers that spanned the North American and European continents, within which the the majority of Earth's population enjoyed a pseudo-Utopian existence, the sense of genuine freedom gained from standing alone on a windswept plain, or feeling a desert's heat, were enjoyed by few. More than that, for Delgado such environments allowed him to escape from the difficulties of his life, however briefly.

But standing on the ridge also awakened ingrained combat instincts. He felt a strong urge to seek cover from the non-existent sniper, coupled with dizziness and disorientation as remnants of long-defunct nobics – the nano-organic boost in cerebrovascular capacity he had so often received for operational purposes – responded to his reaction and sought synaptic bridges no longer present.

The abrupt sense of displacement passed after a few moments, but unsettled him nonetheless. In a hostile environment nobics could be invaluable, enhancing physical capabilities, increasing perception, enabling a certain level of telepathic ability and providing many other useful functions, but they could never be completely removed from the human body, and the residue made it impossible to forget why they had been put there in the first place.

Not that Delgado would want to forget.

He had been with Stealth when he had received his first batch of nobics, his career at its peak; he was respected, valued. It was a time that preceded General Smythe's downfall in the bloody coup that had led to the rise of General William Myson, powered by the huge wealth acquired by his family through selling technology to developing worlds. That

Myson's great grandfather had funded the building of the first habitat tower – *Salvation* – in the Nevada Desert was hardly a handicap: the incredible edifice represented an affirmation of human achievement, and offered a chance to escape the pollution, social decay and violence faced outside; those who questioned whether this was possible were ignored by a global population dazzled by the promise of apparent nirvana.

After that, investment in research, exploration and trade had given way to whatever increased Myson's personal wealth. And as this increased so did his power, with his position at the head of the military enabling him to manipulate political players through bribery and graft. Within a few years Earth's unofficial role as interplanetary arbitrator had shifted to that of galactic bully and thief.

It was a change adopted eagerly by those who were greedy, or hungry for power. Their motives were understandable: Myson rewarded success well, and encouraged those within Structure's increasingly complex bureaucracy to take advantage of any potentially lucrative opportunity. But he was also merciless with those who betrayed him, and even those who demonstrated passive resistance were sidelined, ridiculed or both.

As a result of his own quiet disapproval, Delgado had endured difficult times, assignments for which he would previously have been the obvious choice instead given to younger officers who toed the Myson line. He eventually found himself bored, ignored, spending most of his time on leave, taking courses to learn skills he would never need, or escaping, alone, into surroundings such as this.

So much for rewarding loyalty.

He became aware of the spaniel approaching to his right, but pretended not to notice. The dog moved nearer, becoming increasingly daring. When it seemed close enough, Delgado lunged for the stick – but the animal was too quick and scampered away, joyful in its achievement. Delgado sighed heavily: even a small dog could outwit him these days, it seemed.

He stood upright again and looked back towards the settlement in the distance. He frowned and shielded his eyes with his right hand, as if adopting some lax salute: a dark cigar-shaped object was travelling at high speed from east to west just below the lowest cloud, a thin line of vapour trailing behind it. When the dark object was directly in front of him it stopped abruptly. After a momentary pause it began to increase in size, elongating across the sky. The ice-coated branches stopped creaking as the breeze suddenly ceased; Delgado's breath no longer condensed in front of his face, despite the cold. The spaniel was frozen, erect and alert, one paw off the ground, stick hanging in mid-air between its upper and lower jaws, its tail flickering like a faulty neon sign.

Delgado muttered profanities. He had specifically stated that under no circumstances was he to be disturbed. Lost leisure time would not be credited back to him, he knew that much.

The dark shape expanded until eventually he was standing in a black void – fields, frost, dog all gone. There was a slight pressure in his ears, as if a vacuum had momentarily existed, then Delgado experienced a sudden falling sensation as a new manifestation formed.

He found himself standing a few metres away from a reception desk. There was a smell of disinfectant. The ambient temperature was not high, but it was considerably warmer than his previous environment; his heavy coat had been replaced with a tunic and trousers. Feeling heat on the back of his stubbled head, Delgado looked upward, seeking its source. Broad bands of sunlight cut through the glass-panelled ceiling high above to form oblique patches of light on the marble floor beneath his feet.

Looking to his left he saw people walking across a spacious atrium, the roof above them supported by fluted stone columns. The people themselves were distant, indistinct, but their voices were bright and clear. The sound of their footfalls on the hard floor was like muted, unenthusiastic applause.

Delgado looked back to the reception desk. Behind it sat a woman whose shining black hair was set in tight coils; she was looking down at something Delgado was unable to see. He walked forward and, resting his elbows on the desk, looked down; she was studying an advertisement playing in a magazine of a girl applying eye make-up in a colourful, repetitive loop.

The woman looked up. She was young – only twenty-five or thirty – with skin as pale as milk. Her irises were set with brilliant glowing studs; colourful lipwires decorated the edges of her mouth like tiny glowing spines. Delgado could smell the bubble gum she chewed quite distinctly.

The lipwires sparked bright green as the woman cocked her head to one side and smiled. 'Hello, sir,' she said in a warm, sensual voice that didn't suit her. 'My name's Cindy. I'm sorry your escapist experience had to be interrupted, but you've received an urgent message.' She blew a bubble that popped to form a pink membrane across her chin; she pulled it back into her mouth with a swift lick. 'Haven't you got lovely blue eyes,' she said.

Delgado was unable to decide whether Cindy was real or not, whether returning her flirtation was worth the effort. 'I asked not to be disturbed,' he said. It seemed important to mention this, even though Cindy's manner and appearance had largely diffused his anger. Besides, no-one was interested in anything he had to say these days.

Cindy adopted an expression that was simultaneously apologetic and sympathetic. 'I really *do* apologise, sir,' she said, 'but I'm afraid your privacy request was overridden.'

Yeah, that'd be about right. 'So who's the message from?'

She glanced at a small screen. 'A Commander Osephius, interfacing via PPD frontdesk.'

'Oh, great,' mumbled Delgado, looking towards the atrium. 'Public Protection Department on my back. Hassle from Myson's fucking henchmen – that's all I need.'

'I'm sorry, sir? I didn't quite catch that.' Cindy's lipwires shimmered red; a slender finger coiled a ringlet of hair.

Delgado stood more upright: this could be being recorded, and there were those who wouldn't hesitate to use anything they could get hold of to discredit him further. 'I said that's wonderful, thank you so much.' He smiled broadly; she didn't get it.

'Are you ready to connect then, sir?' Her smile shifted to yellow as she batted long eyelashes.

'No, not really.'

'Very good, sir. Transferring you now.' Cindy's eyes turned to vivid turquoise, her lips to shining copper. Again Delgado felt nausea and vertigo as she, her desk and the atrium all vanished.

He was standing outside the door to the suite occupied by Earth's Commander Supreme, General William Myson. A Hostility Class cyborg stood either side of the door, towering over him. They stared stolidly ahead, mute sentinels skinned in graphite-grey atomex armour, bristling with advanced weaponry.

A half dozen or so vee-cams flitted around the corridor, continuously recording the lack of activity and assessing potential threats that would not arise within the sim; the faint sound of their tiny lift fans was like the buzz of insects' wings. Occasionally one would fly close to Delgado, unfurl a long black proboscis from its snout and drag its tip across an area of exposed skin to check his DNA against the sample in the biocomputer. Each time the vee-cams would buzz quickly away, only to return to repeat the process a few moments later as the details of the manifestation cycled.

'Delgado.'

Delgado turned. Osephius' manifestation had appeared

behind him. He was as tall as Delgado but with a youthful slimness the older man's regular InterCell makeovers were unable to maintain. His eyes were narrow, his nose long and sharp, his teeth uneven and discoloured.

'Osephius,' replied Delgado frostily. 'It's been a long time.'

Osephius didn't smile. 'I guess one of us has been lucky.'

Delgado let that ride. 'Why am I here?'

'Your services are required.'

Delgado adopted a look of surprise. 'What – an aging has-been like me? You sure you've got this right?'

Osephius sighed heavily and looked down. 'You're a sad case, Delgado. There was once a time when I wanted to *be* you – can you believe that? When you were in Stealth – one of the elite. But then, I was just a boy. Easily impressed.' Osephius shook his head. 'Not any more,' he said with a sneer.

Delgado focused on the hovering vee-cams. 'Just tell me what this is all about, OK?' he said quietly. 'This is using paid-for leisure time.'

Osephius chuckled. 'Yeah, it's kind of how I knew where to find you. I've heard you spend more time in manifestations than in the real world these days. Certainly more time than you ever spent in briefings. What's the matter? Can't face the truth?'

Delgado fixed Osephius with a hard gaze. 'If this is some sort of joke, then—'

Osephius held up a hand. 'All right, calm down. Myson's got a mission. And he wants you to do it.' Delgado uncon-sciously stood a little more upright. 'He says he needs someone with experience and skill. Youth is apparently less important.'

Delgado shrugged. 'So what's the job? Save the world and get the girl?'

Osephius blinked. 'You're familiar with the situation with the Sinz and Seriatt, right?' he continued.

'Not really. I don't mix in the same circles as you, Osephius. Not these days. They tell me I'm too old, spend too much time in manifestations.'

Osephius snorted but didn't smile. 'Yeah. OK. Well, basically we've managed to persuade some influential Seriatts that it would be wise for them to form a link with Earth, to ease the growing tensions. You're aware of those, I hope?' Delgado pulled a face. 'Well, that's something anyway. As it's got to be a strong political link, it's felt that the best way to do this would be for Myson to father a child by the *conosq dis fer'n'at*, the assigned bearer to the Seriattic Royal Household. The *conosq*'s name is Vourniass Lycern.'

Osephius paused, and looked at Delgado like a doctor trying to decide whether a patient is capable of caring for himself.

'So,' he continued eventually, 'Myson went to Seriatt, did what he had to do, and returned to Earth with an assurance that Lycern would follow as soon as it was safe – child well on the way and all that. Lycern, however, seems to have decided that she doesn't share her counterparts' enthusiasm for the idea, and has absconded. Now diplomacy's failing, and the Seriatts are becoming increasingly fucked off. So's Myson. It's all reaching critical mass.'

'There's a chance of war?'

Osephius wrinkled his nose. 'Maybe. Who knows?'

'I knew things were tense, but—'

'Always have been, always will be. But if something's not done to sort this mess out soon, something big could kick off.'

'So Myson wants me to fetch the Seriatt, right?'

Osephius seemed to brighten. 'By Christ, Delgado, I think there might be hope for you yet!'

Delgado's mind was already racing. 'Where's the *conosq* now?'

'Enlightenment tracked her ship to Veshc, to the Affinity Group. Our understanding is that the Seriatts remain unaware of her location – so far. But we suspect that those Seriatts who were initially keen on all this are having second thoughts. Myson wants you to go and get her so things can be firmed up at this end before they discover her whereabouts and pull her

– and the deal – themselves. Time's a factor now. Think you can do it?'

'Of course I can do it.'

Osephius nodded slowly and looked Delgado up and down. 'I voiced concerns when your name was proposed, Delgado, I'll tell you that much. I'm not sure you can hack it any more. But for some reason Myson liked the idea of using you. Me? I still reckon he needs someone younger.'

'I do have some experience of Seriatts, Osephius. Well, *mourst* at least. From the Buhatt Rebellion.'

'Ah, yes, of course. That was before I was born.' Osephius smiled thinly for a moment. 'You're right, that may be it,' he said with a shrug, glancing absently around him, 'but I'm more inclined to think it's because you're expendable. Not everyone with your level of experience is tied up or too far away to do this. There are those who would jump at the chance, as well.' He looked directly at Delgado again. 'Still, I guess it's Myson's choice. He's waiting to see you now.' Osephius indicated the door. 'You ready?'

Delgado stood erect and brushed invisible specks of something from the front of his tunic. 'I'm always ready.'

Osephius laughed again, and shook his head as he approached the retscan panel next to the door. He stated his name clearly. There was a click and a faint grinding sound, and both men stood to attention as the thick door began to slide slowly open.

The room beyond contained silhouettes and ghosts. Vortices danced from huge fans in the ceiling, coiling away to shadowy corners. Dark pillars of thinly-veined marble dissected the room into wide portions. At the far end was a huge, domed window overlooking the brittle skyline of the decaying city – a stark contrast to the protective sheer black sides of the towering habitats.

Bright light flooded through the window, turning the scene

within the room to monochrome. Bleached by the brilliance, a group of nymphs were playing a game of some kind in the window. They were always naked, always prepared, their bodies genetically engineered by the finest biotechs to meet Myson's own perverse specifications, their appearance sustained by the latest nanotech evolutions. Bony, skeletal creatures wrapped in almost transparent slithers of alabastrine flesh, they were like pre-pubescent children, burgeoning sexuality and innocent purity combined. Yet despite the truth and depravity of their existences, their huge absorbing eyes were full of love for the universe, and all it contained.

Beyond the window, on a platform extending from the side of the chamber, sat an expensive luxury flier. More cyborgs stood motionless around the sides of the room, partially obscured by the shadows cast by the pillars.

And at the centre of the room, a broad silhouette, sat General William Myson.

The door closed behind Delgado and Osephius as they approached. When they were a few metres from Myson, both men dropped to their right knee and bowed.

'Sire,' they said in unison.

'Come. Stand before me.' Myson hissed the words, as if he could manage nothing more than the exhalation of air.

They stood. Delgado hoped his shock at Myson's appearance was not obvious. The Commander Supreme's bulbous eyes were bloodshot, his skin pallid; he was sweating profusely and there was a certain vacancy to his expression, as if his eyes were unfocused. Delgado could just make out the dark, flea-like specks of robots swarming all over his body, cleaning him, unblocking pores, fighting the yeast infections that were so rife within his sweaty folds. There was something else about him, too. Delgado struggled to define it clearly, but it seemed related to grief.

'Thank you for coming, Commander Delgado,' said Myson slowly. Delgado blinked. Myson dabbed at his moist upper lip with a handkerchief; it seemed a considerable effort. 'We have a slight problem,' the General continued. He paused, his eyes watering as he coughed again in a series of wheezing gasps. He looked at Delgado and Osephius for the first time, glancing between the two men. 'I trust Commander Osephius has explained the situation to you?'

'He has, sire.'

'I have also prepared an infocram file to provide Commander Delgado with more in-depth briefing data, sire,' Osephius interjected. 'He will have time to review this before he leaves.'

'Excellent, excellent. So, Delgado – can you do what I require? Can you bring this cursed Seriatt to me?' His skin seemed to redden as he spoke.

'Of course, sire.' For some reason Delgado felt a compulsion to look at Osephius, but resisted.

'Good, good.' Myson began coughing again. He raised an index finger in anticipation of his recovery. 'It is imperative that she is not harmed in any way, Delgado,' he croaked eventually. 'Do you understand me?'

'I do, sire. I hope to prove myself still worthy of being in your charge.' He bowed slightly, unsure why he was making such a statement: if he had heard such obsequiousness from anyone else he would have spat in disgust.

'Wonderful. I do appreciate that you have found the changes Planetary Guidance has seen since the departure of General Smythe difficult to bear, but perhaps this presents you with an opportunity to begin afresh.' Myson paused as if waiting for a response; none was forthcoming. 'Well, then. Go now.' He waved a dismissive hand. 'Too much time has already been wasted. A vessel has been arranged for your use, I believe. A shuttle?' He looked at Osephius, who nodded.

'It is less likely to attract attention, sire,' the Commander explained. 'I have arranged for a competent pilot to drop Delgado's craft from a larger vessel in high Veshc orbit, then return to pick him up when his objective has been achieved.'

'Very well. By the way, Osephius, what is the situation with the imps being produced for Dassilos? Our, shall we say, *investment* is performing badly.'

'My contact in Inventory informs me that the three squads you have specified will be ready by the agreed time, sire.'

'Excellent, excellent.' Myson nodded slowly and returned his gaze to Delgado, who felt that more would have been said, had he not been present. 'Delgado,' said Myson eventually, 'gather whatever effects you need and report to landing platform fourteen-west. Before you leave, Commander Osephius will ensure that you are imbued with the latest nobic evolution. I understand it remains experimental and occasionally temperamental, but its abilities may prove valuable. Go now. I am relying on you. Indeed, Earth is relying on you, Delgado.'

'Yes, sire.' As Delgado saluted crisply and turned to leave he caught a glimpse of Osephius' face; the younger man's expression was slightly unsettling.

The audience with Myson over, Delgado was dropped unceremoniously from the sim back into his quarters. The room was quiet, much cooler and darker than when he had entered the manifestation. The displacement chair supporting his arms and legs was now cold and unresponsive, no more than the sum of its components: it seemed his leisure time had either expired or simply been terminated.

He stood, tore the visuals visor from his face and walked across to the phone. He passed his right index finger through one of the holographic icons to update the display. Unusually, he had a message: although blank, it carried the infocram file from Osephius.

Mostly sourced from Enlightenment archives, the index indicated that the cram covered the basics of Seriattic culture, physiology, some recent history and miscellaneous other information. There were chapters dedicated to the three Seriattic sexes – *conosq, vilume* and *mourst* – but apparently an image of Lycern was not available. Typical.

Delgado looked at the details and curled his lip: a cram – particularly a hastily prepared one – was just the kind of bullshit that would fuck with the nobics when they were loaded. Osephius knew that. And none of the information was less than a decade old. Info*crap* would be a more accurate description.

Delgado sighed, walked across to the window and slouched against the frame; outside, gusts of wind blew drops of rain that left greasy smears on the glass and swirled layers of grim, polluted cloud. It was chaotic, corrupt, nothing like the natural tranquillity of the winter landscape in which he had chosen to take his virtual walk. The vast, glossy black exteriors of *Soliloquy* and *Zeitgeist* habitats, and the curving transport tracks linking them, made brief appearances as gaps appeared in the cloud; but they existed only momentarily before being smothered again.

He glanced down towards the ground so far below, but the ruins of the city, now populated only by criminals expelled from the habitats or the descendants of those who, for whatever reason, were not fortunate enough to get inside at all, were completely obscured from view. He looked up again and refocused on the face reflected in the window; it bore a resemblance to someone he had once known, but with whom he had not made contact for many years. He was no longer certain he knew that person.

What he did know was that Osephius hadn't told him the whole story. Maybe he was unaware of what Delgado already knew but it was rumoured among the military's higher ranks that as well as the dated hardware units and aging war vessels officially recorded, Myson was also selling advanced nobic technologies and research data to the Sinz for personal gain. Sinz ships slipped through the M-4 wormhole using whatever magic it was that enabled them to do so, then, deal done, they went back to wherever it was they came from.

The possibility that the additional technology could at some point compromise Earth's security did not seem to concern Myson: his personal coffers were swollen by the additional trade. Inventory achieved its targets and official profits as reported to the auditors were great. Everyone was happy.

But the wormhole was only a few light days from Seriatt, and Structure activity so nearby would be making them nervous. Reports from Enlightenment that the Seriatts were preparing to initiate stop-and-search incursions on any vessel entering a yet-to-be-defined exclusion zone around the wormhole now made sense. If tensions escalated into interplanetary conflict, billions could die, the fighting almost certain to spill over into neighbouring systems. This *conosq* – Lycern – was key to Myson's plans. Where Dassilos fitted in he had no idea.

All in all, it stank. It stank like Osephius' fucking breath.

Delgado stood upright again. So, Myson thought they could start afresh, did he? Well, Alexander Delgado had always been one to rise to a challenge. Maybe he could give the Commander Supreme more than he expected, even more than the glittering prize he so desperately sought – show his younger counterparts a thing or two. Maybe he could return his own name to the status of notoriety it had once held. And given the right circumstances and a little luck, maybe he could even bring about a level of change that had, until now, seemed impossible.

Delgado turned abruptly and walked over to the phone. He activated another of the icons. 'Hello? Yes. This is Commander Delgado. I'd like a courier to take me to landing platform fourteen-west. Right away.'

As he disconnected he considered that he might even download a copy of Osephius' infocram to the nobics when they were installed. Just in case.

Two

courting the maenad

The engines failed just after the shuttle entered the atmosphere, their bassy offbeat pulse replaced by the cool sound of rushing air. Delgado cursed Osephius as he opened diagnostic visuals. The information hung in his brain, an opaque sheet rippling gently. The results of the analysis were puzzling. There was no overspill, no FTM waste, nothing; it was as if the turbines had not functioned properly at all. His fierce blue eyes raged. He thought the diagnostics to secondary-peripheral and opened the main core page.

Warning and general status pages overlapped, updated, closed. The nobics made decisions on information priority, then optimised the map overlay in a stream of fluttering colour and shape until only the most essential sheets remained. The entire sequence was processed almost too quickly, and some promising pages were gone before he had time to collate their potential.

Delgado absorbed and compared as a succession of related secondary-peripheral overlays strobed across one another. Raw information surged into him, but it was of little use. He linked directly with the core subsystems, expecting this to make more options available, but no combination of routing sequences or override protocols would bring the power units back on line. In a final effort, Delgado allowed his nobic stream to connect with the shuttle's core: it risked a surge, but

15

he calculated that direct interface between mutually empathetic systems might prove more successful than the clumsy probings of a frustrated human. Besides, he always enjoyed a gamble.

Data packets exploded in his head as the shuttle's core opened its heart to the nobics within him, releasing a prickling rash of new information. Analysis suggested that the turbines had simply died; the core could offer no explanation why and was unable to access information relating to the systems affected as they were isolated from the primary interface. All it could reveal with certainty was that a catastrophic failure of Broughton-Shelley ether displacement units one thru four had occurred. It apologised wholeheartedly for the lack of useful information, and was sorry it could do nothing more to help.

Delgado swore: it seemed that he was aboard a suicidal dinosaur and would just have to deal with it. The wisdom of using an old craft now looked singularly questionable. It was less likely to attract attention, true, but for some reason Delgado had assumed that he was to use a new craft made to look like an old one and given a new universal ID code, not a genuinely old vessel. So much for assumptions.

As it was, instead of a ship whose performance gave him confidence, he was aboard a vessel with technologically dated processes, and a management system that was little use at the best of times. It was not even designed for humans, but the slight Courlow, and with the Courlow an average of one point five metres tall and Delgado a good two metres give or take a centimetre, his tall frame was compressed uncomfortably into the small cockpit. The lower edge of the panel immediately in front of him pressed hard against his shins; his head smashed against the panel above when the craft hit turbulence; his elbows dug into his ribs due to the narrowness of the seat and the proximity of the hull to the left and the central console to the right. Delgado looked forward to discussing the situation with Osephius upon his return to Earth.

He was unable to spend long considering his misfortune, however; for it soon became clear that the data management software was also corrupt. An increasing number of inactive or updated visuals clusters remained in view long after they should have faded, obscuring necessary information, blocking routes to other layers. With his visuals map increasingly chaotic, control-cycling eventually became impossible. He tore the shuttle's integrated visuals strip from his face and tried to maintain a remote link directly through the nobics, but information transfer was erratic and slow. After a few seconds he gave up, disabled the AI core, and went to manual, cold-piloting the vessel through the seat of his pants. His only artificial aid was the scant information his own nobics could feed him, and he wasn't sure he could rely on those.

The shuttle seemed determined to drop its nose and increase the speed of his entry into oblivion with every passing moment. As the atmosphere thickened and the curvature of the planet decreased, he estimated that although the craft was moving at high speed, he might just survive if he could generate some drag and slow the vehicle down a little. The lights of the Affinity installation were visible past the tip of the huge delta wing to his right, the forest where the target was reportedly located a rough texture between the structure and the coast. If he was really careful he just might be able to make a relatively soft landing, repair the craft, complete his primary mission objectives and make the rendezvous with Beech in the slipspacer that had dropped him. It was a long shot, but he had learned long ago that positive thinking was important in times of adversity. Besides, what else was he going to do?

He extended flaps and landing skids, then dared a cautious turn.

He winced as the right wing became absurdly heavy and the shuttle banked far more than he had intended. The increased level of drag slowed the craft dramatically, and it lost so much altitude in a few brief moments that the horizon rose almost level with his line of sight. A multitude of visuals flashed through his brain as the vessel slipped sideways through the air. His seat seemed to rattle in its mountings. He heard a distant bang somewhere behind him.

Despite his low speed he managed to stabilise the craft, but distance was suddenly much more difficult to judge. With the shuttle's antiquated core interface making control of the vehicle almost impossible, he knew his flying time was limited. Turbulence buffeted the craft, and it dropped suddenly; Delgado swore aloud as the top of his head hit the panel above him. He made a mental note: *next time bring crash helmet*.

Through the viewport immediately to his left he saw the forest speeding beneath him. The area immediately below the craft was bathed in orange light from its glowing underside, a shimmering swathe of flaming trees; he was too low, moving too fast. With automated and fly-by-wire systems all but useless, it took all his effort to keep the craft nose-high. An alarm began to shriek; he silenced it deftly. But the huge mental effort required to plough through the mass of data in his visuals maps was largely wasted, and a few moments later he heard a faint rushing sound as the vessel began to brush treetops. The nose dipped sharply. There were a few seconds of raging noise and vibration. Then all was silent.

The pale moonlight cast long shadows. Delgado leaned against a large boulder and dabbed absent-mindedly at his bleeding nose. He contemplated the wreckage, then looked back along the line of broken trees through which the shuttle had ploughed. Several were still on fire; the rest smouldered, an angry, throbbing wound in the forest. It had been a short but eventful trip. One he would remember for a long time to come, if given the opportunity.

He looked at the shuttle again. The craft lay with its back virtually broken, nose half buried in the ground, tail in the air. It was like a creature on heat, waiting to be serviced. The vessel was obviously irreparable: even if the engines could somehow be coaxed into life, it was structurally unsound. This made the success of his mission uncertain to say the least. Failure of almost any system other than the engines would have enabled him to abort and return later, or make a softer landing and consider other options. But luck of that nature was not for Alexander Delgado. Hadn't been for as long as he could remember.

Delgado closed his eyes and allowed his thoughtstream to flow freely, reassessing the mission directive and some of the briefing information in the nobics. The basic objectives were simple enough: find the Seriattic *conosq* named Vourniass Lycern and get her back to Myson with all speed. And, despite his unfortunate circumstances, this remained achievable. OK, so it might be a challenge, but he had to prove Osephius wrong. Some things were a matter of pride. So, that was it: he would try to complete his mission objectives regardless. In other circumstances, he might have found the irony of the whole situation darkly amusing.

He had been attempting to land the shuttle within three kilometres of the Affinity installation, so he knew he was already close to the target. However, while getting to the Seriatt was one thing, getting her off Veshc and to the rendezvous without the shuttle was quite another. Beech would not make any attempt to contact him because her orders were to wait on the far side of the Doghin system to avoid possible confrontation with the Affinity Group, the Sinz, the Seriatts themselves, or – given that Delgado was involved – all three at once. And with the shuttle powerless Delgado could not use its systems to contact her. If it had been any other fucking system . . . but no. She would simply wait for the allotted period, then depart assuming him dead, ably managing to contain her grief for the duration of the journey, no doubt.

Delgado realised that his nose had stopped bleeding. He

blew clots from his nostrils that made dark spots on the ground and looked at the wreckage of the shuttle for a moment longer. At the back of his mind he harboured a suspicion that his situation was not entirely accidental. Perhaps the whole mission was a sham. Or perhaps he was just paranoid. He wasn't sure. It didn't matter. He spat a glob of blood from his mouth and thought of Osephius, Myson and all their kind. Fuck them. Fuck the lot of them. He'd show them what he was capable of.

Delgado stood, checked his bearings, refreshed the geographic and Affinity Group data, then merged silently with the trees. If anyone had seen the shuttle come down, his time would be short indeed.

The trunks creaked gently as the trees flexed in the wind. They were tall and slender but quite closely packed, devoid of foliage until the very top, where thin circular leaves around a metre in diameter spread like organic parasols, filtering the early morning light. Large black birds circled just above the canopy crying loudly to each other; it was as if they predicted Delgado's imminent demise among the bracken and the dead wood and were arguing about which of them was entitled to first sitting at his toothsome carcass.

He headed west to climb the hill that lay in that direction: if his calculations were correct it would provide a natural vantage point from which to meet the target. What he would do then he remained unsure: with the original smash-and-grab option no longer viable, finding and positively identifying the Seriatt was his primary objective for now. He would then have to play things by ear.

When he reached the top of the hill the ground dropped steeply away, the canopy of leaves spreading before him like a rich green sea. The installation emerged from it like a sinister island, a dark haven for the mysterious religious cult known as the Affinity Group. Delgado pulled the enhanced visuals strip from one of his tunic pockets and flattened it across his eyes; his nobics immediately linked into the strip's core and flicked rapidly through display modes, activating stat visuals and passing processed information directly into his mind.

The home of the Affinity Group was a huge collection of architecturally disparate and contradictory buildings. It looked like the remains of a city from a technological dark-age growing organically across the rambling sprawl of a decaying but once glorious empire. Oddly shaped buildings of industrial heritage stood next to palaces with large baroque balconies, ornate spires and elegant crystal towers, many of which were linked by an intricate aerial web of narrow, curving walkways, wide causeways and thread-like monotracks. Thick, dark stains rose diagonally from clusters of great brick chimneys, and an assortment of transports darted from tower to platform to courtyard like parasitic insects searching for food in the mouth of a giant host. The sinister installation stretched almost to the glistering dark green sheet of the ocean, surrounded by a thick, armoured wall.

From the wall itself rose many brittle wooden towers, supporting small guard huts; Delgado could clearly see the people within them as they paced and smoked, chatting and joking with each other. They paid little attention to the weapons they were meant to be manning; the Affinity's strength and reputation obviously bred complacency within. A clutch of tiny visuals appeared in his mind providing information ranging from weapons type to the composition and effectiveness of the guards' personal armour; neither was particularly impressive.

His consciousness suddenly expanded as his nobics linked to an unknown source. A moment later a voice cut through the quiet of the forest. It was faint, but quite close; a non-human male, fairly young yet confident. He was speaking in the warm, mellifluous Counian language.

Hiding behind a tree at the edge of the clearing, Delgado

looked down the slope. A group of people riding bipedal creatures with short, curled horns, brown fur and wide, flat feet were climbing the incline towards him. The riders wore plain, thick cloth garments and elaborate face masks. The masks were decorated with wavy lines in red, white and gold, backed by a matt silver rectangle: the colourful banner of The Ultimate Union. This military pact was formed by three long-dead civilisations for the purposes of mutual protection, one of them had been based on Veshc, and its governmental palace now formed part of the Affinity Group installation. Basic weapons of a type indistinguishable even to his nobics were slung over the riders' shoulders. They wore little or no armour. Nobics and visuals conferred, and a moment later Delgado knew physical details about all those he could see: two strong males he would have to be wary of, and the Seriatt, who seemed to be at the centre of the group. The rest – a variety of weak, immature and nervous individuals – posed little threat.

The animals were snorting loudly, obviously unhappy at being forced up such steep and unstable terrain. When the rocks became too much for the creatures to manage, the riders dismounted and led them. They split into two groups and spread out, fanning left and right, occasionally shouting to each other. Delgado ran to a nearby boulder and crouched behind it, waiting, listening; the sound of his breathing echoed back at him off the rock's grey face. He peered around its coarse, gritty surface and saw one group disappear behind some fallen trees, while the rest struggled to circumnavigate a clutch of large boulders. He turned, leaned against the rock and closed his eyes, trying to extend his consciousness more precisely, attempting to gauge the hostiles' emotions and moods; he recognised excitement, tension and anxiety among the normal traces – an odd combination for a group who were outwardly so relaxed.

A gunshot suddenly split the silence of the forest, the report rolling around the sky like a heavy song of discord. Another followed a few seconds later, a bitter harmony. Delgado looked up at a loud noise above him, and saw one of the large black birds crashing through the canopy; it landed nearby with a dull thud, raising a cloud of pale brown dust. He heard someone approaching and pressed himself flat against the boulder; a moment later a figure appeared, not far away from him, but facing in the opposite direction.

The hunter was panting, grey mist forming on the inside of his visor as he looked for the bird he had killed. Delgado could tell by his movements and the way his cape hung on his body that he was not particularly muscular. New analysis visuals opened: the man was young, unfit, lacking strength of will.

Delgado smiled.

A surge of euphoria emanated from the other man as he spotted his kill. He strode over to it, placed his rifle on the ground and picked the dead bird up by one of its skinny, taloned feet. As he held it level with his face and examined it closely, Delgado assessed the man's gun; it was an old and clumsy four-pulse repeater with short-blade bayonet. Delgado would have to pick his moment carefully if he was to ensure a quick and silent kill.

Delgado took a few tentative paces forwards. As he was about to attack, the hunter turned. Delgado found himself staring at his own image reflected in the other man's visor. His appearance surprised him: there were too many wrinkles, too much tension for one so highly trained. Perhaps Osephius was right after all.

The hunter seemed paralysed, his body rigid. There was a momentary stand-off that seemed to last an age. Then, as Delgado felt his opponent's emotions shift from elation to a combination of panic and confusion, he instinctively lunged for the weapon lying in the dirt.

The hunter leaped for the rifle at the same moment, and they grabbed it simultaneously. They see-sawed, each trying to wrest the gun from the other's grip. The hunter attempted to twist away but lost his balance and fell. Delgado snatched the gun from the other man's grip and brought the butt around in a smooth circular motion, cracking the hunter hard under the chin. He rolled and moaned, fingers clawing at his mask; blood began to seep through the locking seam at the chin. Delgado smashed him full in the face and the latch came undone; as the mask fell to the ground, the face revealed knew only fear.

Silence stretched the length of the moment as, for a few brief seconds, Delgado savoured his power, a sense almost lost to him, sapped by the conspirators of frustration, cynicism and the hierarchy of the new consolidated Structure. He circled the rifle again and stuck the bayonet through the man's left eye.

Blood darkly stained the ground; dying fingers twitched.

Delgado heard the dead man's companions calling for him. He threw down the rifle and rolled the body over so he could undo the wide metal clasps on the back of the corpse's cape. He pulled the cloth from the body, removed his own tunic and threw the cape casually over his shoulders; the garment was heavy, coarse and smelled damp. Inside it were large pockets; he placed his sidearm into one of them hoping the gun's bulk would not be noticed, then quickly grabbed the damaged mask. He wiped blood and saliva from its mandibles and arrangement of tubes, then put it on to his own head. The damaged clasp made it difficult to close, and its loose components were awkward to apply correctly, the sensory pads particularly hard to position against his face. When eventually closed, the inside of the mask smelled oddly metallic. Blood dripped from the fine breather filter mesh just above his nose; the liquid feeder pipe was warm and slimy against his cheek where it had been down the dead man's throat. Fans just above his cheekbones whirred softly; perception drives clicked somewhere near his ears; information was transposed on to the inside of the visor's faceplate in alien text he was unable to read.

Delgado stooped, grasped the body by the ankles and dragged it into the undergrowth, then quickly snatched up the rifle and cleaned the bayonet on the dead man's underclothes. As the hunter's companions approached, Delgado sprinted back across the clearing and grabbed the dead bird. He was just in time.

'Ah, Byrbegch. You have a kill, I see.' It was the group's leader, speaking from the edge of the clearing. His voice sounded thin, muted by his mask's speakers.

Delgado nodded enthusiastically, and held the bird in the air.

'Excellent. Good shooting. We need hunt no longer, for that bird is surely large enough to feed twice this number.' The rest of the party were gradually emerging from the trees and removing their masks. Delgado looked quickly around them, searching for the Seriatt: identify, consolidate, act.

Vourniass Lycern was standing to his right. She had removed her mask, and was undoubtedly the most enigmatic, mysterious creature he had ever encountered. Strong and fit, her physical size was imposing. Yet her beauty was not an obvious, superficial one; quite the opposite. Her features were disproportionate enough to be disturbing; her mouth looked slightly askew, her chin was almost as broad as her cheekbones, heavy and intensely aggressive, and the distance between the septum of her nose and her upper lip was disconcertingly great. It was as if her facial components had been carelessly arranged by someone in a hurry. Yet there was also something deeply attractive about this grotesque Seriatt; confidence, definition – a greater depth he was unable to pinpoint. And so much more.

'We shall make camp here and eat,' the leader continued. 'Byrbegch, choose someone to help you clear this site of rocks while the rest of us find water for the *rutull* and give them some food. They have worked hard to carry our lazy bodies up this hill.'

It was too good an opportunity to miss. Delgado looked at the Seriatt and beckoned to her.

25

Lycern walked over to him, her gait assured. 'Why do you not remove your mask, Byrbegch?' she said, her voice warm and husky even through the mask. 'Surely you are too hot.'

Delgado said nothing, but simply shrugged, glancing at the others as they disappeared down the slope with the animals.

Lycern frowned. Delgado sensed suspicion and mistrust growing within her. She looked at him intently. 'You are not Byrbegch,' she said slowly. Her tone was calm and certain. 'You are a little taller, a slightly different shape. Who are you? Where is Byrbegch?' She glanced around as if her dead colleague might emerge from the trees at any moment.

Delgado checked that none of the party were returning, then coolly released the latch and removed his mask.

'Byrbegch allowed me to take his place on this trip. I needed to escape the walls for a while and he helped me.' He studied her as he spoke, absorbing information concerning her appearance, mannerisms and behaviour.

She narrowed her eyes. 'But I saw him with his *rutull* as we were passing through the gates. I would have noticed your different figure when we were riding, I am certain of it.'

Delgado leaned forward as if sharing a secret. 'The eye often sees what it expects,' he said. 'We changed places quickly so I wouldn't be challenged. We have done it before and not been discovered.'

'I am not sure I believe you,' she said after a few moments. 'Perhaps we should see what Ballassio has to say.'

'No, don't tell Ballassio. I'm not supposed to be here. If he learns of this, Byrbegch and I will both be punished – perhaps you too. We've got away with it so far, why report us now? We've done no harm.'

Lycern looked Delgado up and down. 'I do not trust you,' she said. She glanced over her shoulder towards the others who were beginning to return.

Delgado quickly replaced and re-sealed his mask. 'You must say nothing,' he repeated. 'We could all be punished. Maybe even expelled from the Group.'

Lycern looked at him for a long moment, then eventually nodded. 'Very well, I will not tell him. But be warned: I will be watching you closely, stranger, and shall speak to Byrbegch when we return. Now, help me move some of these stones. We need to clear a space to pitch our tents.'

Delgado nodded and smiled to himself as he hefted rocks to one side: he was still Alexander Delgado after all.

The group sat informally around a large fire in the centre of the wide circle made by the tents. Delgado was relieved that most wore their masks.

The group drank water fetched from a nearby stream heated over the fire, and ate the cooked bird. The creature was surprisingly small when stripped of its dark feathers, and although Delgado's stomach was more disturbed than satisfied by the pitiful offerings of singed meat it received, he slipped the tough slivers of flesh between his mask's sharp-edged mandibles gratefully nonetheless; uncertain when he would next have the opportunity to eat.

He sat directly opposite Lycern. Embers rose from the fire that lay between them like burning fireflies, and even though her mask's dark visor reflected glossy miniature flames, Delgado knew she was looking directly at him. Visuals swarmed in his mind, struggling to relate the odd composite of traces she projected. She was an enigma, and he was fascinated.

Anonymously they stared at each other, their respective masks in opposition as the group sat in silence, listening to Ballassio speak in the calm, quiet voice of someone glad to be sharing his knowledge, experience and wisdom with people who would not dare to question him. Delgado sensed the collective humility and respect of those around him quite clearly. He pitied them. He had once been subject to the restrictions of such loyalty, only to have it cast back in his face.

'My children,' Ballassio said, the snapping and popping of

burning logs in the fire adding sporadic punctuation to his words. 'Some of you will undoubtedly become high priests, but even those of you who do not go through to the Completion Ceremony and embrace the full opportunities that would be offered to you in such circumstances will still play an important part in the future of the Affinity Group. You will carry the beliefs of Lissiam Junoch and the reputation of the group into the next millennium and beyond. I envy you, for that is not my path. Honour,' he continued, 'will only come with the eradication of all non–Affinity thought and intention. Diversification is the way of the foolish. Only strength and focus can result in success.' He clenched his fist in dramatic emphasis. 'At this very moment in our galaxy the effects of disparate thoughts are being felt. As I speak, the tensions that exist between Earth's Structure and the Seriattic Government are heightening. The potential consequences for both sides and, for all the civilisations that may be impacted by their actions, are too terrible to comprehend.

'The irony of their situation is that the efforts they have made to avoid war simply seem to be compounding the situation through lack of communication. The leaders of these worlds are greedy, stubborn and unable to express their true feelings – the feelings which you, as trainees, are currently learning to unlock and utilise. Believe me, were these people Children of the Affinity, there would be no threat of violence between them now. No tension. Their doubts would not exist, and their conflicts would already have been fought – within them.'

Delgado listened and nodded when the others nodded. It was strange to be among members of this sinister, mysterious cult. More disturbing was the fact that Ballassio's words sounded similar to ideas expounded within Structure since Myson's rise to power. The slant was slightly different, true, geared more towards collective awareness, but the underlying theme was the same: capitalise on instability, exploit the misfortune of others.

Ballassio made no mention of what course of action the Affinity Group might take should war break out between Earth and Seriatt, but Delgado knew that if it formed the correct alliances, the Group could only benefit from such a conflict and the destabilising effect it would have on all nearby systems. Recent Enlightenment reports suggested that the Group had entered a period of calm following extended industrial activity, intensive and expanded farming, as well as budgetary tightening; all would prove beneficial if the Affinity Group became isolated, besieged or affiliated with one side or the other in the event of a war, with their resources stretched as a result.

It was generally believed that this would not be their agenda, however; the Group would more probably take advantage of the opportunities for 'acquisition' that would likely arise as smaller, less advanced cultures suffered the consequences of the wider conflict, caught in crossfire as the fighting spread. Details were sketchy, but there were rumours that the Group brainwashed its members into unquestioning obedience using specially adapted nobics, although Delgado harboured doubts about the likelihood of this due to the cost of such technologies. Even administration of the most basic evolutions was limited to the more elite military personnel; mass usage was out of the question.

Ballassio began to speak of the rich rewards that could soon come their way, potential for a golden age of prosperity and growth as the Affinity Group benefited from trade opportunities with worlds sidelined by Earth and Seriatt. As Ballassio spoke, Delgado could feel the Group's collective emotions swelling into a rich glow of expectation and desire. He noted with interest that Ballassio made no mention of the Sinz, and yet he had heard that within the last four standard months there had been three reports of Sinz vessels passing through the Veshc system. Their destination was unknown, but it was unusual for Sinz craft to stray so far from the M–4 wormhole – and unnecessary, given that Myson delivered their purchases direct – so where they were going, and what they were doing, was a mystery.

'It is time we settled ourselves to sleep now,' Ballassio was saying. 'We have a long journey back in the morning. I hope you have all enjoyed this little escape from the confines of the Affinity Group and the strict limitations and disciplines that are occasionally imposed upon you there.' He smiled and looked around at them all. 'When we get back I am sure we shall all be able to concentrate on our tasks and rituals much more effectively, having spent some time outside those high walls.'

He paused. 'One more thing before we retire,' he said. 'I know some of you are soon to be inducted, mainly those of other faiths and planetary origins. Do not worry too much about the ceremony. If you were not to worry at all then you would be foolish, but believe me when I say that you will feel reborn, and able to carry out your duties with all of your souls committed to them. Go now and sleep, my children. We start back to the church at dawn.'

Delgado lay awake, considering his options.

If the shuttle had been flyable, or even repairable, then he would have risked snatching the Seriatt and escaping under cover of darkness. It would not have given him much of a start, but anything was better than none at all. But this was not an option – his skill as an aviator had seen to that. Mental note addendum: *as well as crash helmet, apply for piloting refresher course.*

Despite the dangers it posed, he now had little choice but to enter the Affinity Group installation: he had to find a way off the planet, with or without Vourniass Lycern, and only there would this be possible.

First he would rest. He had several courses open to him, but until he had successfully penetrated the Affinity Group he would not be able to implement any of them and for that he would need all his strength.

He allowed himself to relax, clearing his consciousness of all thoughts and visuals. As the fire outside rustled gently, smouldering logs collapsing, Delgado's eyelids weighed heavy.

Delgado sat bolt upright and grabbed his gun, instantly alert. The surge of energy his nobics had stimulated caused him to tremble for a few moments, until his body stabilised. He was unsure how much time had passed since he fell asleep.

His nobics fed him strong traces of determination and anger emanating from a closing source. He peered out of the tent. A wind stirred the trees; the night air was chill and damp following an apparent rain shower. He saw a dark silhouette loping clumsily across the camp towards him, running between the other tents and the fading glow of the near-dead fire. It was the Seriatt. She was heading directly for his tent.

'Open this and let me in,' she said sternly, tugging impatiently at the small gap when she reached him.

Eyebrows raised, Delgado shrugged, calmly put down his gun and struggled to undo the tent's wet, swollen laces. Cool air washed across his body as she slid through the opening. He caught her scent as she passed him; it was a thick, pervasive odour that stirred something within him. He appraised her form as she turned within the confines of the tent.

She knelt opposite him, her hands on her knees. 'I cannot accept this,' she said, breathing heavily. 'Who are you? Where is Byrbegch? I demand to know.' Her strange face was tight with resolution, her jutting chin resolute.

Delgado sat cross-legged and stared at her. 'My name is Alexander Delgado,' he said coolly, 'but I prefer Alex. I'm a member of the Brotherhood for Affinity Security.'

She looked him up and down, uncertain, wary. Her odd face shifted to an even stranger expression. 'I have never heard of this unit,' she said. 'I believe you are lying.'

He admired her spirit, respected her courage. 'Believe what

you like,' he said. 'We're a secret Order. We maintain intelligence records on Affinity members to track their progress within the group in order to prevent possible infiltration by hostile outsiders. Occasionally we're called upon to control undesirables already within the group. It's an unpleasant task, but sometimes necessary.'

She paled visibly. 'You have killed Byrbegch,' she said. 'Am I correct?'

Delgado paused, reassessed: she already knew the answer. 'I had to,' he said, nodding. 'I had orders to follow. He was considered a threat.'

'These were orders from whom? A threat to what? Tell me.'

'Security – more than that I can't tell you. I am . . .' He spread his hands and shrugged, momentarily breaking eye-contact in a dramatic, theatrical manner '. . . shall we say I am not of the highest authority. You just have to accept that his death was necessary for the good of the group. As do I. You must reveal this to no one. Both of our lives will be in danger if you do: there are those more powerful than you could possibly imagine within that church.'

'You do not have to patronise me quite so heavily, human. I appreciate that I, as a lowly trainee priestess, may know little of the Affinity's internal politics, but it is difficult to think of Byrbegch as any kind of threat. He was a weak and shallow creature – as are the males of most species.'

Delgado smiled again, more broadly this time – the expression felt alien. 'He was obviously good at some part of his evil and treacherous job if he was so convincing,' he continued. 'He had to be killed, believe me; there was no choice. It was for the good of the group.' He was beginning to enjoy the story he had invented; perhaps he should have been an actor.

'I despise killing,' Lycern said, shaking her head and looking away from him. 'I cannot understand the mentality of it. I am *conosq*, a species dedicated to giving life; to take it goes against everything I exist for. This Affinity claims much but offers little. It is a haven for criminals and thieves, not the religious sanctuary it pretends to be. That it is prepared to kill its own members demonstrates the contradiction of it all.'

She seemed deeply moved. Delgado studied the alien's unattractive face, took a moment to explore the distress and grief rising within her. He absorbed her pain and searched for its true source. He was fascinated by it, transfixed by the purity of her emotion. Her skin held a lustrous sheen. He reached out and touched her cheek. 'Don't hate me for what I've done,' he said, frowning slightly. 'I was just the instrument; someone else's tool. It wasn't something I wanted to do, believe me.'

She looked at him again, her expression cold and hard, and pulled her head away from his hand. 'I understand something of your motivation,' she said, 'but know this, Alexander Delgado: unless you have *com tulies vievro* – justification, as you say – you will have to atone for this act of murder. It is *di-fio na'atu*: the ultimate crime. Whether it was your wish or not, you took the life and you will have to pay. That is certain. Seriatts have a saying: "*illios nim guar ehil moe*"; it means "live to give life". Do you see?'

Delgado nodded and pretended to see. But he began to realise that there could be bonuses to this mission that he had not previously considered. If he followed the instincts he felt now, things would change to a greater extent than he could ever have considered possible.

He reached out and touched the lapel of her cape, moving his right hand slowly towards the split at the front. His fingertips barely touched the fabric, yet despite this slight contact the firm resistance of her body beneath was an overwhelming aphrodisiac.

Lycern did nothing for a few moments, then looked down at his hand and placed hers on top of it. 'I will not mate with a killer,' she said, shaking her head and staring into his sharp blue eyes. 'I cannot. I am *conosq*.'

Delgado moved up on to his knees, maintaining eye-contact. 'Is that right?' He slid his fingertips into the split at the front of her cape; her flesh was warm, soft and incredibly smooth. He began to move his hand towards one of her breasts, searching for the weight of that even softer flesh. As he did this he reached out with his other hand and touched her shoulder. She twisted slightly, resisting but then closed her eyes and shuddered, a slight gasp escaping from her mouth, a faint ululation at the back of her throat.

Delgado gently massaged her with his left hand, pulling his right away from her chest and moving it up to her other shoulder. He caressed her. She tilted back her head, her mouth slightly open, and began to sway gently, her breath coming in short, excited gasps. Quietly she began to moan, the sound becoming louder as her arousal increased. Intrigued and painfully excited, Delgado shifted up on to his knees and pressed his body against hers.

Lycern opened her eyes and looked at him. She was flushed, her eyes bright and clear. Their faces were merely centimetres apart. 'Are you sure you want this, Alex Delgado?' she breathed. 'Do you know the power of *conosq*? Can you deal with it?' She gripped his biceps tightly, as if angry or frustrated, and pushed him away from her. 'Are you strong enough to give me all that I need?' Delgado nodded once, a curt flick of his head. He leaned forward again and began to kiss her neck. 'Very well,' she said. She pushed him away again and cast her cape from her shoulders.

She wore nothing beneath the coarse cloth other than an ornate silver pendant that hung from a chain between her visibly swelling breasts. The thin line of glands down her sides and across her shoulders pulsed, glistening with tacky slime. The large cluster of glands at her crotch were secreting a thick white foam that spread down her inner thighs. The scent was rich, sickly sweet, an invidious aroma.

Delgado's heart raced; his head began to spin. He was no longer aware of his nobics functioning. Lycern reached up and placed her hands on his shoulders, pushing him on to his back

34

with a strength and ease that both surprised and aroused him. She quickly straddled his narrow hips and leaned forward to kiss him, her hair falling across his face, heavy pendant resting on his chest, warm flesh smothering him. Suddenly her former anger was lost in a new and passionate mask of pure sexual energy, and her demeanour changed dramatically as she released her true self.

She became increasingly impatient, kissing him with an aggressive, frenzied passion as sadistic as it was erotic. Bites to his neck and face drew blood and she gripped his hair tightly in her fists and clawed at his flesh with her nails, her body flung into wild muscular spasms.

Delgado was caught between euphoria and despair, uncertain where this was leading or how he had suddenly become the one controlled. But his concerns were swamped by a multitude of overpowering emotions. He placed his hands on Lycern's hips as she searched for his heat; when the warm, slippery foam touched him he gasped at the shock waves that ripped through his body. Dull pain in every cell was both agonising and incomprehensibly sensual. He laughed aloud at the glorious torture; but which emotion engendered this he could not have said.

Lycern began to rock slowly when she had fully absorbed him. Her breasts brushed his ribcage in time with the movement, her form a voluptuous mass of flesh. Her motion was the absolute essence of sexual allure, a hypnotising rhythm. Yet to Delgado their coupling was different to any he had known: she was distant, taking from him, using him for her own gratification. And when he opened his eyes he felt a sense of repulsion that instantly countered his arousal, but did nothing to alleviate either it, or his ecstatic agony.

Lycern's face was a monstrous mask. Her lips were engorged with blood, hideous, purple and swollen; her eyes were closed tight, her brow furrowed, tense and moist with sweat. Spittle formed at the corners of her seething mouth as she hissed and moaned a range of surging, throaty sounds indicating an urgent need to slake a basal thirst. Delgado knew this was not right, that he wanted to escape her snare; but his head was in turmoil, his mind unable to focus, his body weak, immobilised. More than that, he found the strength of his own sexual desire for her full yet pliant form impossible to resist. He wanted her to use him, wanted her to abuse his body for her own ends in whatever way she chose – and his complete acceptance of that was the most alarming aspect of all.

Lycern's swollen breasts hung before his face; as he pushed himself up to kiss them she twisted and rolled him on top of her. The air in the tent was choked with the stench of sex and desire as they became truly alive, Delgado as frantic and wild as she, an agonising need rushing through him in this new position of perceived power.

Then, abruptly, Lycern calmed.

Delgado felt her mood shift, as if increasing the distance between them still further. Yet while her face maintained its gargoyle-like appearance, she seemed to become almost serene, as if her former anguish had dissipated completely.

He became aware of a warm sensation around his sides and buttocks. It was accompanied by a smacking sound and an even richer scent, an odour so strong he could almost taste it. He managed to look down at their two joined bodies and saw a thin, opaque film of moist skin growing rapidly away from the glands around her body. It was a sheet of veined flesh, shiny and slick with mucus.

The membranous sac spread from her and began merging with his own skin as he watched; it was as though her whole body was opening to ingest him. He tried to speak, to exclaim, to question – but he could manage only a few anxious gasps.

She seemed to sense the tension in him and briefly rose from her trance-like state. 'Do not be worried,' she said. 'It is the *assissius*. It is natural.' And then, almost as quickly, she sank away from him again.

There was nothing he could do. Beneath him, Lycern remained distant, unmoved. She was in an erotic trance, drawing all she needed from him. Gradually the thin film reached up to his face, and spread slowly across his mouth and eyes until his body was entirely consumed by hers.

Delgado opened his eyes. The morning light filtering through the canvas filled the tent with soothing shades of green. He stared at the fabric above him as it billowed in the breeze. As ever, he was instantaneously alert, his mind reviewing his mission objectives, planning how to proceed, reassessing his situation; but there was also rampant nobic activity that he was unable to access let alone control; it was as if his own interneural systems were assessing their host.

The stench of their mating filled his nostrils still. He tried to remember what had happened, tried to picture it all and savour it again. He immediately became aroused by the images that filled his head. He had heard vague rumours about Seriattic *conosq*, their power, their abilities. The sac – the *assissius* as Lycern had called it – emerged from the sides of her body and had wrapped him like a moist cocoon within minutes. When inside it he had felt something akin to weightlessness, had been overwhelmed by a great peace and an immense sense of inner calm. He had needed to do nothing but allow himself to be carried along by the waves that had pulsed slowly through him, their cadence erotic and bizarre.

Yet this was not a physical sensation – Lycern had not manipulated muscles in order to draw him to the repeated and ever increasing plateaux of rapture he had enjoyed: the things he had experienced transcended the body. It was as if she had caressed a tender nerve with the most delicate touch. Never before had he experienced such a fusion, such a powerful merger between himself and another being.

It had been a revelation.

He touched his head: the mucus had dried to make his hair

sticky and hard. He smiled. Lycern was powerful indeed, capable of changing the course of any number of futures at a whim if she so wanted. If any being could forge the links Myson desired between Earth and Seriatt, it was surely she. But she could be dangerous, too, he could see that.

There was a shout outside the tent: it was Ballassio.

'Listen everyone. We will be leaving shortly. Pack your tent and belongings quickly. I will not wait for the idlers among you.'

But what about impostors, thought Delgado as he pushed himself up. He wrapped the cape round him and fastened the clasp at his waist, then quickly checked his sidearm and put it back into the cape's inner pocket, and placed the mask over his head. He took a moment to adjust to the dry, metallic air it fed to him, then stooped and unlaced his tent.

The morning air was cold and clear, the sky a sharp ultramarine cut by a few slender fissures of brilliant white cloud. The other members of the group were clustered around their tents, which were in various states of disassembly, or loading their already complaining *rutull* with panniers and baskets.

'Ah, Byrbegch,' called Ballassio, who was standing on the other side of the clearing. 'I thought you dead, my son. Take a drink,' he indicated the fire, 'then pack your tent. Quickly, now. We are about to leave.'

Delgado nodded and went towards the fire. Lycern was there, pouring steaming water into a tin mug. As he approached he felt somehow disoriented, light-headed and confused. He frowned, attempting to regain his poise, yet the disruption seemed insurmountable. The effects intensified when he glanced at Lycern, but she could not be responsible for such a weakening loss of control: Alexander Delgado was a controller – had an effect, rather than being affected.

He tried briefly to access his nobics for data on those around him as he walked towards the fire and Lycern, but only a few visuals opened, and these were subdued, offering him little information of use. It seemed as if every one of his main utilities had in some way been infected by a virus. He felt naked, vulnerable, and knew that if his normal functionality did not quickly return, his life would be in danger.

Lycern turned and held the water out to him as he walked the final few metres. He took it from her silently and drank it in a single mouthful, its burning heat ignored. Their masks faced each other in defiance, the ancient, alien motifs on their visors hiding the true emotions behind their mute façades. Each knew the other had secrets, but what these might be, and how immense their gravity, neither could guess.

And at that moment, Alexander Delgado could not have known that the truth behind his situation, and all to which it would lead, would change his life forever.

The journey down to the plain and onward to the Affinity Group's church was not easy. Delgado, who was unused to dealing with creatures as moronic as *rutull*, even if some of the grunts he had dealt with in his time had deserved such a description, found Byrbegch's animal to be an unruly beast with a stubborn nature and awkward disposition. At first he tried to force the animal around fallen trees and larger boulders, digging his heels into the creature's ribs and yanking at its reins. But whatever brutal methods of coercion he tried, the *rutull* would always decide it knew better and go in whichever direction it liked.

Eventually, and although it went against his every instinct, Delgado was forced to accept that he was just a passenger. He stopped trying to control the animal; held the reins limply in one hand; moved with the creature's motion rather than resisting it. Even then, with the journey considerably easier with their battle over, he found staying in the saddle took all his concentration. Indeed, some of the moves the animal attempted were so alarming that Delgado wondered if it was actually trying to scare him. If so, it was failing; he would simply cut the creature's throat if the opportunity presented itself.

Delgado's punishment continued even when the slope was far behind them and they were making their way through the forest using hard, worn and – most importantly – level dirt paths. But as they approached the home of the Affinity Group, its mysterious church, his physical discomfort and underlying uncertainty about how he would get the Seriatt back to Earth were all temporarily forgotten.

The installation was almost completely hidden by the forest, and they came across it quite suddenly as they entered what at first appeared to be a clearing. Towering wooden gates were set in the middle of the relatively small section of wall that emerged from the solid banks of trees to either side; they were comprised of numerous huge timbers, each of which was warped with age and riddled with cracks and knots. The gates were topped by long black metal spikes, and reinforced by broad bands of black metal that stretched from the huge bolts and hinges that affixed them to the walls; each hinge was easily as tall as a man.

On top of the wall to either side of the gates rose wooden towers supporting two of the guard shelters Delgado had seen from the ridge. He shielded his eyes as he looked up: no sign of life. The wall itself consisted of large sandstone boulders honed almost square, fixed by thick layers of dried mud. The aging clay was pale and cracked, but irregular dark patches indicated the moisture that remained in recently repaired areas. The hideous carved gargoyles that sprouted from the wall at frequent intervals, defying attack with their bulging, slitted eyes, pointed ears and probing tongues, reminded Delgado of imps he'd struggled to control during the Buhatt campaign.

Ballassio stopped at the vast wooden gates and waited for the party to gather. By the time Delgado caught up with them the rest of the group had dismounted, and their *rutull* were chewing mouthfuls of foliage torn from the trackside. Apparently hungry, Delgado's animal seemed as keen to eat as the rest of its herd, and kept jerking him sideways as it lowered its head to the ground, resisting his attempts to continue walking.

Lycern, who was standing by the track holding her *rutull*'s reins, watched Delgado's ungainly approach with a level of amusement even her cape and mask could not hide. Now stubbornly refusing to walk, his *rutull* was focused on finding the tastiest greenery available. In frustration he yanked sharply at the creature's reins several times in rapid succession; it stopped chewing and slowly raised its head to meet his gaze, as if prepared to rise to any challenge he might propose, then slowly lowered its head again and continued to eat. Staring fiercely at the animal's neck, Delgado wondered where he might obtain a large, sharp blade.

'Are we all present, then?' Ballassio called, quickly counting the gathered number. 'Excellent. We have made good time.' He turned and pulled a plain black metal staff from a holding vase, then reached out and smashed it against a large square of metal suspended within a wooden frame in the wall. Amplified by some means Delgado was unable to establish, the metal boomed, its reverberating chime deeply resonant. The *rutull* stopped chewing and abruptly raised their heads in prick-eared attention.

A series of faint clicks and knocks could be heard, and a male voice shouted. Then the gates slowly began to open.

The courtyard beyond was large, seething with life. Animals grazed at straw-filled cages or drank at metal troughs. Servants struggled with overflowing washing baskets while men and women of all ages relaxed in roughly constructed bars propped against the outer wall. Children scampered around sheds and wells fighting mock battles with broom-handle swords, their laughter bright and clear. Transports moved along gravel roadways carrying people, livestock or machinery. The air was thick with the combined smells of cooking, dung and vehicle fumes, and although the ground was covered in a heavy layer of dry brown dust, it reflected the sun's heat like a sheet of beaten metal.

Delgado followed the rest of his party into the courtyard and towards a cluster of ramshackle sheds fashioned from corrugated metal sheeting. The walls were uneven and corroded, the roofs dislocated and riddled with holes. Clouds of dust rose from the ground as the indolent *rutull* dragged their feet, reluctant to return to the confines of their stables.

As the party neared the buildings, a farrier with a blackened apron, tanned leathery skin and a thick black beard came to meet them from the dark retreat of his workshop. He squinted heavily in the sunlight and silently took the reins of every animal in one large, rough-skinned hand. As he led the animals away he inspected the hooves of each for signs of damage caused by the inexperienced imbeciles who had handled them.

Ballassio turned to face them. 'My children,' he said, 'in a few weeks' time you will take part in the Induction Ceremony, after which you will be full white priests and begin to learn your true roles within the group. It is a great transition, and a difficult, tiring time; for this reason I would advise you to take a few days' rest. Drink a little, eat, perhaps even enjoy each others' bodies.' He smiled and clasped his hands before him. 'Whatever you choose, banish all stress from yourselves. My part in your training is almost finished, and I will not see you again until the ceremony is over. I wish you the luck of Lissiam, and thank you for making this trip a pleasant one.'

There was a brief ripple of applause, and the group fragmented. As some of the party gathered around Ballassio, Delgado moved close to Lycern. He grasped her right elbow firmly and steered her away; she tensed slightly but did not resist. 'I'll be coming with you,' he hissed. 'There are things we need to discuss.'

Delgado let Lycern lead him across the courtyard to a set of wrought-iron gates in one corner. A guard standing next to the gates watched them as they approached; Delgado noted the position of a large bush which could act as cover should he need it. There was also a wooden trough, which could either be used to hide a body, or yield a makeshift weapon if broken.

As it was, Lycern spoke softly to the guard when they reached the gates and they were allowed to enter without question. Delgado was almost disappointed. Even though this made his task much easier, he always seemed to operate more efficiently when the odds were stacked against him.

Beyond the gates it appeared that they had somehow been transported to another world, a temple of wealth, luxury and comfort that was an affluent and carefree contrast to the relative squalor he had already seen. Silence and tranquillity took the place of noise and confusion. He looked up as a flier passed overhead, and wondered about the possibility of gaining access to such transport. The Affinity Group's security, its control systems and the level of armament with which the installation was equipped were all factors he had to consider.

They walked along a balcony fashioned in generously carved and deeply varnished wood on a delicate and colourful parquetry floor. The balcony constituted one side of a quadrangle enclosing a lush green courtyard sunk some ten or fifteen metres lower. The courtyard contained bushes and shrubs cut into intricate patterns, the flowers blooming upon them creating a dazzling display of brilliant and vivid colour. Pink hexagonal slabs formed pathways around the gardens, and in the centre of the courtyard was a statue of a stalking bird. From the bird's long and elegant bill spouted a sparkling line of water, which fragmented into jewels of dancing light as it arced through the air; across the bottom of the circular stone pool into which these liquid gems fell, there tripped a fragile web of slender golden veins.

They walked along the balcony for a little way, then stopped at a plain black door. Lycern pulled a key from her belt and swiped it through the lock. The latch clicked, and the door swung smoothly open.

The room within was cool, clean, spacious, decorated in the red, gold and white of The Ultimate Union. It was also ornamented with numerous exotic otherculture artefacts. Delgado thought he recognised some as fertility symbols, but gave them only a cursory glance. It was alien mystic nonsense – mumbo–jumbo for weak souls.

Lycern motioned for him to sit on the sofa, then disappeared through a door to the left.

'So what is it you wish to discuss with me, Delgado?' she called back to him.

Delgado glanced around the room, examining objects, searching for clues, looking for any information about the Seriatt that might make it easier to get her back to Myson. Within him many battles were taking place, not least the conflict he felt with regard to what he should do with Lycern. 'I just need to make sure you're not a risk,' he said casually. He scrutinised the small and extremely unusual terminal in the far corner of the room, but was unable to ascertain its type. 'There are certain security procedures to be followed. If too many people learn of our existence our work will become difficult. We have to prevent that. We also need to be sure that *you* are not a risk to security. If you aren't, are genuinely concerned about the welfare of the group and want to help maintain its internal strength, then it might be possible for you to join us.'

Delgado heard a noise and looked towards the door. Lycern was walking towards him carrying a tray set with wine-filled goblets and plates bearing small portions of food. She had changed her clothes, and was now wearing a startling gown of brilliant scarlet silk; the cut of the cloth accentuated the sexuality of her clumsy Seriatt figure.

Delgado became instantaneously aroused despite himself. He looked away, but could only avert his gaze for a few moments before she drew him back. This alien was unattractive, almost repulsive, but he wanted her more than he had desired anyone or anything in his life. The sudden, all-consuming strength of his need was shocking. It denied him the sense of control to which he was so used. And even then, despite the unfamiliarity of this feeling, something about it attracted him. Perhaps it was the fact that she challenged him, and the sense he had of his own authority.

Lycern placed the tray on the sofa next to him. 'Please, you need nourishment after your ride aboard the *rutull*. Eat and drink.'

He watched as she sat on the floor in front of him, then began to pick at the food she had brought: pastry parcels filled with spicy meat, vegetables coated in succulent batter, cold meats, cheeses, hunks of crusty white bread. He found it difficult to detach himself from the situation and view events from an impartial perspective – something he was usually able to do unconsciously. His highly trained military persona was being eroded by the basic human male in him, the dynamism of his most fundamental drives taking control. These were weaknesses, things he had denied for so long – yet now everything seemed to be in question: what he was, who he was, his inner compulsions.

'So when will you tell me who you really are?' Lycern said. 'I am prepared to believe that you are part of some security unit within the Affinity for the time being, but I do not think this is really true. I believe you are a spy of some sort – one of the infiltrators from whom you claim to protect the group, perhaps. Is this the case?'

Delgado forced a smile, but whether this was for her benefit or his own, he would not have been able to say. 'You can think what you like,' he said, his manner cool, offhand. 'If you don't believe the security unit exists, then that pleases me. Secrecy is of the utmost importance if our unit's effectiveness is to be maintained.'

Lycern smiled back. 'If you say this is so, Alex Delgado, then it will do for the time being. But understand that you *will* reveal the truth to me sooner or later. Of that there can be no doubt.'

Delgado was on a knife-edge: if this Seriatt reported his presence to anyone he would be arrested, probably killed. He had to minimise risks. While killing her and aborting the mission was a tempting option, the potentially great rewards for succeeding despite his circumstances were also to be considered, as were the vague plans lurking at the back of his mind. He could still benefit if he conveyed her safely back to Myson, that was true. And despite his feelings for the man, he would be willing to accept any reward the Commander Supreme might wish to offer. But then, in that room so distant from his homeworld, he knew that of the several choices open to him, only one could give him the opportunity to set his life upon a new course.

As he considered this, Lycern suddenly set down her glass and moved towards him. Her pupils were wide; her breasts seemed to be swelling. She knelt before him and placed the palms of her hands on his thighs. 'You can tell me about joining your Brotherhood later,' she whispered, leaning closer. 'But to join with your soul is all I desire now.'

Her breath was a hot sensation, her lips irresistibly tempting. Delgado realised he was trembling as they kissed. He tried to fight it but this only seemed to worsen the tremors: it was involuntary, part of his natural physiology breaking free from the constraints imposed by his nobics and ingrained military training. He hesitated for a moment, fighting her, fighting himself. Yet he felt compelled to reach out, to caress her, to feel her flesh against his own.

He touched one breast with the fingertips of one hand, exploring the firm, smooth shape through the soft fabric, while running his other hand through her hair and down her neck to the glands at her shoulders. Bizarrely, he pictured Myson for a moment.

The soft tissues were already moist, tacky with viscous foam. When he touched them Lycern pulled away from him, apparently incredibly agitated even by this slight stimulation.

To Delgado's eyes, the expression she wore looked close to anger.

Her face stern, she maintained eye-contact with him as she crouched and unbuckled his belt. He sat forward slightly; she opened his cloak in one easy movement and threw it from his shoulders. As she rapidly unlaced the front of her own gown, the pendant around her neck reflected a glint of light. With the smooth flesh of her swollen breasts exposed, the glands around her body secreting their thick white slime in a rich, slippery torrent, she reached out and pulled him to the floor.

The warmth of her body was smothering as he settled upon her, and an immense craving consumed him as he was again absorbed by her body. Their tongues became entwined in a frenzy of frightening strength, and as his body was gradually ingested by the slick opaque sac that spread from her, Delgado found an energy and urgency he previously thought only madmen possessed. His skin tingled as if layers had been burned away to expose the raw flesh beneath. And yet this pain seemed wholly natural, the conflict of resistance and acceptance perversely gratifying in a way he was unable to reconcile.

Far back in his confused, spinning mind, Delgado suspected that he was losing a part of himself to something he did not understand. But at that moment in time, had he been able to comprehend his true situation, he would not have cared.

Delgado touched the GUN-ARM tab on the weapon's butt and waited for the nobics to kick in. A few seconds later a small cluster of visuals appeared in his head, giving information about the gun's status. He thought the main visual forward and activated the operations tab in the top corner. Another visual appeared and the gun began to emit an almost inaudible hum. A further visual opened to indicate that the weapon was armed. A warm breeze made the curtains tremble. His heart beat faster. His mouth became dry. A ravenous desire welled.

He rolled gently on to his side, trying to ignore the need. He was doing what he knew was essential, what to him was just another aspect of his everyday existence. He was Alexander Delgado, Military Intelligence Officer. Such actions were nothing to him: they were what he lived for. Killing the Seriatt now would halve his problems; she was nothing. He would be rid of her and able to return to Earth. He would have failed his mission, yes – but it seemed a small price to pay.

As he lay there he could not escape the subtle scent of her hair, the beauty of her skin, the warmth radiating from her tranquil body. It was an intoxicating combination, such a potent life essence, and he was increasingly suffering its influences, the purity of his life tainted by the intensity of her own.

He knew he had no choice despite what he had briefly planned. He convinced himself he had no attachment, stirred the recognisable, callous Delgado of old. He needed him now, needed that man's strength and leverage, his clarity of vision.

Slowly, silently, he drew up the weapon and placed the tip of its barrel against the base of the sleeping Seriatt's skull. His heartbeat was a series of rapid explosions in his chest. The universe contracted to encompass only the few centimetres that lay between them on the bed. The tip of the gun began to quiver.

Many strong emotions spread through him. He felt sick and hot, cold and weak, utterly helpless and torn. As Delgado closed his eyes and tried to maintain his resolve, his decision was made.

And in that moment, his fate was set.

Delgado sat on a small stool in front of the terminal in Lycern's suite, his knees almost touching his chin; he wondered if it was a piece of Courlow furniture. The antiquated unit in front of him was difficult to operate, largely because of Delgado's difficulty in reading Counian. The fact that there was no link for his nobics did not help matters; instead he was forced to best-guess his way through the assortment of screens that presented themselves to him in the search for a communications pool.

Any wrong move could expose him as an intruder if the group's security systems were remotely in tune – he knew that. But he had little choice. If he was to succeed with any kind of objective – whether it was the one he was formulating in his own mind or the one he had officially been sent to achieve – he had to contact Beech in the slipspacer. She was his only chance now.

He looked back to the bed where Lycern lay. The decision not to kill her had been difficult, but what disturbed him most was the fact that, despite knowing that killing her almost guaranteed his own survival, he had still been unable to commit the act. Not unwilling: *unable*.

Yet now he felt an absurd calmness and relief. Choices remained, but nothing was certain. The nobics he had injected into her were supposed to keep her sedated indefinitely, but the vial had looked damaged when he had pulled it from the butt of his sidearm, and he was uncertain of the health of its contents. If he failed to get her offworld before she woke, his whole plan – such as it was – would be jeopardised. It was no wonder he had a headache.

Delgado looked back to the small screen, rubbing his eyes with his fingertips. He had successfully opened comms channels with what appeared to be a secure relay through local hardline systems. It seemed the only way he could power his transmission was to run the pulse through a substation generator driving a small atmosphere purification unit. The purifier was operating on minimum, and had vast reserves available to draw on at peak periods, meaning that more than enough for his purposes remained.

He bypassed routers and redirected supply to the pulse energiser he had isolated and placed on standby. When the unit indicated it was ready, he input the Doghin co-ordinates and the relevant MI sequence operator code: if he was lucky, the MI ultrabeam would search for the slipspacer ID, and channels would open automatically. *If* he was lucky.

A few moments after releasing the signal, a processing menu was briefly replaced by a direct communications list. He scanned its contents, and noted with some interest that there were at least two plots which, unless he was very much mistaken, were routed to a large relay in the vicinity of the M-4 wormhole. But he did not have time to explore the possibilities. He continued searching and selected a driver that seemed to meet his needs. The list immediately disappeared and a thin grey line stretched diagonally across the screen. It widened, skewed, vanished; words began to form.

SECURE TIGHTLINE ESTABLISHED : VESHC − DOGHIN | | 7342
PRIORITY #4-09 CONFIRMED
ULTRABEAM COMMUNICATIONS START

After a few moments the words disappeared, replaced by Beech's familiar face. She looked red-eyed, and was frowning slightly as she squinted at the viewer.

'Sorry to wake you, Beech,' said Delgado, 'but I need some assistance. Get your ass down here, will you? Breakneck.'

Beech pursed her lips. When she spoke, the tightline compression relays through which the signal was being driven distorted her voice, making it sound thin and nasal. 'What have you done, Delgado?' Her words swirled and faded slightly; a momentary fracture in her voice made his name sound like a sex toy.

'The shuttle's engines went down and I had to make a forced landing,' he said. 'Unfortunately it wasn't a very good one. You have to come and get me. I have the target with me now. If we can get her out of here soon the mission can still succeed.'

She shook her head. 'I can't do that, Delgado. You know I

was specifically instructed not to risk confrontation with the Affinity Group. You're putting a great deal at risk just by contacting me in this way. A skirmish with Seriattic forces has kicked off in the Dassilos system while you've been down there. Myson won't want to waste unnecessary resources in case things get nasty. He already has five squadrons of xip fighters en route, with five more on standby.'

Delgado held up his hands. 'Look, Beech, you're not paid to think, consider or have opinions. Just do what the fuck I tell you. Get that goddamn ship down here and pick us up.'

'I should like to remind you, Commander Delgado,' Beech said slowly, 'that we are of equal rank. I don't take orders from you, I take them from General Myson, and if General Myson says I don't go in, I don't go in. I'm sure even a renegade like you can understand that.'

Delgado blinked, his jaw set. 'Look, Beech,' he said softly, 'this is all to do with the situation with Seriatt, right? Myson wants to establish some kind of direct link, so we need to get this *conosq* back to him. I appreciate your unwillingness to go against his orders, I really do, but we have to take the present situation into account and utilise contingency plans. It's called being adaptable. The success of my mission is only possible if you come and get me. And this mission has *got* to be successful, Beech. Myson is depending on it, God bless his fat, disgusting soul. I'm sure he would reward your bravery and initiative well if I were to tell him you had been instrumental in averting war. You want a transfer to PPD, don't you?' Beech licked her lips, but remained silent. 'The other option of course is that you obey Myson's orders without using any initiative what-soever, then return to him and explain why his precious *conosq* is dead, the war with Seriatt imminent, and his Sinz trade little more than a pleasant memory. It's up to you.'

Beech's image distorted and faded almost to nothing. Delgado cycled through menus. It seemed the purification unit had started to demand more power; soon there would not be enough to push the signal to Doghin.

Beech's face separated into three sections as the signal weakened further; sound became little more than white noise. Delgado opened more menus and relayed power from the Affinity Group's own comms systems and ATC coding units; they were high risk sources, but he had no choice.

'Can you hear me, Beech? Visual is fading. *Can you hear me?*' He cocked his head, listening hard, but heard just a few weak fizzing sounds that may or may not have been a response. There was no way for him to be sure. He re-routed as much power as he dared to the energiser and linked his sidearm to the terminal. The connector – botched together using some wire and old SGN-type couplings cannibalised from the aircon automation unit in the Seriatt's suite – was unstable to say the least; if it worked at all it would not do so for long.

'Beech, if you can hear me,' said Delgado, 'I'm uploading precise co-ordinates and as much information about the landing zone to the slipspacer's core as I could pack into the sidearm. By my reckoning you can land in the courtyard without sustaining too much damage and we'll be out of here before anybody realises what's going on. This is an order, Beech. Fuck! Can you hear me, Beech? *Beech*?'

Sound and visuals faded completely.

'Stupid bitch,' he hissed.

There was nothing more he could do. He hoped his performance as a loyal Structure officer had been convincing. If Beech was going to come for him she would arrive within three or four hours at most. He would give her four and a half, then consider alternatives. If there were any.

Delgado woke to the sound of two or three people shouting and running along the walkway outside, then silence. He pushed himself up slightly and listened; he could hear little other than birdsong and the faint trickling of the fountain in the courtyard. He checked that Lycern was still unconscious, then lay back down and closed his eyes again.

A moment later he heard a whining drone – faint at first, but quickly growing louder. Delgado opened his eyes and stared at the ceiling focusing nobics, trying to accumulate some information.

He got up, ran to the door, opened it slightly. For a few moments all seemed quiet. Then a stream of cannon fire appeared in the sky above him, a great swathe of destructive energy arcing into the distance towards the forest. A few seconds later another joined it, crossing from a different point; a third followed soon after. The noise became a deafening raucous wail as the weapons' raw energy tore the very fabric of the sky apart. Delgado was puzzled by the fact that the three weapons seemed to be aiming at different targets, but had little time to consider the reasons.

He could tell from the general angle of fire that Beech was bringing the slipspacer in low, possibly even below treetop height. Despite their differences he admired her courage and was thankful that she was such a skilled pilot. Handling a slipspacer was difficult in an atmosphere, let alone at low speed and altitude; others would have brought the craft in high and fast then had difficulty finding the precise pick-up point among the buildings, risking a strike at close range.

Delgado briefly glanced down at the courtyard where she was to land. For some reason the courtyard seemed smaller than he remembered it, and despite his unwillingness to consider that he might have made an error in his calculations, he felt a twinge of doubt. Still, if Beech did crash, the fireworks would be magnificent.

Fire continued to rip through the sky as Delgado ran to Lycern. In other circumstances he would have performed basic checks on her condition, but he had no time for such niceties. Instead he simply hefted her up on to his shoulder and made his way towards the courtyard.

She was even heavier than her appearance suggested, as if

her body was incredibly dense, and despite being immensely fit Delgado was red-faced and sweating before he had left the apartment.

He walked to the steps leading down into the courtyard and took them slowly, pausing when he reached the bottom. He had to wait patiently, remain in cover. The cannons were still firing and he could hear people close by, shouting and swearing. His nobics fed him traces of mood from those around him, and visuals opened giving information about the slipspacer. Beech was two miles away, closing rapidly; the craft had not yet suffered any serious damage despite the barrage. He could hear the vessel quite clearly now; its discordant wailing drone sounded remarkably like babies crying.

At that moment, the slipspacer appeared above the rooftops like a dark cloud, its odd, angular shape a bizarre contrast to the curvaceous elegance of the courtyard and surrounding buildings. As it hovered, the gunmen attacking the vessel seemed unable to train their weapons on it properly, and although they scored one or two hits that caused minor damage to unimportant areas, most of their fire was ineptly focused, slashing too wide or high. Razors of return laser fire occasionally sliced from the slipspacer's automatic defence systems, but Delgado knew well that these were largely inaccurate at such close range and could not be relied upon as a source of protection. He would have to be quick. Very quick.

The shrubs beneath the slipspacer began to singe as the vessel sank slowly towards the ground; columns of steam spiralled upwards as the water in the fountain boiled. The cannon fire raging through the sky above ceased as the vessel dropped below the gunmen's line of sight, its engines screaming. Landing skids extended, one of which crushed the stalking bird. As waste gases were released through vents on the vessel's underside, a thick ramp emerged from the hull with a disapproving rumble he could feel through the soles of his feet.

Delgado slipped from his hiding place. As he struggled to

carry Lycern up the ramp he heard a volley of gunfire burst from two corners of the courtyard, faint pops and cracks indicating basic projectile weaponry. He swore, but had to keep running, and hope he was not carrying a corpse full of holes.

When he next looked up he saw Beech standing in the open hatchway, cradling an automatrix pulse rifle in her hands. She looked down at the weapon, flicked rapidly between modes, and began to return fire, streams of light drawing perfect near-silent lines in the air above the courtyard. The hostile gunfire lessened; Beech immediately turned her attention to another source.

'Welcome aboard, Commander,' she shouted as he climbed the ramp's final few metres. A bullet ricocheted off the slip-spacer's hull and passed between them. Beech changed the gun's setting, then took careful aim and released a long burst of corplak tracer that sounded like a long swathe of fabric being torn; for a few moments all hostile firing ceased. 'You look like you're having difficulty,' she shouted. 'Would you like a hand?'

'Thanks very much. Some lifting gear would be useful.' Delgado slumped forward and allowed Lycern to roll from his shoulders, her weight carrying her further into the craft. He grabbed a sidearm from the charge rack in the wall and hit the door override button with his fist to keep it open. Then he lay flat on the floor and aimed. 'Just get this thing into the air and get us out of here, for fuck's sake.' He began firing at a fresh complement of guards without waiting for any kind of response.

'Well, if that's all the thanks I'm going to get . . .'

'If you don't upship now you'll be getting a whole lot more than thanks.' Delgado released a few more rounds, followed by a prolonged burst. Beech shrugged, casually threw her rifle towards him, then sauntered back up to the flight deck, glancing only momentarily at the Seriatt lying on the floor.

More armed members of the Affinity Group began to fire

at the slipspacer from another area of the courtyard; others appeared on a balcony to their right and a volley of shots crossed the space. Bullets ricocheted from the area around the hatch. One hit a panel behind Delgado, showering him with fragments of metal and plastic. The noise from the engines increased substantially and he felt the vessel rise. As the slipspacer left the vicinity of the courtyard Delgado heard the faint *ping* of bullets hitting the craft, a delicate music that somehow managed to penetrate the roar of the engines.

Beech tipped the craft slightly to give him more cover and flew across the complex, heading towards the coast. The disparate nature of the installation was underlined as Delgado peered past the edge of the open hatchway. Above the court-yard, incoming fire came once again from the guard towers; Delgado destroyed two with the automatrix rifle and was aiming at a third when Beech turned the craft and the tower was obscured from view. Cannon fire resumed briefly from other towers when they were forced to climb, but with the need for stealth required on her approach gone, Beech accelerated rapidly and they were soon out of the enemy weapons' limited range.

With the temperature dropping rapidly, the wind raging around him and the floor at an angle of about forty degrees, Delgado had to pull himself up using part of the weapons' charge rack in order to seal the hatch. He looked at the still unconscious Seriatt, who had rolled a short distance as the craft had climbed and was now resting against a bulkhead. Despite one or two moments of doubt, it seemed his plan might work after all.

All he had to do now was deal with Beech.

Beech cycled through a swarm of visuals as the slipspacer powered away from the planet. A small map was dedicated to scanner control in case the Affinity Group decided to give chase, while the remainder calculated the course they would take following their slide into slipspace.

'What have you done with her?' she asked, looking in Delgado's direction with the blank, unseeing expression that indicated intense visuals activity.

'She's in one of the passenger cabins,' said Delgado curtly; he was preoccupied, distracted.

'I take it you used the nobic solution?'

'Had to. She was extremely suspicious. If I hadn't put her out the whole mission would've been in jeopardy.'

'Oh, and it wasn't already? I can't help thinking Myson's still not going to be pleased despite getting his *conosq*. Structure's relationship with the Affinity Group is almost as tense as it is with Seriatt. If this ship was positively identified as a Structure vessel the shit could hit the fan.'

Delgado glanced at the various instruments and displays that surrounded them. He frowned: damage to any one of the monitors or control panels would ramp up his problems. His nobics could help him fly the craft to a certain extent, but no more than on the stricken shuttle, and that had not proved too successful. He would have to think of another way. 'Nothing's going to happen,' he said. 'You did the right thing in coming to get us, believe me. Rest assured that General Myson will be fully informed of both your skill in getting us out of there and your unwillingness to disobey orders. If he's not happy about how things transpired I'll carry the can, OK?'

'Depends what's in the can, Commander. Just remember what you said about the PPD. I risked my ass coming in there after you and I expect to be rewarded in the appropriate manner. I want a transfer to Earth, a shaft–side habitat suite and a private flier. At the very least.'

'You really are a modern Structure operative, aren't you, Beech? OK, if that's how you want it. Myson asked me to send a confidential report as soon as possible, so if you leave the flight deck for a while I'll contact him, inform him of the mission's status and mention the crucial role you've played in its success.'

'We're almost ready to slipspace, but still within range of Affinity ships; if we delay the slide we're increasing the risk of being caught.'

'You know I can't transmit from slipspace, Beech. Just give me a few minutes to send the message and we can make the transition. Or aren't you as serious about getting into the PPD as you implied?'

An alarm began to sound, cutting off her answer, a lazy monotone that seemed to call for apathy rather than action. As she stared at the shielded viewport in front of her, Beech's eyelids fluttered, a complex array of visuals maps suddenly opening in her mind. 'Two Affinity wasps,' she said quietly, almost to herself. 'Chasing hard. Weapons already armed. Still out of range. Closing but slowly. Wait – there's something else.' She narrowed her eyes, analysing and absorbing information. 'That's odd,' she said after a moment. 'It's a Sinz ship.'

'Really? How very interesting.'

'One Affinity ship is breaking off to intercept the Sinz craft.'

'But the other one's still on our tail, right?' Beech nodded. 'Destroy it,' he said. Delgado began trying to link into the slipspacer's nobic interface so he could see what was going on himself: without real-time visuals updates he felt half-blind.

Beech's eyes became visible behind the purple visor she wore as she dropped the maps and looked directly at him. 'It's still out of range. Besides, I have to remind you, Commander Delgado, that orders from General Myson are to avoid confrontation with the Affinity Group at all costs. We can make the slide to slipspace now and the enemy vessel won't be able to catch us. You look like shit,' she said with a frown.

Delgado shook his head. 'Thanks very much. No. Destroy it. As you said, if they realise we're Structure, things could get nasty. They might not have positively identified us yet, and the less chance there is of that happening, the better. Destroy it.'

Beech pursed her lips, as if trying to think of something to counter his argument, but the visor misted over again and she returned to her trance-like state apparently unable to do so. A bank of manual controls lit up to her right. 'Weapons systems armed,' she said flatly.

Delgado found the AI core interface, and his mind was suddenly packed with visuals. After a second spent filtering irrelevant information, his head was filled with much the same data as Beech's. The Affinity ship was no longer closing on them, and would not get close enough to fire if they maintained their speed; similarly, they would be unable to destroy it because it was out of range.

'What's happening with the Sinz ship?' said Delgado. 'I can't focus on it.'

Beech shifted through visuals. 'Difficult to say.'

'I need to know.'

'The Affinity craft seems to be cruising rather than chasing. The Sinz vessel is within range but nothing's happening. And unless I'm very much mistaken, the Sinz craft is an old Reactionary Forces SDV. It's been re-coded and re-specified, but it *is* an SDV. D-type. Interesting.'

'I wouldn't say interesting exactly.'

'What would you say?'

'I'd say it's ironic. I'd also say we'd better despatch our friends here just in case we suddenly find ourselves out-numbered. Watch the other two craft and let me know what happens.' Delgado moved to vessel control cycles and opened combat interfaces. The Affinity craft was still some way behind them, its distance maintained. He reduced all four of the slipspacer's propulsion units to idle and put the braking unit on an extremely narrow spread, focusing the energy tightly to ensure maximum speed degradation. The slipspacer slowed rapidly, its composite containment field envelope ebbing and flowing to negate the physical forces that would otherwise kill the passengers. Delgado felt a slight vibration through his seat as a service panel by his left foot fell open – it seemed that even the high specification generators used by the slipspacer found some manoeuvres taxing.

The vessel slowed incredibly quickly and the distance between the two craft diminished in seconds. This was something for which the crew of the Affinity ship were apparently unprepared. They could neither alter weapons focus to target the slipspacer fast enough to take advantage of its new range, or slow their craft with equivalent speed.

Delgado, who had pre-set weapons focus to one quarter of the crafts' previous separation, simply waited. As the Affinity craft closed on the slipspacer, emotional traces from its crew slipped sideways into his consciousness. He smiled: they were frantic, panicking. A moment later, when the craft was at half initial separation, Delgado calmly released three bolts of plasma. In the 0.2 standard seconds that followed, plasma charge and Affinity craft approached each other at immeasurable speed. Then they met.

Hardware data flared momentarily, then vanished from Delgado's visuals. The rippling confusion of emotional traces he had experienced just a moment earlier were also gone. He opened a real-time viewsheet and focused on the relevant area. There was nothing to be seen: no wreckage, no survival pods, no fireworks display. Destruction was total.

Delgado linked into Beech's visuals. 'What's going on?' he said.

'Nothing. The Sinz SDV has plasma charged in all weapons clusters but has made no effort to move into attack position. For all we know they may have plasma charged as standard procedure.'

'And the Affinity craft is maintaining its distance?'

'Right.'

Delgado shook his head. 'Nothing more's going to happen there, Beech,' he said, closing all main visuals. 'The Affinity craft is escorting the Sinz vessel out of the sector. They won't bother with us now. For one thing we've just destroyed their companion craft and for another they're too far away to catch us. So, now that little escapade is over, perhaps you'd like to go and check on our Seriattic friend while I contact General Myson. Then we can make the slide. She's on B deck, cabin four. Go.'

'You really need to learn some respect for fellow officers, Commander, even those who are younger than you. I know you've been in the service a long time but—'

'Stop your whining and get the fuck out of here, Beech. I need to send this transmission.'

'Well, do me a favour will you, Commander? Watch that monitor there,' she pointed, '– and if you see anything that looks like an ether fibrillation, open combat visuals and call me.' She pushed herself out of her seat and left the flight deck.

Delgado waited for five minutes, staring at the screen she had indicated. This was it: the turning point. He briefly reconsidered what he was about to do, but could see no other way of changing his position. If he was to be true to himself, he had no choice. The combat of the previous few moments had reminded him who he was, but somehow it had left a bitter taste in his mouth. He had gone too far now to be able to suppress his loathing for Structure and Myson, and to act on their behalf in whatever context went against the feelings that increasingly dominated him.

He allowed a few more minutes to pass, then got up and followed Beech to B deck.

When Delgado entered the cabin, Beech was bending over Lycern, examining the Seriatt's face closely. She straightened and turned when she heard Delgado's footsteps.

'Commander,' she said, 'I take it your message is sent and I can now return to the flight deck?'

'My message is sent.' He avoided her eyes.

'And you mentioned my transfer to the PPD?'

'Trust me when I say that you need not worry about your transfer to the PPD, Beech.'

The officer smiled. 'That's good news,' she said. She walked towards him, her hands clasped behind her back. 'It's something I've wanted for a very long time, a goal towards which I've been working. It'll be satisfying to achieve it, however so.' They were standing barely a breath apart. 'I hope we haven't got off on the wrong foot, Commander Delgado. Perhaps you'd like to help me celebrate my future post,' she reached out and touched his chest with the fingertips of her right hand, 'when we've entered slipspace. You're an arrogant man. But your confidence is attractive.'

Delgado experienced a sudden dizziness and disorientation he was unable to rationalise. He found his nobics unresponsive, as if suppressed, and was unable to utilise them to stabilise his body. The room began to spin; his heart hammered in his chest. He felt as if he would vomit at any moment.

Beech was kissing him, her lips warm and soft against his. Yet he experienced the contact as if he was a third party, watching.

Delgado heard Beech telling him that they must make sure the Seriatt was securely fastened, and then return to the flight deck to recheck the calculations and monitor the slide. After that they would go to her cabin and celebrate her promotion in the only manner truly suitable. He saw her turn and walk towards the unconscious Seriatt, but did so in a hazy fug, as if inebriated, drugged or concussed. The dense rush of his own blood was the only recognisable sound, swelling dullness that seemed to emphasise the pressure in his head.

Delgado tried to concentrate, to clarify his thoughts and see his actions through. He followed Beech, watched her. The officer looked over her shoulder and asked him to do something, to assist her in some way he could not decipher. He paused as some part of his mind made him consider what he was about to do, reminding him that this went against everything he had learned, everything he had stood for up to this point, however false and forced that standpoint might have been.

After moments which seemed like an aeon he managed to salvage a sense of his new purpose from the depths of his confusion. He drew his sidearm from its holster. Its weight and shape were somehow comforting, a reminder of other times; times he could not recall in detail. He raised his arm.

The first blow sent Beech to her knees, but she remained upright, as if praying. He moved around to one side of her and looked down at her face. She was staring, her expression one of slight confusion; her mouth was slightly open. The second blow left a wide, dark stripe across the side of her head, growing quickly, matting her hair as she fell to the floor. At the third blow Beech's skull softened, and Delgado knew then that she posed no further threat.

On the flight deck, his head clearer, Delgado plotted a course projection to the only place within range he felt could offer some protection, some time in which to review, plan, and possibly negotiate. First he would need time to decide what exactly he was going to negotiate, however, for although he knew what it was he wanted, how it might realistically be achieved was less clear. He could be signing his own death warrant. In fact, he might effectively already be dead. But he knew the power of the Seriattic *conosq* named Vourniass Lycern, and recognised her importance to Myson. Delgado had to hope that the General needed her as badly as he claimed, since that was the only way Delgado would have any chance of achieving what had become an obsession: the downfall of Myson, the collapse of Structure.

Three

an intemperate charge

Elixiion was a huge leisurestation, a sparkling cylinder of decadence and recreation hanging in space. Patronised only by those wealthy enough to afford its extravagance, it offered absolute escape, the opportunity to 'shed the binds imposed by an existence of virtuality' – at least, that was what the advertisements said.

The resort looked like a gem, radiant and perfect against the infinite depth of its hostile environment. As the slipspacer closed on the station Delgado stared at one of the many screens in front of him, studying the hundreds of ships that were constantly arriving and departing. They were tiny stars cutting smooth, elegant arcs through the cosmos, points of isolation for those within. Brighter points were the automated docking hubs where vessels too large to enter the station would moor, their cargoes or passengers later to be transferred by shuttle. *Elixiion* and its immediate setting was a micro-galaxy, planets and suns moving in perfect synchrony. The equilibrium was maintained by forces unseen, their power almost equivalent to nature itself. Delgado found this both attractive and comforting. His origins lay in such demonstrations of power. It was what had drawn him to this place; it was what would shape his future.

As the slipspacer turned to face one of *Elixiion*'s flat, circular ends Delgado opened hardline communications visuals and linked to the leisurestation's database systems. When the link was securely established he absorbed information quickly, seamlessly, all he needed to know streaming into his brain through the buffer provided by his nobic interface.

A multitude of data pages relating to the station and its systems fluttered in his head, staccato bursts infusing his mind with pre-processed information. He operated in the usual calm, unflustered manner of a long-standing Military Intelligence Officer. Anyone unaware of his internal crisis would think this any normal mission rather than a personal betrayal of all he had ever been.

When the infocram was complete he was able to commune freely with *Elixiion*'s Guest database; the system was receptive to the approach made by Delgado's nobics and was generous in its revelations. Data and stats were soon merging smoothly with his thoughtstream, linking with the information received by his nobics to form a strong overall awareness. He soon knew what he had to do, and the methods he would need to employ.

With the analysis complete Delgado sifted through the data and uploaded modified sequences. By the time the slipspacer was being guided into *Elixiion*'s spaceport, their welcome was guaranteed. But as the vessel lined up to enter the port Delgado felt that, despite everything – all the reasons and determination – he had made a bad decision, been swayed by something so intangible as the intensity of an emotion. Emotions were weakening, that much had been drummed into him long ago. But they were persistent, and he had always been aware that they compromised his ability to perform in the way a dedicated officer should. So he had suppressed both his emotions, and the fact that he recognised their existence at all. He had done this successfully for decades, something that was in many respects an achievement itself, considering his position. But it seemed that, driven by acrimony and hatred, he had reached the point where his feelings were too strong to hold at bay any longer. It was crunch time; time to address who he really was. He sighed and tried to concentrate on the image of *Elixiion* on the monitor in front of him. The leisurestation seemed to represent so much. It was a beginning, an end, a resolution.

The spaceport was a smaller cylinder within the larger one that was *Elixiion* itself, the slipspacer just one in a long procession of ships waiting to be designated one of the small landing bays set around the port's interior. The bays were squares and rectangles filled with white light, blocks of brilliance containing craft of varying shape and size. The craft themselves were blurred silhouettes, a multitude of designs indicating their widespread origins. Delgado was increasingly frustrated by the wait for a bay, which seemed interminable. While the slipspacer was unlikely to be noticed visually, its unique MI signature could expose its military status if the station's AI was alert. In such a case he would undoubtedly be questioned, turned away or possibly even boarded. He instructed the ship's AI to maintain clandestine operation protocols to minimise the risks, but only when the slipspacer had landed in the empty bay assigned to it did Delgado allow himself to relax slightly.

Everything seemed to have gone smoothly, no alarms were raised, no hazards identified. He extended his hyperconsciousness to subtly interact with any organisms and semi-sentient constructs in the immediate vicinity. Nothing seemed out of place; no disguised intent or address was manifest, no appreciation of their identity or that of their craft. Delgado considered that others might say he was demonstrating symptoms of unreasonable paranoia: while extended lack of contact from the mission team would seem unusual to anyone on Earth who might think about it, neither he nor Beech would yet be thought overdue. In any case, theirs was a low-profile mission due to Myson's personal interest and the General's wish to restrict knowledge of it; concern from other, lower-ranking operatives was therefore unlikely. Indeed, if any concern was expressed, Delgado felt relatively sure that this would quickly be quashed by a General keen to maintain secrecy regarding his exuberant Structure expenditure on personal interests.

The containment field was engaged, vents hissing and heaters whining as the environment within the landing bay was established. Now Delgado cast all thoughts of Structure and Myson from his mind and focused on the current situation. His immediate survival was paramount now, and successful absorption by *Elixiion*'s myriad Guests was the key to doing that. Not even a Structure operative saturated with the most advanced nobic evolution would be able to isolate and identify his personal thread among the tangle of those within the resort. But despite his plans for seamless assimilation into civilian life, Delgado knew well that the Seriatt was strong and that, if ineptly handled, could give him many problems he did not need. His course of action was already well set. Besides, he now had little choice: he was too far along his chosen path – if indeed it was chosen – to turn back. And, in many ways, he knew he had destroyed his path as he had travelled along it.

Lycern began to show signs of life the moment Delgado injected antidote nobics into her; a few minutes later she was fully conscious. Although clearly unsure of her surroundings, her awareness and perception were restored with remarkable speed. This disturbed Delgado: it demonstrated her level of mental and physical strength, and while the latter was never in doubt, the former could add to his difficulties.

She looked around the cabin with bloodshot eyes set in an ashen face. When she gazed at Delgado they were filled with emotions he found unrecognisable; when she saw the sidearm in his hand her expression did not appear to change.

'What is happening?' she asked. 'What is this place?'

The blood pounded thickly in Delgado's ears. 'Get off that bed, clean yourself up and let's get out of here.' He tried to nod towards the sink in the far corner of the cabin, but only seemed able to jerk his head awkwardly, and almost lost his balance.

Lycern pushed herself into a sitting position and then off the bed completely. 'Where am I?' She put a hand to her neck. 'And what have you done to me? My entire body hurts.' She touched her stomach. 'I think I may be sick.' She looked unsteady for a moment, then seemed to recover slightly. 'Am I to be interrogated? Or have you interrogated me already?'

'You feel sick because I've injected nobics into your body and they're neutralising the initial dose that knocked you out. It'll pass in a few minutes. You're no longer within the Affinity installation – not even on Veshc. That's all you need to know.'

She walked slowly towards the sink. 'I take it my suspicion that you are not part of the Affinity Group was correct,' she said, glancing briefly at the still slightly bloodstained floor.

'My identity and origins are unimportant.'

'You are from Earth.'

Delgado found it increasingly difficult to suppress the feelings coursing through him, the source of which he was unsure. Nausea welled in him. It was hard to form a coherent response to Lycern's statement. 'How can you be so certain?' he said eventually.

'It is obvious. Your manner, your arrogance, your transparency. I have come to learn that these are characteristics typical of human males.'

Delgado simply watched as Lycern filled the sink with water and bent over to wash her face, following the line of her body through her clothing. A hazy mist suddenly appeared at his peripheral vision. He blinked, massaged his sore eyes and temples with the fingertips of one hand, letting the gun in the other fall to his side; when he looked up again the room was spinning slowly, slices of light and dark shifting and flickering.

His nobics seemed to have become nothing more than a numb lump somewhere in the back of his brain; his testicles felt swollen and his penis throbbed painfully despite its flaccid state. He felt utterly disenfranchised from his own actions. He could not isolate what in his situation or self was causing these overpowering sensations, or determine what their ultimate effect might be, but knew that if they continued, he would not be able to carry his plan through.

That Lycern had so far been correct in every estimation of him made things no easier. His origins and motives, that he had killed the one called Byrbegch – she had been correct in everything. And as he considered this fact, he suddenly felt a compulsive need to reaffirm the power she seemed able to negate and exceed so easily, to prove that he was the one in control, not she. It was a dangerous impulse which in clearer times he would have resisted. But it was then, in that sparse cabin, overshadowed by Structure's eclipse logo painted on the wall to his right, that a new phase in his life truly began. And with it came a determination to reaffirm his self-worth beyond doubt, to step across the threshold of his personal commitment to Structure, to Myson, to the military. And to himself.

'Not only am I from Earth,' he said, sneering absurdly. 'I am a Military Intelligence Officer.'

Lycern stopped washing and reached for the towel in its dispenser. Delgado derived an irrational pleasure from her obvious discomfort. Her recognition of his words was manifest not only by the trace of fear he felt rippling through her, but also by some imperceptible shift in her stance. Yet he also felt abject guilt for what he was doing, as if committing a betrayal to someone close. He continued quickly, as if to smother such sensations, forcing out the words while their meaning remained clear to him. 'I was sent on a special mission to fetch you from the Affinity Group by General William Myson.'

Lycern turned to face him. Her expression was difficult to

judge, her alien features wearing an odd contorted grimace that could have represented any nuance of human emotion. 'I understand,' she said quietly, and nodded.

'That all you have to say?'

'What more is there? Your mission was successful and you are about to hand me over to your superior. Congratulations, Alexander Delgado. You are obviously worthy of your position.'

Delgado stared fiercely at her, yet his discomfort grew in the compressing claustrophobia that wrapped him as completely as her body had. 'We are not on Earth,' he said abruptly. 'We're on the leisurestation *Elixiion*. And I'm not handing you over to Myson. At least, not yet.'

Lycern frowned. But to Delgado her expression also seemed to be one of amusement. 'Either you are as good at navigation as you are at riding *rutull*, or there is a particular reason for this, Delgado. *Elixiion* is very distant from both Earth and Veshc. It is nowhere along the route between the two if my knowledge is correct. What does all this mean? Why have you not taken me directly to Earth – to Myson?'

Delgado was trembling, his heart squirming in his chest. His brow was glossy with sweat. 'Just prepare to disembark and then come to the flight deck.' He turned stiffly and walked out of the cabin; he did not respond when Lycern called after him.

In the corridor Delgado leaned against a dark bulkhead, closed his eyes and breathed deeply. The rhythmic pulse of the aircon fans matched the throbbing in his head as he tried to draw his consciousness from the edge of loyalty and betrayal.

As he rested there, he wondered what illness could have escaped the defences provided by his normally impenetrable nobics. It was virulent and powerful, that much was obvious. Maybe something he had picked up on Veshc? His eyes were sore, his skin rough with a faint rash. The immunisation in the nobics should have protected him. He had been imbued with the latest evolution, the most powerful strain available – or so he had been told. Perhaps Osephius had issued him with a toxic strain, a course designed to kill him after a given period: the period allotted for the duration of the mission. It was not impossible. It would not surprise him. And in truth, he did not care. He simply had to find a way of negating their effects quickly. In his current state he could control nothing, and given his situation, he had everything to control.

Delgado waited until a sense of normality gradually began to return. He opened his eyes and looked around. The slipspacer was, despite its SGX classification as one of the military's most secret and advanced vehicles, grimy, coarse, abhorrent and arrogant throughout. A tool much used to hammer home the stunning conceit of Structure's questionable idealism, the dark text of which was writ in large, unseen letters that smothered every wall. Bleak narrow strips cast long, insidious shadows from every ridge and rivet, and it was in these dense folds that his past lay. At one time he had felt completely at home in such surroundings, an integral component to the Structure machine. But he was no longer sure of his destiny, or if he was able to influence it in any way. He had to consider the possibility that he never had been.

Delgado had almost completely recovered by the time Lycern arrived on the flight deck.

'So why are we on *Elixiion*, Delgado?' she asked as she settled into the seat next to him. 'Despite thinking deeply, I am unable to decide. I cannot see the reasoning behind it. Is this vessel faulty in some way? Were you forced to come here?'

Delgado ignored her.

'You would have been wiser to take me directly to Myson,' she continued. 'This course of action will only cause problems. For you, at least.'

Delgado tried to remain focused on the screen in front of him. Although the information it displayed did not interest him, Lycern's face was reflected in its surface; he watched her, fascinated both by her appearance and the effect it was having on him. 'Why we're here is unimportant. Just do exactly as I tell you when I tell you. Understand? Then I'll be able to get you to Myson in one piece.'

'I think not.' He saw her reflection wear its odd smile.

Delgado glanced at the real Lycern and bile welled momentarily. 'It was what I was sent to do. What makes you think it won't happen?'

She looked simultaneously sad and frustrated. 'I did not say it would not happen,' she said quietly. 'I said it will cause problems for you.'

'Why? Tell me. I've been a Military Intelligence Officer for twenty years. Emotional detachment is second nature. You're nobody, nothing. I will do what I have to do.'

'I pity you, Delgado. You do not understand the magnitude of your situation.'

Delgado stared at her for many seconds, his face a bitter mask. A sense of panic began to grow in him. 'You'll be going to Myson, believe me,' he growled. 'Just do what I say and you'll live to see it. Give me any trouble and I'll kill you. Don't test me on this; it'll be the last thing you do.' He tried then to decide whether she was smiling or not. She seemed about to say something, then stopped herself. Delgado continued, 'We're going to disembark now. I've penetrated *Elixiion*'s Guest management systems and got a suite allocated to us. When we're questioned just keep your mouth shut. Got me?'

Lycern nodded slowly. Delgado sensed patronage in her expression and manner. He pulled his sidearm from its holster and placed it against her mouth and pressed hard, pushing her lips apart to reveal her teeth. His hand was trembling slightly. 'You won't even know what happened,' he hissed. 'Don't fuck with me. Don't even think about it.'

They walked down the ramp, a stiff, tense pairing. Delgado pressed himself close to Lycern, gripping one of her arms

72

firmly with one hand while pressing his sidearm into her ribs with the other. She seemed disconcertingly untroubled by her situation, as if immunised by irrational confidence or greater knowledge. Whatever the reason, Delgado was suspicious of her calmness, unsettled by it. He treated her roughly as a result, gripping her arm with far greater pressure than was necessary.

As they approached the bottom of the ramp, the door on the far side of the bay opened. A diminutive human male stepped through it and began walking towards them. He strode briskly, taking short, rapid steps, the sound of his heels echoing percussively around the bay. He wore a white, one-piece gown fashioned from what appeared to be silk. A long, tapered train dragged along the floor behind him, accumulating dust and grit, and he clutched a lightpad closely to his chest. A false smile petrified his delicately structured face.

'Hi, hi, so glad you could make it, nice to see you,' he called, drawing his hand through the air in a flamboyant arc. He looked past them at the slipspacer. 'I *say*, I do like your vehicle. Very chic. Very fast too, I bet.' He narrowed his eyes dramatically. 'What kind is it? I've never seen anything like it before. What an odd shape it is. I say, aren't you tall.'

Delgado responded to the man's demeanour in an appropriate manner, using his nobics to temporarily apply false mannerisms and speech patterns. 'It's an experimental model,' he said with a secretive wink. 'I test them.' He leaned towards the man and whispered, 'Don't tell anyone about it. The vehicles I test aren't supposed to be for personal use, but I couldn't resist borrowing this one.' He placed an index finger to his lips and winked again.

The man nodded. 'Your secret's safe with me, sir,' he said admiringly. 'Anyway, welcome to the leisurestation *Elixiion*,' he said in a louder voice. 'My name is Shushti Carr and I'm your Guest Representative for this module. I take it that you are . . .' he checked his lightpad and cleared his throat

73

'. . . Damitron Siretia Goghh and Plessidior Fubla.' He looked up and smiled broadly.

'I'm afraid not.' Delgado forced a smile and tried to sound apologetic.

Carr's smile faded instantly. His face looked completely different when relaxed: he looked years older and his whole head of hair moved forward. 'Oh, I simply don't believe it.' He furiously pressed stylus onto lightpad and the device made rapid, high-pitched sounds. 'I don't know what's going on here, I really don't,' he said, scowling at the information scrolling up the pad's screen. 'Every other arrival seems to be designated to the wrong shuttle or assigned to the wrong rooms or something equally annoying these days. This is a freight deck, you know,' he said, glancing up at them. 'You shouldn't be in here at all. Oh, no. You should be in a different area completely. A place where there are carpets and complimentary drinks, not freight-loaders and inventory terminals. I had to dash across here by aircar to meet you. I don't know, I really don't. Changes in management, cutbacks, insufficient staffing levels – you can't provide a good service with such pressures.' Carr looked up from his lightpad; its earlier bleeping had ceased. 'Well, if you're not . . . ooh, do you know, I spent *ages* practising those names – if you're not these people here,' he tapped the lightpad twice; it bleeped sarcastically at him, 'then who are you?'

'I am a relative of Goghh,' Delgado said with confidence. 'A nephew.' Out of the corner of his eye he saw Lycern look at him. 'My name is Cruz. Enrique Cruz. Goghh and Fubla were unable to come so they said we could use their suite. Goghh has had it reallocated to me.'

Carr frowned dramatically. 'Oh, I *see*. Right. You should have a personal allocation code confirming it, then.'

Delgado smiled. 'I'm afraid not. A last minute thing, you see.'

'But you should still . . .'

'No, sorry.'

Carr frowned. 'Oh dear.'

'Is there a problem?'

'Well, I'm afraid I'm not authorised to admit Guests who don't have personal room allocations. It could open the floodgates for illegal aliens and cause all sorts of problems.' Carr grinned awkwardly.

'You could overlook it just this once, though, couldn't you.' Delgado winked. 'I mean, we're obviously not illegal aliens.'

Carr seemed embarrassed and looked down. He squinted at his lightpad, tutted, and scratched a non-existent mark from the top corner with his thumbnail. He looked up, again wearing his rigid smile. 'I had better get some authorisation, otherwise I'll have to fill in a *lot* of forms and be hauled before the overseer. And a power-crazed maniac *she* is. Got it in for me big time, I can tell you. Can't stand the sight of me.' He widened his eyes and paused, as if to emphasise his seriousness. 'If you'll just wait here, I'll see what I can do. Back in a mo.' And with that, Carr turned and flounced out of the bay, his silken gown billowing behind him.

'You are skilful in deceit, Alexander Delgado,' Lycern said as they watched him go. 'A master of trickery.'

Delgado jabbed her with the barrel of the sidearm. 'Shut your mouth and keep it shut. I'm not interested in what you think. I need a place to hide you for a while until I have things straightened out, and that creep holds the key.' When he saw that Carr was strolling back towards them, Delgado finished the sentence with a wave and an even broader smile than before.

'Yes. That's OK,' Carr called as he approached. 'I've got clearance on that. It was a bit of a struggle but the Head Steward confirmed the cancellation of . . . er, well your aunt and uncle, and that you have, um, oh dear –' he glanced at his lightpad '. . . Goghh's rooms allocated. Cruz, wasn't it? That's right. So, sir, madam, if you'll just follow me? Oh – do you have any luggage? If you leave it in your craft for an automatic to collect, it'll be halfway across the galaxy before you know it. You can't trust any of them lately. They're all too concerned with Artificial Sentiency Rights and other such nonsense.'

'No. We have no luggage.'

Carr looked astonished and glanced from Delgado to Lycern. 'What? No clothes, no make-up? Nothing?'

Delgado shook his head. Carr looked at Lycern and she too shook her head.

'Well,' said Carr, obviously taken aback, 'there's a first for everything, I suppose. Very well then, if you'd like to follow me you'll be in your suite in no time.' He spun on his heels and walked so briskly out of the hangar that they were forced to run a couple of steps every so often to keep up with him.

They tramped along a grimy corridor with bare metal walls. There was a distinct smell of rotting vegetables, and the air was uncomfortably cool and dry. The light emitted by the wide, flat slabs in the ceiling was desolate, its faint blue tint chilling the corridor still further.

Droids and automatics scooted rapidly around them with absolute disregard for safety, either their own or that of the three people who had invaded their world, carrying items such as toilet paper and soap to temporarily assuage the seemingly neverending needs of the organics they served. The speeding machines frequently shouted at each other in their artificial dialect, their language colourful and terse. It seemed the tone of profanity was recognisable in any language.

Carr was somewhat embarrassed by the situation. 'Of course, Guests don't usually see this side of things,' he explained. He walked closer to Delgado, lowered his voice and placed the palm of one hand on the Structure man's forearm. 'Do you know, I had this great big speech prepared for your uncle about how sorry I was that his craft had been directed to a service deck, and when I found you weren't him after all it slipped completely out of my head! Sorry about that. But honestly, I don't need this kind of aggravation day after day, I really don't.' He looked from Delgado to Lycern and spoke more loudly, slipping back into his normal pattern. 'Still, now you're here I hope you'll enjoy your stay on *Elixiion*. I think you'll find it one of the most fully featured leisure facilities in the galaxy. If you have any special interests then you can gain information about them either from the Data Dump booths you'll find dotted about the resort, or from the information screen in your suite. Do you have any special interests?'

Delgado shook his head. 'None that you could speak of.'

'Well, you'll be staying in the resort of Countre so I'm sure you'll find something to suit your taste – perhaps something you've never tried before? There's free-fall parachute jumping. Boating and diving on the lakes. There's even skiing and snow-boarding or hunting and tracking in the mountains. If you have more cultural inclinations then perhaps you'd be interested in visiting the museums, theatres and art galleries in Ventria – that's another resort on the other side of the station. You can easily hire an aircar to get there. It's well worth the trip: a great deal of money was spent by *Elixiion*'s owners to secure some of the galaxy's most prestigious works of art, you know.

'In your suite you'll each find an *Elixiion* leisuresuit to ensure you have a comfortable stay. Which reminds me, I'll have to make sure they're changed for ones that fit you: they'll be the wrong size now. Where was I? Oh yes, there'll be a complimentary credidisc worth two thousand units for you to use as you wish, and an *Elixiion* ID chip to clip to your suit. Make sure you enter your own details into those, by the way, otherwise you might be arrested by Peacemakers for impersonating your uncle.' He sniggered at this thought, then paused at a door on their left. He keyed a number into an

ADMIT pad. The door slid open and they moved out onto a high walkway.

There was a lift nearby. Carr walked towards it then spoke into a small grille set into the wall. 'Lift request. Port level nine, cargo section deck one eight four. Two passengers for casting six, deck nine eight one.' Carr turned to face them again. 'This is where I must leave you, I'm afraid. Here's the key to your room – the number's on there – and a bleeper in case you have any problems.' He took Delgado's right hand and placed the objects in its palm. There was an awkward pause as Carr held Delgado's hand and looked up into his eyes, smiling brightly. Lycern cleared her throat and Carr suddenly seemed to become aware of the silence. 'Right,' he said, looking at the floor and blushing slightly, 'as I said, if you have any problems just bleep me and I'll be with you as quickly as I can. Have a nice stay, won't you.' He turned, strode a few metres further along the balcony, gave a final wave, then disappeared back into the service corridor.

With Carr gone, Delgado released Lycern's arm and walked forward a few steps to lean on the walkway rail. Lycern followed him. The view that greeted them was breathtaking. The *Elixiion* resort covered the whole of the cylindrical leisurestation's interior surface like a textural blanket of life. In front of them, above them, below them was an infinite web of artificial features: various types of terrain – forests, lakes, cities, villages, plains – all integrated to form an environment that was as realistic as possible without the restrictions imposed by nature.

Great sparkling accommodation towers rose from the curved surface, a hundred thousand lights glittering coldly. The peaks of snow-topped mountains, bleached and arrogant, serrated the inner sky. Luxurious liners drifted like polished gems across the sparkling blue waters of a hundred seas, cruising through archipelagos, atolls and reefs, and across ornate aqueducts. Wide walkways fashioned from blocks of multi-coloured stone twisted random patterns around bars, cafés and shops in a multitude of residential Guest centres. A variety of airborne vessels – aircars, fliers, shuttles and tugs – drifted elegantly through the air like metal insects, and hundreds of aerial walkways spanned the distances between these features, intertwined with the shafts linking starport to ground like the spokes in some giant wheel.

To their left, at one of the station's flat ends, there was a huge yellow disc, the warmth and light radiating from which as realistic as that of any actual sun. At the opposite end of the station, to their right, was a silver-grey moon textured with craters. The two false bodies faced each other in perverse opposition.

There was a chime behind them; they turned to see that the lift doors had opened. Delgado gripped the gun tightly in his hand. Lycern's stance was proud, upright, strong; Delgado found her strength and confidence arousing.

'In,' he barked, jerking the gun's snout towards the lift.

Lycern paused challengingly for a moment, before she eventually complied.

The large circular fountain in the centre of the main room reflected light from the coloured spot lamps positioned directly above it, casting rainbow threads that undulated across the ceiling. It reminded Delgado of the fountain in the courtyard in the Affinity complex; it seemed so long since they had been there. Other more ambient illumination lit the rest of the suite – discreet pools of warmth in secluded corners, precise beams cutting lines through air.

At the far end of the room was a huge window leading onto a glass-walled balcony overlooking the rest of *Elixiion*. Beside this window was a large bed with sheets of ink-black silk. The overall atmosphere was one of tasteful luxury.

Two leisuresuits lay near the pillows, one-piece outfits of thin grey fabric, lightweight and loose-fitting judging from their shape. The complimentary credidiscs and ID tags Carr had mentioned lay next to them.

'Goghh's obviously wealthy,' Delgado said. 'Probably a fucking politician.' He picked one of the leisuresuits off the bed and held it up against him. 'These are the right size. Carr works quickly.' He began carefully checking the suite's other rooms, peering into the wardrobes that covered the length of one wall, checking empty drawers. He pulled the studded leather chair from in front of the bureau near the bed, stood on it, and pushed up a ceiling panel to peer briefly into the dusty darkness beyond.

Lycern walked across the room to look out through the window. *Elixiion*'s floor rose like a huge tidal wave in the distance. She turned to face him. 'When do you intend to give me to Myson?'

'Nothing's set in stone,' he said as he replaced the chair. 'Best thing you can do is keep quiet and don't try anything. Tell me something before we go any further though: why is he so desperate to get you? Sure, I can see that having a child by you is probably the easiest way to form an unbreakable link with Seriatt, but there must be other ways. What makes you so special?'

Lycern looked away. 'The same reason you will find it so difficult to hand me over to him. Myson does not want *me* to forge peace with Seriatt. That was his original motivation, yes, but no longer.'

Delgado frowned. 'What do you mean?'

She paused, then looked back to him. 'What do you know of my species, Delgado?'

'I'm a soldier not a biologist. I'm more interested in how to kill things than what kind of food they like or how many times a day they shit.'

'*Muscein.*' The word was like an exhalation of breath, a smooth and sultry utterance. Delgado frowned. Lycern had to search for the right word to explain. 'It is a drug – a pheromone released from the *assissius*. It gives Seriattic *mourst* – our sperm-carrying species – energy and sustenance, and increases their fertility. The infants of our race are weak when first born, Delgado. Death is very common, and multiple pregnancies extremely rare. The *muscein* evolved to increase the sexual drive and physical stamina of *mourst* in order to compensate for this. It also ensures the *mourst* continue to return to us as individuals, as they are outnumbered by *conosq*. It is an essential part of mating, and keeps the Seriattic race alive. If you think you could satisfy me sexually without it then you are mistaken: you would have neither physical ability nor will enough. Even an adult *mourst* would struggle, and they are powerful indeed. *Muscein* is like a living entity within you. It demands attention, needs food. If it does not get what it requires quickly enough it will find ways of doing so. It is powerfully addictive, especially in those who are weak. And humans, Alexander Delgado, tend to be particularly weak.'

Things slowly began to clarify in Delgado's mind: his confusion, the symptoms of his apparent illness – and also Myson's appearance when he had last seen him. He maintained his calm exterior. 'So why am I unaffected?' Lycern's face contorted into the grimace he thought represented a smile. 'All right. Say this is all true. Why didn't you go along with the deal? Why run away? You must have known this would raise the stakes.'

Lycern sighed, seemed saddened. 'I used to be a scientist in Seriatt's largest academic facility, Head of Research and Development in our equivalent of your nobic technologies. In many ways we are ahead of you and given Earth's strength in this field, this obviously represents a threat to your planet's position of power. Myson came to Seriatt on what was claimed to be a peace-building mission six standard months ago. It was all a pretence, clear by his words that he was even lying to those supposedly in his confidence, and that he wanted our secrets in addition to peace. He knew who I was and, advised by certain Seriattic proctors and arbiters, courted me in the traditional way. Eventually he said that he wanted to join with me, to build a solid relationship between Earth and Seriatt for the good of the two planets. Seeing the political and economical benefits, my guardians coerced me into agreement.

'It was a charade, a decision already made. I am a member of the Seriatt's Royal Household – the *conosq dis fer'n'at*, revered, worshipped, adored by the Seriattic people. My so-called career was a concession on the part of the *mourst dis fer'n'at*, who understood my need for mental stimulation. While in one sense I was spiritually fulfilled through the offspring I bore, there remained in me the need to challenge myself, to expand my intellect. The lives of *conosq* and *vilume* tend to be limited, in many ways suppressed by the physical strength and dominance of our *mourst* society, despite the fact that there are fewer of them, and this was something I sought to fight against. And in my extreme situation I needed something additional.'

Delgado looked unmoved. 'Continue,' he said.

'When Myson arrived on our world I had just delivered the *Monosiell*, the next Seriattic monarch. He asked for an audience with my guardians in the Royal Household soon after he met me. Conjugation was discussed. Our union. The agreement was made in my absence by those in positions of power: a council of *mourst* and *vilume*. No *conosq*. They decided that I would provide him with an offspring. We joined that night.' She looked up at him. 'But that is all. There was no ceremony. Immediately I saw myself trapped, unable to escape the binds that would so restrict me. My *mourst* and *vilume* counterparts were blind to the fact that he sought access to our latest technological developments. Seeing the terrible potential in what Myson was trying to do, and although I despaired at leaving my beautiful world, the next day, before anyone in the household awoke, I took a ship and escaped to the only place I felt I would be able to hide.'

'Veshc. The Affinity Group.'

She nodded. 'There I felt I could bide my time, and begin to make choices for myself. Maybe I would eventually be able to return to Seriatt – when the storm had passed.'

'What about the child?'

'You assume much, Delgado. There was no child. Myson is a weak man who has abused his body in the way of many humans. He is infertile. I am *conosq*: we are able to tell such things easily. As he spoke of his desire for an heir I wanted to tell him of his inadequacies, shatter the pathetic illusions of his fragile human masculinity. But I realised that this would do nothing to help me, and could even serve to compound my difficulties. Perhaps even Seriatt would suffer. Let him entertain his delusions. They are of his own making and will return to haunt him.'

'So if there's no child, why did you run?'

'Many people suddenly had much to gain or lose. They would have found a way around such a problem. While Seriatts consider artificial insemination immoral, it is a technically simple procedure, and I have no doubt that I could have been forced to comply.'

'So now Myson is tormented by *muscein*, but has neither his key to lasting peace with Seriatt nor the military information he wants.'

'And his chosen *conosq* is in the hands of someone who will also be subject to the power of the *muscein*. The problems are many, Delgado, and not easily overcome.'

'He'll find a way around the Seriattic problem. He wants his sinz deals too badly. And if this *muscein* is too much for him to bear he'll just find another *conosq* to feed his craving.'

She shook her head. 'All *muscein* is different, unique to each *conosq*. Without me to satisfy its hunger he will suffer its full power. By now he will be maddened by it. As will you, in time. You may already be feeling its effects. Imagine them a hundred times as strong. Although you are physically fit where

Myson is not, you will eventually feel as if you are being consumed.'

They stared at each other. The air was tense, expectant. After a few moments, Lycern shrugged her cape from her shoulders. Delgado maintained his poise as he tried not to look at the body revealed to him. It was an almost grotesque form, fleshy folds of skin stippled with *assissius* glands, but utterly erotic nonetheless.

Lycern reached out to him. And despite his inner wish, he had no choice but to go to her. The compulsion was too powerful to resist. He was a prisoner, his ability to detach himself and make clinical decisions taken from him. Smothered by alien emotions he could not understand or rationalise, part of him hated Vourniass Lycern for her intimate violation of his physiology. Yet she had released a facet of his being he had never previously been able to address. It was a time of new awareness.

But even though Delgado felt more alive then than at the times he had faced death, as they joined, his mind drifted back to his mission. The loyalty he felt towards Structure and Military Intelligence, however tenuous now, lingered still. It was a battle inside him, of will, of honour, of self-belief. He did not know which side would be victorious.

Pain woke Delgado. It was not a muscular stress born of exceeding his own physical limitations; it was deeper than that, as though his body were being dismembered and immediately reconstituted cell by cell. His joints ached and shards of pain would occasionally shoot through his groin, anus and inner thighs. The area from his abdomen to his knees would tense for a few seconds in a rolling rippling wave that spread downwards before the muscles eventually relaxed again. The fact that Lycern slept peacefully next to him, the only sign of life in her body the fluttering of her eyelids, did not help matters.

Suddenly he began to sweat, gritting his teeth as he felt the rhythm's gradual return. As the discomfort grew Delgado tried to alleviate its effects through mental processes; it was little use, and again his body was sent into spasm, although the discomfort was slightly less strong than the previous time.

This was linked to Lycern, of that he had no doubt. It could simply be a reaction to the level of physical commitment she had demanded. But it could also be the *muscein* the truth about which he remained uncertain. Delgado considered that perhaps he had been hasty, stupid, possibly both.

Despite his previous reluctance to do so, he retrieved the infocram file prepared by Osephius, loaded to his nobics just before his departure from Earth. He drew the file to prime direct and opened it; a shimmering silvery rectangle appeared to him, upon which were details of the infocram file. He thought his way down the contents list until he reached *Seriattic race: overview*, then focused on the sheet and activated it.

He heard someone speak; it was not an external sound but a warm voice, neither male nor female, nestling somewhere near the centre of his brain; it was unnaturally dry, completely lacking in reverberation. As the voice began a manifestation appeared in Delgado's mind's eye, as if projected onto some invisible screen a few centimetres in front of his face. The first image was of a Seriattic infant, slowly metamorphosing as it aged.

'*Seriatt's dominant race consists of three sexes*: mourst, conosq, vilume. *Seriatts are asexual until puberty, at which point hormonal changes stimulate rapid shifts in both character and physique.*' The image in Delgado's mind stopped changing, and began to rotate slowly; although he had never seen one in the flesh, he knew the peculiar, slender creature was a young *vilume*.

'Vilume *are asexual, generally calm, patient, pragmatic creatures,*' stated the voice. '*Distinguishing features include vestigal sexual organs, a generally androgynous appearance and a slender build. The role of the* vilume *is to care for Seriattic offspring following weaning from the* conosq *until* moulniaq, *the first full ritual mating, after which they are considered adults.* Vilume *guide young Seriatts and*

85

instruct them in the rituals and behavioural mores of Seriattic society. It is an honour to become a vilume, *and when evidence of such a fate becomes clear in a child entering puberty it is customary for the family unit in question to celebrate.*

'Note: *only* mourst *and* vilume *contribute to the genetic composition of offspring. Conjoining of all three sexes is known as* driss lousoue, *and is felt to reflect commitment to the offspring that may or may not result from the mating. While* driss lousoue *are slow, relaxed, yet emotionally draining events often lasting days, part unions, known as* courm lousoue, *and consisting of any combined pairing of* mourst, conosq *or* vilume, *last just hours, and are physically more intense due to their shorter duration. For Seriatts, however, the acts of* courm lousoue *and* driss lousoue *are equally symbolic and passionate . . .'*

Delgado sped forward through the cramdata, the image of the rotating Seriatt presented to him altering again, growing taller, becoming more athletic with greater muscular definition; the skin darkened, and the tiny appendage at the *vilume*'s crotch enlarged substantially, its smooth skin becoming coarse and veined. He switched to normal playback.

'Mourst,' the voice continued, '*are Seriattic males. Averaging two and a half metres in height, they are physically well defined creatures whose main distinguishing features are ridges of ligament across the neck and lower part of the face, which pull down the corners of the mouth. There is a reptilian quality to their appearance, with their dark eyes and slightly scaled skin.* Mourst *are hot-headed, aggressive, brutish creatures, and form the basis of Seriatt's military forces. They also have a propensity to engage in highly competitive sports. The emotional needs of* mourst *are basic, and usually met either by mating or releasing aggression. These often occur simultaneously. The desire for such release can be so strong that it dominates their every action. This is partly due to the power of* muscein, *released by the* conosq *during mating.*' Delgado winced and chewed his bottom lip. The image metamorphosed again: the ligament ridges faded away, the form softening as breasts developed, the trunk thickening as the body gained weight. He increased the playback speed briefly, then allowed it to slow again.

'Conosq *are females, and could be described as anything from voluptuous to corpulent by human standards. Almost as sexually charged as* mourst, *they carry the eggs fertilised during mating until birth. During intercourse* conosq *release a powerful pheromone called* muscein. *This is released from the* assissius, *an opaque sac that emerges from the* conosq *during mating to completely envelop the other party or parties.* Muscein *increases the arousal of* mourst *and sustains them during the mating process. Its presence is also believed to raise fertility levels.'* As Delgado watched, a *mourst* appeared next to the *conosq.* They turned to face each other and embraced, and the *mourst* was quickly enveloped by the *assissius* sac that rapidly spread from the *conosq*'s body; Delgado couldn't decide whether events were accelerated or depicted in real-time. He felt uncomfortable stirrings as the manifestation briefly zoomed in on the glands running down the sides of the Seriatt's limbs and across her shoulders as they produced the membrane.

'*It is important to note,'* continued the dispassionate narrator, '*that* muscein *is highly addictive among* mourst, *and even more so among human males. Its effects are wide-ranging and variable, and care should be taken to avoid sexual contact with* conosq *during operations. There is no known antidote to* muscein, *and any operative affected by it will have to tolerate its effects until its eventual, natural decay. Case studies are extremely rare, but indications are that* muscein *can remain active in a human male for up to three standard years. It is understood that in cultural terms . . .'*

Delgado closed the file and the images disappeared: he needed to hear no more.

He closed his eyes and cursed. What the fuck had he got himself into? How could he have lost his focus to this extent? It was as if all his experience, training and natural instincts had deserted him to the point that he now appeared trapped by events of his own making, tormented by something he did not understand.

He suddenly began to sweat, and rolled onto his side to lean out of the bed; his body arched as he retched violently, but all he managed to produce was a thin strand of bile that pooled on the floor. When the attack had subsided he rolled onto his back again and tried to relax.

He began to experiment with the small control panel he found set into the side of the bed. For a while he entertained himself by adjusting the pressure of the water in the fountain, resetting the lights, altering the opacity of the window and balcony walls. At one point the colourful mural on the wall opposite him flickered, then changed to a virtumex image of male Solliwian *unills* fighting over a female. Narrow vents below the screen released the smell of dung and dust to enhance the atmosphere. The animals growled loudly, and curved horns knocked dully together as they fought. Delgado lowered the volume; steam spouted from flared nostrils as clawed feet stamped dry earth.

Beneath this display of violence was an assortment of colourful animated icons. Delgado explored further. Having specified a language he skipped through their offerings. *Incredible Elixiion!* was a list of boring statistics about the leisurestation: construction data, information about the owner group, power requirements and generation statistics. *Available Services* was effectively a noticeboard advertising translators, horny creatures of various persuasion, cheap drugs and craft for charter to various destinations. Then there was *Elixiion: Entertainment Universe*.

Delgado opened the page and began scrolling through the thousands of activity files that appeared. He sifted rapidly through a series of screens: advertisements, demonstration films, sales previews, sponsor drives and other miscellaneous trash aimed at *Elixiion*'s clientèle. Most was worthless material from an assortment of companies and groups relevant in one way or another to *Elixiion* or its Guests. Delgado was becoming bored and about to turn off the screen when something caught his attention. He backtracked to the image of six humans engaged in sexual intercourse.

He glanced at Lycern, sleeping next to him, and selected TEXT ONLY; words appeared.

INFOTEXT. 43/3424 . . . >234O3E4OJ.

O. PARTIES [OBSCENITY PARTIES]. SOCIAL GATHERINGS WHERE SEXUAL ACTS ARE CARRIED OUT WITHOUT INHIBITION OR REPERCUSSION. ALL PARTICIPANTS ARE VOLUNTARY. NO ADMISSION, ADMINISTRATION OR BOOKING FEES ARE CHARGED. NEXT OBSCENITY PARTY (HUMANOID), WILL BE HELD IN AREA TWELVE, SUITE 267454, DECK 9797, CASTING 4183. ALL RACES WELCOME. GUESTS SHOULD BE WARNED THAT ACTS OF LEWDNESS AND CONSUMPTION OF DEBILITATING SUBSTANCES ARE COMPULSORY TO ENSURE ENJOYMENT AND NON-OFFENCE OF HOST. OBSCENITY PARTIES SHOULD NOT BE ATTENDED BY THOSE OF A NERVOUS, SHY OR RIGHTEOUS DISPOSITION.

DISCLAIMER

THESE EVENTS ARE NOT SPONSORED, MONITORED OR CONTROLLED BY THE MANAGEMENT OF ELIXIION. PARTICIPATION IS AT GUEST'S OWN RISK.

INFOTEXT − 43/3424 . . . >234O3E4OJ − ENDS

The screen returned to its former state, but the words *Obscenity Parties* were highlighted, yellow on blue. Area twelve, suite 267454, deck 9797, casting 4183.

He looked at the Seriatt again; she was still sleeping. A combination of unfamiliar emotions rippled through him as he made a mental note of the address: nervousness, excitement, fear – he did his best to suppress them. Even if her *muscein* was inside him, he felt sure that the drug could not yet have taken him completely, and whatever its power he would not let it do so. Myson was older than he, weaker, and its effects probably more pronounced as a result. Perhaps Delgado would be able to resist the *muscein* rather than be overwhelmed by it. And this obscenity party would surely ease his discomfort, possibly even neutralise Lycern's pheromone completely despite what the infocram claimed. Negating its effects would enable him to make decisions as he should; a skill that seemed increasingly valuable.

The feelings he had for Lycern, Planetary Guidance, Structure, his own future, all required serious consideration, and only when his mind was sufficiently clarified for him to assess his situation properly would he trust his judgement fully. This represented a chance to find the key to control, an opportunity to reaffirm his position and the possibility of regaining his personal will.

But even as that positivity bloomed in him, doubts began to form. Perhaps he had acted rashly, bringing Lycern to *Elixiion*: although it was the place where finding them would be most difficult, it was also one of the likeliest places Myson would look, given the range of the slipspacer. And if Myson found them, what then? Delgado began to realise that, against habits formed through years of military training and his normal painstaking methodical approach, he had acted with neither initial nor contingency plans formulated. Driven by negativity fuelled by raw emotion, he had been weakened by bitterness, and his current situation was the result of that. He had no one to blame but himself.

He looked at Lycern's back and shoulders. A throbbing came, deep within his head. His mind felt numb and empty, his body weak. All of these factors angered him, for he was physically strong, mentally well trained and disciplined in manipulation of the subconscious mind. Despite their physical proximity, the distance between himself and Lycern seemed immeasurable. And yet regardless of this perceived distance and his apparent physical and mental weaknesses, the sight of her flesh stirred demons within him.

His choices seemed to be narrowing, but what these choices were, he was not exactly sure. And more than that, despite his wishes and intentions, he suspected that his feelings for Vourniass Lycern were changing, and his need to escape her invisible clutches becoming more urgent than ever.

Delgado walked, hands buried deep in his leisuresuit pockets. He felt deeply, unreasonably relaxed now his earlier discomfort was gone. It was as if his consciousness were coasting along a smooth plane, the air warm and still, the forward motion steady and unwavering. He wondered if Lycern was still asleep. If she had woken she would be wondering where he was, how he had managed to lock her into the suite. She might even be out on the balcony, looking across the artificial world in a futile attempt to see him. He paused and looked back at the tower in which their suite lay, but the floors and lights were too numerous for him to identify it precisely.

Given the conflict between the two of them, he then began to wonder about the wider friction between Earth and Seriatt, and the state of play in Dassilos. Forces could be engaged in combat around that distant world even now. Snubships could be dropping cannon-fodder imp squads, xip fighters attacking inbound Seriatt bombers out to destroy strategic targets, a Structure fleet massing to assault the Seriatt homeworld. Anything was possible.

But around him the arena was quiet, the only moving things being large automatics, cumbersome machines jerking awkwardly between benches and trees to squirt sharp jets of water into tight corners, rinsing away grime and litter. Delgado watched them, enjoying his solitude, welcoming a few peaceful moments when he did not have to meet the demands of others, provide any answers or enter into complex mental gymnastics. It was a feeling he had long forgotten, a feeling denied him by years of intense commitment to cause, campaign or institution.

He had always enjoyed his own company. As a child he preferred to spend his time alone, playing by his own rules, controlling situations through imaginative processes. Other people had for the most part seemed a distraction, limiting, unnecessary and often obstructive. He was never part of any crowd as a child and it was perhaps this relatively insular existence that imbued him with the drive and determination necessary to succeed within the Military Intelligence system, overcoming the extensive bureaucratic machinations, the political in-fighting, the spin and the whispers. The odds were stacked against him, everyone had said that, but his perseverance paid off and, as was always the case, he got what he wanted in the end. Perhaps it was his self-centred streak that had then resulted in his ability to obtain the required results, whether leading an elite fast-response Reactionary Forces squad to quash a potentially threatening uprising, or as part of the insidious Stealth, with its long-distance angel sweeps, counter-terrorism operations (sometimes terror activities in themselves), and occasional – and unofficial – 'removals'. If he were honest he would say he considered himself imbalanced, maladjusted and dysfunctional. Although such labels would seem negative to others, to him the qualities contained within their broader scope were assets that had shaped him, and continued to shape him still.

Area twelve, suite 267454, deck 9797, casting 4183. The address formed itself in his head as a flat text block on a rogue visual. He examined the situation: the problems were many and complex, but not insurmountable; the possibilities were equally great and far-reaching. A turbine lift was not far away to his right, extending up to the starport cylinder far above him, and down, to the cheaper apartments and suites in *Elixiion*'s skin. GROUND LEVEL, CASTING 6142 said the sign next to the lift door.

'Do you require transport, sir?' the lift asked as he stepped towards it.

Delgado found himself pausing to consider the consequences of his actions, the frustrating nature of his situation; something which in itself highlighted his abnormality.

The lift repeated its question somewhat impatiently.

Many strong emotions and sensations exploded within Delgado. It was a barrage – physical, mental, spiritual. He wanted the Seriatt, that was the truth. But to go to her now would be to admit defeat to something so intangible as emotion, and to become something he had never allowed himself to be: susceptible. He began to tremble; his mouth became dry, his chest taut. He felt nauseous, and an intense pressure built in his head as if he were being subjected to high gravitational forces. He had to reaffirm his self, re-establish command of his destiny – and quickly. Myson might need Lycern in order to avert the war that seemed inevitable, but Delgado had her. And he realised then that with every moment that passed, the war came closer still.

He stepped towards the lift. 'I require transport,' he said.

The lift was hovering in front of him immediately, its tiny containment field buzzing gently, blue pulses rippling.

'Please step in, sir,' said the lift, its tone more polite now Delgado was a customer.

Delgado took a pace forward into the lift, and turned; the doors were already closed.

'Specify deck and casting, sir.'

'Deck nine seven nine seven, casting four one eight three.' The lift immediately swept downward, and although its containment fields negated the physical forces of acceleration as it descended rapidly through *Elixiion*'s levels, Delgado felt a sudden rushing sensation nonetheless.

Delgado stepped out of the lift into a corridor. There were suites on either side; it was warm, hushed, carpeted and thoroughly clean. The air was still. The only sound was the faint, rhythmic pulsing of *Elixiion*'s heart. He walked slowly along the corridor, held secure by the closeness of the walls, the warm amber colour of the low ceiling. He felt as though he were floating, his motion surreal and disconnected, immunised against everything yet certain of nothing. When he came to the address where the party was being held he pressed the pager without hesitation.

He could smell drug cocktails drifting on the air the moment the door opened: potent mixtures, scents and flavours delicate and exotic. A woman wearing a skintight one-piece outfit of platinum gauze stood in the doorway. She was older than she wanted to be: a little haggard, but hiding it quite well with subtle make-up and regular semi-permanent cell shifts. A large snake was draped around her neck; it licked at the air, its black eyes like polished glass. An erect nipple poked through her revealing thin mesh gown. The woman leaned against the door frame and focused just past Delgado. Her eyes were red and watery. She smiled slowly, and blinked even more so.

'Hello,' she said. 'Who are you? Come to enjoy yourself?' She swayed slightly as she sucked on the straw leading into the brilliant red cocktail she clutched in one hand. The liquid flowed from its elaborate container like blood through a vein.

He glanced around the room behind her. 'I'm looking for a party.'

'You've come to the right place then. *This* is where the action is.' She made a sweeping gesture with her hand, but lost her balance and staggered back a few steps before falling on to her backside. She stayed where she was on the floor, sipping at her drink; the snake slid silently away.

Within the room the air was sultry. Delgado felt the miscellaneous drugs being used affecting him even as he stood in the open doorway. His body became somehow disengaged as if relieved of its duties. His consciousness began to slip. He tensed slightly, fighting the involuntary and disarming release.

Inside the suite he could see members of every humanoid race in the galaxy lying, standing or balancing in groups, joined in sexual acts of various type and severity. Oils lubricated intimate parts of bodies anonymous; groans and sighs softened the air; tongues and fingers probed and stimulated, coaxing reluctant sensations. Scented candles around the room heightened rather than disguised a certain sickly odour.

Some people were sitting, watching those participating while consuming potions, sucking on slugs or sticking seed pulses to themselves. Occasionally an individual, pairing or group would stand and join in with the activities of another, caressing, inserting, merging with one body or more. Delgado felt somewhat repulsed, and a tightening at the pit of his stomach despite himself.

'Do you want to join our little party, then?' asked the woman, who was still sitting at his feet. 'I can do things with my friend over here –' she looked around, searching for the missing serpent, then pointed '– over there, that would have you begging for mercy. He's very obliging.' She laughed, belched, spilled some of her drink down the front of her gown. She looked up at him and smiled again, fingers pressed to her lips. 'Don't be shy,' she said, cocking her head to one side. 'Come in and enjoy yourself.' She peered at him. 'You look as though you need it.'

Delgado's mouth was dry. As the snake-woman kicked the door behind him closed with one foot, he looked for someone who might be able to ease his discomfort, and perhaps return to him some self-esteem and control.

Although deep inside he suspected that only the Seriattic *conosq* named Vourniass Lycern could do this, when he made eye-contact with a human female on the far side of the room, he immediately walked towards her.

Sore again. All over. But different this time. And a headache, too; one like never before. It was as if someone was digging their fingernails into his eyeballs and trying to pluck them from his head.

He opened his eyes, winced, immediately closed them again. He decided to listen instead. Other than a faint trickling of water coming from somewhere close to his head, the only sound he could hear was the gentle humming of the aircon. He put his right hand over his eyes and reopened them, gradually widening his fingers to let painful light seep through.

He was pleased by the ceiling he faced when his eyes were fully open. It was a pleasant, bland colour, not too taxing on his recently abused brain. His left hand was warm and soothed. He wondered if he should raise his head. As he was not entirely sure whether this was still attached to his body – which seemed to be numb from the neck down – he did so carefully.

His neck was stiff, so he moved his head gingerly. The party was clearly over. Apart from one or two bodies, the suite was empty. The debris of the night before was scattered across the floor, however. Basins full of dried, dead slugs and empty oil jars lay discarded all around; abandoned sexual aids lay on tables and chairs. One particularly nasty-looking instrument whirred slowly on a nearby table, small studs sparkling.

He then saw why his left hand was warm: he was lying on the edge of a fountain, with his hand dangling in the water. He raised his left hand and wiped it across his face; the water was cool and refreshing. He licked his fingers, then sat up a little further and thirstily scooped handfuls of the water into his mouth, pausing to pick fragments of something from his teeth. He paused for a moment as cold drips ran down his neck, staring fixedly at a particular tile in the fountain. He breathed deeply, tried to relax his muscles. Then, with a determined movement, he sat bolt upright.

This was something he immediately regretted. His head throbbed with renewed ferocity, pounding like a Rell Drummer in a war zone. He clutched the edge of the fountain and fought an intense sensation of nausea. He watched a snake slip across the steps leading up to the base of the fountain and move off towards the kitchen in the far corner of the suite, then threw up into the fountain. He noted with some surprise that his stomach seemed to contain a good deal of food, none of which he could remember eating.

'You OK?' It was a woman's voice, one he did not recognise.

'Yes, I'm OK,' he replied, nodding as much as he dared.

'You don't look OK,' she said. 'You look terrible. Unless you're one of those white-skinned aliens – but you're too big. You're not an alien, are you?'

Delgado wished she would shut the fuck up. 'I'm an alien to someone somewhere. Everyone is.'

'Yeah, but what I mean is, you're human. You are human, aren't you? Same as me.'

He touched his forehead gently. 'I think so. Can't remember.' Delgado looked round to see the woman lying on the floor next to the artificial window, one arm above her head, the other resting across her stomach. She was pretty, but he couldn't decide why. Her blonde hair was cut into a neat bob. Her clothes were loose and rumpled, but for some reason he got the impression that she had not engaged in the activities of the previous evening as fully as many others.

'I'm not surprised you can't remember. You were really into it last night. I reckon you should see a doctor this morning. Get a few tests done. Make sure you haven't, you know, caught anything.' She pulled a face.

Delgado frowned, disarmed by a genuine lack of recollection. 'What did I do?'

She laughed. 'What *didn't* you do is more like it. A lot of people commented on your fingers. Strong but gentle they said. I remember that.' She nodded twice and blinked several times, as if trying to convince herself that she really did remember that.

He wondered what he had been doing that would require strong fingers, and looked at them with interest; they divulged no clues. He saw the snake disappear beneath the cooker in the kitchen.

'What's your name?' said the girl.

'Delgado,' he said, letting his head loll back again. 'Alexander Delgado.'

'You from Earth?'

'You could say that. Been all over though.'

'Where?'

'Here, there. Everywhere.' The conversation was boring him; he massaged his forehead with his fingertips in an attempt to rub away the edges of the pain. Lycern's face appeared in his head, and although her name temporarily escaped him, he knew she was important. He couldn't work out why his mind seemed so empty. 'What time is it?' he said, speaking carefully, trying not to antagonise the demons in his skull.

'Late,' she said, her voice echoing slightly off the glass as she looked out of the window. 'Can't be too sure, but I reckon it must be early evening. Maybe later.'

'Shit.' He stood slowly and massaged his aching thighs.

'You going?'

'Yeah. I've got an appointment with someone important. Know where the can is?'

'An important appointment with someone important. An important appointment with someone important . . .' She repeated the sentence over and over again, trying to speed up a little each time she did so. She stopped only when Delgado raised his eyebrows impatiently. 'Over there.' She moved her eyes slightly to indicate the relevant direction.

When he returned she was standing in the kitchen looking through the cupboards. Her creased clothes clung to her like a jealous lover's stare. 'Want anything to eat?' she asked, hooking her hair over one ear to keep it off her face.

'No thanks. I have to go.' He tried to make himself sound

energetic, despite feeling anything but; this was not only for her benefit.

'I know, I know: you've got an important appointment with someone important. Who is she?' She stooped and began searching through a cupboard in the unit between them.

Delgado frowned. 'No one. Who's who?'

The girl looked up, shrugged, then continued to search through the cupboards. 'Oh, nothing. Go to your no one anyway,' she said. 'Wouldn't want you getting into trouble with no one, now would we? Especially no one that important.'

Delgado watched her. Gravity made her look different when standing. There was something about her he liked; but it was something he was unable to pinpoint. This problem triggered some memory within him, but he could not access it.

The girl stood and turned towards him. 'Go on,' she said, motioning towards the door. 'You're late, remember?'

Delgado moved towards the door, his feet crunching on party detritus. He paused. 'What's your name?' he asked her.

'Celine,' she called, without looking round, her head buried in a different cupboard.

He nodded and turned to leave. 'Watch out, Celine. There's a snake around there somewhere.'

'Thanks. Oh, and . . .'

He looked around the half-open door.

'Don't worry about the pain: it wears off eventually.' She smiled and waved before she looked down, apparently trying to work out how the cooker functioned.

Delgado closed the door and began to hobble down the corridor towards the lift. He blinked rapidly several times, slightly unsettled: 'Don't worry about the pain' had been the favourite saying of a Drill Sergeant he had once had. He wondered if he was going mad.

Delgado drew his sidearm as he stepped cautiously through the slightly open door and into the suite. He crouched close to the nearest wall, automatically opening perceptivity visuals to check for booby traps. He glanced around the room looking for a body, signs of a fight, anything unexpected. Other than a few stripped wires and disassembled components on the floor next to the bed, nothing was evident. Apart from the fountain, the suite was silent and still.

Satisfied he was alone and in no immediate danger, Delgado closed the visuals and stood. He turned to examine the door; wires spewed from the open service panel next to it. Forcing the door to lock through his sidearm's frameware had been ineffective: in his absence Lycern had cannibalised the bed's control unit and escaped simply by opening the panel and undoing his crude adaptation of the door circuitry.

He swore, turned, strode across the room and kicked the studded leather chair. Despite his knowledge of her scientific background he had grossly underestimated her. He despaired at his own stupidity, the apparent failure of his skills, his increasing desperation. Now he faced a damage limitation exercise. Perhaps that had been his task all along.

The air remained thick with her anger, the strength of her presence still heavy. He cursed himself again: this should not have happened. He should not have allowed it to happen, let alone been instrumental in its cause. She had been asleep when he left, so with the amount of time available to her unknown, she would not have waited long before attempting her escape. Although it was unlikely that she had left the station completely, she could be anywhere within *Elixiion* by now.

Delgado walked around the room, hands on hips, mouth twisted bitterly. The bedclothes bled from the mattress towards the kitchen like dark liquid, marking the trail of Lycern's initial movements; he scooped them over one arm and threw them back onto the mattress in frustration, his face grim as he looked at the place where they had so recently made love. He could not help but picture the two of them together, writhing like slowly dying serpents, his own body lost like a grey shadow within her. His mouth suddenly dry, his bones aching and limbs trembling, he turned and sat heavily on the bed. Gripping the sheets between his clenched fists, he closed his eyes and released a long, deep groan of anxiety both mental and physical. Despite his apparent abandon at the obscenity party and the resultant fragility he felt, he desperately wanted Lycern again, and knew without doubt that he would willingly have gone to her had she still been there. It was more than a lustful desire. So much more. It was as if joining with her amounted to a verification of his spirit, the most basic affirmation of his being.

Much had been taken from him in the past few days. He was trained to endure long periods of intense concentration and physical stress, yet his performance was compromised by both the influence of the *muscein* – clearly more powerful than he had dared to consider – and the unfamiliar strength and subtle nature of the emotions it had released. Both were difficult to address, and inextricably linked to recent events. Maybe the pheromone had accessed areas of his psyche too long repressed. And perhaps these areas were home to the real person within him. The possibility that the true Alexander Delgado was only just beginning to emerge was the most difficult of all to accept.

He pushed himself up off the bed and began to pace back and forth in the suite, kneading his forehead and temples with his knuckles. This could not be happening, not to him. He was a Military Intelligence Officer, versed in power, control, the manipulation of others. But events had taken far more extreme turns than he could ever have imagined. He didn't yet know which strategy he would have to adopt to retain control; if control was his now to achieve. Salvaging any measure of what he had originally set out to do was unthinkable: he simply had to play the game to the best of his ability. The consequences of failure were impossible to gauge, the stakes immeasurably high. So, he had to play – and win. He had no choice.

Now he had to find Lycern, for she was the key to his future.

After taking a moment to compose himself Delgado strode out onto the balcony and opened enhanced perceptivity visuals. He looked down into the arena immediately before him. He recognised the area where he had watched the automatics, saw the lift that had conveyed him to the party.

The early nightlife was just beginning to stir Countre's arena: young couples were walking arm-in-arm; older, less active guests were enjoying late meals at intimate cafés; various types of music wafted from bars and restaurants. Above one of the lakes – just visible in the ground's rising curve – speed flyers were performing impressive acrobatics in tiny machines apparently constructed from pure gossamer. Ablaze with powerful coloured lights, linking and looping, spinning and twisting through the air, they were like battling crystalline insects. Onlookers stood around the edge of the lake and somehow, despite their distance, the sound of their cheers and applause managed to reach him.

His visuals proved all but useless, providing no information. Frustrated, he closed them and, although the perspective seemed flat and featureless in comparison, he watched the people below unaided. He wondered if one of those he could see was Lycern. What was she doing? Where had she been? To whom had she spoken? His head still ached deeply, and his mind was unquestionably dull, a blunt tool that was at this moment of little use to him. He felt pressure, as if beneath a great body of water. A white light suddenly drifted across his eyes from the edges of his vision. He became hot, agitated, and anxious. He perceived colours, sounds, sensations on the skin. Someone was suddenly standing close behind him, a thick-set figure in a uniform. He spun around and drew his sidearm, but the person was gone.

Within seconds his mental torment was over, but the residual aftershocks continued to ripple through him, further undermining his strength and will. It was exactly as Lycern had said: the *muscein* was like a living entity, demanding attention, needing food. He needed her now, he recognised that, but whether this was to satisfy his own needs or the physical addiction born of the *muscein* he did not know. In truth, the reasons were unimportant.

A chime suddenly sounded: he had a visitor; Lycern?

He walked quickly to the suite door and opened it; in the corridor outside stood the diminutive Carr, clipboard in hand. Delgado's eyes narrowed.

'Hi there,' said Carr; he appeared somewhat embarrassed. 'Got a bit of a problem. I'm sure it's all a big mistake. Mine probably.' He laughed briefly. Delgado remained stony-faced. Carr continued. 'The thing is, your uncle's turned up and, well he, er, he *says* he hasn't got a nephew.' Carr smiled as if conveying a nugget of humorous news. 'He also says he always uses this suite and hasn't reallocated it to anyone. He's in hospitality now, sipping the best wine I could find, but he's not in the best of moods.' Carr wrinkled his nose. 'I've probably got the wrong end of the stick or something, so I thought I'd check with you before doing anything.'

Delgado took a step forward and looked in either direction along the corridor: it was empty. Carr yelled as he was grabbed by both lapels and hauled into the suite.

Delgado kicked the door shut and pushed Carr back against the wall so that the two men were separated only by the clipboard, which was trapped between their chests. Carr's lips trembled as he looked at Delgado; he appeared to be on the verge of tears.

'As I said,' he whimpered weakly, 'probably my mistake.' He tried to smile again, but this time his lips refused to comply.

Delgado took a step back, pulled Carr forward, and turned so he was behind the small man. Gripping a fistful of the silken cloth from which Carr's robe was fashioned, Delgado began pushing him towards the bathroom. As they walked Delgado knew Carr was speaking, but the words were muffled, lost in the throb of blood thundering through his head. He activated his sidearm with his right hand, changing the settings with his thumb; there was no point making more mess than absolutely necessary, and if he shot Carr with a low velocity pulse at close range, the damage would be minimal, and easier to clean up in the bathroom.

As they neared the bathroom door Delgado accidentally stood on Carr's robe, which was trailing along the floor. Carr's shoulders jerked back and Delgado hopped off the gown, pushing the small man forward. Carr staggered, arms flailing, his clipboard cast through the air to the right. As he stumbled his own feet became entangled in his gown, and he fell forward, impacting heavily against the wall next to the bathroom door. There he remained, motionless.

Delgado stepped across Carr's body and leaned forward, peering at the man's face. Although it was clearly broken, Delgado fingered Carr's neck to check for a pulse nonetheless. He stood again.

'No mess, no hassle,' he said quietly. 'Suits me fine.' He turned and walked across to one of the wardrobes, slid open the door and manhandled Carr's surprisingly heavy corpse inside. There was just enough room to lie the slight man flat when his arms were folded across his chest and his neck straightened. Delgado covered Carr with a couple of bath towels and closed the wardrobe, then picked up the clipboard and stood on the leather chair to hide it on top of one of the ceiling panels. He then replaced the chair and walked to the suite door, opened it, and peered outside: it remained empty.

He glanced back into the suite again, his gaze resting briefly on the wardrobe within which Carr's body lay; nothing looked unusual in the slightest. Unless someone came looking, Carr should not be discovered. Not for a while, at least. All he had to do now was find Lycern.

★

Beings from across the galaxy cruised around each other on the twisting walkways, absorbing the atmosphere of the bars and street entertainment provided by jugglers, poets and artists, while feasting on fast-food and confections. The majority of Guests were human, and Delgado felt uncomfortable among them. He found civilians lacking in focus and entirely unpredictable, their actions and reactions illogical and often resistant to analysis.

Delgado acknowledged, however, that he too was subject to such traits as these civilians possessed. Perhaps he always had been, because his adoption of them was natural. He blamed the Seriatt. She had seemed to offer an opportunity; now she held him trapped.

As he wandered along *Elixiion*'s coloured pathways, the anxiety and guilt the *muscein* aroused in him strengthened the resentment he felt towards Lycern, and his natural stubbornness – part of his character Military Intelligence had forced him to suppress in the name of discipline – began to escape. As his bitterness grew his perception of danger was lost, and this in itself was dangerous. The heady combination of pride and his own unwillingness to accept that he was just another human animal – so brutally demonstrated to him by Lycern, and the all-consuming effects of her *muscein* – was potent indeed.

And yet, despite all the uncertainty that surrounded him, he realised that for the first time since joining the military he had a level of freedom. On the leisurestation *Elixiion* he was anonymous, just another Guest, freed of the automatic prejudice that accompanied his perceived Structure status.

He stopped walking. For a moment he simply looked at the people streaming around him, then made a decision: he would not look for the Seriatt or worry about Military Intelligence, the Affinity Group or the torment of the *muscein*. He would simply look after his own interests, ensure his own survival on terms he set himself. It would be a new and revelatory experience. Delgado's life had been so controlled, so regimented by routine, that such a release could be the answer. He had made no truly personal decisions since joining the military other than those involving the greater scheme of Military Intelligence and Structure. Vourniass Lycern, a Seriattic *conosq*, had drawn his true self to the surface. Yet despite this mental reflection and positive assertion of his worth, within the silver pockets of his leisuresuit, his hands still trembled.

He looked to his left where an artist sat drawing caricatures with charcoal sticks. He was a thin, gaunt man with a narrow beard and long, pointed nose. His intense frown occasionally cracked into a self-congratulatory smile as he extrapolated a subject's character and transferred its magnified image to the canvas. With elaborate flourishes of his right hand he made marks that exaggerated the features of whomever sat before him. Noses and eyes were perfectly enhanced; every trait of each person and the emotions deeper within skilfully accentuated. Eyes had life, expressions were isolated from their surroundings and given new meaning; souls were displayed. Upon appraisal of the artist's work the subjects saw themselves afresh, and marvelled at his talent.

Delgado watched for several minutes, remembering an ex-girlfriend. They had both been young, and she had held deep-rooted aspirations of becoming a great artist. Delgado, keen to make a good impression, had also claimed such an interest, and talked with great enthusiasm on subjects about which he really knew nothing but had researched thoroughly in order to demonstrate a superficial knowledge. He had been exposed as a charlatan during an embarrassing incident at a formal dinner party at her parents' home, and the girl had never spoken to him again. He remembered that her name was Jenny, and that she had blonde hair and carried the warm scent of fresh-baked bread.

He was wondering if she had ever become an artist, and was trying to recall her surname, when the artist motioned for him to sit in the chair opposite. Delgado turned and walked quickly away. He did not want to see himself afresh; many innocent bystanders would be caught up in the release of such monsters.

As he emerged from the gathered crowd he saw water, glinting like a sheet of beaten metal between the trees comprising part of Countre's wood. He stepped off the pathway and headed towards it.

At the shore the water eased off into the false night like a silken carpet, enhanced by occasional lines of silver. The water smelled fresh and its coolness reflected on to his face. Waves plashed gently against the shore.

Away from the lights and noise of the main arena it was surprisingly dark. Looking along the shoreline he could see couples tied in knots of knees and elbows, kissing, caressing, whispering. He saw one such pair toss sticks into the lake and watch them drift slowly away. They kissed and smiled at each other, lost in the intimacy of their moment. Delgado recognised their closeness, and was uncomfortable with the feeling of envy that lurked somewhere deep within him. He could neither address his feelings nor understand them.

His life had been one of unemotional distance; he had been separated from everything by both physical space and his military existence. Was it possible that these emotions, repressed and abused for so long, were taking their revenge while he was weakened? Had the necessity of hiding his feelings, of immunising himself from potential harm, rendered him incapable of experiencing true emotion? He did not know, but the accusation had been made towards him by others in his past. The fact was plain and disturbing: he appeared to be an emotional void, bereft of the experience of feeling. And now, with his deepest and long-suppressed emotions stirring, he did not know how to identify or control them.

Solitude apparently heightening his anxiety and confusion, he moved back into the wood, walking swiftly towards the light, where obscurity might be found among strangers.

As he pushed his way through the trees, the thin branches

whipping against his face, he stumbled across a couple making love. Their leisuresuits lay next to them, hastily discarded like the skins of snakes. They did not see him. The male was on top, his face pressed hard into the young girl's shoulder, his pale, skinny body thrusting urgently, tensing and flexing like a single muscle as he realised his primal instinct. The girl's knees were drawn back almost level with her shoulders. Eyes tightly shut, her forehead was compressed into deep ruts, so intense was her desire, so deep her greed. Her breasts jarred in time with her partner's exertions and she gasped repeatedly, a series of breathy exclamations. Her bottom lip trembled as she approached her peak, her gasps rising in pitch until they eventually became inaudible. The male's guttural utterances also rose, extended, aggressed, then faded.

Delgado staggered past the exhausted couple, his face grim and taut, his mind spinning. After a few steps he paused by a tree and bent double, vomiting around the base of its trunk. The sticky liquid he produced coated its bark like a thin membrane. His legs were weak. In his mind twisted a confusion of images and dreams. He was being manipulated by forces he did not understand, torn by the battle between desire and eroticism and basic human feelings. It was the bloodiest battle he had ever fought, and the first in which he had not been confident of survival. He pushed on through the trees, scared and angry. He needed her. She was the cause of and answer to his agony, essential to his continued sanity, and possibly even the key to his future existence.

When he burst back into the crowded arena he looked for a bar, a café, anywhere there would be people he did not know who might help him forget. Simple alcohol and the emptiness induced by a few powerful slugs in the company of strangers might numb him sufficiently; and perhaps when he surfaced from the depths of the resultant stupor, all would be well.

He pushed through a group of people who were watching a fire-eater performing tricks on a unicycle. The clown rode up to Delgado and mimed something at him, dancing back and forth on his single wheel. As the crowd laughed, Delgado saw only a blurred, painted face. He shoved his way past everyone and strode into the nearest bar, where he collapsed at a table. His body was glossy with sweat; nausea and pain racked him. In the flickering vacuum his mind had become, he feared the onset of insanity.

For a while, Delgado sat perfectly still, concentrating on the table in front of him, cradling his head in his hands until the intensity of the attack had lessened. When he felt a little calmer he looked around. The bar was dark and quiet in contrast to the bright, crowded walkways outside. It was incredibly hot; condensation dripped from the ceiling like tiny, molten pearls.

To his right sat a small, thin person – non-human by Delgado's estimation, although he was not certain. Black hair was slicked back across his scalp, but it was too long and unkempt for the person to be Mars Militia. His face was deeply tanned and leathery, as if toughened by prolonged exposure to natural sunlight; numerous fresh cuts and bruises added further texture. He peered at Delgado, one badly bruised eye almost shut. The alien appeared drunk, and did not seem to blink even with his good eye. Delgado wondered whether the alien had suffered most as a result of whatever altercation had occurred, or whether the other guy was in an even worse state.

Delgado let the heat of the bar soak into him and watched the passing people; they were happy, laughing, having a good time, looking for new experiences. A familiar figure appeared momentarily, but was immediately obscured. His heart thundered in his chest; his pupils widened; his mouth produced excess saliva and he hardened almost instantaneously as the *muscein* raged. He stood on the footrest of his barstool and squinted, searching.

Lycern's head drifted between anonymous shoulders and was gone.

Delgado leaped off the stool and ran after her, scattering chairs and tables.

The crowd was a sweating mass of bodies radiating heat. Delgado found himself carried along as he searched frantically for Lycern. He pushed between two tall, black–clad figures and emerged into an open space. The voices of the people around him formed a rampant cacophony: laughter, shouts, jeers, wails, jokes, gossip and other minuscule fragments of their lives momentarily invading his own. He spun in a tight circle, desperate to find the possessor of his will; and then he saw her, standing between a sculpture and a stall selling ices. He rushed forward, desperate, maddened. The crowd parted as he started to run. He called her name, screamed it incoherently as the masses swarmed and obscured her. When he reached the spot, she was gone.

He caught sight of her again a moment later, heading towards a data dump booth. He bumped into someone as he ran, stumbled and fell to the ground, hitting his head on a kerbstone. Blood briefly blinded him, and his cut head throbbed. People came to help him, but by the time they had raised him to his feet Delgado's awareness had returned; he snatched his arm sharply away and ran onward.

He was too late. Lycern was no longer at the booth. Her aircar, taken from the lot nearby, was rapidly shrinking, powering into the air on twin trails of dark vapour. Delgado was stunned for a moment, shattered at losing her after being so close. He was breathless, on the verge of tears – mentally and physically exhausted. Then he turned and looked at the data dump booth where she had hired the machine. There was still hope.

'Data Dump!' exclaimed the over-enthusiastic voice issuing from the speaker grille as he approached it. 'All you need to know about *Elixiion* and more! Insert any form of tender token to utilise.'

On the screen a friendly digitised *Elixiion* Host beckoned to passing Guests, encouraging them to part with money in exchange for access to the wealth of information locked within his hard shell. Delgado stepped closer and studied the keypad to the left of the screen and the credidisc slot next to that.

'Hungry to learn more about this marvellous resort?' the machine asked. 'Come and enjoy the feast of knowledge stored within my huge memory. Hire aircars. Visit the other side of the station. Book theatre tickets, restaurant tables, excursions and much, much more. My name is Yulos. Let me assist you.' Yulos looked out somewhat pleadingly.

Delgado fished the credidisc from the pocket of his leisure-suit and seated it on the small circular depression in the data dump's façade.

'Congratulations, friend,' Yulos exclaimed, 'you've made a wise choice. You're from Earth, aren't you? I can tell, you know. Tell me, good human, what is it that I can do for you this fine day?'

'That aircar,' said Delgado, pointing vaguely into the empty air where Lycern's flier had once been. 'Where's it going?'

'I'm tempted to say something about manners,' said Yulos with seriousness.

Delgado took a deep breath. 'It's a friend of mine,' he said evenly. 'I need to know where she's going.'

'Ah. Had a lovers' tiff, have we, friend? Never mind. All's well that ends well. Ships that pass in the night. A bird in the hand is worth two in the bush. Never a dull moment and all that.'

Delgado tried to maintain his calm. He wiped blood and sweat from his brow. 'Can you help me or not?'

'I don't know, sir. All bookings and hire details are private, just between the client, the car and the system of the car's owner. I could scan over the owner's files and pretend it's a peacemaker matter, I suppose. Checking up on Guests or something. But a search like that – which could put me in serious trouble if I were to be caught . . .'

'How much do you want?'

'The search will cost you five two hundred pulses. Want me to go ahead?'

'Yes.'

'Very well, sir. Deducting from your token. Scanning now.'

Delgado rapped his fingers on the screen's surround. Faint music began to spill from the unit's speakers. On the screen Yulos performed a slow and frustrating mime of searching high and low in his totally empty and completely white environment. When the search was complete he returned to the front of the screen, grinning cheerfully at Delgado.

'Got the information you want, sir,' he said triumphantly.

Delgado waited long moments, but the information did not seem to be forthcoming. 'Well, can you tell me where she's going, please?' he hissed.

'Of course I can, sir. But that will cost an extra five hundred pulses. I've got profits to make, you know, budgets to meet.'

Delgado nodded, his face twisted and gently thumped the screen surround. 'Never mind Yulos, more like my fucking loss. Yes. Go on, go ahead, take the fucking money.'

'Thank you, sir. Deducting now. She is going to area twelve. But, my oh my, that's a rough place over there. There's a bar called Gessio's Place that attracts all sorts of lowlife. You'd better take some peacemakers if you want to make sure there's no trouble.'

'I'll take the risk.'

'OK, but don't say I didn't warn you. You'll want to hire an aircar now, I suppose, to go after her. All the ones you can see parked behind me are booked, but I think there's one in area nineteen that I may be able to procure for you. I am friendly with the controlling system over there.' The image stooped forward as if sharing a secret. 'It's an old unit, but I can get it here quickly if you want it. *Do* you want it?'

'How much will it cost?' said Delgado.

Yulos smiled, stood upright and grinned. 'I like your style, friend.'

*

Yulos was right about the aircar being old. It was so old, in fact, that Delgado had been tempted to demand a refund when he saw it land in Countre. It was uncomfortable, noisy and unrefined. The machine was powered – if that was the correct word – by a single, piston engine that, to an ear as unfamiliar with such aged technology as his, seemed to be misfiring. The vehicle was scarred and battered. The tyre on its small single tail-wheel looked only half inflated. He had to climb a ladder that descended from the fuselage in order to clamber into the cockpit, which was extremely basic, equipped only with a physical joystick, LCD instrumentation and an autopilot unit. As far as he could gather there was no AI technology of any kind. Certainly no nobic interface. As the machine taxied on to the runway, Delgado's confidence in its ability to convey him safely to his destination was not great. He reflected on the fact that he had recent experience of crashing, which might prove useful.

Once airborne, the aircar followed exactly the same flight path as Lycern's; something only made possible by yet another payment to Yulos. The action of revealing the intentions of one Guest to another – whatever their relationship – apparently contravened Clause 1875 of his Guest Interaction and Information Dissemination Guideline Document. But upon further deduction from Delgado's credidisc, Yulos had proved willing to overlook the moral overtones on this occasion. Just for Delgado's sake.

As the aircar crossed the countryside between *Elixiion*'s more populated areas, the huge grey buildings of Countre gradually dispersed until eventually the only constructions Delgado could see below him were outposts of various sizes, scattered through the artificial wilderness. He squinted as he tried to make out more detail. His visuals were able to offer little clarification, but there seemed to be both pastoral and arable farming, trawlers fishing on the larger lakes, the occasional amenities installation and one or two specialist Guest entertainment zones. Forests and woods provided dark coarse patches.

The distances between the resorts were great, more extensive than Delgado had anticipated. Countre and Vinyess were just two among dozens of similar resorts around the interior surface of *Elixiion*, all of which were joined by wide groundcar highways. From his position these highways looked like strong, dark bands rising parallel to each other at regular intervals up the curved interior of the station. The roads were linked by narrower tracks to form a matrix of distribution and access routes, while the lifts to the spaceport were spines drawn thick into each resort.

Close to a line of mountains, the aircar began to descend. The stone-like grinding of the engine in front of him deepened in tone, the vehicle tipped on to one aged wing-tip, then slowly began to spiral downward.

As the aircar circled, rapidly shedding speed, Delgado saw a small settlement, the buildings clustered like a rash at the foot of the mountains. The streets were narrow apart from the two main arteries, which crossed each other through the centre of the community. The streets themselves looked deserted, the buildings in a poor state of repair. Although some were barely more than sheds, those lining the two main roads seemed more substantial. Each gaudily painted building was four or five storeys high and fronted by a great porch. Elaborate wooden carvings painted in equally blinding colours decorated the eaves and chimneys.

The aircar sank lower until it was circling a flat grey strip on the outskirts of the settlement. The engine quietened still further, flaps extended from the wings with an asthmatic wheeze and the vehicle slowed almost to stalling speed. It maintained an altitude of about twenty metres for a few seconds, then sank the final distance, flared, and made a precise three-point landing. Delgado relaxed slightly as a sheet of dust and grit rose to obscure his view in the turbulence of the aircar's propeller. As the machine slowed and taxied towards the parking area, Delgado noted that no other aircars were present.

A feeling of unease rippled through him as he walked away from the vehicle and approached the buildings. It occurred to him that the settlement looked deserted. Indeed, he had seen no signs of life from the air; even his visuals had remained dormant, and seemed reluctant to respond to his attempts to rouse them. He began to suspect that Yulos had been less than honest, and briefly entertained ideas of dismembering the booth and spreading it across a broad area. That'd teach the greedy little fucker.

Clouds of dust rose with every footfall as he crunched his way across the gritty ground at the outskirts of the settlement. The atmosphere was dry and somehow cool despite the relatively high ambient temperature, as if the air was somehow less dense. The fact that he was in the foothills of a small mountain range was irrelevant: the air within *Elixiion* would be maintained at a fairly constant pressure throughout, he was sure.

Faint music began to trip through the streets. Delgado stopped and listened for a moment, frowning. He then continued, walking past a large building and turning onto one of the outpost's main thoroughfares. He paused; the music was coming from somewhere nearby, from within one of the buildings. He did not have to walk much further before he discovered exactly which.

It was a bar, rundown and unkempt. The word 'saloon' slipped sideways into his mind from a history lesson long ago. The blue neon sign above the entrance crackled, buzzed and flickered as sparks danced behind it. Two sections of the sign were unlit, numb limbs on a lively body: *ssio's pla,* it said. As he climbed the wooden steps of the porch the sign buzzed even more loudly, sparked, then popped. Delgado looked up: the *pla* part of the sign was no longer illuminated.

He pressed his palm against the door and pushed.

Exotic music exploded at him, a rich mosaic of strange and mellifluous textures, harmonics and layers of cold, gaunt tones that rattled his bones. The music was boosted by the clamour of many voices in a multitude of languages. The lush, wet-grass smell of cheap, factory-farmed slugs thickened the dense environment still further.

The bar's interior décor was subdued. The walls were painted dark brown, the ceiling almost black. Windows were small and few, illumination being provided by two pairs of spotlights on either side of the room, which cast sickly yellow pools across tiny areas. The only other light was from the screen on the autosnax dispenser next to the bar. This threw stripes of red and gold across the nearest tables, warming the faces of those who sat at them, and reminded Delgado of the banner of The Ultimate Union. A fan spun lazily in the centre of the ceiling, oscillating slightly as it stirred the heat. It had the lethargic motion of a unit exhausted by constant use.

Delgado began walking towards the bar, but had taken only a few steps when he saw Lycern. She was on the other side of the room talking to a man wearing the grey and black uniform of the New Buhatt Military Coalition, formed on the planet by a 'cartel of interested parties' following the quashing of the Rebellion. He was either a Captain or a Lieutenant, but Delgado was too far from the man and insufficiently familiar with modern Buhatt uniforms to distinguish his rank precisely.

The two of them were laughing with each other, making jokes, openly flirting. The Buhatt was gazing with lecherous longing at Lycern's cleavage as she rocked with laughter at something he had said. Their mutual falsity both frustrated and angered Delgado. He felt a rage rising within him, fuelled by the clamour of what seemed like a thousand unfamiliar voices in every part of his head, screaming, laughing, taunting. His muscles tensed, relaxed, tensed again. He felt incredibly alert, awareness of his surroundings passing even the boundaries of perception offered by his fully active nobics; yet it was a surreal, disconnected awareness, itself dangerously false.

Then, suddenly and impulsively, acting independently of the world around him, freed from its constraints and protocols, Delgado's course was clear, his actions instinctive.

He pushed his way through the throng and grabbed Lycern by the upper arm, twisting her round to face him. When she saw him her eyes widened. He grinned maniacally and leered towards her, his face ruddy with anger. Blood thundered in his ears and the incessant voices grew louder and louder, until they were an unintelligible cacophony of raging angst desperately trying to escape from within him.

Lycern tried to wriggle free but Delgado tightened his grip, purposely trying to hurt her. She winced and said something that was lost in the overall noise. The Buhatt stepped forward and tried to lever them apart with one arm. So great was his desire for violence as a way of venting his pent-up frustration, Delgado almost welcomed his interference. For a moment the three of them were a clenched fist of tension, unmoving in the midst of the bar's tumult. Faces turned towards them; people stepped back, making room for whatever was to come.

As the Buhatt tried to push his way between Lycern and Delgado, the Military Intelligence Officer released his grip on the Seriatt and threw a punch. It landed squarely on the Buhatt's chin and he staggered backwards a few steps before falling against a table, scattering chairs, drinks, other patrons. The Buhatt rolled across the floor and jumped quickly to his feet. A small sizzler was clutched in one hand; it fizzed and spat like an angered creature, venomous and agitated. Other armed Buhatts appeared behind him.

Delgado faced the group, sweating and breathing heavily. His muscles were twitching, the voices roaring in his head, his vision tunnelled by the dark shadows of hate and desire. 'Come on, come on,' he hissed under his breath. 'You don't know who the fuck you're dealing with here. Come and see what I can do. Come and spill your stinking guts.'

The Buhatt stood in a fighting stance and spat words at Delgado in his bitter, acid tongue as he dabbed a bleeding lip. Lycern stepped in front of Delgado, faced him, and said something muffled by the voices and his own thudding blood. He stared angrily at her, uncomprehending. She spoke again, then took a pace forward and touched his arm; he flinched as if stung, his eyes wide. Lycern took another step. Delgado glanced from Lycern to the Buhatts and back again. He caught her scent as she got closer to him, and the thick, intoxicating aroma that seemed to have been in his head since their first meeting filled his nostrils again, a sickening combination that stuck at the back of his throat. She reached up and placed the palm of one hand on his cheek; her flesh was cool against his and he felt instantaneously reinvigorated. Suddenly, through this simple contact, his need was temporarily sated. And with this release returned his strength and determination.

Delgado gripped Lycern's wrist and twisted it away from his face. He pushed her to one side and in a fraction of a second his sidearm was drawn and primed. A multitude of nobics visuals flashed open in his head as mind and weapon linked in an automated fusion of biotechnical and electronic processes. Before either party had realised what was happening he had killed four of the Buhatts with clinical accuracy and minimum wastage, and was priming for the rest.

He stared at the remains: stinking, smoking pools of putrefaction branded into the floor. He looked around; the other customers were staring at him, terrified, incredulous; some took a step back when he looked at them. And for a moment Delgado tasted the power of old: the true power of a Military Intelligence Officer; the power of a killer.

He looked up and saw two grey/black uniforms slipping quietly to the back of the crowd. Delgado felt that they were hiding, but he knew they could also be going to fetch help. He looked at Lycern. For some reason she had vomited and was sobbing; mucus was trailing from her nose; her cheeks were red and wet with tears. Her face wore a pained, pitiful expression. Delgado hated her then, but knew well that he also had other feelings which were far too complex to address.

His mind clarified by the Seriatt's touch and his own violent release, he grabbed Lycern's wrist and dragged her out of the bar into the deserted street, pulling her roughly towards the waiting aircar.

They didn't speak until they were back in the suite.

'What did you think you were doing?' Delgado's face was taut.

'I was trying to escape. What did you expect me to do? Sit here and wait for your return? You are even more foolish than I thought, Alexander Delgado. I learned that the area is popular with ship crews. There are brothels and gambling is legal so that is where they go. I hoped to meet someone who would be able to convey me to safety. Somewhere other than here, at least. You must have expected this. I do not want to go to Myson.'

Delgado swallowed as he thought about it, felt perspiration on his forehead. He leaned close to her. 'Next time I'll blow your brains out when I find you – understand me?' Lycern said nothing. He jabbed her left shoulder with the fingertips of his right hand. She took a few steps backwards. Delgado took a pace towards her and reached out, gripping her shoulders firmly. 'Do you understand?' He shook her as he spoke, emphasising each word with vehemence. When she still did not respond, Delgado leaned so close to her that he could see the veins in her eyes. He began to tremble. When he repeated the question with forced anger, she simply stared at him. She was his prisoner, yet it seemed that he was also hers. They both knew that she had the power to manipulate him.

Lycern's head snatched sharply sideways as Delgado slapped

her; his signature was written red in her flesh like a brand of ownership. She turned her head to face him once again; he saw only purity and resolve in her eyes. She could defeat him simply through being herself. He could respond to her power in the only way he knew, and in truth it was a way that indirectly served to weaken him.

Delgado released his grip and let his arms drop to his sides. Forced to look away from her, he found his eyes inadvertently fixed on the wardrobe in which Carr's body was hidden.

Lycern reached out, gripped his chin firmly between the fingers of one hand and turned his averted face towards hers. She stepped closer to him, squeezing his cheeks so hard his mouth was contorted into a comical grimace. She stared into his eyes for many seconds then pressed her warm, soft lips against his, firmly yet gently.

It was the most intimate contact Delgado had ever encountered, a disarming action filled with passion and meaning. It encapsulated everything he knew that was erotic, arousing and animal; yet it was simultaneously tender and restrained. Her scent was overpoweringly rich, choking in its concentration, and despite all his training and capabilities, he could do nothing to assuage its effects. Instead there was an instantaneous and reciprocated transmission of energy, an infusion of ultimate belonging shared between them. Her tenderness was a powerful foil to his physical strength, the appalling antithesis of everything he was and all he knew. It highlighted so many of his weaknesses, and the fact that power was not necessarily the key to unlocking the will of others. Delgado wanted to step back, deny her ability to control him through such basic manipulation; but he could not, for he had lost the ability to reason. All he knew with certainty was that her *muscein* was a demonic spirit torturing him from within.

'Do not think me weak,' she said softly.

He tried to say 'I could not,' but as she pulled him to the bed with her, he began to realise for the first time that he was effectively her slave, held in bondage. How he might break free from the invisible binds that restrained him he could not see, but he knew that he must if he were to survive. And soon.

Lycern was pressed close to him, her full and fleshy body warm against his muscular frame. When she spoke, her voice was little more than a breath in his ear.

'Will you answer me a question, Delgado?'

'Ask it and find out.'

'Why did you bring me here? You could have completed your mission easily. Yet you did not. What were your motives?'

Delgado absently studied the patterns of light tripping across the ceiling. 'I guess it was power. That's what it boils down to.'

'Your power?'

He said nothing.

'I do not understand.'

Delgado thought about it. He was not entirely sure the reasons he had imputed to himself were the ones which actually drove him. But they seemed the most credible, the ones that were most easily justifiable. 'I'd had enough. I felt betrayed. I'd given them everything, served well, contributed to the ongoing propagation of Structure's opinions across the galaxy throughout my career. I was respected, valued, sometimes even consulted when new campaigns were planned. We were involved in a programme of human expansion, of learning from other cultures, of *giving*. There were occasional skirmishes and peace-keeping asides that interrupted the flow, such as the ongoing problems with Seriatt, but overall the human race was growing in ways more than physical.

'Then Myson came to power and everything changed. He's neither politician nor soldier. He has money, that's all. He built an army of mercenaries and challenged the position held by General Smythe through force and by bribing half the Planetary Council. Eventually there was a bloody coup and

Smythe was deposed. Structure, Military Intelligence, Stealth – they all became part of Myson's own private empire, tools for satisfying his debased whims. He wanted none of the old format, none of the progressive policies, and anyone who resisted the changes he implemented found life difficult to say the least. You slept with one eye open and a hand on your gun after the coup. If you criticised him openly you didn't sleep at all. Well, it was either that or over-consumption of *tersip*.' Delgado smiled thinly; Lycern clearly didn't understand. He sighed and shook his head as he continued. 'Of course, there were those who embraced the new opportunities for the inhumane treatment of others that presented themselves under his rule, that's true enough. Many of my colleagues were happy to adopt roles as rapists, torturers and sadists on back-ward worlds whose inhabitants didn't know how to defend themselves against skyships, blastplate and high-intensity plasma weapons. But I wasn't one of them. And that was my biggest failing. I gave my life to Structure's military, but when the balance changed I was unable to change with it.

'They knew pretty quickly that I'd prove troublesome in the long term. It was obvious: I kept overruling orders in the field, using less firepower than I was told, fewer skyships, fewer grunts. Sometimes I'd use more, but it was usually less. It wasn't because I simply wanted to disobey orders. I just felt I was in the best position to make judgements on situations. When they said to use forty skyships and weather conditions meant at least thirty of them would be destroyed with no measurable gain, I simply sent up fewer instead because that way our losses were minimised and we made the same kills. So gradually I was moved to the sidelines. Myson knew he couldn't have me killed or get rid of me overnight because we shared too many sympathisers, people who knew and respected me but were also aroused by the personal growth and fulfilment opportunities he offered. But if he kept me out of his way, I could do no harm.

'Over time Structure became his toy, and now he looks for conflict wherever he can, controlling his minions through *driette* slugs and the promise of financial reward. He has no pride, no interests other than his own. He's just greedy.' He looked at her; his pain threatening to surface. 'I joined the military to do something worthwhile and that became impossible. I wanted revenge for what he'd done to all I'd been and wanted to be. He took it all away.'

'So why do the people of Earth allow him to continue if he is so corrupt? Why has no attempt been made to stop him?'

Delgado snorted. 'History. His grandfather funded the first habitats and passed on the legacy. John Myson had a huge fortune built on selling technology to developing worlds. His personal funds gradually overwhelmed Earth's financial market, and those of many other planets, to the extent that he had controlling stakes in almost all influential corporations, and large holdings of smaller players. It increasingly destabilised all the cultures – and sometimes even systems – in question. So he commissioned the first habitat. Self-contained, fully self-sufficient, utilising every technological advance, the building – if you can call it a building – was home to five hundred thousand people. They turned their backs on the pollution, decay and crime they were continuously forced to fight outside, and enjoyed a new life within. The programme offered everything, and within a few decades the majority of Earth's population lived in Myson habitat towers. William Myson is a descendant of the man who gave most of the human race safety, security, health and luxury, all for free. Why would they resist his rise to power?'

Lycern paused. 'But I still do not see what you hoped to achieve by bringing me here, by kidnapping me. Surely such an act cannot help your cause or redress your perceived injustices. You cannot regain your former status through this act. You will simply make things worse. Correct?'

Delgado thought. 'I wanted recognition. I wanted respect.' His words tailed off.

She nodded slowly. 'You had not anticipated the *muscein*. Now you are finding it difficult, as I said you would, to be without me.' She pushed herself up in the bed and leaned across him. 'So what will you do now, Alexander Delgado? Now that you have made a trap and cast yourself into it.'

Delgado tried to avoid inhaling her aroma, or looking at her strange Seriattic face or the deep, dark cleavage before him. But the temptation was strong, the need stronger still. The *muscein* beat a determined, incessant rhythm. And it was then that he reached a decision. 'There's only one thing we can do,' he said calmly. 'Only one way to beat Myson.'

She looked at him intently.

'Go to Seriatt.'

She seemed unsure whether he was serious. 'But our respective worlds are on the brink of war, Delgado. There really would be no return to the life you once had if we went there. Seriatts are tolerant in such circumstances, and it is unlikely that you would be persecuted, but you would surely be considered a traitor on Earth. Could you accept that?'

'There's no other choice as I see it. We'll have to take our chances. I'll organise a ship and we'll get out of here as soon as we can.'

She smiled; it was a strange contorted expression, as if she were eating sour fruit. 'This is good,' she said. 'We need to be together. Things bind us; many things.' She sat across him, glands beginning to foam. 'I know you understand little of my race, Alexander Delgado, but at a certain time in life *conosq* enter *sheyaq*. It is . . .' she paused as she sought a suitable translation '. . . the time of singular commitment.' She pressed herself against him, smearing the glutinous gel that was spreading from her across their two bodies with an enthusiasm and arousal that propagated the gel's production. Soon it covered them, a stinking slime, a fetid corruption that literally glued them together. 'I was unsure at first,' she gasped, her breathing becoming rapid and intense as her arousal grew, 'but I feel I am approaching that time, Delgado: *sheyaq*. You are the one I am to be with – I know it. And my return to Seriatt with you will be welcomed, my former indiscretion forgiven. I feel it.'

'Got a crystal ball, have you?' he uttered tensely.

'What do you mean?'

'It doesn't matter.' Delgado wished to protest, to prevent yet another physical onslaught that he simply felt unable to take. But the necessary words and actions would not come to him. His blood pounded, his entire body seemed to ache. Yet within a few moments of once again being ensnared by her form, the pain had vanished completely, to be replaced by a glorious sense of peace.

But deep within his lulled brain, he knew: the possible war with Seriatt was but a minor battle compared to the one that would rage within him when he did what he now knew he must. Afterwards he would allow himself twenty minutes' rest, then slip out while she slept.

When Delgado returned Lycern was sitting on the bed wearing one of the complimentary bathrobes; she seemed impatient and frustrated. The smell of cooked food was strong in the air and she was rubbing her belly in a gentle circular motion as if she had eaten too much. He automatically checked the wardrobe – the door remained shut.

'Where have you been?' she asked. 'You left no message. I feared all kinds of possibilities.'

'I went to find us a ship to get out of here,' he said. 'A fast one.'

'Your use of past tense implies that you were successful. Am I correct?'

'Of course I was successful.'

'You are an arrogant human.'

'Well, you seem to doubt my capabilities.'

'I tend to doubt everybody; it is a trait demonstrated by most *conosq*. When do we leave?'

'Tomorrow. The ship's being prepared for departure. It arrived only a few hours ago and the Captain wasn't expecting to leave again so soon. He needs to restock with provisions and fuel, then he'll be ready.'

'And it will take us to Seriatt?'

'Yes. He seems a good enough man for our needs. I made him a substantial payment to ensure he keeps his mouth shut. It was almost all that remained on my credidisc. Besides, he's got no idea who we are.' Delgado inwardly marvelled at his ability to create; it was a skill he had forgotten he possessed.

Lycern moved off the bed. 'You have done well,' she said, walking towards him.

Delgado narrowed his eyes. He could see the radiance in her skin, the music in her eyes; he knew what was coming. 'What did you expect?' he asked quietly. 'Failure? A half-hearted effort? Sorry to disappoint you.'

'I expected no less than this. But perhaps not quite as quickly.'

She stopped walking when she was about a metre away from him. Delgado licked his lips, swallowed, tried to look away. Lycern tugged at the cord tying her robe and allowed the garment to fall to the floor. For a few moments she simply stood, naked before him. She seemed even more corpulent than he remembered, as if she had been changed by some unexplained process, her skin stretched, her folds slightly deeper, her body somehow even more absorbing than before. Yet illogically, her muscles seemed more defined at the tops of her thighs and around her waist.

She stepped forward and curled her fleshy yet sinuous arms around his neck, pressing her naked self against his clothed body. Delgado felt simultaneously repulsed and aroused, a tormenting combination he was unable to counter. He cried

126

aloud as she coiled tightly, nipping the skin of his neck while roughly fondling the lump at the groin of his leisuresuit. As he gave in and embraced her broad body, she easily released the clip to his garment.

A few moments later they were a single unified entity, a joined consciousness encased in a repugnant mass of gel, shuddering at the centre of the room.

Delgado wished he could sleep as Lycern did: deeply, solidly. So great was the energy she expended during their unions that she fell asleep the moment her *assissius* began to dry up and shrivel away to the fine grey powder it left behind. But for him such rest was all but impossible: he was made restless by their sexual acts, physically irritated.

He quietly dressed and reflected on the events of the past few days. He had changed – *been* changed – beyond his own recognition since his meeting with the Seriatt. She was a curse on his soul. A glorious, corrosive curse. And although his core instincts and abilities remained, they were much diluted. He knew without doubt that he could not be without her, that she had become an integral part of his existence. She represented a threat to all he was, and all he ever could be. So it was with a great battle of will that he embarked upon the course to which he found himself committed. The sooner events were underway, the sooner his problems would be solved. Or so he hoped.

He picked his sidearm off the floor next to the bed and traced a fingertip along its casing: it was smooth, perfectly contoured to his grip. He wondered how many beings had died at the discharge of the weapon; he had lost count long ago. The gun was part of him, part of his life; it was a true representation of his adult existence, an icon for what lay within him, beneath the layers of his current torment. He placed the sidearm in a pocket of his leisuresuit and glanced back at Lycern: still she slept.

He walked across to the table next to the door; a bowl of fresh slugs had been placed there by a cleaning automatic the previous day, a selection of wild creatures that slimed across each other in an orgiastic slick. It seemed Goghh's apparent wealth was supported by a taste for expensive recreational narcotics – farm-reared creatures possessed none of the lustre displayed by these examples.

They were strangely captivating and somehow beautiful – beautiful in the same way as Lycern. Delgado took one of them from the bowl and held it up in front of his face. He looked at the shiny, glistening creature. Its antennae waved slowly; its muscular foot rippled. At that moment Delgado felt weak, and needed the illusion of strength the creature could provide. Besides, what harm could it do him now?

He squeezed the slug with his fingertips. The creature grew warm and even more moist; vapour rose from it. He looked at the animal, considered what it was, how it had come to this point in space and time. Then, after a final moment of hesitation, he placed the fleshy muscle into his mouth.

As he rolled it around with his tongue the result was instantaneous and intense, his mind twisted by the creature's toxic release. He became breathless, panicky. The power of the slug's juices distorted his mind and perception. Decisions were suddenly easy – the course for his actions clear and the necessary will instilled in him.

Delgado went to the dataview screen and sat on the floor in front of it.

He scanned the main menu and quickly found what he needed. 'Access Technical Services Information,' he said. 'Guest Communication Options.'

A menu scrolled up the screen.

'Specify service requirement.' The voice issued from a speaker, desolate and unemotional.

The screen throbbed in time with his heartbeat as he sucked at the slug's sticky flesh. Colours blended together, the words fusing on the screen. He pulled the slightly shrunken slug from his mouth and cast it to the floor. As the request tripped from him, he was controlled by a deeper sense of purpose.

'List available frequencies for ultrabeam transmission to deep space relay stations.' The screen updated. Text appeared: ULTRABEAM TIGHTLINE FREQUENCIES. Three columns followed, a mammoth list of bandwidths and pulse frequencies. They appeared and disappeared as quickly as they were used, reserved or released, billions of communication transactions occurring every second.

'Ultimate destination details are necessary for an accurate analysis of frequency, power and tightline pulse requirements. What is the ultimate destination of your transmission?'

Delgado hesitated and picked a fresh slug from the bowl. He closed his eyes, placed it into his mouth and chewed, waiting for the effect of the substances already within him to be amplified. He hated himself, but fought the compulsion he felt to spit the vile creature from his mouth, for he knew he needed the immunity the slugs provided.

'What is the ultimate destination of your transmission?' The words were repeated with no change in tone.

He opened his eyes. The decision had been made; there was no turning back. He spoke quietly. 'Transmission destination is Universal Identifier Code 4197-876H4.'

'Plotting.'

An array of star charts appeared on the screen, relay and booster stations blinking green. A yellow line marked the first short segment of the route the signal would take. A narrow block of text scrolled up the right side of the screen. He was able to read it, but comprehension and meaning were unattainable in his abused state.

'What is the priority of your transmission? High priority transmissions incur an additional fee.'

'Are you related to a datadump called Yulos, by any chance?'

'Repeat please.'

'I said, it's a high priority transmission.'

'This communication will cost three hundred standard units. Do you wish to proceed?'

'Yes.'

'Please insert a valid currency chip.'

He placed his credidisc in the circular indentation on the unit's fascia.

'Thank you. The currency has been deducted from your Guest Account. This credidisc is now empty. You may purchase further credidiscs via a Spenidex account. When do you wish to send this transmission?'

'Immediately.' He was shaking now, his breaths short and snatched. Tears welled in his eyes, absurd physical responses. There were too many questions, too much time wasted. He picked up two slugs at random, tilted his head back and squeezed them above his face. The slime they released trailed into his open mouth and across his cheeks and neck, a thick line of rich toxicity that rushed him headlong into near oblivion. Moments later his entire body was numb, and the hollow sense induced by the previous slugs expanded immeasurably until his self-awareness was lost in an indistinct haze. He vaguely heard the word 'plotting' as images of disparate fragments of his life streamed through his brain. He waited as communications links through ultrabeam energisers were negotiated, frequencies for the transmission secured, links through relay stations all across the galaxy reserved. Pointless statistics about required tightline strength and signal output flashed onto the screen.

'Details set. Transmission will take four point two standard hours to reach Universal Identifier Code 4197–876H4 from initial pulse. The final relay will be fourteen standard minutes before the cold signal reaches the target receptor. Begin your transmission now.'

Delgado paused for the briefest moment, then moved closer to the screen and began to speak.

★

Delgado was sitting on a chair on the balcony, his feet resting on the rail. When Lycern walked out to join him, sleep still had a firm hold on her. He glanced up. Her gown hung open, revealing her body beneath; her eyes were bloodshot from hours of sleep. Delgado quickly returned his gaze to *Elixiion*'s magnificent vista.

'Get dressed,' he said.

'Your tone is urgent.' She rubbed her eyes and leaned against the balcony door. 'Why?'

'We're getting out of here. Ship's almost ready. Come on; it's time to leave.'

She crouched beside him. 'How long do we have?' she said.

Delgado pushed her away but did not look at her. 'No time for that,' he said. 'You've got time to shower and dress, that's all. Then we must leave.' She stayed where she was, simply looking at him. 'Go!' His voice cracked slightly.

After a momentary pause Lycern stood and walked towards the bathroom without speaking.

Delgado recalculated his timings. Unless he had repeatedly missed something stupid, his estimations would tie in nicely with their departure. He closed his eyes, linked his fingers beneath his chin and concentrated on focusing his nobics into their standard configuration. Despite his weak physical and mental state, this took only seconds. He then linked into *Elixiion*'s communications management core. There he observed, absorbed, refocused, and soon had what he wanted. When the relevant fragments of information had been sent to the remote system, distant but rapidly closing, everything was in place. The chain of events could not now be broken. He smiled grimly: it was one of the most clinical manoeuvres he had ever performed.

Delgado walked briskly along the corridor in *Elixiion*'s spaceport. He was several paces ahead of Lycern, who was struggling to keep up.

Delgado stopped for a moment and looked at a map set into the corridor wall. 'Not much further,' he said, more to himself than to Lycern. 'The ship should be ready and waiting.' He opened a basic timing/stat visual and hoped he was right. As the Seriatt's sensuous aroma began to reach him, he quickly turned and walked on.

A few minutes later Delgado looked back. Lycern was clearly in some discomfort. Her face was red, her breathing laboured; beads of sweat were visible on her face. Delgado surmised that although Seriattic *conosq* enjoyed great stamina during intercourse due to the agitated *muscein*, when exerting themselves without its benefits they were prone to problems; no doubt this information was contained somewhere within Osephius' infocram, but he had no time to access that now.

Part of him pitied her, and he felt a compulsion to reach out and help; but this was opposed by a stronger, darker need to revel in her anxiety, as if this might somehow alleviate his own suffering and perhaps help him justify what he was about to do. She looked at him and opened her mouth as if to speak, to plead for a moment of rest, but before she could do so Delgado had spun on his heel and was striding off along the corridor.

He arrived at the bay door half a minute or more before she. He stood, his expression impassive, yet he also seemed restless, pacing back and forth as he waited. When Lycern arrived, she was breathless, unable to speak. She leaned against the wall to recover, wheezing asthmatically. Delgado felt his mouth dry and his heartbeat quicken. As Lycern leaned forward and placed her hands on her knees, trying to regain her composure, a strand of drool trailed from her mouth. Delgado was forced to look away, and stared at the door intently as if he might be able to see through it to what waited beyond. By now a visuals representation was unnecessary: his nobics already told him that his message had been received and acted upon. He glanced at Lycern, looked each way along the corridor and then back at the door. But this was no time for indecision. Although he made no move to help or comfort her, he found it difficult to maintain his distance let alone his resolve.

'Are you ready now?' he said when she seemed to have recovered a little.

She nodded. 'I think so. Let us continue. I am eager to return to Seriatt.'

Delgado opened the door.

The bay was large, and appeared empty: all that confronted them was a vast expanse of white, the only colour the throbbing orange glow of the containment field around the portal at the opposite end.

But Delgado knew.

They stepped into the bay. For a moment, as the door closed behind them, Lycern looked puzzled. Then she saw the craft to their right, close to the bay wall. It was a svelte machine, dark and brooding in the clinical bay, squatting on its landing gear like a beast poised to pounce. A shallow tail curved away from its slippery hull like a dorsal fin. At first she smiled as she beheld the vehicle that would convey her back to Seriatt. But her expression soon changed as she saw the craft's name – *Miscreant* – emblazoned below Structure's familiar eclipse logo. She looked from the ship to Delgado, back again.

The PPC was an ultra-fast vessel, a design that utilised a combination of slipspace and hyperstream techniques to move low density cargoes across extreme distances in minimum time. They were notoriously expensive to run, and due to their speed the safe passage of such vessels required complete co-operation from the independent ATC groups controlling the different sectors and subsectors of any given route. That such a vessel had been sent for Lycern – and so quickly – was an indication of the Seriatt's importance to Myson. Delgado was certain it was nothing to do with his own involvement.

Lycern looked at Delgado through eyes filled with rage and pain. 'What have you done?' she whispered. As she spoke, a ramp began to descend from the craft's smooth underside, and a moment later a number of slim figures clad in black leather were walking stiffly down it, short-stem pulse rifles clutched to their waists. Their uniforms were like second skins, their visors as glossy as polished rock.

Delgado looked at the approaching silhouettes, held his chin high, and responded to Lycern with assurance. 'Myson gets his Seriattic *conosq*, I complete my mission. Everybody's happy. Except you. And Beech, I suppose.' He shrugged. 'But that's life, I guess.'

Lycern stared at the line of troopers walking regimentally towards them. But, then, behind these automaton represent-ations of Structure's power and evil, was something even Delgado had not expected: William Myson himself.

Seated in his huge throne, he was surrounded by a clutch of nymphs, who constantly fanned him with a rainbow display of large *careth* feathers. His gargantuan figure was even larger and more obscenely ridiculous than Delgado remembered it. His thighs dripped from the sides of his chair; his neck was a succession of thick fleshy folds; his head was a huge, bald dome. Metal supports extended from the sides of the chair to support his fat, flabby arms, and a fur-lined metal collar took the weight of his huge skull. He dabbed at his forehead occasionally, mopping beads of sweat.

The troopers surrounded Delgado and Lycern in silence, their disdain evident. They parted to allow Myson to enter the closed circle. The General looked haggard, and appeared to be in considerable pain. His skin was grey, his eyes tired and bloodshot. The robots teeming across his flesh seemed to have doubled in number. He was trembling slightly.

Delgado sank to one knee and bowed low. 'Sire' he said; Lycern remained motionless, her face rigid.

'Commander Delgado,' said Myson slowly, staring at Lycern. 'Come, stand. You have brought me my desire, my pain, my death.' Lycern took a step forward and opened her mouth to speak. Myson motioned quickly at one of the troopers. The figure immediately raised his weapon and it released a single bolt of light that knocked the Seriatt from her feet and threw her several metres across the floor. Myson looked at her prostrate body for many seconds, running his right index finger along his lower lip. He seemed to be battling something within him, struggling to prevent some kind of outburst or escape. 'The Seriatt has ideas above her station,' he said eventually, looking slowly and calmly back towards Delgado. 'She thinks I am interested in her opinions and fantasies. How typical of her race. And how mistaken. You,' he indicated four troopers, 'carry the *conosq* into the *Miscreant*. You two nymphs accompany them. Ensure they do not harm or abuse her.' As they obeyed, Myson appraised Delgado with his eyes cold and bitter.

'I expected to be reunited with you both in more familiar surroundings when I gave you this assignment, I admit. The message revealing your location was brief, Delgado, lacking detail concerning events. So, why did you come to the leisurestation *Elixiion*? And why did you wait so long before contacting me?'

'Sire, forgive me my ineptitude. It was necessary to bring the slipspacer into close quarters in order to escape from the Affinity installation. We were chased by Affinity ships when leaving Veshc and the slipspacer suffered some damage. The extended evasive manoeuvres we were forced to perform in subspace meant we ran low on fuel, and I was therefore forced to bring the vessel here and adopt covert operation procedures. A cover was successfully maintained but I had to be cautious, which is why contact was not made sooner.'

Myson nodded slowly, thoughtfully. 'And what of Beech? Where is she?'

'Dead, sire. A lucky shot from an Affinity vessel decompressed part of the slipspacer. There was no way of saving her. The craft was similar in performance and firepower to a xip fighter and evaded detection until launching its attack. In truth we were lucky to escape at all.'

'Losing Beech is unfortunate. She had great potential.'

'I was forced to draw on all my experience, and utilise all my skills, sire.' Delgado spoke firmly and with conviction, but could not prevent a slight tremor in his voice as he glimpsed Lycern being manhandled on to the troopers' shoulders and carried with much effort up the ramp into the *Miscreant*. He felt nauseous, light-headed. He blinked, swallowed, felt a rivulet of sweat trickle from his right temple down the side of his face.

'You seem disturbed,' said Myson, still staring at Delgado, his eyes slightly narrowed. 'I wonder if there is anything you would like to add. Anything you have not told me about the mission or your time here on *Elixiion*.' He raised his eyebrows and cocked his head slightly to one side.

Delgado returned the General's gaze. 'No, sire. There is nothing.'

For a few moments Myson remained silent. Then his chair began to buzz loudly as he started turning it through one hundred and eighty degrees. 'Very well,' he called back. 'You will be fully debriefed once we return to Earth. Let us depart immediately. I am needed there, and my marriage to the Seriatt must take place soon if war is to be avoided.'

Delgado bowed again. 'Sire.'

As Myson made his way towards the *Miscreant*, Delgado stood and watched. As he looked towards the vessel he thought of Lycern. Cramps ran through him, he felt an intense rawness of skin, as if it had been stripped and salted. He tried desperately to maintain his composure as his mind spun, and an array of distorted sheets sporadically opened and closed, his nobics seemingly trying to link with a non-existent sub-system or core within the Miscreant. He could do nothing but bear his torment, allow the feelings to pass, and reflect upon their obvious cause.

136

★

The cabin door hummed deeply as it opened. Delgado spun around and saw a young Reactionary Forces Officer stepping into the cabin. He folded his arms and leaned against the doorframe. The officer was thin and short, his skin deeply pock-marked. He was chewing a small red slug, rolling it around his mouth. His tongue and lips were stained crimson by its release, his teeth pink. The slug looked old and dry. 'General Myson wants to see you,' he said with a sneer. He looked Delgado up and down. 'Better straighten yourself up, bucko, or he'll have you for lunch.'

Delgado strode forward until he was close enough to smell the officer's breath. 'Don't presume to tell me anything about the etiquette of meeting a General, you arrogant little fuck. I'd done it a hundred times before you were born. And you will address me as *"sir"*. Understand, soldier?'

The other man blinked once, slowly. His expression was complacent, cocksure. 'I haven't got to show you any kind of respect or acknowledge your supposed rank. You're nothing. You're just a pile of shit who used to be nobody anyway. Just shut up and move out.'

Delgado gripped the officer's throat in his fist and lifted the smaller man from the floor, pushing him back until he was pressed against the dark bulkhead on the other side of the corridor. As Delgado squeezed hard, the man's eyes widened and he made a small, high-pitched noise. His face became increasingly red. His lips began to turn grey, then blue. The slug he had been chewing fell to the floor.

The two men became frozen in time: one could see death rushing headlong towards him, along with the loss of his peripheral vision, the other was enjoying the taste of a power almost lost.

When the officer seemed to be on the verge of sexual euphoria, Delgado released his grip and let him slide slowly down the wall.

The officer was shaking visibly, and looked considerably less arrogant than he had a few moments earlier. He avoided Delgado's eyes as he began to walk along the corridor, rubbing his throat. 'This way,' he croaked. 'The general wants to see you, right now.' Delgado clenched his jaw as the other officer uttered derisive words under his breath, but did nothing in response. For the time being.

Instead he followed him in silence through the PPC's grim black arteries. The low ceilings and insidious dark shadows were typical of a Structure ship; despite its seductive exterior, within it was threatening and evil, arrogant and crass in every aspect, a vessel for the transportation of Myson's ego, a conduit for his greed.

The officer stopped at a door engraved with the eclipse logo. 'Wait here,' he said. 'They'll summon you when they're ready.' He looked Delgado up and down again, as if about to utter some final, bitter remark, but then simply walked away. He stopped and turned as he began to merge with the ship's dark walls further along the corridor. 'You're scum!' he shouted hoarsely, stabbing the air with an index finger. 'Military Intelligence will be well rid of you, Delgado. You're the worst kind of officer there is. I hope you burn in hell. Everybody does. You're a fucking joke.' He turned again and strode assuredly away.

Delgado walked a few steps, his fists clenched. 'Important business dealing with a faulty toilet somewhere is there, *boy*?' he shouted. The officer did not answer. Delgado had to fight hard to suppress the rage rising within him. 'If we ever meet again I'll show you parts of yourself you never thought you'd see. Remember that.' But the man was gone.

Delgado calmed quickly and waited patiently in the corridor, hands clasped behind his back, rocking on his heels. The metal floor grids clattered slightly as he moved, the noises of the ship amplified by his solitude: air hissed through a filter and unspecified liquids rushed through pipes above his head; a good-natured argument roared in a cabin somewhere to his right; a faint alarm indicated some minor crisis on a lower deck.

The door behind him whined quietly; Delgado turned.

Tiny spotlights blazed like microscopic suns, illuminating corners of the room. Ample swathes of luxuriant black fabric were draped around the walls and from the ceiling, ripples in the rich material shining like mercury waves. Myson was sitting on a large white throne at the far end of the room smiling like an idiot, as he chewed gently on a fat slug. Delgado judged from the slug's aroma that it was a particularly potent species: *runias* or *goorgem* perhaps. Two nymphs fanned Myson slowly.

Lycern was lying on a chaise longue to Myson's left, leaning on one elbow and sipping brilliant green liquid from a heavy, plain glass goblet. She, too, was playing with a slug, teasing it between the fingers of her right hand. She would squeeze it occasionally and watch the thin strands of slime that trailed from it with fascination.

Although smiling and apparently relaxed, when she did glance in Delgado's direction she seemed to look straight through him, her expression like that of one who is seeing distant yet amusing events. She appeared to be slightly aroused: her breasts and thighs were swollen, threatening the seams of the new and unfamiliar gown she wore. In places the thin cloth was darkened by the gel being secreted by the *assissius* glands beneath.

Delgado's body reacted immediately at the sight of her, and he was forced to look away.

Myson spat his slug onto the floor and beckoned to Delgado. 'Come, my soldier, enter!' he shouted. 'Stand before your General.' He placed a fresh slug into his mouth and sucked hard, savouring its release.

Delgado stepped forward until he was just inside the doorway. Guards stood to each side of him, sidearms drawn.

Myson pulled the fresh slug from his mouth with a smack and slowly, theatrically licked slime from its squirming foot. 'Step closer, Commander Delgado,' he called, gesticulating extravagantly, his intonation and tone exaggerated and ridiculous. 'We have important matters to discuss. Important matters indeed.'

Delgado took a few more steps, his hands still calmly clasped behind his back; the guards moved with him. As Myson settled back into his chair Delgado glanced at Lycern; she was clearly traversing an entirely different dimension to his, a surreal plain of mysterious events. Myson noticed the direction of Delgado's gaze and smiled. 'She is looking well, I think. Do you not agree, my soldier?' He reached out and patted the Seriatt's thigh, pushing up the hem of her dress. He rested his hand on her soft flesh and teased one of the glistening *assissius* glands with a fat thumb; she closed her eyes, shuddered and gasped.

Delgado clenched his jaw and stared hard at the eclipse emblem on the wall above Myson's huge head, gorge threatening to rise.

'You are jealous,' said Myson quietly, nodding. He leaned forward. 'And rightly so. Vourniass Lycern is, like all *conosq*, capable of many wonderful and fearful things. Controlling the minds of men is just one of them.' He raised his eyebrows briefly and made a sweeping gesture with his hand, but his eyes were heavy-lidded, drowsy. 'This is why we are here now, Delgado. Do you know what we need to do? We need to talk about the future. More precisely, *your* future.' He sat back again smiling. 'I know you have coupled with Lycern. It is obvious in your manner, in your physical discomfort. When I questioned her deeply about it she revealed to me your real reasons for going to *Elixiion*.' He wrinkled his nose. 'I understand these. But I nevertheless consider what you have done to be an act of grave treachery. It can be considered nothing else.' He paused for a moment and sucked hard on his still-squirming slug. 'Obviously I take such things very seriously, and can appear to be neither lenient nor foolish to any degree. As a result, only one course of action is open to me.

'It is a shame, Commander, for although the Planetary Council has not agreed with you on many occasions since I came to power, and your inability to adapt to new procedures and strategies has often made things very difficult for us, you have served for much of your life, and some of the tactics you have developed – particularly during your time with Stealth – have proved most effective. It is because of this that I felt impelled to treat you with a little more respect than I would any other traitor.'

Myson looked across at Lycern. 'My Seriatt is with me again,' he said quietly, 'and before you die I wanted you to understand just how suitable she is to be my wife and bear my offspring. It was destined to be so, and your attempt to take her from me, to use her for your own gain, was doomed from the start.' Myson nodded at the two nymphs, who put down their *careth* feathers and stepped towards Lycern. She smiled like a child dazzled by angels, giggling as they helped her from her seat and guided her into a room to the right. When the door was closed Myson continued. 'We are soon to be married on the moon of Monas,' he said with satisfaction. 'When the planet's rings diffuse the sun's light during the fourth quarter, we will join in the ancient Yethrendin ritual and seal our bond by publicly consummating our marriage, thereby linking Earth and Seriatt in the most intimate, sacred way. Lasting peace will be assured. And a satisfying future for all. Most importantly, she will provide me with a politically acceptable heir to whom I can leave my legacy, and who can guide Earth into the future.' He smiled at this. 'How does that make you feel, Commander?'

The two men stared at each other. Myson leaned on his elbow and chewed one of his obese, ringed fingers, clicking the jewelled metal on his large, square teeth. A thousand messages passed between their unblinking eyes: one challenged, savouring a conquest; the other had rage in his veins, adrenaline, pure love and a million repressed dreams, all of which were coursing through him like lava.

Delgado felt immobilised, transfixed by the power of the Commander Supreme, seated before him like a god. His entire life had been geared to such moments as this, and even when faced with the loss of Lycern and his own life being forfeit, he was unable to rebel. It was ingrained loyalty, a bitter unbreakable chain of constraint. Only now did he realise the extent to which his true self had been denied, his every action programmed into him.

'Of course. You are right, sire,' said Delgado, shaking his head. 'I was foolish to think that I could . . .' He appeared lost for words. 'I only hope that you can find some measure of forgiveness and understanding within yourself, and perhaps spare me my life.' Myson wore a broad grin on his greedy, arrogant face and seemed to be enjoying Delgado's discomfort as he cowered before him.

Delgado continued. 'Would it be possible for you to forgive me, sire,' he asked humbly. 'To find mercy in your supreme soul? I know such a request leaves me no honour, but I deserve none after my recent actions. The only excuse I can offer is that I was not of sound mind. I know you will understand my reasons in the light of your experiences with the *conosq*, and can assure you I will—'

Delgado spun, grabbed the guard to his right by the shoulder, pulled the man around and held him to his chest. Within a breath Delgado had snatched the guard's sidearm. While the second guard was still turning, a look of complete surprise on her face, Delgado fired.

For the briefest instant the woman's face distorted, her features becoming somehow warped, as if melting. Her eyes flared into swollen scarlet spheres; the autosighters at her temples glowed white hot, charring her flesh. A moment later, her head shattered. Glistening fragments of bone, brain, blood and nanocomponents sprayed the wall behind her, tinting it a grey-flecked scarlet. The headless torso fell to the floor with a deadened thud, limbs jerking.

The guard Delgado was holding flailed, shouted indecipherable words. Delgado wrenched him round, put the barrel of the gun to his forehead and fired.

As the body fell Delgado turned and flung himself bodily towards Myson.

His momentum rocked the General's throne despite the man's great size and weight, and the chair tipped backwards almost in slow motion. Myson kicked his fat, flabby legs like an upturned turtle and grabbed at a length of fabric draped from the ceiling; the fabric tore, and the cloth fell on top of them. In the sudden darkness Delgado could hear Myson's laboured breaths close to his right ear as the enormous man writhed weakly. As they struggled, the length of cloth was pulled from his face by one of Myson's kicking legs. Delgado brought his hand up and saw a light on top of the gun blinking a solemn red message. He knew what he had to do.

The light continued to blink, his right index finger poised over the trigger.

But he could not fire the weapon.

Killing the Commander Supreme of Military Intelligence – and thus effectively of Structure – was beyond him, as it would be beyond anyone in the Service. Delgado hated everything Myson and his new Military Intelligence stood for, from the corruption and erosion of standards on Earth to the massive slaughter that had been so needlessly instigated for capital gain throughout the galaxy; but the fact that he was the Commander Supreme remained, and touched something at Delgado's core. Even though he held new morals and a deeper understanding of what his own existence meant, the mental block that Myson's position established in him was too great to overcome.

143

Delgado flicked the weapon in his hand around and, against every instinct rising in him even then, clubbed Myson with its butt. Myson's cries briefly became more urgent, but as Delgado brought more blows down onto the cloth covering the man's huge skull, they quickly faded, and his writhing ceased.

Delgado stood, and looked down at the heap of fabric. There was no going back for him now. There could be no return to the familiarity and comfort of Military Intelligence no matter what miracle might save his life. Upon recovery Myson would order his death and his name to be erased from the Military Intelligence biocomputer on Earth. Thus he would be gone forever, with no record that he had ever existed at all, no better than the scum who scavenged the streets outside the habitats.

Delgado turned and strode towards the door through which the nymphs had taken Lycern; it opened automatically.

She was naked, lying on her back on a large, round bed. One nymph was sitting astride her, massaging oil into her stomach and breasts with smooth, slow, circular motions of her tiny hands; occasionally she would tease the *assissius* glands around the *conosq*'s body and giggle at the sudden secretion of slime. The other nymph was standing at a table next to the bed, laughing and playing with the brutal sex toys she had found there.

The nymph at the table looked up. When she saw Delgado and Myson's empty, upturned throne in the room beyond, she dropped the circular, multi-bladed device she was holding, threw her hands to her face and screamed a string of ultra high-pitched, incoherent sentences. The other nymph turned, and also began to scream.

Their shrieks reached new heights as Delgado walked towards them, but when the nymph at the table darted past him out of the room in a blur of pale, bony flesh, the other instantly fell silent. Delgado waved the barrel of his gun at her, and she slipped off Lycern's legs and ran after her friend, her legs and buttocks glistening with massage oil, her bare feet struggling to find purchase on the smooth floor.

Delgado looked at Lycern; her eyes were glassy and bloodshot – she seemed only semi–conscious. He walked across to her. She reached out and touched his forehead with her fingertips.

'Wet,' she said. 'Warm, too.'

Delgado looked down at himself; he was covered in the guards' blood and brain matter. As he looked up he felt a dizzying surge in his nobics, but the sensation was gone before he could establish its cause.

Lycern tilted her head slightly, her expression one of great sorrow. 'Have you killed someone, Delgado?'

He glanced behind him. 'We'll talk about that later. Right now we've got to get out of here.' He blinked rapidly and shook his head as he felt another nobic swell; it was like a whirlpool, sucking in information, preventing him from accessing important data.

She frowned hard; the expression pulled lines across her wide face. She seemed to be on the verge of tears. 'That is not good,' she said, shaking her head and looking past him. 'Taking life is wrong. You should not take life unless you are prepared for your own life to be taken. Giving life is all that matters.'

An urgent shout echoed somewhere outside. 'Come on, we've got to get out of here.' Delgado tried to move Lycern, but she gripped his arm tightly and refused to budge.

'There is something I must tell you, Alexander Delgado,' she said.

Delgado glanced from Lycern to the door and back again. 'It'll have to wait,' he replied. He struggled to close a series of datasheets that had unexpectedly opened his mind. 'No time now.'

'It is useless, Delgado. You must go without me,' she said, and began to sob gently. 'I cannot move.' She laughed

145

suddenly. 'I cannot even stand. You must leave us, escape, save yourself. You are strong enough to withstand the *muscein* withdrawal. It will be painful, but will fade in time.' Further shouts came from the corridor, guards quickly closing in. 'Go now,' she said. 'Go quickly.'

Delgado felt nauseous, his skin clammy, his head aching fiercely as his nobics continued to reel. He stood upright and took a few paces back, returning Lycern's anguished gaze. Pain and love were communicated between them, an affirmation that their relationship was more than physical. A battle between logic and emotion raged within him, compounded by the increasing fluctuations of his nobics; it was as if someone was trying to contact him, but was prevented from doing so by some kind of barrier.

There was a further shout from outside; an alarm sounded loud and shrill. Delgado felt the approach of death like a closing net. And despite the intensifying storm in his skull, he knew he had no choice.

He kissed Lycern briefly but passionately, then he opened a cluster of combat visuals, turned and ran.

A screen flickered to his right, a small black square imparting essential information that no one would read; he was vaguely aware of that. But the rest of the universe had shrunk to a black pinpoint at the centre of his mind.

The tube down his throat and the needles in his arms and neck were slightly distracting, but he knew their presence would dissolve as he sank into normally inaccessible realms, his mind fully absorbed by the approaching blackness.

The PPC had left *Elixiion* soon after his escape. The troopers had searched the immediate vicinity for him, but their efforts were typically half-hearted and unhurried. So, hiding in the bay's observation room, he had watched the PPC rise silently, turn and depart, beginning its journey back to Earth. And even as the vessel was leaving, Delgado knew he could not let

Lycern go, despite the sense in doing so. The *muscein* controlled him, that was true enough, but his feelings for her were much stronger than that; stronger than he would be prepared to admit.

So, struggling to overcome his nobics' continued volatility, he had used them to link into *Elixiion*'s systems, fraudulently credited his chip with currency, and chartered a personal micropod.

At first he had wanted to run, escape the memories, deny his past the right to exist, and program the pod to take him to the nearest non-Military Intelligence controlled settlement, however primitive; he had even considered the Affinity Group. But, overcome by emotions stronger than any he had previously experienced, he knew no escape was possible.

The pod was slow but had sufficient range to get him back to Earth. In stasis he would cover the huge distance to his home planet, his body recovering as time elapsed. Then, when the pod entered Earth's system and slowed, its systems would re-engage and he would be drawn from the depths of his extended unconsciousness. Somehow he might then be able to find Lycern again. His earlier actions had seemed right, fitted in with normal procedures, his training and instincts; but he realised then that he had changed to such an extent that he could no longer rely on his instincts to guide him. He was on his own, without even the comfort of habit or familiarity.

As the chemicals fed to him by the pod's deepsleep programs began to take effect, gradually calming his errant nobics, his mind replayed fragments of images and brief slices of time that seemed even more vivid than when they had actually occurred. His escape had been bloody, and many people had died because of his anger and pain in the short time it had taken for him to get off the PPC. Fuelled by an emotion more powerful even than lust, desire for glory or hatred, he had cut down all those who had stepped into his path with more enthusiasm than at any time during his military career. It had

147

been the most satisfying hand-to-hand combat he had ever experienced. But the price had been great, for he knew without doubt that Vourniass Lycern, the Seriattic *conosq* who had poisoned his blood with her alien being, had all but crushed the person he had once been.

He had realised the true weight of grief in the past few hours, and nothing had prepared him for its magnitude. Now, in the darkness of the tiny capsule, all seemed unimportant, lost, without reason.

While enough consciousness remained in him, Delgado focused his nobics and reached out to see if he could reach Lycern again, and communicate with her in some small way.

She was just within range.

When he joined her mind he was confronted by a puzzling array of unfamiliar traces and fragmented emotions. The maddening nobic fluctuations ceased, abruptly and completely. And so, despite his semi-conscious state he released more nobics to analyse Lycern's responses, striving to overcome her increasing distance from him and merge more fully with her mental processes. She seemed to be unconscious or drugged, so deeply transient was her mind. But a sense of incompatibility remained, a feeling of separation; it was something Delgado could not resolve. He floated above her, peering into her thoughts. And then, in a moment of stark revelation, the cause of his current symptoms and the disorientating nobic surges he had experienced suddenly became clear to him.

She was carrying his child.

He knew it with no shred of doubt. It was the culmination of everything that had happened, every emotion and experience they had so far shared. But he could not go to her, could wrest neither her nor his unborn child from Myson's grip. This knowledge caused the most agonising pain he had ever known.

The screen to his right suddenly darkened, and somehow he was saddened by its loss; it was a final abandonment.

148

As the point of light at the centre of his brain faded, his pain and longing were total. And he knew then that the recent events played out aboard the PPC had not been the end of an episode, but only the beginning.

Through the pod's thick transparent hatch the last thing to register in Delgado's mind was the flickering light of the tiny craft's displacement wake. It fluttered gently, its rhythm like the beat of a baby's heart.

Four

a fissure avowed

A dull, undulating pain washed through Delgado's body. He allowed his consciousness to return only gradually, forcing his nobics to open in small batches rather than with their usual overwhelming flood. But it was hard work: the system was unused to periods of sensory inactivity, and was eager to get back into action. Delgado kept his eyes closed for as long as he could, exploring sensations, absorbing, assessing.

Then he remembered: Lycern, Myson.

His child.

His mouth was dry, his throat sore; he parted his lips slightly and drew in cool air. The feeder tube in his mouth rubbed against the back of his throat and made him cough; he snatched the warm, slippery pipe away and cast it aside. But the speed of this action only heightened his discomfort and made his head throb intently, and he was forced him to remain motionless for a few moments.

Eventually he found the strength necessary to move one heavy arm, and reached up to touch his head. He pulled off the electrodes, stuck to his scalp like cancers, then plucked the needles that had monitored the drug levels in his sleeping body from his arms. He rubbed sleep from his eyes with his fingertips before opening them, and ran his hands through greasy hair. He rubbed his face, trying to awaken himself, and found he had more stubble than ever before in his life.

The chamber's canopy was already open, so he eased his legs round and pushed himself up to sit on the edge of the cocoon. He felt weak, his mind dulled by his prolonged comatose spell. In a sharp and determined movement meant to take his body unawares, he stood up quickly.

His head spun as he walked across to the storage compartment, where he grabbed a two–litre compact water cell. He activated the reconstitution process and waited for the liquid to form. When the container had expanded fully he unscrewed the cap and almost emptied it in a single draught. The cold liquid bloated him uncomfortably, but he was immediately refreshed.

He looked at the deepsleep cell with contempt; he could not understand those who persisted in using these antiquated devices from the time prior to the slipspace breakthrough. Upon leaving *Elixiion* he had thought the chance to rest would do him good, give him time to recover both physically and mentally; now he was less certain of the wisdom in this. He turned and walked towards the shower cubicle. Perhaps a good soaking would put things right.

Later, when he had washed, shaved both his face and his head and dressed, he walked through the hatch and up on to the control deck, where he sat in the pilot's seat. Through the small viewport to his right Saturn's rings swept through the heavens like bands of rough fabric. Pure sunlight released shards of vivid colour trapped within the rocks and crystals like a jewelled halo. At frequent intervals large, dark gaps in the glittering display indicated the workings of one of many mining units whose crews constantly plundered the meagre mineral resources offered by the tiny fragments of rock. It amazed him that the mining companies still thought the work a viable proposition, given the increasing profitability of importing such products from other worlds. Perhaps subsidies paid their bills and their work continued merely as a form of routine.

More importantly, though, Delgado was concerned to find that he was still so far from Earth. Quite why this should be he was unsure: he had double- and triple-checked the course programming before entering the sleep cell. The only possible explanation was interference from the military base on Titan; he had heard reports of systems of ships passing close to the moon during his time with Stealth. The pod had used almost all its energy in the initial acceleration push, after which the craft had proceeded steadily on its way; but now it had slowed short of his destination, he had no means of propulsion. The only way he could get to Earth from this point was to navigate into the shadow of a liner or freighter and try to slip onto that vessel's displacement wake as it accelerated. There were plenty of candidates, but the move bore many risks: the pod could be crushed in a larger ship's containment fields as it manoeuvred, or – if he positioned the pod incorrectly – it could even be ripped apart by shifting gravity wells as the tow vessel accelerated. But he could see no other choice: the pod now had a very limited range, and landing anywhere other than Earth would make things even more difficult.

He found the comms desk and opened a general communications channel with the intention of intercepting some ATC transmissions to ascertain the IDS of possible host ships. His nobics would be able to isolate any signals that might be of interest, after which things should be relatively easy. But instead of the garbled hiss of ultrabeam pulses he had expected to hear, there came a lazy, apathetic voice:

'– to be boarded. Repeat: this is the Customs Vessel *Damascus* calling unidentified vessel. You are violating controlled spacelanes without authorisation; prepare to be boarded. Repeat . . .'

The pilot had to make three attempts at guiding the battered *Damascus* into a stable approach line before he succeeded in docking with the pod. Delgado breathed an unimpressed sigh of relief. He had initially despaired at the pathetic attempts of the so-called pilot to dock, but managed to remain philo-sophical in the face of possible death by musing over the advantages of being boarded. However, the aborted attempts came increasingly close to disaster with each effort, the *Damascus* almost colliding head-on with the pod the final time it had been forced to power-up and go round again.

When the two ships did eventually come together, Delgado was knocked to the ground by the force of the impact and banged the back of his head against the deepsleep cell. He stood quickly and dusted himself down; he would only be able to take so much from these people.

The green light next to the hatch flickered for a moment, then remained lit; the door seals hissed as air passed from the pod into the connecting tube leading to the Customs ship. A rim of white light appeared around the edge of the door as it began to open.

'All right, OK, step back there, Customs Officers approach-ing. Make way, please.'

'Why do you always have to be so, so . . . *over the top*, for pity's sake? What do you think this is – some kind of a gameshow?'

'Oh, shut up. You're just upset because it was me who got through the door first again.'

'I am not.'

'Yes, you are.'

'I am *not*. Hello – who's this then?'

The two androids looked at Delgado for the first time. They were worn machines, old and beaten, primitive designs. Their voices issued from grille speakers set into their chests; a few simple marks on their scarred faces were supposed to represent features. Delgado felt them scan his body and heard the computer behind him jar into life as they tapped into the pod's management and navigation systems. Delgado returned their unwavering gaze, stony-faced. For long moments the units stood motionless, as though all their consciousness systems had been switched off by some distant controller. Delgado could almost see the messages passing between them as they communicated with the pod's systems in undertone, their complete lack of activity betraying the use of this ancient language.

The shining blue faces of both androids were modelled on people Delgado recognised. The one that had boarded first looked like Governor Schlass, a woman who had wielded immense power in Military Intelligence in the time leading up to the Buhatt Rebellion, but had since been forced to seek asylum offworld. Whether this was through genuine mental deterioration or the result of a Structure plot to get rid of someone who was both a nuisance and a threat was unclear. The other machine was cast in the image of Marshall Deron, a slimy character who had 'cleansed' Structure's workforce of 'subversives and inappropriates' during the period immediately following General Smythe's downfall. They had been black times indeed, and Delgado thought it quite ironic that these two old workhorses – undoubtedly doing their best for the Customs Department in their own way – were fashioned in the images of two of the most detested people in Structure's history.

'Looks like we've got ourselves a runner,' said Schlass to Deron eventually.

'Hmm. Maybe, maybe.'

'What do you mean, maybe? He looks good enough to be a runner if ever anyone did.' Schlass leaned close to Deron, positioning itself as if whispering into its colleague's ear despite the location of its speaker. 'We only need to process one more runner to meet our bonus target,' it said in a loud whisper. 'This is an opportunity too good to miss.'

'Hmm. Don't you feel that there's something not quite right about him, though?'

'Such as?'

The two androids looked at Delgado, their blue eyes cold

and unblinking. The one that looked like Deron linked its fingers at its waist and cocked its head to one side. The one that looked like Schlass rested its hands on its hips; somehow it managed to look frustrated despite its fixed expression.

'Can't put my finger on it,' said Deron eventually, 'but there's definitely *something*.'

'Well, I think he's perfect,' said Schlass with a shake of its head. 'He's in an unregistered vehicle, plotting an uncharted course, potentially endangering both military and civilian shipping. What more do you want? He might actually be a runner for all you know. You'd better search him.' Schlass looked at Delgado and leered forward, trying to adopt an intimidating stance. 'What's your name, fella?' it said, clearly trying to sound threatening. 'And what are you doing drifting through a busy shipping lane without guidance from Advanced Trajectory Control, eh? That's just not on, you know.'

'My computer malfunctioned,' said Delgado calmly as Deron tentatively patted his clothing. 'I was trying to get to Titan for repairs when the drives went down. I had to—'

'See?' said Schlass, wagging a finger. 'Not a leg to stand on. I say we bag him and run with the loot. Titan for repairs, indeed. A likely story. Pah!'

'Oh, I don't know. You know I've never been too keen on that sort of thing.'

'What sort of thing?'

'Well, I mean, it's breaking the law, isn't it? You know.'

'Oh, for pity's sake! How do you think Grade Ones get to be Grade Ones, eh? They don't go around doing everything by the book and trusting their scores to chance, do they? No, they make their own luck. Honestly, you're so naïve sometimes. You've got to take some risks if you want to keep up with the rest of the crowd.'

'Hmm. Maybe. It still doesn't seem right somehow. He has got an impressive-looking gun, though.' Devon held up the sidearm for Schlass to see.

'Ah, now you'll have to trust me. I know I'm right. Where shall we say we found it?' Schlass walked through to the flight deck and looked around the main console. He stooped and pointed underneath the pilot's seat. 'Under here?' it called back.

Deron shrugged resignedly. 'Whatever.'

Delgado realised he was being set up. Capturing illegal aliens trying to get into Earth's system was everyday bread and butter stuff for Customs, and thus worth little in the points system on which their bonus levels were based. But capturing a smuggler of *collini* root or a similar substance could put them within reach of a valuable award.

Schlass walked back over to them. 'We'll say we found it under the pilot's seat, OK?' Deron nodded. 'Good. I reckon we can get two, maybe three hundred points for this.' It looked at Delgado again. 'What's your name, runner?' it said, jabbing a finger in his direction.

'This is outrageous,' he replied firmly. 'I'm not required to say anything until I have a human or class four AI construct legal adviser present. This is a set-up. You've got it written all over you.'

Deron looked down at its own chest. 'No,' it said, pointing at small characters embossed upon the metal surface, 'that's just my serial number.'

'So, a *professional* smuggler, eh? Know your rights and legal position, do you, buddy boy? Well, you're in the hands of the Customs Department now, son, so don't get smart with *us*. Understand?'

'You tell him.' Deron nodded emphatically.

Delgado nodded and tried to appear worried.

'Well, that's just fine, then. Behave yourself and you'll find we're pretty reasonable guys. What's your ID number?'

'As I said, I'm not required to give you any information without legal advice.'

Schlass became somewhat agitated; it plucked microcuffs

from its belt and flicked on the charge switch. 'All right, that's it. Come on, turn around.'

Delgado was assigning nobics and projecting scenarios. He knew which of the two machines he would have to take out first as the other could probably be bullied into helping him; it was just a matter of picking the right moment.

Schlass repeated his command; this time Delgado complied. 'That's better. Now put your hands behind your back.'

Delgado did as he was told but looked over his shoulder as he did so. 'Look, I understand that this is probably routine procedure, but do you think I could have my hands in front of me? It feels as if I've been in that deepsleep cell forever and a day. My muscles haven't really relaxed yet. Don't tell me you're as barbaric as we are.'

There was a pause. Schlass looked at Deron. 'What do you think?'

'Oh, it'll be all right. I can believe those things aren't very comfortable, and we are using him to meet our bonus target, after all. And what if he's found guilty? I'd feel really bad about that.'

Schlass stood upright, clearly astonished. 'Found guilty? Found *guilty*? When was the last time you heard of a smuggler being found guilty? Everyone knows it's all a propaganda show. You amaze me sometimes, you really do.'

Deron shrugged. 'Well, you never know . . .'

'OK, turn around. You can have your hands in front of you.'

Delgado turned. 'Thanks,' he said. 'Where are you going to take me?'

'We're not really supposed to say,' said Schlass as he fixed the microcuffs around Delgado's wrists, 'but I don't see that it can hurt. You'll go to the Customs Department Building on Earth and be processed there.'

'A bit like food!' joked Deron. Delgado and Schlass looked at it blankly. 'I'm sorry,' it said, and looked at its feet.

Schlass continued, keeping his eyes on Deron for a moment: 'As I was saying, you'll be taken to the Customs Department Building, your arrest will be processed, and then you'll have to wait until the Judgemaster can see you.'

'How long is that likely be?'

'Well, the Judgemaster's a pretty busy fellow, you know: he's got all sorts of business to do, not only Customs stuff. But it should only be a few years, I reckon. After that he'll come and see you, say there's insufficient evidence or something like that and let you go. It's a bit of a rough deal for you, I suppose, but that can't be helped.'

Deron stepped forward. 'Look,' it said, 'we feel really badly about this, but if we don't bag you now we've got no chance of meeting our target this quarter. Sorry. Think of it as a kind of holiday.'

Delgado decided to change tactic; while being locked away for years while awaiting a trial was not something he was too keen on, he knew that these two fools were probably well armed. And despite Deron's obvious cowardice and insecurity, if Delgado destroyed Schlass here on the pod he had no doubt that the other machine's automatic programs would take control, strip any restricting character traits and allow him to fight more effectively. He leaned forward and sneered into their faces. 'Look, you two don't know who you're messing with here. When I get out, you'd better watch your backs because I'm going to be looking for you. Do you understand?'

Deron glanced at Schlass with concern. 'What does he mean?' it said, obviously worried. 'What *does* he mean?' It looked back to Delgado. 'What do you mean?'

'He's bluffing.'

'But what if he's with the Mars Militia or something? You know what they're like.' It addressed Delgado. '*Are* you with the Mars Militia?'

'That's only for me to know, Rusty. It's up to you to decide whether you want to take the risk or not.'

158

'He is part of the Mars Militia, I know he is. I think we should forget all about this and let him go.'

'Look, I'm telling you he's bluffing, now shut up for God's sake.'

'Well, I don't want any part of it. The Mars Militia will—'

'Shut up! He's hardly in a position to hurt anybody, is he? He's handcuffed, he's our prisoner and he's going to help us get that bonus. Mars Militia my tin ass. Those people don't fly around in shitty little ships like this. They plant bombs on passenger liners and kill tens of thousands of civilians at a time just to get into the headlines.'

Deron thought about it for a moment. 'Hmmm. I suppose you're right.'

'You're damn right I'm right. Now let's get him on to the *Damascus* and back to Earth. The sooner we get him processed, the sooner we get our bonus.'

The *Damascus* had, despite its size and appearance, modern, highly compact displacement drives, and they were approaching Earth within three hours. Delgado felt some trepidation as the planet swelled before him: he was now committed to specific actions not of his own choosing, and he disliked such freeform situations. What he had to do was clear to him, but the lack of options and unclear process of events troubled him.

'Contact Advanced Trajectory Control,' said Schlass, who was sitting in the pilot's seat.

'I have, I have. You don't have to tell me everything you know.'

'Well, have you got a descent rate?'

'Yes, it's already fixed.'

'And aligned?'

'And aligned.'

Delgado shook his head as the two machines squabbled. They encapsulated everything he despised about the path humans had taken on Earth: petty bureaucracy and greed took precedence over issues that were vital to the survival of the human race. That these traits had even permeated the world of AI constructs reflected the level to which humans had become obsessed with these issues, and in turn themselves.

He experienced a faint light-headedness as containment field generators took over from the ship's displacement drives and the *Damascus* turned. As Earth reappeared from behind, drifting right and rising in the frame of the small window at his shoulder, he could see the outlines of some of the old continents – the Americas, Europe, Asia. But even though the land masses were easily distinguishable, their internal borders were almost completely lost, the small countries that had once made the planet so culturally rich long since abandoned as the populace had compressed itself into the ten main population centres, and then compressed still further into the Myson habitats. From orbit, the new urban areas looked like huge grey leeches feeding on the planet's surface, sapping what meagre resources remained.

The *Damascus* shuddered and rattled as it entered the atmosphere, an orange glow wrapping it and obscuring the view below. Delgado was not sorry that he could no longer see the planet towards which they were heading. The view brought back too many memories for him; his past lay there, waiting to trap him.

A few minutes later the craft banked hard left, and as it dropped below the lowest cloud Delgado eyed the city with undiluted cynicism. It seemed exactly as he remembered it: dirty, desperate, decaying – like Earth itself. He pressed his face against the thick glass and looked down. The largest buildings – the great habitats and the Military Intelligence building itself – appeared to be huddled together in mutual protection, as if those who remained outside somehow posed a threat.

The *Damascus* turned again, and as Delgado hung in his straps he heard a distant electronic voice saying something about crossing a beacon; an alarm briefly sounded, and small blocks of text scrolled up a screen inset into the back of the seat in front of him. They levelled for a moment then turned again. The distinct mushroom shape of Military Intelligence Supreme Headquarters drifted around, then swelled in the windshield as though being inflated as they approached it. The Customs building was visible just beyond.

Military Intelligence Supreme Headquarters was the same place it had always been. Dark, menacing, the dome-shaped edifice, supported by a thick single column, sprouted from the earth like a mutant fungus. Innumerable flier platforms linked by spiralling tracks jutted out from the building. Constantly arriving and departing vehicles – xip fighters, freighters, diplomatic craft – danced anxiously around it like flies feeding on a beast not yet dead.

The *Damascus* skewed and rocked in turbulent air as it began to descend through the thick clouds of the lower atmosphere, which sweated a grim poison that left greasy streaks across the window. Delgado looked into the bland soup as the vessel passed the upper levels of the Military Intelligence building, and saw things he remembered of Earth: past events, people he had killed, people he had known and respected.

As the craft ploughed through the dense, exhausting vapour, he remembered how as a child he had imagined that the clouds were huge and magnificent skyships, stretching from horizon to horizon, drifting ponderously through the air like gigantic creatures tamed by men, beasts of burden ridden for gain. He had since learned to his disappointment that the men he had come to know seemed incapable of taming such creatures. True, they were interested enough in personal gain, but as far as the creatures were concerned, slaughter was their only sport.

A gust of wind threw the *Damascus* sideways through the sky and Delgado was plucked back into reality. He looked at the two androids. Their blue heads were bowed towards the instruments in front of them as they tried to deal with a minor crisis of some kind. Delgado realised he would have to make his move soon.

The whine of their craft's engines deepened as it slowed. Rows of harsh, cold lights became illuminated on one of the largest landing platforms at the top of the Customs building. As they blinked their solemn message of welcome, Delgado began to feel increasingly unsettled.

'We're going too fast, can't you slow down?'

'We're not going too fast at all.'

'We are. Look at that: three eighty-four . . .'

'A pilot now, are you?'

'No, but—'

'Well then. Don't talk about things you don't understand.'

'But it just seems . . .'

Delgado glanced at the microcuffs; there was no way he could get them off now, but having his hands in front of him was a definite advantage. Between the two androids' shoulders the Customs building was getting ever nearer, and once there escape would be difficult. He narrowed his eyes as he looked back at the vast, sinister edifice that was the Military Intelligence building, as though that would be sufficient to penetrate its exterior. Lycern, Myson, his unborn child – all were there, of that he was certain.

He was pressed against the window as the *Damascus* banked, and the Military Intelligence building drifted out of sight. He looked ahead at the banks of screens. Soon, he knew, the droids would hand the *Damascus* over to City Control, after which its systems could not be overridden.

He checked on the androids. They were quiet now, watching screens, monitoring engines, keeping an eye on other traffic, possibly communicating with some remote system via an undertone channel; it was time to prepare.

'Third marker,' Deron announced. 'Prepare for hand-over.'

Delgado squinted and looked through the window; he could no longer see the Customs Building, but knew it must be close. He watched as Schlass struggled to focus the containment fields and keep the *Damascus* level as the atmosphere played rough with its aging frame. Delgado felt the vehicle slow somewhat, saw Schlass release another field to increase lift.

'Hand-over in one minute; speed three ten; descend to one three eight four.'

Schlass pushed the small joystick forward slightly, and eased the containment field into a shorter, narrower spread with its left hand. Delgado lifted his hands from his lap, controlled his heart rate, his breathing, his entire body: he could not let either machine sense his mood.

'Hand-over in thirty; drop to one two five five; maintain speed.'

As Schlass began to perform the manoeuvre, Delgado shoved forward, and clubbed the pilot around the back of the head with the edge of his microcuffs. The android's head smashed into a screen; it shattered under the impact. His head buried deep within the unit, Schlass became a convulsing mass of electricity and blue flame. Delgado quickly leaned the other way, grabbed the astonished Deron with his tied hands and began to repeatedly pound the machine's head against the lip of the window behind it.

Deron pleaded with Delgado to stop, squealing in a way that reminded him of the nymphs aboard Myson's PPC. He beat the android until its head began to fragment, its words dissolving into a nonsensical montage of random consonants and vowels. Eventually, when the unit's head was totally destroyed, all that emerged from its chest speaker was a series of incoherent noises. Delgado continued to pound its metal cranium against the hard surface for longer than was necessary, sating a hunger within.

Then Delgado looked up and saw that the *Damascus* was plunging towards the grey mass of the street. Schlass's lifeless body was slumped against the joystick, pushing the craft down at increasing speed. Delgado leaned as far forward as he could between the seats and tried to pull the android away from the controls, but its body was rigid. He was able to lessen the craft's descent rate only slightly, and as the *Damascus* closed on the crumbling buildings and deserted roads, Delgado knew that he could do nothing to save himself. In a final short prayer to a god in whom he did not believe, he said goodbye to Lycern, and to the child he had never seen.

The initial impact followed soon after.

A warm, damp wind smoothed across Delgado's cheek, gradually drawing him from the black depths of unconsciousness. He opened his eyes, but otherwise remained motionless.

Awareness came. He was slumped forward, his feet higher than his head, his body angled across the two rear seats in the *Damascus'* small cockpit; he could see little other than his slightly gashed right forearm, which was in front of him. The lack of any other pain in his body concerned him, and he wondered if he had suffered injuries so severe it had simply given up. Again the wind caressed him. Something vibrated above him, making a noise like that of a dying insect uselessly beating its wings. With caution, he raised his head.

The side of the *Damascus* had been torn away as the craft slid along the street; he found himself looking not at a control or instrument panel, but at a dark, damp road. The vibrating sound was caused by part of the main hull which was rattling noisily in the gusting wind. He looked down at his body, relieved to see that he was wholly intact, and that his feet readily complied when he tried to move them. It seemed the reason he felt no pain was because he was relatively unharmed. Cautiously, he pushed himself up, swung his legs round until he was in a sitting position, and looked out through the *Damascus'* open side.

Derelict buildings stared down like toothless witches, the

empty eye sockets of their windows absorbing what little grim light there was. They were old, decaying structures, abandoned many years before by those drawn to Myson's towers. They were all around him – imposing monolithic representations of all that humans had become.

Delgado moved across the seats and slid down on to the road. For a time he crouched behind the loose section of hull, watching, waiting. The air was humid and thick, a foul-smelling poison. Pools of water lay around him like black traps reflecting dark and glossy images of decomposition and death. Far along the road he saw a tangled mass of wire and charred blue metal; he realised that it was one of the androids which had arrested him, but was unable to recognise which one. The other was nowhere to be seen.

Yellow light suddenly burst from the rear of the wreckage of the *Damascus* with a sound like breaking ice, briefly illuminating the whole area around him in its sickly glow. Delgado recognised it as an unchained containment field: if the generators were damaged the energies within them could link at any moment and cause a sizeable explosion. Not enough to cause widespread destruction, but capable of proving unhealthy for anyone in the vicinity at the time. He looked around again; about five hundred metres down the road was a building partially eaten by the co-conspirators of neglect and time. Only three walls remained standing, and although he was unsure if it would stand a field chain explosion, it was the most stable cover he could see. Still bound by the microcuffs, Delgado slid to the ground and ran towards it.

When he reached the building he looked back along the street at the *Damascus*. The shadows had already released several figures, who were moving stealthily towards the crashed vessel. More appeared, inspired by the nerve of the first. Soon the vehicle was alive, rapidly being disassembled by a swarm of street dwellers. Delgado, who had never seen street people so closely before, watched in amazement and admiration at their discipline and focus. The small army worked as a unit, using small tools to carefully remove body panels, retrieve instruments, strip the seats, lighting and wiring, all in eerie silence. They were a single, living entity, working together for their collective benefit.

A large Structure flier bristling with guns and shields suddenly appeared above a rooftop in the distance. It hovered briefly, and when it began to move silently towards the wreckage the scavengers immediately ran for cover. A few moments later the flier was hovering directly above the *Damascus*, its shadow cold and grey. Thin, barely visible lines of red light linked the two vehicles as the wreckage was scanned. When the flier crew was satisfied that no survivors were to be found, the machine moved gracefully away across the city, occasionally scanning things Delgado was unable to see.

The warm breeze strengthened and whined around the ruins; rain began to fall. Delgado realised he would have to find more substantial shelter. He looked down at the microcuffs that bound him; the design was simple, and he doubted they had any anti-tamper mechanisms built in to punish a would-be escapee. He looked around, found a particularly sharp-edged lump of rubble and began to smash the cuffs against it. The pounding quickly cut his wrists, but he continued to hammer the device until it failed and dropped from him like a dead creature. He turned to look along the street, planning his next move.

Then a blow to his head stole consciousness from him.

The smell permeated his consciousness first: a damp mustiness that reminded him of a former campaign, waged in uncomfortable and frustrating conditions. Then some sounds filtered through: voices, hushed and secretive. According to his nobics there were five of them, four males, one female, all on the far side of the room. They were arguing among themselves; he detected discontent, frustration, anger, traces of mischief.

Delgado partially opened his eyes. He was facing a yellow-painted wall. The paint was old, and large flakes were peeling away to reveal the damp, disintegrating brickwork beneath. He closed his eyes again and listened carefully, filtering out the voices to concentrate on background noises. He heard water dripping; an old and noisy computer downloading infocram data near to the arguing people. An ancient e-suit buzzed softly.

The talking stopped. Delgado felt a ripple of anxiety, but whether it was his own or came from one of his captors he was unable to distinguish. There was movement. His nobics suggested that four people had walked towards him, while one remained on the other side of the room. A moment later one of the group was standing next to his shoulder, leaning over his face.

'He's still asleep.' It was a female voice, soft and husky but with a hard edge. 'We should leave him: he looks as though he's been through hell.'

Then a male: 'Fuck that. Kill him now, before it's too late. If he wakes up he'll—'

'Shut up, Lox.' Another male, his voice softer than that of the first.

'But we don't know who he is. Or anything else about him. Just because he was wearing Structure cuffs doesn't mean he's on our side, Bucky.'

Male. Bucky. Leader?

'Sure,' said another male voice, deep and nasal.

'See? Even Clunk agrees with me. This guy could be an undercover purifier – how are we to know?'

The female again. 'Oh, come on, Lox. You think Structure's really likely to waste a flier and two droids, and risk the life of a purifier, just to get some intelligence on the streets? Get realistic.'

'Why the hell not, Girl? They've done more stupid things before now. You think we should kill him, don't you, Clunk?'

'S'pose.'

Bucky and Girl support each other. Clunk noncommittal, impartial. Third male – Lox – antagonistic, trouble.

'We're not going to kill him,' said Bucky firmly. Delgado began to focus on everything he said, the way he said it. 'Girl will look after him for now and when he comes round we'll ask him a few questions. Like Girl says, Structure hasn't got funds to waste on the stuff you're suggesting, Lox. Myson's not interested in us, or anything outside his precious habitats. I reckon this guy was smuggling something and there was some kind of problem with the flier's hand-over. Software crash, something like that. Clunk, you stay with Girl and make sure he doesn't try anything if he wakes up, OK?'

'Sure.'

There was a pause, then Bucky said: 'Lox: I think Headman wants you. You better go help him out.'

'Oh, man . . .'

'I'm going up top,' Bucky continued. 'Let me know if he wakes.'

'Yeah.'

'And Clunk – don't fall asleep.'

'Sure.'

Delgado listened as Bucky walked away, then felt the bed shift as someone heavy sat on the end of the mattress.

'Careful, Clunk,' said Girl, 'you'll break his goddamn legs. Move up a bit or sit on the floor, for Christ's sake.'

'Sure. OK.'

Delgado felt the bed shift again as Clunk stood up, and then felt Girl pull his gashed arm away from his body and begin to dab something onto it. It stung like hell, but Delgado remained motionless.

When she had finished tending to his wound Delgado allowed himself to relax, and took the opportunity to drift off into a light sleep despite the burning in his arm: he would need to rest while he could. He released some nobics to pain relief and some to constant awareness; if the one called Lox returned, he wanted to know about it.

A strong vibration was running through the bed; it was so loud the rusting metal frame was rattling against the wall, loosening brickwork and flakes of paint. Delgado opened his eyes and cautiously raised his head, startled from a sleep which had gone from the light slumber he had intended to an almost comatose state.

A man – or something resembling a man, at least – was sitting on the floor at the end of the bed. His head was lolling, resting on one of his huge, thick shoulders: the vibration in the bed was caused by his snoring. This, Delgado assumed, was Clunk.

All over Clunk's face, neck and arms, and visible through his clothes on the rest of his body, were ridges of what appeared to be a carbograft body enhancement; but the application had been a bad one. His dark skin seemed to be covered in a primitive form of radioshield cell graft that had failed to knit at molecular level, so that the separate units had bonded erratically into rigid, random lumps rather than the smooth and virtually impenetrable shell it was supposed to be. To Delgado it looked like a FleshArmor design, albeit a very old one, but he could not be sure. FleshArmor had ceased operations years ago, unable to compete with cheap Lyugg imports of similar products.

The graft had rendered Clunk's flesh hideously textured, an angular array of points and tiles that were so incoherent Delgado doubted they provided much if anything in the way of protection. His features looked small and oddly delicate on this frame despite the deformation of his mouth and eyes.

'Like a drink?'

Delgado turned his head sharply to look over his shoulder: it was Girl. Delgado immediately assigned nobics to find out why she had been able to startle him.

Girl was slim and very young – not more than twenty-five or thirty. Her skin was fresh, alive, her eyes blue and bright. She had a friendly, heart-shaped face, her features well proportioned; nothing like Lycern. Her blonde hair was cut in a short bob, and it reminded him of the girl he had met on *Elixiion* the morning after her obscenity party; he frowned when he could not remember her name.

Girl was wearing an old Military Intelligence nuworld scoutsuit: tough cadmex ranging trousers and matching bolero tunic with integral oxyfeed and body moisture recycling unit. The buddymatch attachments on her chest – designed to allow pooling of scoutsuit resources in emergencies – were scratched but looked unused: there was no gum residue around the seals. The suit was mostly olive green with grey trim and brown fur lining. It was also three sizes too big for her; for some reason Delgado found this oddly attractive.

'Like a drink?' she repeated, raising her eyebrows and pointing at the mug in her hand.

Delgado nodded. She handed him the mug and he drank the water it contained gratefully. He hoped it had been filtered in some way.

'Clunk.' Girl went over to the snoring lump of flesh at the end of the bed and shook him vigorously by the shoulder while Delgado drank. 'Clunk!'

The huge man stopped snoring and opened his eyes. He raised his head slowly and looked around the room, at Girl, then at Delgado. His eyes were bleary. It seemed to take a while for him to appreciate where he was and what was happening. But when he realised that Delgado was awake, he pointed in a sudden, silent panic and began to tremble, gagging on words that would not come to him.

'It's OK, Clunk,' said Girl, resting one hand on his enormous left shoulder. 'It's all right. Just go and fetch Bucky. I won't tell him you fell asleep.'

The huge man looked into Girl's eyes, frowning, searching

170

for reassurance. He glanced at Delgado, then stood. 'Sure,' he said, suddenly completely calm, and shuffled towards a doorway on the far side of the room.

Girl turned to Delgado again. 'Want to sit up?'

Delgado stayed where he was, only pushing himself up when Girl moved forward to help him. He looked round the room. It seemed to be a basement or warehouse of some kind. Narrow, slatted windows ran round the top of the high walls filtering grey light into alternating slices of light and dark that cut the space into segments of density. The pot-holed concrete floor trapped black liquid mirrors; a pile of rubbish in a distant corner trembled as a rat larger than any Delgado had seen before scrambled across it. Directly opposite him an old cooker stood between a large metal sink and an antiquated refrigerator.

Further along the wall to the left was a man sitting in front of a bank of screens, most of which were blank. He was rocking back and forth as if hearing a slow, rhythmic beat, his head occasionally twitching. He was wearing some sort of large, cocoon-like suit, and had his arms and legs drawn inside its fur-covered shell; the feeder connectors, data exchange couplings and environment filters glinted like a hard metallic rash on the suit's soft surface. Most of his body was hidden in shadow, but a slab of silver light fell through one of the high windows directly onto his face, releasing his features. His eyes were closed, as if in intense concentration or imagining horrific images. His mouth was slightly open; a thin strand of saliva trailed from one corner. His muscles looked taut, as if he was in some kind of physical pain. A second man was leaning over him, watching one of the active screens very closely, his face bathed in the milky light that radiated from it.

In the wall behind these two men were several deep recesses containing piles of bedding, cupboards, small lamps and what looked like variously sized weapon cases. As Delgado tried to establish what kind of weapon each one might contain, movement caught his eye; the man who had been standing next to the rocking figure was now walking towards them.

'He's awake, then?' Delgado recognised Lox's voice immediately. He was tall and thin, his small and sinister eyes partially covered by his straight, lank hair. He walked with an arrogant, slouching gait that exuded confidence; Delgado sensed from some imperceptible aspect of the man's attitude that this was a pretence. His clothes were uniformly black and loose-fitting. Strips of wire and mechanobe culture cells protruded from almost every one of the numerous pockets on his trousers and long jacket. 'Kill the bastard, Girl,' he said as he approached, brandishing an index finger. 'Kill him before it's too late. You should've let those cronos have him. We don't need this shit.'

'Shut up, Lox. We do what Bucky says, OK?'

'Yeah, yeah, sure. Always do what Fucky says.'

She ignored his comment. 'Did you and Headman do OK?'

'Yeah, well. I guess. We cracked the new landing codes, no problem. Now we just have to upload some gibberish in the new format and all hell should break loose.' He turned and pointed at Headman, who was still rocking in front of his screens. 'He's just makin' sure he's downloaded all the stuff we need.' He shook his head, then turned back to face them. 'Goddamn fuckin' creep scares me sometimes, though. I don't reckon he lives in this world at all. Crazy head shit, man —' he tapped his temple '— it's fuckin' him up big time. I don't reckon there's no turning back for him now. Still, it's his funeral. I better go and see if he's done.' Lox turned and walked back over to Headman; he flinched and looked at Lox with fire in his eyes when tapped on the shoulder, and only returned to his former state after a few minutes of placation from Lox. The latter looked back over at Girl as the other man resumed his easy rocking. 'See what I mean?' he called, shrugging.

Delgado heard footsteps from the doorway and looked to

his right: Clunk and Bucky were returning.

Bucky's face was serious, filled with wisdom and experience that seemed beyond his obviously young age. He was neither tall nor slim, but possessed a certain solidity and steadfastness Delgado thought the others would probably find reassuring. His short curly hair emphasised the roundness of his face. His hand was at his hip, resting on the HiMag blaster that went with the black purifier suit he was wearing, both undoubtedly taken from a person long-dead. Bucky walked confidently up to the bed; both Girl and Delgado looked up at him, expectant. 'How long's he been awake?' he asked.

'Just a few minutes.'

'Has he said anything?'

She shook her head. 'Nope.'

Bucky leaned forward. 'What's your name, man? Where are you from?'

Delgado just looked at him.

'Maybe he doesn't understand you,' suggested Girl.

'Maybe he does and he just doesn't want to let on,' said Lox, who was walking back across to them. 'Kill him now, Bucky, while you still have the chance. I'm not joking here, man.'

'Shut up, Lox. I'm as suspicious as you are, but we're not barbarians.'

'No?'

Delgado met Bucky's eyes. And in a moment of absolute clarity, he saw far beyond the young man's face. Messages passed and links formed between the two men instantaneously, an immediate and mutual respect generated as they communicated in ways that transcended the conscious mind. If either had been asked to explain the sensation, neither would have been able to: it was the bond of kindred spirit, a meeting of like souls, the reunion of lost twins.

'I can understand you perfectly well,' said Delgado quietly. He noticed that his words possessed an unusual clarity of enunciation.

'See?' said Lox, pointing a finger, 'I told you. Now will you kill him?'

'How do you feel?' asked Girl, ignoring Lox. 'You had a bit of a rough landing. We watched you come down – thought everyone aboard had had it.'

'I'm fine,' he said. 'Nothing for you to worry about.'

'Interrogate him, Bucky. He's Structure, I can just smell it on him. It's a stench.' Lox wrinkled his nose to emphasise his point.

'I'm not Structure.'

'You would say that.'

'Lox thinks that you're a purifier come to get some word on the street situ,' said Girl, leaning forward and smiling in a way Delgado liked. 'He's a bit paranoid sometimes.'

'I'm not paranoid, I'm just careful. And we can't be too careful, Girl – you know that. I say we kill him. He's an unnecessary liability.'

'I'm not wearing a purifier suit,' said Delgado. He glanced from Lox to Bucky. 'Maybe I should be the suspicious one. Besides, why knock me out if you're so friendly?'

'That was Lox. He doesn't like to take chances.'

'Yes. I can believe that.' Delgado cast Lox a thin glance.

Lox was about to speak, but Bucky held up a hand. Lox shook his head and stormed off towards Headman.

'So who are you, man,' Bucky asked, 'if you're not Structure?'

'Just a trader. Got picked up by Customs when my systems went down.'

Bucky turned to Lox and Headman who were sitting together in front of the bank of screens in the far corner. 'Lox,' he called, 'ask Headman to access records of incoming ultra-beam signals to the Customs Department and see if there's anything on a smuggler being picked up.' Lox waved one hand in a manner that could have been construed as either dismissal or acknowledgement, and turned back to Headman. Bucky sat down on the edge of the bed; Delgado noticed that he had opened the catch on his holster. 'So what's your name?' Bucky asked.

Delgado was impressed by his friendly-interrogator act. He paused for a moment before answering, and considered whether to give them a false identity. In the end he decided it wouldn't help him, and might only cause problems if they found out that he had lied. Besides, he had little to lose and, given the evidence of recent events, he felt as though he had been denying who he really was for most of his life. 'My name's Alexander Delgado,' he said, before he was able to change his mind.

Bucky nodded. 'Right. OK, Delgado. So you say you were picked up by Customs?'

He nodded. 'Out by Titan.'

'Were you smuggling?'

'No, that's the worst part about it. I was going to be framed by a couple of droids. They were keen to meet quotas. Wanted an upgrade of some kind, I think.'

Bucky and Girl looked at each other and smiled. 'They do have a habit of doing that,' said Girl. 'But why did the Customs flier crash? Usually it's because we've been interfering with the codes.'

Delgado shook his head. 'I wasn't going to lose years of my life for two greedy droids so I trashed them while we were coming in. I thought I could get control of the flier and speed out to a settlement in the Dead Zone. But there wasn't enough time. Complications.'

'You nearly killed yourself.'

Delgado shrugged. 'I had to take the risk.'

'That was some gamble.'

'There's a gamble in everything.'

Lox walked over to them. 'No record of any pick-up or arrest this morning. He's Structure. Kill him.'

'Hang on, hang on. You know what these customs droids

are like, Lox, they never register pick-ups when they're supposed to. I tell you what, check out a name: Alexander Delgado.'

Lox walked away again, muttering something under his breath and shaking his head. Bucky appeared to hear him, but let it pass.

'So,' said Bucky, 'if you weren't smuggling anything, where did you come from?'

'That's not important,' said Delgado. 'But I'm not your enemy.'

'I'll decide what's impor—'

'Got it,' called Lox, running back across to them. 'Alexander Delgado – Reactionary Forces Commander, no less. I told you he was Structure. Now will you kill the fucker? Please say yes, Bucky.'

Bucky frowned. 'Where was this information?' he asked.

'Headman got it from deep searching databases.'

'It wasn't on the Military Intelligence biocomputer?'

'No.'

'Did he check the biocomp?'

'Well . . . yeah.'

'So if he's Structure why isn't he registered in the biocomp?' Bucky half turned and looked up at Lox.

The man shrugged. 'How the fuck should I know,' he said sulkily. 'Headman just scanned maps and followed links to the Military Intelligence propaganda database. The name was in some old compressions relating to Buhatt, and some military stuff from Smythe's era. Nothing in the biocomp, though – nothing current. But then, come on, let's face it, if he was dropped in here by Structure to infiltrate the streets they'd take his name off the biocomp, wouldn't they? Come on, man, let's just kill him now and put the sucker out of his misery. Why take the risk?'

Bucky, Lox, Girl and Clunk all looked at Delgado. Even the mysterious Headman glanced across from the corner. Lox gradually seemed to be convincing his friends that his logic was sound; even Girl was starting to look doubtful. The room was noticeably quieter, more tense.

'So what's the story, Delgado?' asked Bucky. 'Why's your name linked to Military Intelligence and in their propaganda files, but isn't registered on the biocomp? Bit of a contradiction, that. Clear it up for us.'

Delgado felt very tired, as if all the things he had recently experienced had suddenly caught up with him. He pressed his fingers into his eyes and moved them in small circles. He sighed, let his shoulders slump. Everything that had happened to him had eroded his confidence and self-belief. He could no longer pretend, was too weak to continue fighting everything and everyone he was faced with. He looked up at Bucky. 'My name is Alexander Delgado,' he said. 'I was a Commander for—'

'See? I told you! Kill him! Fucking do it, man.'

'Shut up, Lox,' said Bucky patiently. 'Let the guy finish.'

Delgado stared hard at Lox for a moment, then continued. 'As I was saying: I was a Commander for Military Intelligence. Reactionary Forces. I was a Stealth operative for a while.'

The group shifted uneasily. Lox whistled.

'Why do you say "was"?' asked Girl.

'I no longer serve Military Intelligence.'

Lox laughed. 'Come on, man, you know as well as we do that no one, but *no one*, leaves Military Intelligence, let alone Reactionary Forces. Not ever. Except in the final ceremony.'

'We had differences. I absconded, they captured me, I escaped. That's why I was picked up in a dead flier on the edge of the system, and about to be processed by two dodgy Customs droids.'

Headman made some strange guttural noise on the other side of the room; Lox turned and walked over to him.

'I'm not sure I believe you,' said Bucky. 'Like Lox says, no one gets out of Military Intelligence. Once you're in, you're in for life. Maybe we should do as Lox suggests. We don't want Structure knowing where we are. Purifiers would obliterate this whole area – three square kilometres – if they had a clue. And anyway, why come back to Earth if you've got Military Intelligence after you? That's suicidal.'

'I've got some personal business to attend to.'

'With whom?'

Delgado said nothing.

Lox appeared again; he looked a little embarrassed. 'Headman reckons he's found some highly classified secure-data units in the Reactionary Forces section of the biocomp core. And I mean real deep; ones he's never seen before. He came across them by accident a few minutes ago. He says they contain hot shit about certain officers and campaigns. There's a recent Death Instruction out on a Commander Alexander Delgado; no details, just kill. Big reward, too. Maybe we should kill him and claim it. What do you think, Clunk?'

The big man shrugged. 'Sure. S'pose.'

'Couldn't they have planted those files just to fool us into believing his story?' said Girl, whose scepticism had obviously grown. 'If they were going to send someone down here for whatever reason they'd make sure the cover was watertight.'

'I hate to admit it,' said Lox, 'but I don't think so, man. They don't know the power of the Headman there.' He jerked a thumb back over his shoulder. 'That guy can get into places there aren't even places. He's a weirdo but he's good, I'll give him that. They'd stick the stuff where it could easily be found by your average netliner if this was a set-up, not hide it away under layers of encrypted security pass codes accessible only to the Planetary Council. Headman reckons what he's found aren't the complete intelligence files, just notes the biocomp's using as memory. Even he can't get to the full story.'

Bucky looked at Delgado again. 'So you go AWOL, they capture you, you escape, and now they want you dead: what

the fuck have you done, man? And why come back to Earth
if you know they want you so bad?'

Delgado paused for a moment, weighing his response
against the position he was in. He was traumatised, exhausted.
Continued deception seemed pointless. 'He has my child,' he
said. There was no reaction from the group. 'My child's
mother and William Myson are together. She knows the
foetus is inside her but he, as yet, does not. At least he didn't.
And if he does, he may well think it's his. He wants an heir
from her and when my child is born he may well believe it's
his, and if he knows it's not he's not likely to care too much.
I have to get to them, to my child. Even if I die trying, I have
to do it.' Delgado looked down with a single shake of his head;
his shoulders slumped as pure emotion swept through him. It
was all true, and he could not rest until his aims had been
achieved. His revelation was the release of his inner spirit, the
salvation of all he was.

'What makes you so sure it's not Myson's child? What if
she's lying?'

'She's a *conosq*. She told me Myson's impotent, and I believe
her. I also know the child she's carrying is mine. I've no proof,
but I know.'

Lox raised his eyebrows and whistled at a slightly higher
pitch than before. 'Wow. Can't afford too many enemies like
that, man. And Myson an empty vessel? Boy, imagine if that
got out.' He chuckled slightly.

Bucky frowned and glanced at his two comrades then back
to Delgado. 'You must realise that you haven't got a chance of
getting to him: Myson's the most powerful human alive.
When he's on Earth he's right at the top of the MI building.
You ever been on the streets? You wouldn't even get near.
You should've got as far away as you could while you had the
chance.'

'I *can* get to him,' hissed Delgado, tension welling. 'I've
been trained for decades to do just this kind of thing and I have

the experience to back it up. Besides, I have friends I'm sure
will help me if I can get inside. And even if they don't want to
help me, I'll get to him somehow. There's too much at stake.'
Delgado's lips were trembling; there were tears in his eyes.
The strength of his feelings shocked even him, but his sincerity
was clear, both to those around him, and to himself.

'It's an awful big risk to take on your own, man,' said Lox
quietly.

'Maybe we can help you, huh?' said Bucky.

Delgado looked up. 'Why would you want to help me?
What would you get out of it?'

Bucky shrugged. 'Maybe nothing,' he said unemotionally.
'Maybe everything.'

Lox seemed to agree. He looked at Delgado in a
mischievous, mistrustful way. 'Yeah, man,' he said, 'maybe
everything.' He leaned close to Bucky. 'Or maybe we could
get our asses scorched by blaster fire, huh?' He turned and
strode away from the group across the room.

Delgado looked at each of the other gang members in turn;
their eyes were sparkling, their faces – apart from Clunk's –
alive with new vigour.

The group sat on a scattering of cushions in one of the recesses
eating a mixture of rice and sliced meat. Delgado looked at the
meat with some uncertainty, then glanced into the darkest
corners of the room; there seemed to be fewer rats around than
before. He hesitated: in the past he had caught animals and
eaten them before they were dead in order to survive, but rats
were unclean, disease-bearing. He looked at the brown meat
he held between his fingers for a few moments, his nose
slightly wrinkled. With resignation he closed his eyes and ate
the meal heartily, seeking the nourishment he knew only meat
could provide.

'What's his story?' he asked Bucky as they ate. He nodded
towards Headman. Other than Clunk, who was sleeping, he

was the only member of the gang not to join in the meal; he remained in his dark corner, rocking gently, eyes tightly closed.

Bucky turned to look. 'Headman? He's our spider. He used to be a mercenary hacker, double- and triple-agenting for rival companies in industrial espionage. It paid well, he was given a home, flier, ten days holiday a year. But when the four big corporations merged and moved inside the habitats, he was suddenly out of a job and on the streets. He never managed to get back.' Bucky shrugged. 'Who knows, maybe he never wanted to. But one thing I do know: he can dip into any database or file pool on any system and get the information we need. Or log on to an ultrabeam shot from halfway across the galaxy and keep us up to date with what Military Intelligence is doing. He can even talk directly with semi-sentient navcomms on spacecraft. And he doesn't have any nobics to help him. No way, man. Sometimes he needs Lox here to help him crack an access code or establish a messenger protocol, but he's pretty much our eyes and ears. He doesn't use those screens much, just absorbs the information from the suit. It's quicker, and doesn't leave a signature – if he's careful. Having that jack stuck in his skull means he knows exactly what's going on and when, without too much interpreter lag, too.'

Delgado looked at Headman again. Thick streams of wires led directly into the suit from a netstream jack on one wall. This looked extremely non-standard, heavily adapted from various sources to allow the multiple links required by hard feeds and infocrams to work together. It was a clot of lightweight switchways, held together by generous lengths of tape. The link disappeared into the suit through a port at Headman's waist. A wide, multi-coloured ribbon emerged from the suit at the back of its thick, rubbery collar, and linked to an interneural coupler at the base of Headman's skull. It was this stubby metal socket that connected his mind directly to the net. 'How does he translate the information? How can he tell you what he can't see?' Delgado asked.

Bucky stopped chewing for a moment. 'Well, that's why we call him the Headman: because it's all in his head, man. See that suit he's wearing?' Delgado nodded. 'That's a first generation Martian Formersuit. Back when they thought they could terraform Mars, the workers didn't have much equipment with them because of the transportation costs. They used those suits to interface directly with the computers on Earth. Any information they needed was ultrabeamed straight into their heads as and when required, with mechanobe culture implants acting as a buffer for the most frequently accessed information. All the interneural data compression and infocram technology in use today – CyberWeb, cramwave pulses, undertone, even some of that hyperconsciousness stuff you military guys have – was derived from the mixture of mechanobe nanotechnology and biotech gear originally developed for the colonies. You're not supposed to cram for more than one hour at a time, but Headman's zipped into that stinking suit for twenty-two hours a day, so it's no wonder he's gone a little strange. In fact, he's so screwed up from directly interfacing with every code format in use that he hardly speaks any more, and then only usually to Lox. We reckon he even thinks in code.'

'He comes off there sometimes,' said Girl, 'but like Bucky says, he's alienated himself, lost the social skills he needs to integrate with the rest of us. He can't handle it for long.'

'He tells us when the purifiers are coming to this area,' said Bucky, 'or when there's a pile of shit going down at Military Intelligence or Structure that we can gain something from or help to stir up. Pretty much everything we do is controlled by what he sees in his head. I guess he has quite a lot of power.'

'Which means Lox does, too,' Delgado observed.

Bucky raised his eyebrows but said nothing.

Delgado scooped a handful of rice and meat into his mouth and looked at Clunk. He was sleeping in a dark corner, snoring even more loudly than before. 'What about him?'

182

Bucky had to swallow food before speaking. 'You remember the SWAP?'

Delgado thought then shook his head. 'Must've been before my time,' he said.

'No, no – ten years ago at most. The Structure Wealth and Advancement Programme.' He searched for recognition in Delgado.

'I must've been on a campaign,' he said. 'You tend to lose track of what's going on when you're out in the field.'

Bucky shrugged. 'OK. Well, the SWAP was started with the aim of placing people into isolated alien cultures to integrate with the indigenous intelligences to assess the possibility of securing trade agreements, arms deals and other shit like that before anyone else did.' He paused to pick a sliver of gristle from between his teeth. 'They needed people who could integrate without having to wear e-suits and stuff. You stand out like a sore thumb on a non-con world if you can't breathe the atmosphere.' He chuckled at the thought. 'Clunk's a result of early experiments into altering human physiology to suit different planetary conditions – forced shape-shifting, if you like. He used to be a thief. He could transfer funds from your credichip to a smartcard linked to a small remote terminal and shoot the data to a personal fund halfway across the galaxy without you ever knowing it. But when he was caught, instead of a formal sentence he was assigned to the SWAP. Which was funded by Structure, of course.'

'So what happened?'

'From what we can make out – and bear in mind that his vocabulary is now pretty limited – he was supposed to go to a planet on the Bissyan spiral, whose race had virtually mastered telepathy. The military thought this could prove useful in the field: no interneural hardlinks, no waves for the enemy to pick up, no temperamental nobics needed to build a hypercon-sciousness. Clunk was supposed to go there, try to learn the basic processes of thought transmission and send the information back so it could be backwardly extrapolated here on Earth, and Military Intelligence could learn how to use it.

'The planet's atmosphere had a low oxygen content, so they increased his lung capacity. His skull was enlarged so an experimental ultrabeam transmitter could be fitted inside his head, then he could get the information back using a network of microsats placed in orbit around the planet and not draw attention to himself with masses of equipment or power use. As it was, the transmitter was faulty and fried part of his brain almost as soon as it was fitted. The planet itself was fried when Structure and the Lyugg Political Bureau started arguing over who was going to get trade rights following contact. Apparently the Lyugg had a similar scheme to SWAP in operation and Clunk happened to wrongfoot their efforts. There was much diplomatic activity and tit-for-tat expulsions, but in the end it was clear Structure was going to lose out to Lyugg so a Reactionary Forces Gunship "accidentally" lost control of a new weapon it was allegedly testing, and destroyed pretty much the whole place.'

'Now I remember *that*,' said Delgado. 'I thought it really was an accident though. There was hell to pay afterwards, if I remember. Reparations, compensation – the lot.'

'Right,' nodded Bucky. 'You got it. Well, it was the end of the argument: no planet, no problem. So Clunk wasn't needed, of course. But rather than waste money keeping him in a prison or having him executed, they shoved him out onto the streets where they thought the purifiers would get him. And they are, as we all know, funded by the People's Cleansing Tax and therefore no drain on Structure coffers. Things are a bit cloudy after that point. He can't tell us much about it. First we knew of him was when he stumbled in here one morning trying to find something to eat. He's been with us ever since.'

Delgado put his bowl down, then wiped his hands and looked at Bucky. 'So what about you? Where do you come from?'

'You don't need to know about me,' he said, avoiding Delgado's eyes and concentrating on his rice. 'I'm just a survivor.'

'But where are you from?'

'Somewhere I couldn't stay.'

Delgado saw he had touched a nerve, a sensitive area where weaknesses could lie. He filed the information away. If it proved a danger, then he would be prepared to deal with it. If he needed to, he could probably find a way to exploit it.

He looked at Girl, but she knew her turn was coming and held up her hand. 'Don't ask me,' she said, 'I just exist. My head is empty of everything from before the time Bucky and Clunk picked me out of the rubble of a building destroyed by purifiers. Sometimes I get bizarre flashes, like dreams, but nothing useful. I don't know where or when I was born or where I came from, so I can't tell you anything other than that these guys are my family now.'

'The relationships do vary, though,' said Lox. Everyone seemed to ignore this comment.

'What about you, Lox?' asked Delgado. 'How did you get here?'

'No real story,' he said, screwing up his face as he concentrated on trying to clean his bowl of every last grain of rice. 'I'm just a good, honest subversive, man. I'm waiting for the day Military Intelligence falls, and when it does I'll be the first to dance and be in there to mete out the justice. Structure and Military Intelligence do anything to get what they want regardless of the cost, you know that. But one day all the shit they've dished out will come back to them, an' I'll be right there stirrin' it up. You, man? I'd have killed you where we found you without asking any questions. And I might still, so just watch your back. In my experience, anyone from Structure isn't worth shit.'

'Thanks very much.'

'Think nothing of it.' He finished the last of his rice, licked each fingertip in turn, and threw his empty bowl into the corner where Clunk was sleeping. It bounced off the man's huge chest, but although he stirred briefly he didn't wake. 'So what's the plan?' Lox said to Bucky. 'We just gonna let this guy come in and rule our lives for us? Personally I think we should test him somehow; make sure he's really on our side. You know, like we discussed. We've only got his word that he's no longer part of Military Intelligence, after all. It's one thing to say something like that, another to act the part. We all know how ingrained their training is.'

'Did you have something particular in mind, Lox?' asked Bucky.

'Headman told me earlier that a Military Intelligence Diplomatic Vessel is leaving MIHQ pretty soon. He couldn't tell us who was going to be aboard, but he says it must be someone important because there's an escort of half a dozen Detachment Vehicles waiting in orbit.'

'And you're suggesting what, exactly?'

'He shoots it down.'

All eyes turned to Delgado.

'That a problem, man?' said Bucky.

Delgado said nothing.

The rain was warm and smelled of chemicals. The large drops slashed diagonally through the hot night air like chromium insects. The clouds from which they fell were themselves great swirling creatures, swelling and shrinking in the buffeting wind. Occasionally they were illuminated in various shades of red and green by the navigation lights of descending fliers. The city itself was a dark concoction of indistinct lines and textures, its definition softened by the rain. The old city was like a plain of rotting vegetation spread all around them, while the habitat towers directly ahead were silver-studded columns, rigid and indestructible.

Delgado and Bucky stood on the roof of their building

beneath a metal sheet that had slipped from the top of the aircon housings. Rain dripped from its thin edge in a cascade of polished gems that were absorbed by the dark pools at their feet. Delgado stood with his arms folded while Bucky held the Jutt rifle. Its small screen washed his face with faint green light, casting shadows that distorted his appearance.

'Nice view,' said Delgado, squinting at the distant habitat towers.

'This is one of the few high buildings left around here,' said Bucky. 'Don't ask me why; just seems to have escaped the purifiers' wrath. It was a shopping mall before everyone moved into the towers, I think. Something like that, anyway.'

Delgado glanced at the Jutt rifle, whirring quietly in Bucky's hands as it scanned and assessed the immediate area. He hoped they didn't have to wait too long. Jutt rifles were notoriously temperamental.

He looked across the city again; between the nearest habitats he could see the vast mushroom that was Military Intelligence Headquarters. The only sign of life within the gigantic building was that the landing platforms became briefly illuminated as vessels arrived or departed; otherwise the place was dense and cold, isolated and impenetrable. Delgado shifted uneasily; not only had it been his spiritual home for decades, but Lycern and Myson were almost certainly there now.

As was his child.

He felt as though he could reach out and touch the building, feel its coarse texture beneath the palms of his hands and purge himself of his pain through the distant caress.

Bucky walked to the edge of the building and studied the Jutt rifle's tripod stand for a moment. He stepped back under the sheeting and wiped his forehead on the sleeve of his purifier tunic. 'Goddamn rain stings like fuck, man,' he said, resuming his examination of the Jutt.

'Look, is all this really necessary, Bucky?' said Delgado. 'You really want me to shoot this ship down? Tell me what the point is. And what if it crashes into a habitat and kills ten thousand innocent people? What if the containment drives combine and half the city's destroyed in the explosion? Is that what you want?'

'That's an awful lot of "what–ifs" there, Delgado,' he said without looking up. 'You're not trying to get out of it are you, man?'

Delgado scratched his head. 'I really couldn't give a shit. But I know you know I'm telling you the truth, so why do we have to go through with this? It's just to satisfy the others, isn't it? It's some kind of battle you're having with Lox. How close am I?'

Bucky paused for a moment. 'Well, it's like this, see.' He paused and fingered microswitches, adjusting the large weapon's settings and priorities. 'Me and the guys talked about it, and the way we see it is this: if you're really "out" of Military Intelligence and hate Myson as much as you say, then you won't have any problems shooting down one of their ships. Chances are they're just off to do the normal barbaric, nihilistic, Mysonesque stuff anyway, so it won't be no great loss.'

Delgado watched as Bucky studied the gun's information screen. He recognised something of himself within the young man's angry frame: the bitterness that permeated Bucky's soul was old and distant, and yet it clearly affected everything he did. Unlike Delgado, though, he was driven not by the need to prove himself to himself, but by the need to prove himself to others, those who had probably doubted his abilities when he was young – his friends, his superiors, maybe even his family. Delgado had taken another route; one that, rather than satisfying that need by allowing him to achieve a specific goal, had merely disassociated him and obscured his aims. His parents had never believed he would really join Military Intelligence, and had expected him to drop out right up until the Induction Ceremony, whereupon he would return home and adopt a 'respectable position' – the normality and acceptability they so desperately wanted from him. Only Delgado's grandfather had known the true depth of the young man's feelings, even though they had never spoken of them openly. Joining Military Intelligence had been a form of escape for Delgado, a way of postponing the things he really had to face; but if he had been killed while serving then he would not have regretted his decision in the last moments of his life. That his career had been so successful was an unfortunate coincidence and not, if he were truthful, something he had worked hard to achieve. Delgado believed Bucky had taken a more honest route, fighting for what he believed in rather than what he thought would get him somewhere. And whichever way Delgado tried to twist the facts, he recognised that the choices they had made, the different paths they had taken, had brought them both to the same place, at the same point in time, and with the same goal. He was deeply saddened by this fact, for only one of them had had the strength to be honest with himself.

'Where are you going, Bucky?' Delgado asked quietly.

'What do you mean, man?' Bucky asked. He frowned as narrow lines of text scrolled up the rifle's small screen, but whether this was in response to the question or what he saw was unclear.

'Well, Lox seems intent on subverting Military Intelligence and Structure, bringing them down and moving into power himself. But it seems less important to you somehow; you seem almost happy here, content with your lot.'

Bucky flicked the gun into lull mode; his face altered shape as the screen darkened. He looked up and stared into Delgado's eyes for a long moment, then looked out across the city's shining black night. 'This gang's going nowhere, man,' he said in a sigh of despairing honesty. 'Lox lives in a world of his own making, and gets so worked up about things, so enthusiastic, that the others get carried along with him – well, when I say the others I mean Girl. Clunk hasn't got enough brain cells left to make decisions for himself and Headman exists pretty much on a different plane altogether. I know we'll probably all just end up being added to the purifier body count, but what right have I got to take their dreams from them when that's all they've really got?' He looked at Delgado again; his face was bitter, his emotions brittle. 'Sometimes, when we've trashed a purifier or brought down a Reactionary Forces shuttle or something, we all get a real buzz from it. But me and Lox look at each other and, despite that euphoria, that satisfaction, we both know, man – I can see it in his eyes. We both know that it's crazy to even think that we have a chance of bringing Structure down or making even the tiniest difference to what they do in the long run. But we don't say anything because the day we do that, when our dreams are gone, is the day we really lose. Then we might as well just go and wait for the purifiers to come and fry us.'

Delgado stared at Bucky and realised that the young man was expecting an answer or some kind of challenge. Instead, Alexander Delgado looked out into the dark sky, and waited for the Military Intelligence craft to appear.

The information Headman had given Lox proved to be not absolutely accurate, and they were forced to sit on the damp roof looking out into the rain for several hours. They spoke little. Bucky occupied himself by checking the gun's systems and making sure its plasma generation orbs remained clear: any hint of cloudiness indicated an impure energy charge, which could result in an explosion strong enough to rip off a man's head.

Delgado could think about nothing but Lycern, Myson and his child. He wondered what the future held. Myson was one of the most powerful beings in the galaxy; Lycern was the *conosq dis fer'n'at*, the assigned bearer for Seriatt's Royal Household. The tension between the two worlds was historically great, founded in mutual mistrust and misinterpretation. And while Delgado knew that the Seriatts were a harmonious and peace-loving race on their own world, he had heard that they were also intensely proud, and defence of their honour and culture was an intrinsic facet of their collective personality. What they would do if Delgado got to Myson and Lycern and did what he felt he must, which would have a direct impact on their royal bloodline and place both worlds in a position of political instability, he had no idea. But it was too late to go back now: in his own mind he was committed to a course, and he had to see it through.

The rain stopped abruptly; the sound it had made on the metal sheet above them ceased, and the silence of the night air descended upon them.

'The powerful sound of nature,' said Delgado.

'Yeah, man,' said Bucky, glancing up into the sky. 'We're nothing when you come to measure it: we can change the consistency and composition of the stuff that falls from the sky, but we can't stop it from falling. You know, this area was quite dry until they built the habitat towers; now we get some rain most days. Yet the Dead Zone's dry as it ever was. Dryer, maybe.'

From the darkness of the stairwell door to their left, Girl appeared. She was sweating and breathless. 'Lift stopped ten floors down,' she explained, pausing to get her breath. 'Had to run to tell you: Lox says Headman says the ship will lift any minute. You'd better make sure the gun's charged and set up.'

Bucky and Delgado looked at each other.

'Ready, man?'

Delgado nodded, raised his eyebrows. 'In the words of Clunk: "sure".' He took the heavy, antiquated rifle from Bucky, hefted it up onto his shoulder and walked to the edge of the roof. He carefully placed the weapon in its cradle on top of the tripod, locked the securing bolts, checked the safety catch.

With the gun settled securely, Bucky reached past Delgado and activated the weapon. It hummed more loudly than before. The small screen became illuminated, displaying details of the software checks it was performing and its overall sentiency levels. The plasma orbs glowed discreetly. Delgado noticed that there was a hint of cloudiness in one of them, a slowly swirling spectre. He decided to ignore it.

'Seems OK,' Bucky said eventually. 'You ever used one of these things?'

'Many times. Single discharge per generation, plasma regeneration time of half a second, maximum of twenty discharges per standard minute.'

'That's what I'm told.'

A voice from behind interjected: 'Which doesn't give you long, man, so you better not fuck up or we'll throw you off the top of this goddamn building before you can shit yourself.'

Delgado and Bucky turned: Lox, Girl, Clunk, and even Headman were standing on the roof behind them. Lox was at the front, arms folded, a cynical expression on his face; Clunk was standing at the back, huge and blank-faced; Girl and Headman stood to either side of Lox. Girl looked concerned, like a child who had inadvertently walked in on an adult argument she did not understand. Headman – who was still wearing his Formersuit – looked utterly dazed. It was the first time Delgado had seen him close up: his eyes had a yellow tint, and were set deep in dark sockets; his mouth hung open, displaying tiny sharp spikes for teeth; his lips were little more than thin pink lines drawn on to his pale face. Delgado thought he looked like someone who had been to the very brink of death, decided he liked it, and was going to stay there.

'Come to see the fireworks?' Bucky asked the small audience.

'Yeah, man – wouldn't miss this for the world,' laughed Lox. 'Headman's dug up some serious shit about this guy.' He gestured at Delgado. 'Says he was a major league Reactionary

Forces player and an ex-Unit Leader for the Stealth Squad. I can't wait to see how he performs. He's one of Military Intelligence's finest.' He looked at Delgado. 'Get ready, man: that babe's gonna upship any minute.'

Delgado met Lox eye to eye and perceived the level of the man's hatred for Structure and Military Intelligence. He admired him for his clarity of thought, and envied him his ability to allow the feelings to exist. Only now was Delgado beginning to realise that he too held such hatred. Such belief and passion was the catalyst of change, and although Delgado knew that Lox would need to tame his wild zeal if he were to achieve his true potential, he had no doubt that the young man was capable of making his mark upon the social and political horrors which now existed on Earth. *If* that was what he really wanted to do.

Delgado turned and knelt down in front of the Jutt rifle, his above-average height making it awkward for him to settle comfortably into its elaborate framework. He glanced around its instruments and controls and adjusted the position of the screen slightly, pushing the small square directly in front of his face. He gripped the rotating controls on the ends of the two stalks extending from the side of its casing with his fingertips. Drawn on to the gun's display was a grid pattern, subtly overlaid on to the city's outline; tiny cross-hairs moved around the image as he manipulated the ends of the stalks, the relevant settings changing with each target he selected. Delgado thumbed the autosense button, charged fresh plasma, tried to prepare himself for what he would soon have to do.

A few moments later a large, dark disc began to rise slowly from a landing platform somewhere on the other side of the Military Intelligence building; it was a dense shadow, darker even than the night sky. The gun focused on the craft automatically; motors gently whirred in the mounting as it adjusted position. Information scrolled up the screen: range, plasma charge level, bearing, target proximity. The cross-hairs slid smoothly across the image on the screen until they were locked on to the craft. Delgado waited. He glanced from screen to ship as the weapon set mass and distance plasma charge parameters. All he had to do was thumb the trigger. All he had to do to kill many of those with whom, despite all the differences between himself and modern Structure operatives, he shared something unique: a love of Earth.

The spacecraft rose slowly upwards. It became a huge flaw in the sky, like a dense slash of light reflected from the face of some great and terrible blade. It hung motionless. A ring of lights tripped around its waist, while a thick electric-blue haze rippled beneath it, a shimmering ghost. Delgado shifted his grip slightly, licked his lips, cleared his throat. His heart thundered despite his nobic address; his adrenaline glands were in full flight; sweat trickled down the nape of his neck. The words WEAPON READY flashed in the top right corner of the small screen. Delgado flinched as the gun bleeped quietly next to his ear.

Delgado did not fire. He remained motionless, looking at the ship's silhouette as presented on the screen. Information about proposed target statistics, plasma strength and the gun's status flickered on the left of the display, rising upwards in a narrow column. The stand moved slightly as the ship rose a little further away from the platform. Again the weapon bleeped. The icon flashed urgently.

Delgado switched off the gun's autosense functions, disabled the enhancement screen and released the controlling stalks, folding them back into their slots.

'Told you he wouldn't do it,' called Lox.

The lights on the distant vessel shifted from blue to red to signal the imminent activation of the more powerful drives that would push it out of the atmosphere. Two escort craft circled distantly. Delgado stood, rapidly disconnected the gun's stand couplings and heaved the weapon on to his shoulder. It swayed as he shoved the screen away from his face to give him a clear view. He was now reliant on his eyes, his skill, his mental abilities. No nobics were assigned to the task; the weapon was able to utilise none of its automated capabilities. He took a few final seconds to collect himself, aimed, then released a single bolt of plasma.

For an infinitesimal fraction of time the group watched the sparkling ball of energy spin across the city, illuminating the world below as it passed. Then it merged silently with the vessel, seemingly absorbed by its smooth dark shape. Nothing happened for a moment. Then the craft began to oscillate slightly, an almost imperceptible shift in attitude just visible enough to be incompatible with the vessel's normal motion. The deep throb of the lift engines suddenly rose to a shrieking howl; loops of escaping containment field energy spat wildly across the sky, huge swathes of concentrated power lashing into the night. The spinning vehicle seemed to glow from within. The lights at its waist flickered briefly before they died.

Then the craft exploded.

As pieces of the ship spun into oblivion, scattered by its enormous centrifugal force, the wall of sound slammed into them. Shards of white hot material were flung across the city sky, instantaneously igniting, melting, searing or scorching anything they touched. Then the brilliant flare that had existed so briefly disappeared to leave an eerie emptiness, hundreds of new fires, and burned lines on the retinas of those who were watching.

Delgado dropped the gun without switching it off and turned to look at his spectators. The city was aflame behind him, red and angry. Smarting embers linked together to form larger, hungrier animals; he was a silhouette in a burning shroud. 'Deny my honesty now if you can,' he said, his face grimly twisted. 'I've just betrayed everything I once lived for. Alexander Delgado, Military Intelligence Officer, is dead.'

They stood facing each other: Delgado and Bucky in the

stinking, stinging rain that had once again begun to fall. Lox and the others stood in silence by the stairwell door.

Lox broke the silence. 'Come on,' he said, angling his head towards Girl and Clunk but not taking his eyes off Delgado. 'Looks as though we've got ourselves an ex-Military Intelligence Officer on the team. Not too sure I like it, but that's the way it goes. We better go down and check the net, Headman. Structure will be wanting to know who shot down their ship.'

Lox, Girl, Headman and Clunk turned and disappeared into the stairwell, quickly absorbed by the blackness that waited there for them. Delgado and Bucky were left alone on the roof, motionless, silent. Bucky sniffed and looked across at the multitude of fires that had been started, then walked the couple of steps to the edge of the building. He stopped there, put his left hand in his jacket pocket, and rested the other on the butt of his purifier sidearm. The rain patted gently on his tunic, flattened his hair in a shining slick. Delgado recognised something in Bucky's stance and felt a vague flickering in his hyperconsciousness that concerned him.

'Still,' Bucky said, looking across the city, 'I suppose a Military Intelligence Officer sent out by Structure to infiltrate the streets would be prepared to shoot down a Diplomatic Craft; it could all have been fixed up. They'd know he'd have to do something like that if he was going to convince anyone he was on the level. I reckon it'd probably be the only way he could do it, because there's no way *all* the information about him could be taken off the web. Yeah, I reckon the whole thing could be a set up. Structure could cope with a few civilian casualties, collateral damage, acceptable losses. They could send up an unmanned ship as a lure, put out a few informative newscasts, tell the populace just enough to cover themselves and say its destruction was a tragic accident.' He turned and looked directly at Delgado. 'What have you got to say about that, man?'

Delgado paused, then spoke quietly. 'I think you're a very

cautious man, Bucky – and that's a wise trait. But if you've any doubts left after what I've just done then you'd better kill me, because I can tell you quite truthfully there's no greater pain in the life of a Military Intelligence Officer than to kill one of his colleagues. And if my instincts are right, then I believe I may have just killed very many indeed.' He looked about him to check that the others really had gone, then turned back to the youthful gang leader in front of him. Time for another gamble; if he had misjudged Bucky's feelings it could be his last. 'Come on, Bucky,' he said, 'you've got a powerful weapon there –' he nodded towards the HiMag blaster '– why not use it on me now and claim the glory? Tell the others I tried to kill you and that you had to kill me; you'll be a hero. And Lox'll be really pissed off that he missed it, even if it does prove that he was right all along. Come on, Bucky. Do it. Do it now. I represent everything you're fighting against. Kill me.'

Bucky looked awkward and pensive and shifted his feet. He narrowed his eyes in the wind that had started to gust; a tear streamed from the corner of one eye. His fingers drummed on the butt of the blaster, then he turned away from Delgado and looked across the decaying city towards the habitats. 'I can't,' he said simply.

Delgado laughed. 'Oh come on, Bucky, that's pathetic. You don't expect me to believe that a hardened street runner like you can't kill a Military Intelligence Officer in cold blood. What kind of a gang leader are you? Come on, kill me. I deserve that much respect, regardless of what side you think I'm on. Treat me the way you'd treat any other Structure scum.'

Bucky turned; he seemed angry or upset or both. 'I can't.'

Delgado looked at the expression on the boy's face, searched his consciousness. 'Why not?'

Bucky looked down at the powerful sidearm strapped close to his hip and caressed its smooth, black grip with the palm of his hand. He looked up at Delgado and smiled ironically.

Delgado thought he could see tears in the young man's eyes that were not born of the breeze. 'It's useless,' he said flatly. 'This gun is inoperative. I couldn't fire it if I wanted to. No charges, no plasma, no weapon, no use. No fucking hope.'

Delgado looked at him intently. 'You're serious, aren't you?'

'Oh, I'm serious all right. OK, so I've got this baby,' he patted the weapon, 'but I tried to fire it as soon as I got hold of it to see how powerful it was and found it was dead. No sentience, no nothing. I don't know shit about weapons, Delgado, but I know when they're dead, and this one's all but cremated.'

'So why wear it?'

Bucky shrugged, pulled the weapon from its holster and looked at it intently. 'None of the others know it doesn't work. I suppose it's a power thing. Reminds them that I'm capable of killing purifiers. But even then I was lucky. See this?' He tapped the side of the gun's chrome housing. 'This is non-standard, right? The purifier I got it from was young, new to the service, I reckon. Wanted to stamp his identity on his weapon. *Bond* with it, like they tell them to in training, yeah? So he bought this nice, shiny, non-standard snap-on accessory. It was lucky for me he did, too. But unlucky for him. It was the light reflecting off it that meant I could get a clean shot in first. Stupid fuck. I guess it absorbed some of the charge and got fried.' He put the weapon back into its holster and clipped it shut, then looked back across the city. 'It stops them trying to get rid of me, I guess. The others, I mean. And sometimes I think they would, too, especially Lox, man. That guy's crazy enough to think he can survive without me, even though I know that he's really pretty scared about where we're at despite what he might say and do.' He shook his head. 'Like I say, man, this gang's going nowhere. I kinda see it as my job to make sure it stays that way.'

'Very noble.'

'What?'

'I said I think it's very noble, this thing you're doing. You seem to have it all weighed up, Bucky: don't take too many risks, keep your head down, survive. Trying to protect the others as well is incredibly generous. But have you considered that it might not be in their best interests? If they die while they're trying to get somewhere, at least they'll go out with a little self-respect. As it is they have no choice in the way they exist because you manipulate their lives with a useless weapon. That's quite incredible. And dangerous.'

Bucky could no longer look at Delgado; instead he walked closer to the edge of the building. 'Maybe you're right, man. Maybe I should give it all up, let them go. Maybe they're better off dead than following me. I don't know any more.'

Delgado stepped forward and stood next to Bucky. He looked down the side of the great building; there were almost no others in the area above one hundred metres tall. All had been destroyed, raped and ravaged by the bitter conspiring demons of age and neglect and the people's lure of a more prosperous, luxurious life inside the habitats. 'But you do have a choice,' said Delgado. 'You can make a difference. Lox's ideas aren't as ridiculous as you seem to think.'

'I can't see it. What can we do? We have Headman but no serious weapons, no money, no influence, no contacts. How can we hope to achieve anything? Structure is too powerful, man. We're nothing. And worse still, we're *outside*.'

Delgado looked at Bucky and saw an immense sadness in the youth's face. He realised that the young man was fighting the worst enemy he could have: himself. 'There may be a way,' he said quietly. 'There may be a way.'

The tone in Delgado's voice made Bucky look at him. 'What do you mean? How could we do anything that would make a significant difference?'

But Delgado did not answer: he was looking over Bucky's right shoulder. Bucky turned to see what he was staring at. He saw great elliptical shadows, rising slowly into the sky in the distance.

'Purifiers,' said Bucky. 'Boy, those Structure goons are sure on the case tonight. Must've been able to pinpoint the source area of that shot real quick. Not too difficult, though, I guess. I kinda knew this would happen.'

The skyships moved across the skyline as they watched, slowly changing formation until they were a line of craft ten wide and three deep. A few moments passed as they hung motionless above the broken spire of a derelict church, adjusting their relative positions. There was a pause, a few minutes of stillness and eerie silence. Then the firing began.

Thin, piercing blue flashes illuminated the city for the briefest of moments as the skyships came to life. And although the weapons themselves made no noise, even across the separating distance the screams of dying people could clearly be heard.

'Will they come directly to us?' asked Delgado.

'No, man, that's why they're trashing at least three areas. The attack would have been unexpected, so they'll only have a rough idea where it came from. They'll cover areas surrounding the one they really think was the source, just to make a point. A lot of people on the streets will die tonight because of what we've done. But the people they're killing now would have died soon anyway. Shooting down a major Structure vessel right where they could see it probably gave them the biggest boost they've had in a very long time. Besides, death is all most of them have got to look forward to. We're lucky: we have a fairly secure base, warm and dry places to sleep; most people down here don't even have clothes.'

They looked across the city again; the large, dark discs were moving slowly towards them. The intricate web of sharpened light emitted by their weapons filled the world below with death and fear. Delgado had only ever seen purifiers from above before – while aboard fliers heading to Structure's military orbital way-stations — but to witness the unleashing of their power at first hand was a stirring experience. Each release of energy meant the death of someone on the streets, the execution of a sentence without trial — and in most cases without a crime, other than that of being unfortunate enough to be born at the wrong time, in the wrong place, or to the wrong people. They acted on behalf of the prosperous, righteous people in the habitats, cleansing the world of the filth and degradation that thrived and threatened them outside their beautiful, Utopian, self-contained worlds.

Most people were unaware of the truth behind the purifiers. They were seen as heroic Structure officials doing a job that was both dangerous and laudable; they were well paid and respected for their courage and skill, guaranteed attention at parties, thanked by everyone for removing the threat posed to society by those who scavenged on the edges of humanity. But the truth was far different. Most purifiers were rather more keen to meet their quota of kills, claim the resultant bonus and get home safely than pursue the artificial glory so generously bestowed upon them by the populace. Delgado had heard about the low, slow passes made over the streets, picking off as many targets as possible from the safety of their aerial transports, followed by the rapid, cursory sweeps that were sometimes made on foot if the body count was low. All but the youngest and most naïve purifiers knew they had no chance against the seething anger of the people on the street, those who had been abandoned and were despised by a society too complacent to care what became of their unfortunate counterparts, blindly ignorant or unwilling to consider the fact that it was they who had engineered the inequality in the first place.

The skyships crossed into the same area as they, and the machines spread wider, adopting a new formation. After a momentary respite from the sickening carnage, the frequency at which the weapons were being fired was doubled.

201

'Come on,' said Bucky. 'We'd better get downstairs. Those things'll be here pretty soon.'

Delgado followed without a word, unsure whether he felt a greater connection with the victims of the purifiers' terror than with his former Structure colleagues who controlled the deadly craft.

The purifier gunships cast an insidious shadow across the area throughout the night. The light from their weapons' release strobed through the basement's high windows in cold staccato flashes. The group was quiet and solemn for the remainder of the evening, which was mostly spent huddled around a monitor Headman had specially activated for them so they could see the communications patterns emerging from Military Intelligence Headquarters. But whether their sombre mood was because they knew the ferocity of the purifier attack was the result of their actions, or was merely their normal reaction to Structure's flexed muscle, Delgado was unsure. His nobics detected mixtures of fear, anxiety, elation and frustration from the group, but could not isolate specific sources. He determined to follow their example and keep his mouth shut.

Later, when the Structure transmissions had evolved into a recognisable pattern and the mutual decision to sleep had been made, Bucky told Delgado that he could share his sleeping area. But although the heap of clothes Bucky called a bed was comfortable enough, Delgado found it difficult to relax: there were too many conflicting emotions and feelings within him, too much of his past at odds with both his present and future. Once — how long ago it seemed now — he had been so certain of who he was and where he was going. He had been part of Structure, military machinery that served a well defined and useful purpose. Now he felt skewered by uncertainty, every fibre of his being doused in flammable liquid which could ignite at any moment. So much had changed in his life in recent times that it was difficult for him to accept that he was still the same person.

He rolled beneath the pile of clothes, trying to keep warm, using every technique he knew in an attempt to induce sleep. But the noise and light from outside was soon accompanied by the sound of Girl and Bucky making love next to him, their muffled, urgent moans a whispered lamentation in the fractured silence as they sought comfort in each other. Delgado was both aroused and tortured by the *muscein*, angrily stirred by the sounds of their joining. Lycern's pheromone threatened to surge through him, a distant storm that could bring with it as much devastation as could be apportioned by the purifiers. He closed his eyes and tried to ignore the steady motion of the clothes to his right, assigning nobics to the areas of the brain which seemed most affected. The technique was successful to a certain extent, but long after the pile of clothes next to him had ceased its gentle sway, small pockets of fire continued to rage within him.

Half an hour or so passed and sleep seemed no closer. He repositioned himself in the bed and looked around the dimly lit room. Headman was still in his corner, still linked to the net, still slowly rocking. As Delgado watched, Lox emerged from his recess, went to Headman and spoke quietly to him. Delgado felt Lox's concern and Headman's frustration at the interruption equally clearly. There was a brief discussion, an exchange, then finally Headman was persuaded to take some rest. He stood, stretched, and removed his elaborate suit as a reptile sheds old skin, then moved into the darkness.

Clunk, meanwhile, was sitting in a chair by the entrance to the basement, guarding his comrades; he was snoring loudly, his gnarled and angular chest rising and falling slowly, hands clasped together on his lap. Delgado wondered about the risk Clunk posed to the safety of the group. He could obviously not be trusted with important tasks, and did not seem to possess the cognitive powers to grasp concepts, basic or other-wise. If the group were really to enter Military Intelligence

Headquarters with him as they had suggested, Clunk represented a potentially fatal problem that would have to be addressed.

Hours passed, still he did not sleep. Despite some measure of fear and discomfort at his standpoint beneath the issued wrath of Structure, Delgado could not help but admire the purifiers' attack. The gunships – visible as grey shadows through the high windows – passed slowly and methodically, crossing and re-crossing the area. They were thorough, their patterns precisely calculated to inflict maximum damage with minimal risk. There would be a pause as the craft adopted a new formation, then the barrage would begin again. Not a square millimetre of the ground below the gunships was left untouched. The screams of death and cries of hatred seemed neverending, joining with the sound of falling debris in a bitter symphony of human destruction. Delgado increasingly sensed unease born of guilt in himself.

He reached over the pile of blankets covering the now sleeping Bucky and Girl, and deftly removed Bucky's blaster from its holster. The weapon appeared to be in extremely good condition; it was a relatively new model judging from the serial number. Using a technique once shown to him by a weapons engineer on Buhatt, but unsure if he had remembered the correct string, Delgado pressed a sequence of touchtabs and waited. A few moments later a light above the gun's main screen became illuminated, and the screen itself a backlit green. The secondary screen remained dark.

He accessed the emergency operations functions and guessed his way to the maintenance procedures database. He touched various onscreen icons; the weapon hummed and vibrated very slightly. He touched INTERNAL ACCESS. There was a warning that some components posed 'a potential hazard to health'; Delgado muttered something about it being a gun. He pressed the release catches; the casing opened smoothly and he peered inside.

Although he had demonstrated some knowledge of the Jutt rifle's operating procedures, Bucky had said he knew little about personal sidearms. This was clearly true, as the internal magazine of his 'useless' weapon held an almost full vial of quite exceptional, expensive and certainly non-standard issue, self-generating 200 core activattak spinbarb solution. As long as the frameware of the weapon into which it was loaded was powerful enough to cope with the realtime data upload requirements, the ammunition the vial was able to produce – a complex fusion of intellisense data processing modules and cellular aggressors freshly generated for each shot – were capable of stripping a creature the size of a human male from flesh to bone in a fraction of a second. It was certainly not standard for such a weapon, and beyond the means of any purifier unit to assign to their crew. He chewed his bottom lip, wondering if he could remember how such a system might function.

Within a few minutes he had managed to re-establish enough sentience in the weapon to enable its perception functions to communicate with the ammunition delegation system. A few minutes later he thought he could probably repair the weapon completely. He settled to this task, pleased for the distraction it would give him.

Meanwhile, death continued to rain down on the world outside.

Delgado worked on the gun for a further two hours. As he was tinkering with one of its more basic functions – OWNER RECOGNITION/SELF DISCIPLINE – the firing outside suddenly stopped. The light in the basement stabilised. The stillness and silence were oppressive. Delgado knew what it meant: now the skyships would descend until they were just above street level, drop rope ladders, and the black-clad men and women of the Cleansing Unit would descend. On the ground they would scan for signs of life, kill anything careless enough to get in their way and, once they had a personal body-count high enough to guarantee some sort of bonus, retreat hastily back to the safety of the gunships. Delgado lay perfectly still, closed his eyes, concentrated on focusing his nobics. Visuals opened; there were many new presences all around him. He sensed fear, anxiety, resentment, some sexual arousal.

Occasional bursts of blaster fire raged on the streets above with a sound like that of breaking ice, frequently accompanied by a scream or shout which would echo off the walls of the dilapidated buildings before fading. Silence returned after a few minutes of this and, with it, the stillness of the dead. The emotional traces his nobics had fed to him began to fade: the purifiers were withdrawing. He opened his eyes and continued to work on Bucky's sidearm.

As he probed deeper into the gun's physical framework circuitry he noticed that an information link hidden behind a cluster of wiring had become detached from its port. He reconnected the short grey ribbon and turned the gun over to look at its small secondary screen; colours were washing across it in rippling waves, spiralling horizontally. The display stabilised after a moment; the words THREAT LEVEL HI appeared. He watched them rise up the screen, skip back down, rise up, then steady. THREAT LEVEL HI. The words began to flash, and were joined by numerous other warnings and details of default setting options.

He glanced around and brought his nobics to a state of alertness, forcing his mechanobes to produce the chemicals he would need for optimum assimilation of combat data. Light-headed as a result, he felt a definite source of malice and anxiety somewhere nearby; probably within the building. He looked at the screen again: THREAT LEVEL XTREME. He quickly reconnected the gun's major ports, closed the casing, and hoped that he really did know as much about weapons system repair as he thought.

He twisted round slightly; the blankets moved with him, a

trailing extension of his body. He looked round the walls and windows, trying to pinpoint the hostile's position. Clunk snored loudly; Bucky rolled and mumbled something in his sleep. Then Delgado saw movement in the corner of his eye: a slender shadow in the open doorway.

The purifier's skinny silhouette moved slowly, like some kind of insect, using distinctive Structure methods to absorb and process information. Delgado felt it was a male. Light reflected off his visor and creases in the slick black, skin-tight uniform, the design having changed since Bucky had obtained his. As he moved further into the basement, Delgado saw the blaster in the intruder's right hand. He became partially obscured by one of the supporting pillars, but Delgado saw him crouch and slink along the farthest wall, cautiously approaching the still-snoring Clunk. Delgado clutched Bucky's gun to his chest. The purifier came fully into view only when he was right next to Clunk's giant frame. He was making the most of his clear advantage: judging how many people were in the room, where they might be, deciding on target order. He was taking his time, collating, assessing, just as any good operative would, given such a gift.

Delgado glanced down at the gun in his hands and hoped it would not let him down. The intruder stood slowly, smoothly, his decision made. He pointed his sidearm at Clunk's head; the tip of the barrel was no more than ten centimetres from the big man's skull. In the instant that existed between his seeing the purifier arm his weapon and the single flash of its activation light, Delgado knew that he could not save Clunk; his job was one of damage limitation.

The basement filled with raucous noise and hot, intense light.

At exactly the same moment that the purifier discharged his weapon, Delgado rolled. He took half the bedclothes, Bucky and Girl with him, and lay stretched across the cold, wet floor. The blaster was at arm's length as he fired four cluster shots in rapid succession. His arm kicked up with the recoil from each shot as the blaster spat four groups of its potent, semi-intelligent ammunition in short, deafening snaps.

The first shot cluster concentrated on the purifier's head, but the first two rounds were not targeted correctly and simply grazed the side of his skull, stripping his visor and comm unit and embedding themselves deep in the wall. But the force of this initial impact knocked the man off balance, and as he fell backwards a bizarre expression formed on his face as the remaining rounds tore deep into him. They combined instantaneously to shred the soft parts of his head. Some found their way deeper, too, passing through his now empty eye-sockets to deal with the contents of his skull. The frameware assigned different areas of his body to the second cluster. His chest was torn open, his ribs shredded, his internal organs destroyed. It gave preference to most vital organs in case the man should somehow have survived the work of the first rounds. Most of the rest of his body was taken care of by the random designation of the last two clusters, whose constituent units separated in transit to chew the muscles in his limbs and the small amount of tissue that remained in his torso.

When the ammunition's work was complete, all that remained was a glistening pile of soft, charred flesh, and the distinctive stench of death. Thin whispers of smoke rose from the slimy residue in lazy trails. No solid part of the purifier that remained was larger than a man's thumbnail.

Delgado remained prostrate as the others gathered around him: Bucky and Girl were both pulling on clothes, swearing hard; Lox was zipping up his trousers; Headman was already back in his comm suit and reattaching himself to his terminal, a distinct air of panic in his movements.

'What the fuck happened?' asked Bucky, eyeing the gun in Delgado's hand.

'Goddamn mother's trying to kill us all, man,' said Lox. 'Shoot Clunk first then pop the rest of us off while we're asleep. Shit – let's kill him, man. Slow and painful. I told you he was bad news all along.'

'Wait a minute.' It was Girl; she had walked over to Clunk's chair and was examining the remains on the floor. She placed one hand to her mouth and poked at them with her toe. 'There're two bodies here,' she mumbled. She turned to face them. 'Looks like a purifier.'

A solid silence wrapped them. Delgado accepted a hand from Bucky, who pulled him up off the floor. They all walked over to where Girl was standing. That there were two bodies was obvious: Clunk's was still sitting upright in the chair, decapitated quite cleanly by the brute force of the purifier's basic HiMag blast, but otherwise intact; the purifier was just a collection of stinking organic materials irregularly interspersed by bits of his black uniform and weapon; but his visor and comm unit lay some metres away, virtually undamaged.

'You kill that purifier, man?' Bucky asked, pointing. Delgado nodded. Bucky looked at the others. 'Well,' he said, 'anyone here still has doubts about Delgado being on our side had better voice them quick and make them good, because the guy's just saved our sorry skins.' Nobody spoke. 'Lox: you still got a problem with him, man?' Lox shook his head solemnly, still gazing at Clunk. 'Girl? Headman?' Neither answered. 'Right, so we're glad to have him on the team, OK? Guess we owe you big time, man.'

Delgado shrugged. 'I was trying to save myself, that's all.' He slapped the blaster into the palm of Bucky's hand. 'This gun of yours is pretty useful.' Bucky looked at the still-warm weapon.

Delgado looked across at the bodies, and felt something shift uneasily inside him.

The two corpses were buried together in a makeshift grave of rubble and dust in a building as far from the mall entrance as they thought they could get to quickly and safely. Bucky mumbled a few words, and although the lack of special ceremony for Clunk surprised Delgado, he thought it a good sign. He was surprised when the young man also said something for the purifier. It was not much, but enough.

The group then returned to the basement, where they sat in a solemn circle. Clunk's death was more than the loss of a friend; it was a defeat for the whole street community – the community they felt they represented.

'Well, man,' said Lox with a sigh, 'I reckon this calls for some payback. Shit, Clunk's dead. He was never much of a conversationalist, but I liked him, y'know? He was good to have around. Kinda like a big little brother. You had to look out for him.'

Girl nodded but said nothing, staring fixedly at the ground in front of her.

Bucky looked at Lox and shook his head. 'How're we supposed to do anything, man?' He spoke with a resignation that made Delgado immediately tense. 'We haven't even got many proper weapons. I'm as keen to avenge Clunk's death as you are, but you'd better tell me how you plan to do it because I can't see a way. I don't know – maybe we should just accept that he was unlucky.'

'Just let them get away with it? You can't be serious, man. Purifier scum blew Clunk's head off.'

'We did shoot down one of their precious ships, Lox,' said Girl quietly, without looking up. 'If we hadn't done that then they probably wouldn't have come out here in the first place. It's a war. These things happen. We just have to face reality. As a group we achieved a lot and lasted a long time, but something like this was bound to happen to one of us eventually.'

Lox looked at Delgado. 'What about you, Mr Reactionary Forces? What do you think?'

'I've already told Bucky what I think.'

Lox looked quickly from Delgado to Bucky and back again. 'Oh, I see. Well what *do* you think, man? What little plan have you two been hatching? You want to kill us all and claim the reward? You go along with that, Bucky, man? You just prepared to roll over and die like a fucking junkie, because I—'

Bucky launched himself at Lox. His momentum knocked the other man off his seat and they rolled across the floor wrestling, flush with a sudden release of anger and pent–up emotion. Both scrabbled to get a grip on Bucky's blaster, which had been knocked to the ground. Bucky kicked the weapon and it skidded along the floor away from them, coming to rest by the wall. Girl and Delgado jumped up and grappled with the two men, trying to drag them apart. It was difficult to get a grip on either of them, though. Delgado clutched handfuls of cloth and tried to twist Lox round, but the youth was intensely angry, his strength concentrated by the sudden surfacing of suppressed resentment and jealousy. With gritted teeth and bulging eyes Lox lurched forward and slipped from Delgado's grip. He dropped to the ground, rolled and finally managed to get a firm grip on the blaster. With a swift flick of his thumb, the weapon was primed.

The armed weapon waved around in the air, humming audibly as Delgado and Bucky pushed Lox's arm away from them so the gun was pointed towards the ceiling. Girl was trapped between them; she stretched up and bit Lox's wrist so hard that he yelled aloud. When she raised her head, Delgado saw that there was blood on her teeth. Delgado glanced at Lox and saw fierce rage burning in his watery eyes.

Bucky threw a few weak and badly aimed punches. One caught Delgado on the temple. Lox struggled and kicked out, trying to wriggle free of Delgado's grip. All four were shouting, none loudly enough to be heard above the overall tumult which was echoing loudly around the bare-walled basement. Girl clearly wanted to fight but space would not allow it. She grabbed Lox's hand, but instead of biting it she pressed her thumbnail on to the cuticle of his as hard as she could. He yelled again and this time the weapon dropped to the ground and into the pool of dark water at their feet.

And as quickly as it had started, the fight was over. The four of them stood in a tense, sweaty huddle by the wall. Lox was clutching at his wrist, which was bleeding slightly. His flesh had red indentations the same shape as Girl's teeth. Bucky was stubbornly pulling his clothes straight. Headman – who had watched the entire mêlée from the comfort of his chair – simply looked at them, his normal, ghostly expression unchanged.

Delgado looked at Lox and Bucky in turn, trying to contain his frustration and anger. He noticed that he was trembling very slightly. 'This is your biggest fucking problem,' he spat. 'You're your own worst enemies. You should be channelling this resentment and energy into positive action. You two,' he jabbed a finger vehemently at Bucky and Lox, 'are so wrapped up in getting at each other that the obviously strong bond between you is wasted. Lox, stop fantasising about being leader of this gang and wishing you were the one who was sleeping with Girl and try to support Bucky when he makes a decision. He might just listen to you a bit more and, who knows, might even learn to respect your opinion. Bucky, don't resent Lox's bond with Headman or the fact that you can't get information without them. Use him, learn from him, appreciate his skill and respect his ability to focus. The power to succeed is here; you just need to harness it. Don't let Clunk's death be wasted. Learn, work together, become a focused unit. One of the best things about being in the Military was the comradeship, the fact that you could count on everyone else to back you up. It gave you the strength to do things you might not have been able to do in other circumstances. You were one, bonded, fighting the enemy. That's what you need.'

The two young men looked like children caught stealing. They avoided each other's eyes, and also Delgado's. He knew that he had touched exposed nerves and addressed taboo subjects; he was uncertain what the outcome would be, and found analysis of their individual emotions difficult.

Slowly, reluctantly, and with Lox grasping his still bleeding wrist, they seemed to reach an unspoken truce. Gradually they relaxed slightly, and by silent, mutual agreement went and sat on the upturned boxes behind Headman. Delgado picked the blaster from the water on the way; as he sat down he noticed that Girl was very close to him. He glanced at her, and was somehow uncomfortable with the expression she had on her face. He was aware that both Lox and Bucky had noticed her expression too, and this made him feel even more uncomfortable. Jealous rivalries he could do without.

'So, Alexander Delgado,' said Lox, 'just what is this great plan of yours?'

'Yeah,' said Bucky somewhat sullenly. 'Just what?'

Delgado shrugged. 'I've got to get into Military Intelligence Headquarters; maybe you want to help me do that. You expressed an interest before — or was that bullshit?'

Lox raised his eyebrows and an index finger, exaggerating a look of sudden enlightenment. 'Oh, right. Of course. Suddenly it all becomes clear. You want us to help you get into MIHQ because having more people involved in the operation lessens the chances of your being among those who will inevitably get killed. Very nice, man, very neat. I can see why you've risen so high up the military ladder.'

Delgado cocked his head to one side. 'I'm quite happy to go on my own, Lox. Having you lot along, with your lack of discipline and limited combat experience, wouldn't exactly guarantee success. You decrease my chances, if anything. Don't think you'd be doing me any favours. I could manage quite well on my own.'

'Yeah, sure.'

'I mean it. I've got nothing to live for now other than the possibility that I might be able to get to Myson, Lycern and my child. And I've got plenty of experience of clandestine operations to do it on my own. I have to get to my son. I thought you wanted to help me. I'm sorry if that's not the case. Maybe you would rather sit in this stinking pit for the rest of your lives. You might cause a few minor waves by uploading infected codes to the ATCs, but they don't last long. You need to do something that'll make a real difference. Something tangible. And to do that you need to attack from within.'

A long silence followed. Delgado looked at each of them in turn. Lox was toying with a mechanobe culture; Bucky was looking up through the blank, grey windows running around the top of the basement, apparently admiring the red and amber stains of the approaching dawn; Girl was looking directly at him, her chin resting in her hands, eyes wide and bright.

'Say we did come in with you,' Bucky said. 'What would we get out of it?'

Lox sat upright. 'Hang on a minute—'

'Shut up, Lox. He's right: we can't spend the rest of our lives here.' He looked back to Delgado. 'Well, man – what?'

Delgado took a deep breath. 'I'd be lying if I said that our chances of success were good, and I can't guarantee that any of us will survive. But I've always believed that it's better to try and fail than not to try at all. In my experience anything is possible if you have the right attitude and believe in it enough.'

Lox looked at him sceptically. 'You really think it could be done, man? You *really* believe we could get into MIHQ and then get to Myson?' He snorted and looked at his feet. 'Christ, I think you must be even more crazy than the Headman over there.' He laughed fully; it completely changed his appearance.

'It does sound pretty incredible,' said Bucky, nodding.

Delgado shrugged. 'OK, fine; I'll go in by myself. You've obviously got no ambition or real dreams. You think you're fighting the good fight down here, that you'll eventually do some damage. But I can tell you that you're making no difference whatsoever. Do you know what kind of funding Structure assigns solely for the Cleansing projects?' They looked blank. 'I'll tell you: fifteen billion NDs per season. How can you expect to fight successfully against resources like that? They immediately replace every purifier gunship you destroy or crewman you kill with another. Their strength and power are never put at risk. You're an irritation to them, nothing more.'

They looked surprised, dispirited. He sensed their collective mood beginning to shift.

'But this is Military Intelligence Headquarters we're talking about here, man,' said Bucky quietly, a measure of defensiveness in his voice. 'It's not some lightly guarded automatic maintenance workshop; it's the governmental palace for the Planetary Council, the central controlling point for Military Operations, Structure, Stealth, the end of the whole fucking line.'

Delgado leaned forward, suddenly becoming animated. He spoke with genuine verve and passion. 'And that's *exactly* why it'll make a difference, Bucky. If we can kill Myson, Structure will be weakened at the core. For God's sake, it might even collapse! You couldn't begin to imagine the power and influence the man has. No one outside Military Intelligence knows what he can do, nor do half of those within it. Without him the whole pack of cards could come down.'

'OK,' said Lox, 'if you're so keen for all this then answer me just one question: how do you propose to get *into* the most important building on Earth when everyone comes and goes there aboard a flier? How, man? We can get landing codes without much problem thanks to the Headman, but how are we supposed to get ourselves a bird?'

'Could shoot one down with the Jutt,' mumbled Girl.

'Be no good if it was all shot up,' said Bucky. 'They'd be on to us as soon as we tried to lift anyway.'

'And why is it that you think you can do something if you get in there, man?' Lox continued. 'How come you're suddenly invincible? If you're not Military Intelligence you'll be gunned down the moment you're recognised, same as us. There's a price on your head, remember?'

'I'm not invincible,' said Delgado, 'but I have to get in there and do what I have to do. It's as simple as that.'

They were all silent then, each of them contemplating the risks, and the possible rewards. They cast uncertain glances at each other, and occasionally at Delgado who, although aware of a definite change in mood, was unable to tell which way the consensus would finally go. Lox examined his wrist; Bucky looked at the floor and scratched the back of his neck; Girl continued to stare at Delgado.

'Listen,' Bucky said, 'I can't speak for the others, but if you really want to do this, if you're really going to try and get in there, then I'm with you. Hell, you need someone with you.'

'You going to leave us here, man?' said Lox. 'You just going to fuck off with Mr Military Intelligence here? What kind of shit is this?'

'You don't have to come,' said Bucky calmly, 'but if Delgado's going then I'm going with him. I think it's time I moved on.'

'But you can't just go,' said Girl. 'You're our leader.'

Bucky shook his head slowly. 'You don't need me,' he said. 'You only think you do. Lox here is as good as anyone to give you direction.'

Lox looked at his feet. 'You're kinda like furniture though, man. Old furniture. But kinda comfortable.'

Bucky smiled. 'I guess I'm supposed to take that as some kind of half-assed compliment. But you could do it, Lox. You and Headman. Keep fighting the purifiers and some day you'll break through, take control, live the way you've always wanted to, as proud men. I've just got to do something a bit sooner than that. I might get killed, but I think I've got to try.'

Lox looked awkward. 'Not sure I want to though, man. I suppose I like things the way they are. Don't know if I could really, you know, pull it off without you.'

'I'm going with Delgado, Lox, so there's your choice: stay here or come with us.'

'But there aren't any weapons, no way to get in, no nothing.' He looked at Delgado. 'How do you seriously expect to get to Myson, huh? What about all the guards and cyborgs and shit?'

'Despite what you may think,' said Delgado, 'internal guarding is minimal because it costs too much and is generally considered unnecessary. This is MIHQ we're talking about here. Who would be stupid enough to try and infiltrate its walls and kill the Commander Supreme? No, the biggest problem is finding a way in from the ground.'

Lox sighed and rubbed his eyes. 'Well, that's one hell of a problem to have, man.'

Bucky looked at him. 'Not for you. Not if you aren't going to be there.'

'Shit, man, how long have we been together? You think I'm just going to let you wander off with this lunatic to get your head blown off? You're even crazier than I thought.'

Bucky's frown flattened into an uncertain smile; undefined emotions seemed to be released between himself and Lox. Bucky looked at Girl. 'What about you? It's your decision. If you don't want to come then we'll all understand. Maybe I can ask Chris Meikle to give you room in his bunker in the Dead Zone. He's a bit odd, I know, but you'd be safe there.'

Girl appeared incredulous at this suggestion. 'Palm me off onto that fucking creep? Well, thanks a lot, Bucky. Christ, you amaze me sometimes.' She looked at Delgado. 'Despite Bucky's obvious wish to send me to spend the rest of my days with a race-rigging drug bandit in the Dead Zone, I would like to come with you. Any objections?'

Delgado shook his head. 'Just leaves our friend Headman.' He looked over his shoulder at the gently-rocking figure.

'I think it's best if we don't tell him just yet,' said Bucky. 'I'm not quite sure what his reaction's going to be to all this.'

217

'Whatever you think. When it's light enough we'll go up to the roof and see what we can see.' He pointed across the room into Lox's sleeping recess where a plundered piece of Military Intelligence equipment lay on a table. 'Those teleculars operative?'

'Sure, man,' said Lox. 'You can see into the middle of next week with those.'

The air was hot and thick, difficult to breathe. Harsh, unbroken sunlight sharpened edges, clarified detail, bleaching the entire city. The glossy black surfaces of the habitats' huge, featureless sides simply reflected multiple images of the dazzling star, as if boasting about its inability to affect them.

They were sitting in the shadow cast by the dislocated roof of the aircon housing. Although it was cooler – and safer – than in the sunlight, the metal sheet seemed to radiate dull heat which throbbed down on to them in regular pulses.

Delgado was looking across the city through Lox's old teleculars: he had noticed when on the roof with the Jutt rifle that his visuals seemed confused by the towers' combined mass, but the teleculars should be immune to such interference. The city was dominated by the shape of MIHQ, which erupted from the ground like a huge plume of thick, poisoned water, rising higher even than the habitats. It shimmered gently in the heat haze, as if trapped beneath a film of liquid. The brittle glass surfaces of the various bulbous structures that protruded from the building reflected momentary shards of light, slivers of brilliance that made the higher levels glitter, as if dusted with jewels by some great and generous god.

The sky was filled with fliers, darting, hovering or circling; starships, freighters, military cruisers and transports moved more slowly. There was even the odd xip fighter, cutting a precise course through the other vessels as if not bound by the same physical laws. The dark stains left on the perfect blue sky by the older, less efficient engines weaved convoluted patterns as the vessels made the push into orbit or cruised down to land. Engines screamed, whined or thudded dully depending on propulsion type, but these were the only sounds to be heard; in the rare moments when no vessels were close enough to hear, the utter silence that descended was disturbing.

Delgado focused on the Military Intelligence building and increased the teleculars' magnification and enhancement to maximum. He fidgeted slightly. Military Intelligence had been his life – in many ways his saviour – and the most hallowed place in the universe for him for a very long time. To try and destroy it must surely be the act of a truly bitter soul.

'See anything, man?' asked Bucky. 'Think we can get in?'

Delgado shook his head. 'Not sure,' he said quietly. 'Nothing's obvious. All the flier platforms are too high up and guarded by cyborgs; all street-level entrances were sealed decades ago. An aerial approach would definitely be preferable from a tactical viewpoint, but I just don't know how we can do it.' He handed the teleculars to Lox, who was sitting next to him. As the man put the softly clicking, whirring device to his eyes, Delgado rested his elbow on his knee and pointed. 'See that large, domed window near the top on the left-hand side?'

'Uh-huh.'

'That's Myson's private chamber. Lycern is sure to be close to him, but whether she'd actually be in there, or in a chamber of her own, I don't know. Whatever the case, we need to move as quickly as possible once we're in. We spend too much time wandering around with our heads up our asses, we're bound to get into trouble.'

'Yeah, man,' said Lox. 'If we could fly right in there we could do some serious damage before they knew what'd hit 'em.' He looked for a minute or two longer, then stood, handing the teleculars to Bucky. 'Man, it's too hot up here for me,' he said. 'Christ, if it's not stinging rain it's blistering sun. Jeez. I'll go back down and maybe see if Headman can find out anything about the building's construction; the original plans might show us a weakness or something we can take advantage of. Don't know what excuse I'm gonna give him, though. Personally I think we should be straight with him, tell him what's going on.' He turned and walked towards the stairwell door. He paused and called back to them, 'You want me to tell him now?'

Delgado thought about it for a moment. 'Whatever you think's best,' he said.

Lox nodded, and disappeared into the darkness.

'What if we can't get in, man?' said Bucky. 'What then?'

'It's just not an option,' Delgado said evenly. 'Either I get in there, or I die trying.' He looked deep into Bucky's eyes. 'Understand?'

Bucky looked away from him, and back across the city towards Military Intelligence Headquarters without replying.

When they returned to the basement one of Headman's small screens – a highly compact collapsible – was set up on top of a stack of large solid units. It was flickering slightly, animating their features with thin grey light. Headman was looking at the softscreen with a blank expression on his face, rocking from one foot to the other as if uncomfortable or frustrated; he didn't look at them as they approached.

'Find anything useful?' asked Delgado.

Lox looked up and shook his head. 'Nothing. All the construction files must have been picked up by Structure and either classified or erased long ago. Guess they're not so stupid where some things are concerned.'

Delgado nodded towards Headman who was staring at lines of apparently indecipherable code on the small screen. Occasionally, as he manipulated the displayed information via his interneural link, one of his fingers would twitch, or he would nod his head almost imperceptibly, and the text would scroll upward or the screen change completely. The movements were so slight it was unlikely they would have been noticed by anyone not looking directly at him. 'What's he doing now?'

'He's trying to log on to the Structure newscast line to see if there's anything about that ship you shot down. It won't help us, but it'd be interesting to see what damage it did.'

Delgado's lips twisted, but he said nothing.

The screen darkened and an image began to form: Myson, Lycern, a number of Myson's advisers and a clutch of naked nymphs. A voice issued from the speakers; it had the monotonous, detached tone so typical of all Structure newsline commentators.

'. . .and General William Myson will leave for Seriatt in six days with his new Seriattic wife and conosq dis fer'n'at Vourniass Lycern. This morning the Princess's Courtiers confirmed that the heir to Myson's empire is due to be born very soon. The conosq dis fer'n'at was examined today by doctors, and although Seriattic custom forbids the use of scanning techniques to view the infant within the womb, Conosq Lycern is reported to have said she is certain the child is male.'

Delgado stared tensely at the screen, compelled to watch but desperate to avert his gaze. The broadcaster continued.

'. . . although the child is half-Seriatt, it was also confirmed today that he is indeed destined to become Structure's next Commander Supreme. General Myson would not be drawn on whether or not this visit to the Princess's homeworld was in any way linked to diplomatic complications concerning the couple's marriage, and rumours of contractual obligations between the two worlds not being met. Neither would he comment on the rumours of Sinz warships gathering in the vicinity of the M-4 wormhole, or the growing tensions on Dassilos and the potential overspill of the civil conflict there given the recent involvement of Structure forces on the government side. When questioned about the loss of four xip fighters during an incursion on the planet, General Myson would only say that the matter was being dealt with.'

Lines of ice were running through Delgado's veins. He

began to tremble violently as the *muscein* erupted with greater ferocity than at any time since he had last been with the Seriatt. Without warning he lurched forward and vomited, the sticky, yellow liquid expelled from his stomach spattering the soft-screen. The others turned and looked at him in surprise; he simply stood, unable to speak, trembling as if fevered.

The infant within Lycern's womb was, he knew with certainty, his own. Myson would protect his Seriattic *conosq* by whatever means he could, particularly if the Dassilos situation was worsening. Yet Myson was infertile; Lycern had said so with such certainty that it seemed impossible to refute. Besides, Delgado knew within himself that the child was his own. He knew with the same certainty that he had known of battles lost. Or sometimes won. Yet at that moment in time, he had no idea in whose favour this particular battle would swing.

All he wanted now was to be with Lycern, comfort her, satisfy the strong protective urges he felt while she carried his child to term. Such emotions were new and unfamiliar. And despite being aware of their normality, he was unsettled by their potency, his inability to suppress them and that he, Alexander Delgado, could be affected by them at all. He had always felt himself to be beyond the reach of such forces; they were experienced by ones weaker than he. But perhaps he was just the same as all other men. Perhaps that was not a bad thing.

Five

homecoming

Delgado slept restlessly for an hour or two. Vague recollections of dreams he could not remember fully haunted him when he woke. They left powerful trace emotions.

Girl, Bucky and Lox had prepared a meal for him; it consisted solely of a strange fungus that Girl said Clunk had grown in the corner of his sleeping space; she told Delgado that it was rich in vitamins and would make him feel better. Although there was not much of the light, flaky food to share between them, it did seem strangely nourishing despite its lack of substance and questionable origins.

'Funny as it seems, this stuff was what he cared about most of all, I think,' said Girl, spooning a forkful of the dark green flakes into her mouth. 'He used to talk to it every night before he went to sleep. He couldn't say much – you know what he was like – but he grunted and stuff. He was obviously saying something important to it. He was all right, old Clunk. I'll miss him.'

She paused as Lox, who had finished his meal quickly and was once again trying to repair the malleable softscreen, swore furiously. The screen's tiny biotech components were suspended in a rich protein slime sandwiched between its two outer skins, and were difficult to pin down. Even the pair of UHG surgical teleculars clamped to his eyes, whirring and buzzing fiercely as they tried to convert the relevant information

223

and project it on to the lenses, were incapable of processing such a high level of detail as quickly as he needed them to, and the information was updated far too slowly to help the frustrated Lox. His face was compressed into tight lines, his temper frayed. He swore again and threw one of his tools to the floor.

They ate in silence for a few minutes, then Bucky leaned across and whispered to Delgado, 'Any idea what Lox said to Headman?'

Delgado shrugged. 'Not exactly. I know he's told him what we're intending to do, though. He said Headman would let us know his decision when he was ready, not before.'

'We can't wait forever.'

'I know.'

They looked across at Headman. They were surprised to find that he was not sitting at his terminal as normal, but was in the corner of his recess looking back at them. They stared at each other for a few moments, then slowly, the strange man stood. It was an agonising movement that seemed to pain him. He began taking faltering steps across the room towards them, and stopped just a few metres away, looking at each one in turn. His bitter eyes were dark and unrevealing, his breathing coarse and unnatural. His skin was textured by many deep pock-marks and scars and held a grey pallor. When Headman eventually spoke, his voice was like water cast on to hot stones, the voice of a ghost. And yet, even though he seemed to struggle to find the words necessary to convey his message, his voice was lucid and clear.

'Despite what you may think,' he said, 'I can hear and understand you quite well. I have always been able to do so, but preferred not to . . .' He shrugged and his voice tailed off, the effort required to explain his reasons apparently too great, or simply considered unnecessary. 'Lox has told me of your plan to enter the Headquarters of Military Intelligence,' he continued. 'I have decided to come with you. No one should be allowed to sell people's lives for profit. It has gone on for too long. Myson must either be killed or overthrown. Delgado represents the best chance of this occurring.'

Bucky looked at Delgado. 'What does he mean by selling lives?'

'I don't know. You say he's been immersed in that suit of his for a long time. Maybe he's not in quite the same reality as us. He might see things from a different perspective.'

Bucky looked up at the tall, gaunt figure standing before them. 'What do you mean?' he said, carefully enunciating each word as if Headman were a child. 'Who's been selling lives?'

'Myson.'

There was a pause, uncertain glances. Even Lox pulled the surgeon's visuals from his face; their hard rims left red rings around his eyes.

'But *how* has Myson been selling lives, Headman? What do you mean?'

Headman frowned as if the answer was so obvious that he could not understand why they failed to see it. When he did eventually speak, the words burst from him like water breaching a dam. 'Myson has several military units of Division size which he sells as mercenary forces to whoever has money enough to pay for their services. He does not care who his customers are. Just that they can pay.' He paused, breathing hard, sweating visibly; it was as if he was panicking, having suddenly realised that he was the centre of attention. 'The proceeds go to many personal funds he has set up specifically for the purpose. He effectively sells the lives of Military Intelligence operatives for his own profit.'

Delgado felt as though a black hole had appeared in his body, a warm, slippery emptiness that spread through every part of him, sucking in matter. The implications in Headman's accusations were too wide-ranging and terrible to comprehend. But he had to know, to clarify the obscene possibilities and face them head-on. 'Do you know where he's used these soldiers?' he asked hoarsely. 'How long has he had them?'

'Many years. There are files detailing payments for their most recent use supporting the rebels on Secourna. They are still on that planet now, but,' he ran a trembling hand across his shining forehead and took a deep breath, 'because of the pressure from Structure to produce results he has been forced to put more resources into the Structure campaign. The rebels and the mercenaries are now being overrun by the sheer weight of *official* Military Intelligence troops and Reactionary Forces squads on the planet. Soon the rebellion will crumble, and the mercenaries will be killed. He will consider that an unfortunate loss, but not one he will be unable to overcome. He can find more, given time.'

Delgado was numbed. Many odd experiences were suddenly explained, things that had always troubled him fitting seamlessly together: the Reactionary Forces badge he had found in a chest of drawers on Buhatt when only the Infiltration squads were supposed to have been on the planet; the words of Commander Paul Wilkes as he had died in Delgado's arms on Dinsic: 'Fear the enemy who befriends you, Alex, for no one can hurt you more . . .'; the mysterious unplotted troopships occasionally traced leaving campaign theatres, their residuals put down to ether-ghosts on the scanning equipment. Then there was the unusually strong resistance of the rebels on Buhatt, who seemed to have an uncanny ability to predict Reactionary Forces' assault strategies. The answer was clear now: they had been fighting themselves.

Delgado had no doubt that Myson was capable of such a miserable betrayal of his own people, and that the evidence of such actions could easily be lost to the Planetary Council in the bureaucratic slush that existed between the far-flung bio-systems of Structure, Military Intelligence, Reactionary Forces and their many sub-divisions – Inventory, Infiltration, Enlightenment, Assimilation, the Public Protection Department . . . the system was so complex, a division of men could easily be lost.

He wondered bitterly how many of Myson's mercenaries –

probably just normal Military Intelligence soldiers following the orders of their Commander Supreme – might have been killed by troops under his own command? How many men and women had enlisted to protect Earth, as he had done so many years ago, only to be killed whilst feeding their leader's ego and adding to his already immeasurable wealth?

Delgado looked at Headman again. 'How do you know this?' he asked. 'How can you be so sure?'

Headman shrugged. 'I have worked it out over a period of time from various pieces of evidence: communications listings, payments, records of Military Intelligence troopship movements: many were updated at unusual times, and I concluded that this was because they were being falsified to cover his tracks. Read between the lines and follow some logical links and the evidence is all there. Of course, Myson had to keep details of all these transactions to himself, but he is not clever enough to hide the files very well. For me, finding them was relatively simple.'

'Why didn't you mention this before, Headman?' asked Girl. 'Why didn't you tell us what you'd found?'

Headman looked at her with his cold, deathly eyes. He paused before answering. 'What could we have done?' he said flatly. 'If we had threatened Myson's enterprise he would have had people down here to kill us within hours. They have a fairly precise idea where we are, I know they do. They have left us alone because we keep the rest of the street people relatively calm by striking on their behalf. I know this because I have seen the files kept on our group. There are many who would love to have the opportunity to come down here and have some sport with us. On the last purifier sweep there were extensive communications throughout Structure and Military Intelligence. The purifier who entered our base was a rookie, and did so in error. And while many considered the destruction of the diplomatic vessel to be the final insult, the decision was made to punish all except ourselves.'

'Punishment enough in itself,' said Girl quietly.

'Exactly.'

'I can't believe it,' said Lox. 'You say they know all about us? Why didn't you say something, man?'

'There was no point.'

'Well, I say we pay Myson that visit sooner rather than later,' said Bucky.

'I agree, man,' said Lox, shaking his head, 'but you're forgetting one important thing: we still have no way to get into the place. All this big-time, bad-ass action-talk is great, but how do we go about putting it into practice?'

'There'll be a way, Lox,' said Delgado. 'We just have to find it.' He looked up, his expression unreadable. 'And find it we will.'

The attitude within the group seemed different from that point onward: there was an urgency, a newfound purpose. Delgado and the gang had been unified by the betrayal they had shared, and this cemented their relationships. Headman's revelations gave them a goal, something to achieve and a reason to achieve it; and the difference in their new enthusiasm for life and the arousal of their collective human spirit was visible in everything they said and did. Headman started to interact with the group, and once even laughed at something Lox said as they were trying to download the day's landing clearance and personnel ID codes. Everyone had stopped what they were doing and watched them, until they too had become infected by the man's new vigour, and the whole basement echoed to the sound of their laughter.

Delgado suggested that he and Girl should go to the base of the Military Intelligence building to check out any possible access points and the surrounding area. As they were preparing to leave, Bucky seemed to be having doubts.

'You'll be careful out there, won't you?' he said. 'Don't take any unnecessary risks.'

'Your concern is touching, Bucky,' said Delgado, 'but I'm a
. . . I *was* a commander for Reactionary Forces, remember? I
can take care of myself, and I'm pretty sure Girl can too. Now
it's quite a way, so we may not make it back before dark.
Under no circumstances are you to come looking for us if we
are overdue. Understand?'

Bucky nodded reluctantly. 'Did you decide on weapons?'

'Girl's got your sidearm and I've got the Jutt rifle.
Headman's managed to cannibalise it into a pretty small unit.
It's got less power, but it's lighter and much easier to handle –
it doesn't need the stand any more.' He pulled the bulbous
cylinder from his shoulder. Thick bands of brown tape
covered Headman's handiwork around the muzzle and grip;
the single plasma orb on top looked singularly askew and
unsafe, and was attached by tubing of unidentifiable origin.
'It's a pretty basic adaptation,' said Delgado, turning the
weapon over and examining it, 'and we don't think it's going
to be too accurate. It can't be armed for too long without
being fired either, because the power pack was part of the
stand and only a small part of it could be transferred. But that
shouldn't be too much of a problem. It'll do the job if it has
to.'

'Right.' Bucky nodded again, yet still seemed uncertain. 'Is
there anything specific you want us to do while you're out?'

'Just go up to the roof occasionally and keep an eye on
things. And get Headman to keep an eye on net activity in case
we can learn anything from that. Despite what he said I reckon
we'll have touched a nerve with the diplomatic craft and they
may not be satisfied yet, particularly having lost one of their
brave young purifiers.'

Bucky looked at them for a moment, then made a gesture
of farewell and walked away.

Delgado and Girl walked up the stairs from the basement
and through the disintegrating ground-floor level of the mall
to the building's entrance. The glass door was shattered,

sparkling fragments scattered down the marble steps leading down to the street like spilled jewels. They stood on the top step of the partially collapsed entrance foyer obscured by shadow. Delgado listened, waited, sought potentially hostile traces. The sky was overcast now, but the air was still thick and warm. Recent rain had varnished the ground. Thin, pale grey clouds below the solid, darker cloud base above sped through the air as if fleeing. The silence was infinite and impenetrable; nothing stirred. The wide road was deserted. The city seemed to have shrunk in on itself. It was an injured creature, dying quietly.

In the distance to their right, clearly visible above the dilapidated buildings and surrounded by habitat towers, the dark shape of Military Intelligence Headquarters dominated the skyline. From this low angle the landing platforms were short slender spines against the brighter sky to the east, fliers dancing around them as if performing some kind of courtship ritual. Delgado leaned close to Girl and whispered, 'We'll move from cover to cover. I'll go first, you follow. If anything happens and you're on your own, try to get back to the others.'

She nodded once, and they began their journey through the deserted streets.

They had to move cautiously, crouching in doorways, slipping into alleys, hiding behind piles of rubble. They would move forward a little, stop, wait, watch, constantly aware of the possibility of attack. Clusters of shadow lay all around them, and their weapons and clothing would be rich pickings for anyone who succeeded in surprising them. Delgado also recognised that although he had the advantages of military training and enhanced perception, he was unfamiliar with the territory, and knew little of those he might face.

As a result of this forced caution their progress was slow, and after two hours they had covered only a fraction of the distance to Military Intelligence Headquarters. The sky was beginning to darken, the weight of the already heavy clouds increasing with the threat of rain. They ran from the doorway of something that might once have been a chapel and into a dark alley between two buildings. Here they crouched, pressing themselves against one wall. The alley was strewn with debris and sun-faded litter, riddled with racing rats. Delgado suddenly realised how hungry he was.

He peered out, glancing at the sky. 'We'd better get under cover before it starts raining,' he said, breathing heavily. 'We don't want to get rainburn. We'll end up looking like Headman.'

'What a vain fool you are,' observed Girl humourlessly, eyeing the buildings across the street.

'Maybe, maybe.' He checked the plasma orb on the Jutt rifle for clouding; it seemed clear enough. He shuffled forward and peered into the road. All was quiet, grey, still. His consciousness tingled very slightly, and out of the corner of his eye he saw movement in the gap between the two derelict buildings on the opposite side of the road. He raised the Jutt and brought it round in a wide sweep, thumbing PERCEIVE. The gun registered nothing.

'What is it?' asked Girl.

'Don't know – nothing maybe. I could have sworn I saw movement. I'm not usually wrong. Not in these situations.' He waited for a few more seconds, staring at the alley and surrounding rubble, the derelict building to the right. He aimed at the chapel, the alleyway, the scorched remains of a flier, crashed long ago. Nothing moved. He lowered the rifle reluctantly.

'That looks like a good place.' He indicated a building a little further along the road. 'Looks pretty stable. Five hundred metres at most. If we can get in there we can shelter from the rain, then continue when it stops.' He looked at the sky; the first drops were already beginning to fall. 'I don't think it's going to be a downpour, but we don't want to get wet if we can help it. I'll go ahead first and make sure the place is clear. If I enter the building then you follow, but not before. And if anything happens to me, don't put yourself at risk. Wait here until you think things have calmed down, then try to get back to Bucky and the others. OK? Got that?'

'I can defend myself, you know, Delgado – I don't need protecting. Especially not by you. Thanks all the same.' She smiled bitterly.

'I appreciate that, but if we both get screwed then it's all over. At least this way one of us might survive.'

Girl thought about it for a moment, then nodded and checked the clip in her gun: the vial of spinbarb solution had been removed for possible future use, replaced by large-bore snub rounds with explosive tips. They were not subtle or advanced, just effective, cheap and relatively accurate in all conditions.

Delgado stood and checked up and down the street one more time. He paused for a moment, studying the alley where the movement had been. Satisfied all was clear, he stepped into the road.

He ran along the street, half-stooping; the only sounds he could hear were the faint slapping of his footsteps on the damp road and his own breathing. The building looked almost wholly intact, apart from a couple of broken windows. He was pleased; they would be able to rest, eat, shelter from the rain, then move on refreshed.

When he was within a hundred metres of the building he sensed feelings of malice and greed, fear and excitement. They were strong, intense. He stimulated an extra surge of adrenaline and opened perception and awareness visuals, glancing urgently around him as he ran. Despite his heightened awareness, nothing was immediately apparent. Concerned for Girl's safety, he turned and ran backwards several steps, splashing through puddles and pot-holes in the road. As he concentrated on the alley opposite her position, the feeling of threat became more dense. He stopped running. Shoulders heaving, he raised the rifle and thumbed the PERCEIVE button again. He glanced down at the gun's tiny screen. Although no danger was registered and he still saw nothing, he felt certain something was wrong: the feelings he sensed were just too strong.

Girl was about to be attacked.

He instinctively flicked off the Jutt rifle's safety catch and armed the weapon; the rifle began to hum and vibrate. The plasma orb glowed brightly.

Nothing happened: no hostiles appeared, no fliers above the rooftops, no purifiers on foot. Was his hyperconsciousness playing tricks on him? Was he going mad? The *muscein* could conceivably have affected his nobics, but there was no way of telling. Whatever the case, the street was empty despite the strength of his intuition.

He could see Girl peering round the corner of the alley. She made a circle with the thumb and forefinger of her right hand. Lacking an enemy, Delgado felt empty, flat, impotent. He lowered the Jutt, shaking his head and frowning. What was happening to him? He turned.

Three figures stepped into the road ahead of him, appearing from hidden alleys, behind walls, released by the very fabric of the city between him and the building towards which he had been running. He entered a flaw in time; seconds warped and stretched as Delgado lived the next few moments in freeze-frame.

The three men looked calm, confident, relaxed in the familiarity of their environment. One of them was smiling. They raised their weapons in unison, as if controlled by a single consciousness. Delgado absorbed the small details that were suddenly clarified by his isolation: the long scar on the right cheek of the man to the left; the tattered clothing, old breather mask and hollow, deathly eyes of the one in the middle; the antiquated sidearm of the one to the right.

Delgado crouched, raising and priming the already armed Jutt rifle in a reflex action. The gun trembled as the first charge of plasma began to form in the glowing orb; the fragment of time it took became aeons as the energy built in a rapid stream of colliding charges.

Then his weapon died, became nothing more than a collection of components. The plasma orb faded, the weapon stopped trembling, the screen went blank. Betrayed by the power of his own instincts, he had armed the rifle too early – now it was useless. In the instant that followed, the realisation that he could not defend himself was stark and clear, the ramifications numbing: his life was over; he would not see Lycern or his son. Everything he had ever done, every decision he had ever made, every mistake, every achievement – all had conspired to bring him to this moment. And it all seemed so pointless. Such struggle, and for what? The cosmos froze. It was as if he had slipped through a fissure in time and space. The increasingly heavy rain popped and crackled on the stark road. There was a drum roll of thunder.

Delgado heard a thin fizzing sound and a snap. The head of the man in the centre of the three exploded, showering his colleagues on either side with its dark and shining contents; the torso remained standing for a second then fell to the ground. A huge hole appeared in the chest of the man to the right, and he staggered backwards until he hit a wall. He slid slowly to the ground and sat in a puddle, looking down at the blood bubbling from his exposed lungs and shattered ribs. His head slumped as his remaining life essence slipped away. The third man looked stunned and glanced at his two dead colleagues, then back to the still-crouching Delgado. He screamed incoherently. But although Delgado saw the man's lips move, he heard nothing other than the dull rush of blood in his own ears. The man began to run forward. He took two, maybe three determined strides. Then Delgado saw a flash of brilliant blue light as the man discharged his weapon in a torrent of rage and fear.

Raindrops burned into the man's face. They made small red indentations in his flesh as they impacted, hastening his decomposition. Half his head had been taken off by Girl's shot – an area from just behind his right eye, diagonally across to his left ear – which she had caught as he had turned. The exposed area of his remaining brain was charred black and smoking thinly, the skull cleanly sliced through. His eyes were half open, red-rimmed, staring; his slightly parted lips exposed rotting teeth stubs. He had an odd expression on what was left of his face; it was almost one of relief.

'Thanks,' said Delgado. 'I had no chance.'

'Don't mention it. You'd have done the same for me.'

'You're a pretty good shot.'

'Yeah. Suppose. Shit, I sound like Clunk.'

They stood in silence for a few moments. Delgado felt somewhat unsettled. He knew that he could not have saved himself, and he had faced such a scenario only once or twice in his life; the experience of facing his own mortality head-on got no easier to handle. That this should happen to him on Earth was bitterly ironic. Perhaps it was some kind of bizarre justice; perhaps Lycern's warnings of atonement were true. Maybe he had already started to pay for his mistakes, his deceits, his whole miserable lie of a life.

He looked around him; they were standing in the open, exposed, vulnerable. Confrontation with death and the implications in Girl's life-saving action had made him forget the danger they still faced. This in itself was an all-too significant reminder of the loss of his ability to control himself and tap into whatever resources he needed. He took Girl's hand in his and pulled her away from the corpses.

'Come on,' he said. 'Let's take their weapons and get under cover.'

They removed what arms they could find on the three men,

then began to jog towards the safety of the building. As he ran, Delgado glanced up at the sinister edifice of the Military Intelligence Headquarters. Its imposing shadow was cast even without sunlight, its clutches inescapable. He knew he was close to Lycern and Myson now, in ways more than physical. As he entered the building in which he and Girl were to hide, he glanced at the structure again. They were there, somewhere in the dark labyrinthine corridors and suites, subject to Myson's whims and perversions. Delgado had to get to them, exorcise the ghosts of everything that had gone before. Not only for them, but for himself.

He had no choice now.

They sat next to the small single window, which was covered in green lichen. Girl was checking her weapon while Delgado watched the fumes rising from the pools of rainwater in the road through the clean circle he had made in the glass.

The room itself was small and cold. A portion of the rear wall was missing, revealing further debris beyond. Bare brick reflected every sound, and the thick smell of Girl's damp hair combined with the stench emanating from the pile of human faeces in the corner created an almost choking aroma.

Girl loaded a new clip of ammunition and checked her gun one final time. When she had finished she put the weapon down and looked at Delgado. She sighed, clearly uncomfortable with the situation. 'Do you feel bad because I saved your life?' she asked.

He glanced at her, then looked back into the street, frowning. 'What do you mean? Why should I feel bad? I'm alive, after all.'

'You just seem, I don't know, frustrated. As if you resent me. As if you think you should have been able to look after yourself.'

He shrugged, but didn't look at her. 'Maybe. I don't know. Does it matter?'

'Not really. It's nothing to be ashamed of, though.'

There was a moment of silence. Delgado looked up. Girl was staring at him; the pupils of her blue eyes were wide, sparkling, alive. Ripples of hatred fluttered through his consciousness, and although this was obviously a distortion of her true feelings, it nonetheless betrayed the intensity of her emotions. She slowly pushed herself up until she was kneeling in front of him, then she reached out and ran one of her scarred hands gently across his head. The sense of her fingers running through his hair felt odd, for so long had it been cropped. She slipped her hand down behind his neck and pulled him towards her. As they came closer together she leaned forward and kissed him. She stroked the nape of his neck and shuffled forward on her knees, pressing herself against him.

Delgado could taste the fungus they had eaten earlier, and the smell of her drying hair was strong as it fell across her shoulders and brushed his face. But the scent of the dust, wet rubble and decay surrounding them was also suddenly clarified in a stark contrast to the animal arousal growing between them; the pattering of the rain on the road outside was sharpened by the softness of their breaths, which in turn intensified the silence beyond. Battles raged within him, the man he had once been fighting for supremacy with the man he had become. He was increasingly uncertain which was his true representation, and with this uncertainty came a frustration born of his overwhelming fatigue, waiting like a predator to trap him when he was off-guard. He was weak, confused, tired of fighting.

Resistant, unwilling to let go of the vestigial remains of his former self that represented so much of his life to this point, Delgado reached around Girl's neck with one hand, and despite the contradictions and conflicts he felt, began to return her kiss.

She sat across him, unfastening her tunic. 'This was always

going to happen,' she breathed, their lips still touching, her pelvis beginning to move in small, slow circles. 'It was inevitable.' Her tunic fell open; she took Delgado's hands in hers and brought them up, pressing them against her breasts, now contained only by the dirty, thin thermal vest she wore.

Delgado's head spun wildly. He kissed her neck then pushed her vest up seeking the warm flesh of her breasts. She threw her head back and laughed as he nuzzled, complaining about the scratching of the stubble on his face, writhing with growing urgency. She looked down at him, her face suddenly serious, demanding. Her desires converged into a single need. She gripped his hands and guided them down to her hips, to the waist of her already half-undone trousers.

Delgado pushed her trousers further down, baring soft, pale flesh, revealing the first hint of dark hair. She shrugged off her tunic completely and pulled her vest over her head. As she struggled with the laces on his trousers he reached round and clenched fistfuls of her hair in his hands. She arched her back, gasping in a wild combination of pleasure and pain that made Delgado reel. His mouth was dry, his stomach tight. He felt sick, out of control, estranged from himself as his mind slowly drowned in a maelstrom of unmitigated lust.

But then he experienced a moment of sudden clarity, and felt a sadness more intense than he had ever felt before. He pulled Girl roughly away from him, his arousal instantly lost. 'I can't,' he hissed, looking down, trying to push her off him. 'I can't.'

Girl laughed at first, but when she realised his true mood her expression changed. 'What's the matter?' she said. 'Not good enough for you?'

'It's nothing. Just forget it. This isn't what we need right now.' He tried to move, forcing her off his legs. She shuffled back along the damp and dirty floor on her backside in a pathetic, ridiculous posture, feet wide apart, knees together, trousers hanging limply from one ankle. Delgado stood and began pulling his clothes back into place. He avoided her eyes as she did the same; but inside him there was no confusion about his reasons for rejecting her.

He looked across to her. 'I'm sorry,' he said. It sounded feeble and he immediately regretted the words.

'Doesn't matter.'

'It's not you.'

'I said it doesn't matter. Just leave it.'

'Maybe before. . .'

'Look, Delgado, *it doesn't matter*, OK? Forget it.'

'Don't mention this to the others,' he said. She looked at him, eyebrows raised, unsmiling. 'It could cause problems,' he explained. 'We don't want any unnecessary jealousies – the wrong thing said at a vital moment. We're acting as a unit. We need to be strong.'

Her manner was abrupt, her body tense, but she nodded.

Delgado walked across to the door, opened it a fraction and peered out. 'We won't stay here long,' he said. 'The rain's stopping and we need to get there as early as possible. We'll eat, then bc on our way.'

Girl looked at him bitterly. 'Sure, Delgado,' she said. 'Whatever you say.'

The rest of their journey was uneventful. They spoke little as they made their way through the seemingly deserted streets, but Delgado noticed a heightened level of aggression in Girl that had not been there before. He considered himself lucky that she was on his side.

The Military Intelligence building grew closer, and as the sun descended behind the brooding shape and the habitats clustered around it, solid slabs of rich orange light penetrated the gaps between; they turned the buildings into dense black obelisks, highlighting their unnatural status on a world that remained as beautiful as in times of prehistory.

When they were almost at the building's base the wide cap

of the immense mushroom-like structure blocked out the sky: it was as dominant as the ethos it represented, overwhelming, merciless in its presence.

They slipped between two buildings as the last of the daylight faded, edges and lines gradually being smudged away in the half-light. The alley was filled with sodden, rotting litter, corpses in various stages of decomposition, the unsalvageable remains of two burned-out vehicles. They crept forward until they reached the end of the passage; it was blocked by a mound of rubble at least three metres high. They paused at either end of this barrier, indicated silently that they were ready, then began to climb.

When they reached the top they lay flat and looked over the edge. The road on the other side looked fairly well maintained and ran right past the base of the Military Intelligence building. The building's circular shape was lost at such close proximity, and the wall appeared flat. Above, the main column of the mushroom was entirely featureless until the lowest and least important flier platforms, about five hundred metres above street-level. The rest of the platforms – the largest and most frequently used – were far higher, on the top half of the mushroom's cap. It was a magnificent fortification, and a perfect representation of the human attitude to waste and failure.

Delgado knew that internally the building was divided into roughly six sections: the lower half of the stalk held the environment maintenance units while the upper half held quarters for the menial workers. The administration and clerical offices were in the lower part of the cap, along with Structure's propaganda, publicity and funding departments, and quarters for any military personnel on Earth. Above that were the military campaign command centres for both Military Intelligence and Reactionary Forces, and service bays for the wide assortment of vessels used by Structure's forces. The final – and largest – section was devoted almost entirely to William Myson. An area was also set aside for the accommodation of his nymphs and a host of hospitality suites where offworld dignitaries could be entertained and courted. Finally there was Myson's personal chamber: the room where he sat, chewing slugs and using his nymphs to realise his sexual fantasies.

Girl shuffled across the mound of rubble and lay alongside him. 'I still don't see how we're going to get in there,' she whispered. 'I've never seen it from this close up before. It's huge. What if we have to go all the way round it before we find an entrance? And what if we don't find a way even then?'

'There's got to be a way,' he replied. 'There's always a weak point. Always.'

They carefully edged over the top, crawled down the other side of the rubble and crept along the street, skirting the base of the building. After about half an hour they stopped beneath an aging, disused groundcar flyover. They sat in a dark corner against one of its support pillars.

'Do you think we should go back?' asked Girl. 'Perhaps we should see what the others think of all this.' She looked along the side of the building that stretched away into the distance, then back to Delgado. 'This is going to take forever.'

'Let's wait until morning, have a look further round, then decide. If we can't see a feasible way then we'll have to go back and rethink.'

She nodded, then frowned. 'It just seems a little bit—'

Delgado held up his hand. 'Ssh.'

'I can't hear anything.'

'Then listen.'

They both heard it then – a distant clattering rumble: machinery of some kind. They jumped up and ran to the next pillar, looking along the dark, deserted street. A large vehicle turned a corner about two hundred metres away. It was at least twenty metres high and thirty long, with a sloping, windowless front. Two slim, rectangular headlights cast weak pools of yellow light on to the road ahead of it. It was powered by a raucous old engine and rattled and squeaked its way noisily through the decayed city on huge metal caterpillar tracks. The immense sound it made reverberated off the walls of buildings. A few seconds later an identical machine turned the corner and followed the first; another soon followed that. The three machines trundled in single file along the road in pre-programmed, automated innocence.

'It looks like an automatic to me,' said Girl. 'But I've never seen one like that before.'

The two of them ran from pillar to pillar, following the cumbersome machines for about twenty minutes until the three vehicles moved into a bay set deep into the Military Intelligence building, the entrance to which was marked by old, faded lines on the road. Delgado and Girl crept into the bay behind the last of the vehicles. They pressed themselves against a wall as huge floodlights came on above them. The automatics' engines revved and great folding doors opened on their roofs. Then, between the brilliant lights above them, other doors opened, folding up into the building. Delgado stepped out a little and looked up: he saw silver chutes rising vertically, quickly fading into darkness. The automatics' engines revved higher still until the vehicles vibrated and rattled on their great tracks. They could hear a loud grinding sound within. Then, above the roar of the engines, Delgado discerned a rushing noise like waves on a distant sea. He looked round, then up into the chutes; a moment later great torrents of refuse began to descend from all three openings.

After the last of the rubbish had fallen the huge trap doors shut, the doors on the automatics' roofs closed, and the floodlights were extinguished. The automatics roared in the sudden and deeper darkness as their engines idled noisily. Then the noise increased, and the machines moved off, turning in a laborious circle to retrace their route, clattering their way along the road and crushing all that lay before them.

242

Delgado looked up at the blackness, trying to make out the seams of the doors; they were lost in the floodlight glare that remained on his retinas. He looked at Girl and smiled. 'This is it,' he said. 'We've found our way in.'

The others greeted the proposal with mixed feelings.

'You really think we can get in that way, man?' Bucky looked doubtful. 'Vertically? Up a refuse chute? Shit.'

'Quite literally,' said Lox without smiling.

Delgado nodded. 'No problem. The automatics remain stationary and the chute doors above them stay open for a couple of minutes after the last of the refuse has fallen. All we have to do is climb on to one of the automatics then pull ourselves up into the chute above it. We managed to get a few weapons while we were out there, too. Not much, but they're better than nothing.' He indicated the arms they had retrieved from the bodies of the men Girl had killed.

'So, say we get in,' asked Lox, 'what do we do then, man? Apart from get covered in crap.'

Delgado pulled a face and shrugged. 'We just have to play it as we go along, think on our feet. I have a feeling I know what we can do, but we'll have to wait and see. It's our best option, though. The only option we seem to have.'

'What about a flier? We could still try to get hold of one.' The newly invigorated Headman still spoke quietly, but now had far more to say than anyone had ever thought possible. 'Next time the purifiers come this way we could bring one down and use it to get to the upper landing platforms.' He pointed at his bank of screens. 'I could download clearance codes.'

Delgado looked thoughtful. 'The risks are great, but not the chances of success. I gamble, but only when the odds are slightly favourable. Even if we assume the vehicle is going to be flyable after we've brought it down, and that we can land on one of the upper platforms, the moment we disembark people will see that we're not purifier crew and that'll be it. If we go in through the refuse chutes I think we can get right into the heart of the place without anyone knowing we're even there.'

'OK, Delgado,' said Bucky, 'let's say we do it your way. Say we manage to get up into these refuse chutes, and say we manage, somehow, to find a way out of them and into the main building. What do we do then, man?'

'Well, despite my recent history I'd like to think that there was still someone within Military Intelligence willing to help me. And Myson's little self-help enterprise scheme won't be popular.'

'And if they won't help us then we go out in a blaze of glory and take as many of the bastards with us as we can,' said Lox.

The rest of the gang agreed with him, and proceeded to give each other hearty back-slaps. Delgado turned away.

Ignoring protestations that they were already fit, Delgado arranged a training programme to prepare the gang members for the assault. These consisted of a number of gruelling exercises intended to improve their physical strength and stamina, and mental meditation exercises to help them focus their minds, and heighten their instinct and perception capabilities. Delgado would occasionally catch Bucky looking at him – particularly when he was talking to Girl – and began to suspect that he knew something of their brief wrestling match out on the streets. He never said anything to confirm Delgado's suspicions, however, and Delgado was not about to put their relationship at risk by mentioning it first.

The evening before they planned to leave, Bucky and Delgado went up onto the roof of the mall for a final visual check of the immediate area, and the first part of the route they planned to take. The air was still and humid. Clouds hung in the pale sky above the largest groups of habitat towers, gradually increasing in density.

Delgado looked across the city towards the Military Intelligence building with the teleculars, rapidly scanning the terrain between. The enhancement lenses picked out only a couple of things: a few scavengers feeding on a carcass in a road a few blocks away; two thin, bony bodies joined in frantic sex in a pile of rubble that had once been a flier servicing depot, their desperation not born of any heightened level of lust, but because a quick mating was necessary if they were to survive it. He panned across to the right. The teleculars bleeped; he followed the small arrows that appeared along the bottom of the display.

Through the window of a building in the next area, he saw a crouching figure. He thumbed the AUGMENT button on the teleculars' underside, and the walls of the building evaporated to reveal the room within. It contained a woman; she was giving birth. Delgado increased the teleculars' magnification until he felt as though he were in the room with her.

She was squatting, gripping the frame of the window on the other side of the room with both hands. Her naked, dirt-smeared body was glistening with sweat. Her head was arched back, forming thick wrinkles at the back of her neck. Although she was facing away from him, Delgado could tell she was screaming.

The baby's head was just visible. As her body flexed, elongating with each contraction, each scream, the dark blue, blood-smeared dome emerged a little further. The woman released one hand from the window frame, placed it beneath the child's head and gave a final, agonising push. The child slipped from her body onto the floor, a slimy parcel of bone and skin. A boy. Delgado shivered and blinked rapidly.

The thin, exhausted woman turned and sat on the floor, the umbilical cord trailing from her, gathering grit. Her face contorted; the placenta slipped from her. She held her son up to one of her flat, empty breasts and licked the child's head, shaking him gently, trying to encourage him to take what

245

nourishment he could get from her. But Delgado could see that the child would never do so; within seconds the woman knew too.

Intense emotions exploded within him, and he was dizzied by a sudden rush of concentrated *muscein*.

He handed the teleculars to Bucky.

'Thanks. See anything?'

'Nothing important,' said Delgado quietly. He hoped Bucky could not see that he was trembling.

Bucky put the teleculars to his face and made adjustments to the display. 'You really think we'll have no problems getting into the building through these refuse chutes?'

'We'll be OK. We've done as much as we can for now anyway.'

'Right.'

There were a few moments of silence. 'Where were you from originally, Bucky?'

Bucky kept the teleculars to his eyes. 'I'm from the country,' he said. 'A farmer's son. There are a few small communities still do that, you know. Try to eke out a life for themselves on the land. They grow a few puny crops, raise bony, diseased cattle and a few hogs.' He paused, lowered the teleculars. 'I came here to escape the grind, the labour day after day after day, all to barely survive. Just because we happen to be outside.' He looked at Delgado and laughed briefly and bitterly. 'Now look at me. Fat as a sow, huh.' He looked back towards the habitats. 'Yeah, well. I thought I could get into one of those things somehow –' he gestured towards the black towers '– get a suite, a job, a *status*. If I could do that then I figured maybe I could get a message to my folks, perhaps bribe a purifier to pick them up and get them in. I had it all worked out. Jesus, I was so naïve. There's no way for me to get in front out here, and any purifier would rather kill you for the bonus than risk get caught smuggling outsiders. Could get cast out for the trouble himself, right? So, now what do I do? Barely survive.'

246

'Couldn't you go back?'

Bucky snorted. 'You're joking, man. Even if I wanted to go back there's nothing to go back to. About six months after I left I heard my parents had been killed in a Reactionary Forces exercise. The whole fucking area was burned training new recruits to survive desert conditions before sending them off to fight the Mars Militia,' he said quietly. 'Fucking pointless that was, too.' He put the teleculars to his eyes again and continued to scan the city, as if the small device could shield him from his own memories.

Delgado tried to think of something to say.

'Don't worry, man,' said Bucky as if sensing the other man's thoughts. 'Wasn't you personally, after all.' He lowered the teleculars again and turned to face Delgado. For a moment, as they looked into each other's eyes, they were joined. Both knew that whether or not they were successful, Structure had made them the people they were. And both knew that it could destroy them yet.

They were ready to leave the basement in the fading light of the next evening. Headman had downloaded all refuse collection times directly, having traced the information back to MIHQ, starting at an automated maintenance compound for larger automatics situated on the edge of the Dead Zone. While this could have given them a little latitude in how long it took them to get to the building, no one wanted to hang around on the streets for any longer than was absolutely necessary. For this reason their route was carefully planned to ensure their arrival would coincide with a refuse drop.

Before leaving they checked they had everything they would need, then switched off the power, trashed Headman's netlink terminal, all the screens, net and power supply cables and finally all the storage media. The last thing they did was put all their personal belongings in a pile in the middle of the room and set fire to them. As they watched the blaze take hold and the thick, noxious smoke pooled ominously beneath the ceiling, they knew there was no coming back; this was their turning point, their entry into the future.

They divided the few weapons they had between them, and left the building in complete silence. Smoke billowed from the mall doors as they descended the steps to the street, finding its way up from the basement. None of them turned and looked back.

Delgado kept an eye on Headman as the group moved through the streets. He was wearing his heavy, cumbersome suit despite the heat and manoeuvrability problems it posed. It was a precaution, he had said, in case he picked up anything important through the satcomm link. But he was struggling to keep up. The night was exceptionally warm, and he was sweating heavily. His mental distance had also returned as he tried to decipher the rich information the suit was feeding into his brain. Physically, his feet were restricted by the suit's hem, which was narrow at the ankles; he hobbled along like some bizarre geisha girl, having to work twice as hard as everyone else to cover the same distance.

As darkness closed in, Delgado pulled the group together in an alleyway. 'Keep your eyes open,' he whispered. 'We don't want to get caught on the hop, but don't fire your weapons unless it's really necessary.' He looked at Headman, who was standing at the back of the group. He looked pale and was frowning slightly, his concentration obviously intense. 'Are you OK, Headman?' asked Delgado.

Headman closed his eyes and pressed a finger to his inter-neural link, applying slight pressure to the coupling. His frown deepened. Everyone was looking at him. 'Not sure,' he said slowly. 'Some odd stuff circulating. Can't work it out. Give me a few minutes.'

'We haven't got a few minutes, Headman. You'll have to try and keep up and let us know when you work it out.'

'Don't try to screw him, man,' said Lox, casting Delgado a severe glance. 'If he can't keep up then we slow down, right?'

Delgado stepped close to Lox and spoke quietly. 'Have it your way. But if he slows us down too much then we'll have to consider losing the netlink. He's a liability if he's keeping us on the—'

'Purifiers.' Headman spat the word. Everyone looked at him again. 'Special Structure Directive to cleanse this area. Maximum intensity,' he continued. 'Purifiers already launched. Heading this way now.'

'Shit.'

'Shit is fucking right, man,' said Lox, looking up into the sky. 'They must be aiming to wipe us out.'

'We'll have to try and get to the Military Intelligence building before the gunships get here.'

'Oh, come on, man,' said Lox, 'we need to get to cover. We don't stand a chance otherwise. We've still got a fair way to go by your reckoning.'

'Maybe it's a mistake,' said Girl, looking doubtful. 'They've only just cleansed this area. Maybe they won't come at all. Headman doesn't look too well. He might be wrong.'

'No mistake,' said Headman flatly, his eyes now open. 'Purifier gunships will arrive in . . .' there was a pause '. . . fifteen standard minutes.'

Bucky looked at Delgado. 'What do we do, man?' he asked. 'Go on, or stay here and ride out the storm?'

'Shit, man you can't just—'

'Shut up, Lox! Come on, Delgado. What do we do? It's your call.'

Delgado looked around them. The few buildings that were standing did not look particularly sturdy: one good blast from a gunship and they would all be crushed beneath a pile of rubble. And although the Military Intelligence building was temptingly close their chances were slim either way. 'We continue to move,' he said eventually.

'Oh, come on, man. Let's just get under cover before we get fried. Tell me what charred lumps of meat can achieve.'

Delgado stepped up to Lox and grabbed his jacket. 'We've got little enough chance of success as it is without staying around here to get torched by purifiers. We need to move out of this area and we need to move quickly. Now shift your ass.' He pushed Lox backwards.

'Jesus, man,' said Lox, pulling his jacket straight, 'you're so fucking screwed up you're prepared to sacrifice everything to get to this *conosq* of yours. Even our fucking lives.'

Delgado faltered. The power of the *muscein* could push him to kill Lox if he let it, but he also knew that the younger man was right. 'That's got nothing to do with it,' he hissed. 'We either move, or we die. So we move.'

Lox paused and glanced at the others. 'But what about Headman?'

'He'll be OK,' said Bucky. 'You can keep up with us can't you, Headman?'

Headman did not respond: he was staring blankly into space, absorbing cold data.

Soon the purifiers were directly above them, the sky obscured by the great, dark discs as they moved in tight formation. Their lift fans groaned like tormented creatures, a deep and resonant sound that trembled bones. The group felt static charge prickle across their bodies as the gunships' scanners swept the ground. Then the sky became filled with precise shards of deadly, sharpened light.

In the stroboscopic discharge of the gunships' weapons, Delgado saw figures rising from the rubble all around them, flickering silhouettes granted momentary existence by the terrible, destructive rain. Rapidly alternating light and dark rendered them epileptic. Terrified people ran blindly down the middle of the desolate street in a desperate bid to escape, almost as if they were unaware of the purifiers' intentions or capabilities. They had no chance.

The Structure vessels were unwavering in their accuracy, and struck down those below them until the road was littered with clots of charred, stinking flesh. The gang fragmented as the attack intensified. Delgado crouched in the corner of a derelict building; Girl ran into an alleyway some distance to his right; Lox, Bucky and Headman disappeared across to the other side of the road where they were absorbed by shadow. For several minutes, as the purifier group adopted a looser formation, a single gunship hung directly above them. A ceaseless torrent of plasma rain slashed from the weapons around its girth as it culled the few people who remained alive beneath it. The rotating turrets on its underside caught escaping stragglers with cold precision.

Eventually the gunship stopped firing and moved away like a violent storm. A numb silence replaced the throb of its powerful generator. Delgado recognised it as the quiet that follows every battle: absolute, impenetrable, narcotic – the silence of death.

Along the street he saw Girl emerging from the alleyway; he beckoned to her in a sharp, urgent gesture. She glanced up and down the street then began to run towards him, half-crouching, sticking to the outline of the frail buildings and debris. Delgado glanced over his shoulder, from the gunship to Girl and back again. When she eventually reached him Delgado saw she had a long, narrow scratch on her right cheek, and that her nose was bleeding.

'You OK?' he asked.

She nodded. 'Sure. I tripped when I dived into that alley and fell against a wall. Nothing more.'

'I didn't think you'd get away with it in there,' he said. 'Thought they'd spot you for sure. You're lucky.'

'One wall has collapsed,' she gasped, nodding toward the alley. 'There was a pocket formed by some of the rubble so I climbed into it. I pushed myself as far back as I could and kept

251

still. The whole lot could've come down on top of me if they'd hit close by, but there was nowhere else to go. Where are the others?'

'They ran off that way somewhere.' He looked across the road. 'I don't know exactly where.' He stepped forward. The lone gunship was hovering above the road about a thousand metres away. A sudden burst of deadly lashes fused an area of the road beneath it. A little further along the road a person ran from a partially collapsed building; they had crossed barely half the highway's width before the gunship focused. A cluster of weapons rotated on their stems, then fired simultaneously. The body was torn apart. Flesh burned and blood boiled as purity came a little closer.

Delgado grabbed Girl by the sleeve. 'Come on,' he said, 'we have to find the others.' Keeping a cautious eye on the gunships, they slipped across the road.

The sturdy façade of the buildings was deceptive, and concealed a sea of rubble stretching far into the distance. Delgado estimated that as much as two whole areas had been utterly destroyed. Columns of smoke rose from burning mounds; the unmistakable stench of charred flesh was thick in the air.

'They can't have survived this,' said Girl with resignation.

Delgado began to pick his way through the devastation. 'Never accept defeat until captured or dead,' he said to her. Yet as he struggled across the desolate wasteland and the crushed reminders of a past time, even he doubted that Bucky, Lox and Headman could have survived such total destruction.

He stopped abruptly, tilted his head.

Girl was close behind him. 'What is it?' she asked.

Delgado put a finger to his lips, then began to move towards the sound, slowly at first, then leaping silently and confidently between mounds of rubble. He stopped and listened again: it sounded like someone coughing. He waited while Girl caught up with him, then they both moved forward. Delgado climbed onto a larger mound of rubble and stopped dead. Girl came up behind him and looked over his shoulder.

In front of them was a crater; in the centre of the crater was Bucky. He was kneeling next to Lox. Headman was close by.

They could distinguish between the two men only because Headman's face was still recognisable; just about. Lox was just a blackened, distorted lump of skin and bone, his body melted into a smooth, contorted shape. Oddly, there were small parts of him which seemed to have escaped the destruction: a fingernail attached to a charred stub protruding from the main torso; four teeth, more absurdly white and perfect than they had ever actually been, rising vertically from the black rectangular lump that would once have been his face; a single eyelash, which appeared to be in completely the wrong place, just below the four white teeth. Headman was about twenty metres away, and although he too was dead, he had not been burned. Delgado and Girl crouched either side of Bucky, who was kneeling next to Lox, staring down at him. His face was red, wet with tears. Girl put an arm around him.

'What happened?' asked Delgado hoping he sounded sympathetic.

Bucky's words came in faltering bursts. 'Headman,' he pointed. 'Building. A wall from that building. There was an explosion. It collapsed and he was crushed, hurt, trying to crawl over to us, to safety. But the suit slowed him down too much. When he collapsed Lox went to try and help him, to pull him under cover. A gunship came. Lox was in the open and – zap – they lit him up like a fucking . . .' he held up his hands and spread his fingers wide, then shook his head and looked at the ground. A single tear dropped from his cheek and exploded in the dust. 'Guess Headman must've been dead before Lox even went to him,' he said quietly. 'Otherwise they would've zapped him, too. Jesus, man. Look at them.'

They looked. Rain was starting to fall, beating an irregular rhythm. The mark made by Bucky's tear was lost among numerous others.

'Come on,' said Girl, 'we have to go.' She stood and walked over to Lox's body.

'We should bury them,' said Bucky as Delgado helped him to his feet. 'They deserve that at least.'

'We can't. There just isn't time, Bucky.' The young man blinked rapidly as he looked at his friends' bodies. Delgado recognised the ghosts of emotions that had once also haunted him. He saw realisation and acceptance grow in Bucky, then a determination, fuelled by anger and desire for revenge. Despite his bravado, Bucky had been uncertain, his self-confidence eroded by the gang's failure to achieve anything tangible. But the last of that weakness was leaving him now, driven out by the deaths of Headman and Lox. Delgado saw the change. He nodded. 'Don't let them win,' he whispered, stepping close. 'Use this anger and grief. Don't worry about the pain. Feel it, savour it, remember the strength and energy it gives you. Use it and turn it against them.'

Girl walked back over to them and handed Delgado a small torch. 'I found this near the body,' she said. 'It belonged to Lox. God knows how it survived.'

Bucky looked at the torch in Delgado's hand, and then into his eyes. Both knew that in the next few hours their futures would be decided. Delgado handed the torch to Bucky. The young man looked at it briefly, then put it into his pocket.

They sheltered next to one of the thick, wide flyover struts, waiting for the automatics to approach. Girl leaned up against the huge pillar and slept; Delgado and Bucky kept watch and talked.

'I guess you've taken a lot of lives in your time,' said Bucky, looking into the night.

'Suppose I have.'

'Ever save any?'

Delgado thought about it. The possible political argument was that his actions for Military Intelligence had saved many millions of lives by preventing numerous small wars across the galaxy. But it was not a safe viewpoint. 'Can't say that I have,' he said.

Bucky looked across at him. 'Well, let me tell you, man, before you came along I was just about ready to kill these guys, and then myself. Lox, Headman, Girl, Clunk – everyone. So I guess you could say that, in effect, you saved their lives.'

Delgado looked at him, uncertain whether or not he was joking. 'Why would you want to kill them? Why would you want to kill yourself?'

Bucky looked uncomfortable. 'Like I said, man, we were going nowhere, just about surviving by the skin of our teeth. All that stuff Lox used to say about us bringing down Structure?' He shook his head. 'It was all crap, man. Crap. We all knew it, too. But we went along with it anyway. Don't ask me why.'

'But you're doing something now, Bucky. Lox, Headman and Clunk aren't here to share it with you, but that's not your fault. They made their contribution.'

'But all this is down to you, man. What did I have to offer them? Nothing. Maybe this is all a mistake too. Maybe we should just blow our brains out now and get it over and done with.'

'If you want to change your mind about this little trip into MIHQ then fuck off and take Girl with you, Bucky. I'll go in on my own. I don't want people I can't rely on to back me up. It's a liability. I won't get my brains burned because you're wallowing in self-pity when I need you to fire a gun.'

'Oh, we'll be coming in with you all right. I was just thinking out loud, that's all. You think I'm prepared to stay out here after all that's happened? Jesus, I'm fit to kill someone tonight.' He sniggered slightly, nervously. 'And to tell the truth, I'm not that bothered who.'

Delgado nodded. 'That's better – keep that in your mind. Just make sure it's not me you happen to be pointing your gun at when you fire it.'

Bucky smiled. 'I'll try, man, but I can't promise any . . .'

Delgado held up a hand; Bucky stopped talking. They listened. Through the still, silent night they could hear the clatter of the approaching automatics, their caterpillar tracks crushing debris as they made their way towards the waiting refuse chutes. The first of them turned the corner a few moments later. Delgado reached around the pillar and prodded one of Girl's shoulders.

'What do we do?' asked Bucky as the three of them huddled together, watching the automatics approach. 'Do we climb up onto different ones, or what?'

Delgado shook his head. 'No. We'll concentrate on one machine: the one nearest to us. Girl's a little shorter than we are, so she might need a hand up into the chute.'

'I don't need a hand from you, old-timer. I can look after myself.'

'Sure you can. But we don't know exactly how large the gap is from the automatic roof to the chute. It'll be better if we're all together, just in case. I'll go first, then Girl, then you, Bucky. When the machine stops I'll climb up, and as soon as the rubbish stops falling I'll get into the chute. You two follow as quickly as you can, OK?' They both nodded.

They waited until the last of the three automatics had turned the corner, then ran to wait for the machines beneath the overhang. The three great vehicles trundled along the road, then turned into the bay. Each one of them stopped precisely beneath its designated chute. The huge floodlights came on. The vehicles' engines revved. Just as the automatics' roof doors were opening, Delgado began to climb up the caterpillar track of the one nearest to him.

The ascent was not easy, the treads narrow and slippery from the rain. The automatic trembled so violently as tons of refuse fell into the vehicle's hold that Delgado almost lost his grip. But soon he was standing on the narrow lip around the machine's open roof doors, trying to ignore the intense heat from the floodlights just above him and the thick stench coming from the vehicle's intestines. He looked down; inside the automatic's body, rapidly spinning silver blades reflected cold light as they cut larger pieces into slivers like some kind of hideous digestive process.

He looked down at Girl; she had started to climb the track but her clothes kept getting caught. Delgado knelt and reached out to help her; she stubbornly refused to take his hand.

The refuse stopped falling just as she struggled onto the machine's roof. Delgado looked down; Bucky was already halfway up the track. He looked up again. The chute opening was about a metre above him. In the centre of one of the chute's sides he could see a chain set into a groove around ten centimetres deep. The chain was black with oil and looked well maintained, but Delgado could not decide its purpose. Staggered at half-metre intervals around each side of the chute were indentations set in the walls, rectangular holes containing small round nozzles.

Delgado looked down: Bucky was almost on top of the automatic. 'We haven't got much time,' he called above the roaring engines. 'I'll go first. I'm a little taller than you.' He stood up again, judged the distance once more, and jumped.

Delgado grabbed the narrow lip that ran around the edge of the chute, but gripped only with his fingertips. He kicked his legs in mid-air, trying to swing himself up into the silvery chute. He got one leg up onto the rim, but seemed unable to get any further. Just when he thought his grip would fail he felt Bucky grab his other foot and push him up; it was just far enough for him to grab hold of the chain.

Despite being slippery and slick with oil it did not move, and he used it to pull himself up. When he was a little way into the chute he was able to stick his fingers and the toes of his boots into the nozzles and climb more easily. When fully inside the chute he shuffled around into a sitting position, pressing his back against the wall with his legs to support himself in mid-air. He reached down and offered his hand to Girl, who was standing on top of the automatic; she glanced behind her at the still-turning blades inside the machine, then back up to Delgado. This time she did not refuse his help.

They both helped Bucky, and he was barely inside the chute when the doors beneath them began to close and they were plunged into an impenetrable darkness. Beneath them they heard the automatics' roof doors close, then the sound of their engines rose briefly before fading as they moved off into the night.

They were all precariously balanced, pressing themselves flat against the wet, slimy metal walls, trying to maintain their grip on the slippery surface. Delgado braced his left hand firmly against the wall to support his weight, and pulled Lox's torch from his pocket. He switched it on and placed it between his teeth, looking at the doors beneath them. Cautiously, he transferred his weight to his fingers, then pressed on to the doors with first one foot, then the other. He tried a couple of times to test their strength, then gradually released the weight from his arms until he was standing on the doors unsupported. He stamped his feet a couple of times, then jumped up and down. Bucky and Girl were quick to join him.

'Nice place you brought us to here,' said Bucky as he looked round, his voice echoing dully off the close metal walls. 'Nice smell, too.' He looked at the sides of the chute and saw his own warped reflection, distorted by slight undulations in the metal. It was oddly coloured by the slime and the weak light from Delgado's torch. 'Just look at all this lovely shit, man,' he continued with a sneer. 'All this lovely Military Intelligence shit. Christ, it smells like the inside of a fucking corpse in here.'

'How high are these chutes?' asked Girl, looking up into the darkness. 'And how are we going to get into the main part of the building now we're in here? Answer me that.'

'You sound like Lox,' said Delgado without looking at her. Instead he gazed up, holding the small torch at arm's length. Its weak light failed to penetrate the darkness above them, and the chute simply faded from silver to deepest black. He examined the chute's sides; apart from the indentations containing the nozzles and the chain and groove, they were completely smooth. He shone the torch directly at one of the nozzles; it was small, round, matt silver. A drop of some unidentified colourless liquid hung from it. He reached out and touched it, letting the cold droplet spread across his fingertip. He placed it under his nose and sniffed. 'Seems to be water,' he said, 'with a trace of detergent.' He rattled the chain slightly in its groove. He shone the torch upward to follow its line until the light would carry no further, then examined the walls closely. 'I think,' he said, 'that this,' he rattled the chain again, 'is for some kind of cleaning device.' He saw their puzzled expressions. 'Look at the walls. There are scratches, scores in the metal in circular patterns. I think they're made by rotating wire brushes, and that these nozzles,' he tapped one, 'are for squirting water into the chutes when they are being cleaned.'

Girl raised her eyebrows. 'So what does that mean, Mr Military Intelligence Detective Person?'

'It means that this cleaning device is going to have to be serviced at some time, so there should be a way into the main part of the building. If we can find the machine, I bet we'll find a service door. And what is a door but an entry point?'

'An exit,' said Bucky quietly, looking up into the darkness.

Delgado either didn't hear him or chose not to: he had already put Lox's torch between his teeth, and started to climb using the nozzles as foot- and hand-holds, occasionally gripping the chain.

'What if the thing starts working while we're climbing?' Bucky called up to him, his voice echoing in the confined space. 'Say these chutes are cleaned after every refuse drop. What do we do then?'

Delgado stopped for a moment and looked down at them, briefly removing the torch from his mouth to speak. 'We'll probably get wet,' he said. 'All I can suggest is that you don't hold onto the chain: that's probably what drives it along and you might lose your fingers. Now get a fucking move on, will you?'

Bucky looked at Girl and shook his head. A moment later they too were climbing.

The cleaning machine was an elaborate array of bristles, blades and sponges attached to a sturdy metal frame. It lay like a dormant alien creature in a large cavity in the chute's wall, a cave-dwelling creature waiting for food to pass. Delgado, Girl and Bucky hung from the walls occupying a smear of dully reflective silver trapped between pools of infinite darkness. They seemed to have been climbing for a day and a night, but Delgado reckoned it had been twenty minutes at the most. They were hot and breathless, their fingers ached, and their feet were sore, cut by the sharp edges of the countless nozzles into which they had been wedged during the climb. He knew they could go no further.

'So you think this is it?' asked Bucky doubtfully. 'You think this is our way into Military Intelligence Headquarters, man? Shit. I just don't believe this.'

Delgado said nothing, but adjusted his grip, climbed a little further, then stretched across the chasm and pushed one arm past the arrangement of brushes. The bristles were made of wire as he had predicted, and scratched his arm as he felt around behind the machine.

'Be careful,' said Girl. 'That thing could take your arm off.'

Delgado extricated himself from the device a few moments later. 'There's a door behind there,' he said. 'I know we haven't climbed far up into the body of the building, but we should at least be level with the workers' quarters. If we can get out of here we're bound to find a way up to the higher levels. All we've got to do is wait until this thing moves off and force that door open.'

'How long do you think it'll be? I don't reckon I can hang on much longer.'

'We shouldn't have to wait too long. Like Bucky said, these chutes will probably be cleaned after every refuse drop. And if you look at the scratches in the walls you can tell that the device moves upward first. I'd say it goes to the upper levels so that all the gunk gets washed downward. Then it probably moves down again to clean away the residue.'

'Very probably,' said Girl.

Delgado simply looked at her; her face was oddly tinted in the dim silver-grey light.

Ten minutes later a light on top of the cleaning machine became illuminated, and the device began to hum. More lights could be seen at the machine's heart; it whirred and clicked softly.

Delgado glanced at Bucky and Girl, then climbed quickly down until he was below the machine with them. 'I think this is it,' he said. 'I hope it does go up first. Otherwise we've had it.'

'At least we'll be clean when we die,' said Girl grimly.

'Absolutely. No doubt about it.'

A deep hum filled the chute, quickly becoming a loud whine as the machine emerged slowly from its hiding place. It paused for a moment in the centre of the duct, supported by the wheeled struts that had extended from its sides. The brushes suddenly started spinning rapidly, flicking away the scraps of food, litter and the other miscellaneous junk that was stuck to the walls; they flicked down past the three humans, odd pieces sticking to their faces and blinding them. The chain suddenly became taut, and the machine began to rise.

When it had moved far enough away Delgado pulled himself into the space it had left. He reached out and helped Girl into the cube with him. Bucky managed to manoeuvre himself in a little way, but there was not much room and he was forced to sit with his legs dangling in the chute, watching

261

the cleaning machine rise above him. He glanced nervously at the water nozzles. 'Is there a door?' he called back to them.

Delgado was busy fiddling with something. 'Yeah,' he said, his voice booming even more loudly in the close, box-like confines. 'I'm just trying to see if I can force it open. It's a cheap mechanical lock. Typical Myson shortcuts.' He tinkered for a few minutes, then they heard a satisfying click as the lock came undone. The service door swung smoothly open and light flooded in from the corridor beyond. There was a roar as every nozzle in the chute began to spray water. Delgado and Girl dropped into the corridor outside; Bucky rapidly drew his legs out of the shaft and dove after them.

'That was close, man,' he said as he stood. 'Christ, would you look at that.'

They looked into the chute; there was a torrent of water so strong it would have pushed them to their deaths had they not escaped in time. Bucky's trousers were wet from the knees to the ankles.

Delgado closed the door, shutting away the noise. 'Come on,' he said, looking along the warm, quiet corridor. 'Now things really get tough.'

Actually being inside the Headquarters of Military Intelligence, so close to the heart of Structure, Stealth, Reactionary Forces and the PPD – all the things they had been fighting against for so long – was clearly a strange and exhilarating experience for Bucky and Girl. But as they followed Delgado along the dark corridors, they voiced disbelief, not so much because they were there, but at the illusions that were shattered.

Girl looked wide-eyed at the dirty walls and ripped floor covering, the cracked, exposed maintenance panels, the clusters of rusting pipes running through the ceiling above battered tiles, many of which were missing or water-stained. 'I thought it'd be plush, luxurious,' she said, shocked. 'You

262

know, kind of affluent. But it's like an old mining station out on the belt.'

Bucky kicked a pile of litter lying on the floor by the wall. 'Look at this,' he said. 'No one gives a shit.'

'Structure's main source of controlling power, the instrument of Military Intelligence's success, is the fear it generates,' said Delgado. 'Well presented propaganda can be an effective tool, believe me. I think only those who have witnessed the truth of this place can understand that fully. For the most part, Military Intelligence and the rest of the governmental system is constructed purely from what people believe, not from any actual power or genuine policy. There is no great plan, no tangible strength to speak of. Not any more. Myson's taken all that.'

'Christ, man,' said Bucky, shaking his head, 'I wish Lox could see this. He'd be pissing his pants at how long we've been messing around. We could probably have brought this place down long ago.'

'I wouldn't be so sure, Bucky. Despite appearances, the majority of those in here – the workers, the cyborgs, the grunts, the officers, even some of the sentient automatics – have been brainwashed by what Myson seems to offer. They'll defend Structure and the Planetary Council to the end – as I once would've done. Most of them think Structure will look after them, or that they'll get some kind of reward for their loyalty. But there's no honour here, no faith, no trust. You look out for yourself and fuck the rest.' Delgado looked around him. 'That this place has a cold heart is something I've only recently realised,' he said. 'We'd better be quiet now. We're coming up to the residential section where the menial workers live – the people who have to do all the stuff the automatics say is below them: laundry, cleaning blocked toilets, fetching contraceptive pulses or whores for officers, stuff like that. Most of them are junked up on slugs half the time, so if we're challenged just watch yourselves. They can be unpredictable.'

They started to pass black metal doors which ran along either side of the corridor. Each one was engraved with a name. Delgado glanced at one: 2194 ROBSON. They passed more doors. They could hear the people behind them arguing, crying, fucking. The noise flowed around them like the waves of a stormy sea, rising and falling with each door they passed, a sense of desperation carried by their current. It seemed that no one was happy within the dark and sombre confines of the Military Intelligence building: there was no song or laughter.

The corridor ended at a lift door – a black and battered gateway to the higher levels of the building. The lift door opened silently as they approached and the three of them stepped in. Delgado pressed a button, there was a momentary pause, then the doors closed again and the lift begin to rise rapidly through the building.

'Do you have someone particular in mind who might help us?' asked Bucky. 'You got some card up your sleeve, man?'

'I think he has plenty of cards up both his sleeves,' said Girl.

Delgado looked at her. She was challenging him, he knew, but to what end, he wasn't sure. He didn't know if he wanted to find out.

When the lift door opened again and they stepped out, a kaleidoscope of emotions stirred in Delgado. There were so many memories. The place had held total influence over the decisions that he had made in his adult life. Now, in pursuit of an alien and the only child he would probably ever have, he was finally beginning to realise who he really was, and what was truly important to him. This journey of discovery had been difficult and disheartening, yet he sensed that, in time, he would be sorry he had not started it sooner.

'We nearly there yet, man?'

Delgado half-turned. 'Sure,' he said. 'It's just around here somewhere.' He stopped a little further on: PAUL ORMEROD – PUBLIC PROTECTION DEPARTMENT.

264

Bucky and Girl stood to his right. He looked at them both: they seemed expectant, tense. 'This is it,' he said. 'Are you ready?' They both nodded. 'Good. Whatever happens, let me do the talking. Don't say a fucking word.'

Delgado knocked on the door: three loud, confident raps.

Ormerod shouted something short and offensive from within, then in a loud voice demanded to know who was knocking on his fucking door at this hour of the fucking night when he was trying to do some fucking work. Delgado did not answer, but knocked again. There were more frustrated, impatient sounds.

Ormerod opened the door sharply and looked directly at Delgado. He had leathery skin and many wrinkles. His black hair was slicked back across his fragile skull. His face was gaunt, and there was little weight on his bones. For a moment he appeared not to know his visitor, but then a glimmer of recognition began to spread across his tanned face. 'Well, I'm damned,' he said. 'Alexander Delgado. I've heard rumours about you, Al, and that's for sure.'

Delgado saw suspicion lurking behind Ormerod's deep brown eyes. His abandonment of Reactionary Forces and betrayal of William Myson would certainly be common knowledge by now. 'For God's sake, man, I'm surprised at you. You know you shouldn't believe anything you hear in this place.' Delgado tried to summon his old smile, but felt his face tighten. 'We're above such things, surely.'

'Depends what you hear,' Ormcrod replied. He looked at Bucky and Girl. 'Who are these two? Those aren't Military Intelligence uniforms. Not current ones, anyway.' He squinted, peering closely.

'They're friends of mine.'

Ormerod said nothing for a moment, but looked warily at the three people in front of him. He clearly sensed that all was not right. 'What's going on, Delgado?' he said softly, narrowing his eyes. 'What do you want with me?'

'I can't tell you here. Let me in and I'll tell you things you won't believe.'

'I've already heard many things I can't believe, Delgado. Not much detail, but they say that you've abandoned Military Intelligence and Reactionary Forces in favour of the Affinity Group. Tell me that's not true.'

'I can tell you in all honesty, with my hand on my heart, that that's not true. If it were, I wouldn't be here now, would I? Now please let us in. We're more than just acquaintances, after all, you and I.'

Another door opened a little way up the corridor. The sound of voices burst from the room: people saying goodbye. Ormerod stuck his head into the corridor and looked along the row of doors. A pool of warm orange light had spread across the floor and the wall; an arm and half of someone's body had already emerged into the corridor as they paused to say their farewells one final time. Ormerod looked at Delgado, Bucky and Girl. Delgado's demeanour was steady and unwavering, completely calm and relaxed. The sound along the corridor grew louder. Ormerod looked nervous and uncertain. Delgado raised his eyebrows.

'You'd better come in,' Ormerod said finally, and stood to one side to let them pass.

Most of Ormerod's suite was in darkness, the only sources of light being a short row of spotlights on the wall to their right, and the terminal softscreen set up on the table beneath those lights. Further down was his bed: a large, circular affair surrounded by an elaborate arrangement of poles and drapes, almost certainly designed for far more interesting activities than sleep. A kitchen area took up most of the opposite wall. To their immediate left was a large wardrobe and a door which, Delgado knew, led to the bathroom. Other than one or two small photographs – Ormerod's military graduation, Ormerod standing on an anonymous battlefield looking down at a charred corpse, a young and beautiful woman lying on Ormerod's bed — there was not much in the way of decoration.

Ormerod walked to the softscreen and spoke to it gently. 'Save file, preformat and ultrabeam secure to Commander Oplimier, Mars Colony West. Closedown.' He picked up the screen, softened it, then folded it into a small, neat square and placed it in a drawer beneath the table. He walked across to the wall and flicked on more lights; the room seemed to expand in the new brightness. Ormerod indicated that they sit around the table. As his three guests took their seats he went to the refrigerator and produced a bottle of strong beer for each of them.

'So, how are you, Delgado?' said Ormerod as he sat at the table. 'It's been a long time. You had less hair last time I saw you, that's for sure. What have you been up to? Fighting the Seriatts?'

Delgado smiled. 'Something like that. How are things going in the Dassilos system? Any developments? Last I heard, Structure was being drawn in.'

Ormerod raised his eyebrows. 'It's not good,' he said. 'Dassilos has quietened a little but tensions in general are growing. A deal to set up a demilitarised exclusion zone looked on the cards, but the talks have collapsed. The Seriatts destroyed three of our xip fighters patrolling freespace just two nights ago and things went rapidly downhill. They said the craft were violating a controlled area and refused to turn back after repeated warnings. No pilots survived, but the fighters' AI reports concur with what the Seriatts are saying as I understand it. The decision was made not to retaliate in case the other Andamour worlds decided to blockade or engage militarily. The Planetary Council held an emergency session and for a while it looked like it was all going to blow up big time. Even Shaw was in attendance, and he doesn't get out of bed much these days. But nothing happened. Rumour has it that it was Myson and

Myson alone who prevented an all–out assault being launched on Seriatt. God knows why. He hates the fucking Seriatts. He must want these Sinz deals of his to keep going through real bad.' Ormerod looked up. 'But all this is besides the point, Delgado. What I want to know is, why have you and your friends here decided to pay me a visit? When I spoke to Osephius he seemed to think we wouldn't be seeing you again.'

Delgado thumbed a rivulet of condensation that was running down the outside of his bottle. 'We need your help, Paul,' he said.

'I think you need the help of the gods, Delgado. I don't know what you've done, but you're certainly not flavour of the month around here. Especially upstairs. ' He pointed at the ceiling and swigged his beer. 'My sources tell me that if they're not talking about the Seriattic situation they're talking about you.'

Bucky shuffled in his seat; Girl bit her bottom lip and looked tense.

'I'll be straight with you,' said Delgado. 'There's no one else we can turn to. We go back a long way, Paul. That counts for something, doesn't it?'

Ormerod smiled and nodded. 'Yeah, that counts for something all right, although I'm not too sure what. I'm hardly in a position to help you, to be truthful, whatever it is you're after. But now you're here I guess there's not a lot I can do about it. You going to tell me what this is all about or do I have to hazard a guess?'

'I've got to get to Myson. That's all you need to know.'

'"Get to" sounds a bit ominous, Al.'

'OK, let's just say I need to see him.'

Ormerod shook his head. 'I know we fought together once, but I've got too much to risk. My career. My rank. I don't think. . .'

'I can tell you something that will make you want to help us. Something which is against every ideal drummed into us

268

about Military Intelligence, ourselves, our worth. Forget my personal reasons for this, Paul. Think about what's important to you, to all General Smythe's officers.' He stared deep into Ormerod's eyes, trying to arouse some measure of the passion they had once shared.

Ormerod frowned and smiled at the same time; he seemed uncomfortable. 'What do you mean, Delgado? Not many of General Smythe's officers are still alive. It was a long time ago. No one mentions him much around here any more. No one who's got any sense, anyway.'

Delgado took another swig of his beer and leaned across the table. 'We fight against our own,' he said, his voice a hoarse whisper. 'Myson has a whole unit that he sells to whoever wants to use it, whether they're friendly or not. Most recently they were used on Secourna, before that on Buhatt. I was there, Paul. Ordering attacks. Attacks against our own comrades, all to line Myson's pockets. He might even have sold our troops to Seriatt. Christ, there could be a war in the offing in which only one side would be fighting.'

Ormerod sighed heavily. 'Yeah, well. We all know it goes on, Delgado, and that it's not in the best interests of those who have to go to the theatres in question, but what can be done? There are economics in everything, you know. Half the military forces would have nothing to do if Myson didn't arrange things like that. He gets some extra pocket-money, Seriatt gets some top-notch, highly trained grunts, the grunts get battle experience, everybody's happy. Except those who die, I guess. What does it matter, at the end of the day? Most grunts expect to get killed within three standard hours of arriving at a campaign theatre anyway. Jump from a snubship, fire a few HiMag rounds into the air and get one in the head. What's the big deal? That's what war is.'

Delgado stared at him. 'You mean people *know* this goes on and no one tries to stop it?'

'Of course people know. I can't believe *you* didn't know.

Christ, you really have been left behind, haven't you, Delgado? No one tries to stop it because anyone who questions it is – well, dealt with. Troublemakers have a habit of disappearing suddenly. What's the point of stirring things up when what's going on doesn't directly affect you? None of the officers are put in danger so why worry. He's not stupid enough to put the intelligent ones at risk.'

'My God. How long has this been happening?'

'Since Myson came to power. It was one of the first things he did.' Ormerod pulled a face. 'You *must*'ve known about it. You know he bought most of the Council to get into power, don't you?' Delgado nodded grimly. 'Yes, well – it all grew from there. Everyone's involved in some way. Myson even has a say in what the Mars Militia do and when they do it. If he's got a political crisis on his hands here, or some Bill he wants to get through quickly, he has the Mars Militia plant a bomb on a starliner to divert attention. He even sorts the security out for them so they can do it without getting caught. Believe me, if people start becoming anxious about the current situation with Seriatt he'll have them do something like that and the spotlight will move away from the interplanetary crisis. That sort of thing's been going on for centuries and it's not going to stop now.'

Delgado shook his head. 'But people die. Our own people.'

The others looked at Delgado and saw far into his soul. This, they recognised, was a man struggling to retain his own identity in the face of events and revelations so powerful that he had been mentally destabilised. His hands were trembling, his eyes were red, his mind was barely his own. All he had believed in, all he had worked and fought for, had turned out to be a lie.

Ormerod was the first to speak, but his voice was somehow different in the light of Delgado's obvious torment, as if he had seen another side of a man once thought undefeatable. A man who had been brought to his knees by personal betrayal, and the power that had ensnared almost all men at some point in their lives. 'I might be able to help you, I suppose,' he said quietly. 'We do go back a long way. It's risky though.'

Delgado looked up. 'How?'

'I can help you get a clearance code that will allow you access to Myson's level. I'm PPD, you were once Stealth; the guys up in Control wouldn't dare refuse to give us a code if we tell them we want to see Myson. But that's all I can do. I'm not about to get myself killed for you. And if we get stopped then you've got a gun to my back, OK?'

Delgado sighed. 'Sure. No problem.'

Ormerod nodded. 'OK. We'll go right away. I want you out of here as soon as possible. No offence.' He looked at Bucky and Girl. 'You two stay here and don't make a sound. We'll come back for you.'

Delgado saw Bucky's tension. 'It's OK, Bucky,' he said. 'We can trust him.'

'Guess we have to,' said Bucky, avoiding Ormerod's gaze.

Six

segue

Ormerod spoke constantly as he led Delgado through corridors and into lifts towards the Control Centre. The talk was mostly of people Delgado had once known, names from the Academy days, people who had not made it as far up the career ladder as they. But the names were nothing more than familiar-sounding words to him now; their lives had diverged from his long ago, when they had taken easy options or found niches in places not of their choosing, but which were fairly acceptable nonetheless – an easy task to perform if you had the right, or perhaps wrong, connections and attitude.

It seemed from what Ormerod was saying that, for the most part, they were unhappy, bored or frustrated people – trapped in prisons that were essentially of their own making. Delgado had no sympathy for them. You got what you deserved, and if you sat back and simply accepted what came your way, then the odds were stacked in favour of your being dissatisfied with the result. Delgado had been wary of making such mistakes, and always kept his mind focused on his personal targets. And yet, even though he had achieved his aims – and so much more besides – he had still had occasional pangs of discontent during his time in the service. Now it looked as if it had all been a waste of time anyway.

'. . . so,' Ormerod was saying, 'because his engineers couldn't charge the pulse energisers for his communication line to

Myson, he failed to carry out the orders. They lost three ships to Lyugg pirates out on the rim as a result. Myson had him brought back and publicly skinstripped over in habitat nine. They say it was weeks before he died. Mind you, he was unconscious for most of the time so it wasn't as entertaining as it could've been.'

They turned a corner. A large black metal door stood ahead of them. Words were painted upon its dark surface in stark white letters: PLANETARY GUIDANCE CONTROL CENTRE: NO UNAUTHORISED PERSONS OR AUTOMATICS BEYOND THIS POINT.

Ormerod stopped at the door. 'You'd better stick close, let me do all the talking. They probably won't be bothered who you are, as long as I've got clearance. Let's just hope no one recognises you.' Delgado nodded once, and Ormerod pressed the buzzer at the side of the door.

'Yes, what is it?' The speaker rattled slightly as the deep voice issued from it.

'Paul Ormerod, Public Protection Department Unit Fourteen: ET Liaison and Purifier Control. I've come to register an audience window with General Myson.'

There was a long and stubborn silence from the speaker. Ormerod smiled at Delgado; they both pictured the irate and less than polite gesticulations and colourful language that were no doubt hammering off the walls of the Control Centre. A sound like that of a heavy metal object being dragged along a concrete surface briefly issued from the small speaker, followed by a slightly less irritated voice than before. 'Very well. You can come in – but be quick. You know the procedure.' The speaker clicked loudly as the man signed off.

Ormerod stepped forward and looked directly into the eyescan strip. A thin band of red light washed down his face as it took his retina pattern.

'Wait, please,' said a deep, artificial voice. Long seconds passed. Delgado glanced at Ormerod, uncertain, slightly tense. Then: 'Identity confirmed.'

The door opened.

Inside, the room was dim and smoky. Several people turned and looked at them as they entered; their faces were coloured the thin shade of green that glowed from the screens in front of them. They all looked red-eyed; the men were unshaven. There was little noise other than the low mumble of one or two controllers confirming what the computers on Earth would have already told the ships' onboard systems. There was also a strong, repugnant smell of stale sweat and *tersip*, the stimulant most controllers were forced to use despite the risks of fatal strokes or seizures.

The terminals at which the workers sat were grouped in banks of four, each assigned a different system sector to control. The wall on the far side of the room was a giant screen split into eight smaller screens. This facility seemed to be of great use to the controllers, as the wall screens gave them a much wider overview of their control area than the small ones in their desks. Unfortunately, there were twenty banks of terminals to these eight larger screens, so arguments about whose turn it was to make use of one of the wall divisions were almost constant, the official roster largely ignored: by and large it was first come, first served.

The main desk was empty. Ormerod looked around the room and walked over to a short, bald, stocky man Delgado did not recognise; he assumed he was the owner of the voice from the speaker. Ormerod leaned towards the man, placed one hand gently on to his shoulder then whispered something to him. Delgado focused nobics and opened perception visuals; he caught traces of excitement, frustration, impatience, arousal – an inconclusive everyday mix from which he could glean little of value. The controller glanced at Delgado as Ormerod continued to whisper, then the two of them walked towards the desk.

'Well, come on then, I'm a busy man.' The controller stooped over a screen set into the desk, revealing a mole on his chin that sprouted a cluster of wiry hairs. He squinted and frowned. His face was an even more disturbing shade of green than the others in the room when he stared at the screen. 'Come on, come on', he muttered. I haven't got all day. This bunch –' he pointed at the screen in front of him, which from their viewpoint was invisible '– have got four new incoming pilots to work with, and they haven't got a fucking clue. They should give all the piloting jobs to females by default: much more in the way of self-control, far less ego to bruise and *much* more consistent. But hey, that's just my opinion, and who the fuck gives a shit what I think?' He shook his head and sighed, obviously already aware of the answer.

Delgado and Ormerod stepped towards the little man. He was young, but looked old, his face a collection of assorted wrinkles, lines and creases that seemed to move together like a serpent's scales as he formed different expressions. He seemed too serious for his age, and Delgado felt that just below the surface of his harassed exterior was a creative person, stifled and frustrated in his unfulfilling job. When the little man stood fully upright he was little more than five feet tall. Delgado wondered if the post of flight controller – although not well paid or particularly interesting – had once appealed to him because of the power it offered.

'Now then,' the controller said fussily, 'you say you're going to see General Myson?'

Ormerod nodded. 'We have important business and need to see him soon.'

'Doesn't everybody want to see someone soon? You say you're PPD?'

'That's right.'

'Yeah, I figured as much. What's your file number?'

'Four oh one seven oh eight nine.'

The stressed little man rapidly switched between screens, then keyed the information into the terminal. They saw the reflection of the screen update ripple across his face. 'You're

Paul Ormerod,' he said, his voice flat, unimpressed. 'Public Protection Department, ET Liaison and Purifier Control.'

'Yes, I know. I just told you that, didn't I?'

The controller jerked his head towards Delgado. 'Who's your friend?'

'He's a Reactionary Forces Officer. He'll be coming with me.'

'Fine. I'll need a name and file number.' Neither Delgado nor Ormerod spoke. The controller looked up. 'Well? You do have a file number, don't you?'

'I've been on Covert Assignment offworld,' said Delgado. 'I haven't been given a new tag yet.'

The controller frowned. 'You should still have a file number, son.'

'It was deleted pre-assignment.'

The man raised his eyebrows. 'Rubbish. What do you mean it was deleted? Who deleted it? When?'

Delgado leaned forward and glanced around as if to check no one would overhear them. 'Stealth Squad,' he whispered. He tapped the side of his nose and winked. 'Can't say more than that. Confidential.' He leaned even closer to the man. 'Now just get the fucking clearance sorted out or I'll have you skinstripped before you can draw breath, understand me?' He flared his eyes and smiled thinly.

The controller seemed slightly doubtful, and took in Delgado's somewhat shabby appearance: the stains on his uniform, the smell wafting from him, his unkempt hair and considerable beard. Other controllers were also beginning to take an interest. Delgado felt uneasy and knew that Ormerod did too.

'I'm not sure about this at all,' said the controller slowly. 'I don't like threats, whoever sees fit to issue them. I think I'd better check with General Waylian.' He flipped open the lid of the phone next to him and the small screen flickered into life. 'General Waylian's office, please,' he said. He rapped his fingers on the desk, glancing from Delgado to Ormerod and occasionally at the large wallscreen behind him.

While he was waiting for a response, panic erupted on the far side of the room. A siren started wailing; several large red lights began to flash; a number of controllers ran to a particular console and huddled around it. A computer-generated voice could be heard in the background: 'Collision imminent. Abort orbit line placement. Collision imminent . . .'

The controller glanced over his shoulder at the chaos, and then at the woman who had just appeared on the phone. She was asking what did he want, please, as she was far too busy for childish jokes. Didn't he know that she was . . . He tutted and closed the phone lid.

He glanced up at Delgado and Ormerod. 'I'll give you both clearance this time,' he said quickly, 'but if there are any problems, I wasn't involved, OK? I've got to go. Type in the details yourselves, will you? Touch here,' he pointed, 'to generate an access card loaded with the clearance code for the lift.'

Delgado and Ormerod both smiled. 'Sure,' called Ormerod as the man turned and hurried away. 'Thanks for your time.' The little man raised a hand in acknowledgement.

The two men stepped behind the desk and studied the screen. It did not take long for them to find what they needed, and within minutes they had clearance to visit Myson's level at some time within the next four standard days.

As they they left the room, the impending collision seemed to have been narrowly averted, but the ensuing confusion was clearly going to take considerable time to sort out.

'Wait here,' said Ormerod. 'I'll be back in a minute.' Before Delgado could speak Ormerod had turned and was walking across the room towards the controller. He spoke briefly to the man, then returned to Delgado.

'What's up?' Delgado asked.

'Oh, nothing,' Ormerod replied casually. 'Just making sure he knows who he's dealing with.'

As they left the room, Delgado risked a look behind him; the controller and several other men were staring after him, their faces hard and resolute.

Bucky and Girl were still in Ormerod's room when the two men returned. They were standing beneath the spotlights beyond the table, as if both had been pacing up and down while they waited. In the warmth of the room they had placed their tunics and weapons on Ormerod's bed, yet they looked disarmed by more than just a lack of ordnance.

'You OK?' asked Girl as they entered the room. 'You were gone a long time.' She glanced at Ormerod then back to Delgado. 'We were starting to get a little worried.'

Delgado nodded. 'Everything's fine.'

'So we're fixed up?' asked Bucky.

'Yup. We've got a hot ride straight up to Myson in this little ticket.' He held up the card for them to see.

Ormerod was getting more beers for them all. 'You realise he's got some decent guards up there, don't you?' he said as he reached into the fridge. 'I don't know what you intend to do – and I don't want to know, to be quite honest – but you won't be able to just walk in there.'

'Let us worry about that,' said Delgado flatly.

Ormerod turned; he had four beer bottles in his hands. He made to speak, then saw the weapon in Delgado's hand. 'What's going on?' he said. He half laughed. 'What the hell do you think you're doing, Delgado?'

Delgado was completely calm and relaxed. 'What do you take me for, Ormerod?' he said. 'You really think I was going to fall for that? You know me better – and I know you, too. I may have been gone a long time but I know how this place works, the kind of loyalty it breeds. You, Osephius, you're all the same.'

Ormerod laughed. 'I don't know what you're talking about.

Come on, point that thing somewhere else, will you?' He held out the beer for Delgado to take.

Delgado shook his head. 'You know I can't do that, Paul. I saw you talking to that guy in the control room. I just hope you're as greedy as I think you are. Put the drinks down and get over there. Move.'

Ormerod's expression changed. After a moment's hesitation he stepped forward a couple of paces and placed the bottles on the table. 'You surely can't think you can get away with this, Delgado,' he said. 'What are you thinking of? For Christ's sake, listen to me. Why throw everything away like this? It's not too late to salvage some of it, you know. Surrender yourself to me here and now and we can sort this mess out, Alex. I can vouch for you – say you've been mentally unstable, suffering from Post Traumatic Stress Disorder or something. It's insanity. Come on; give me the gun—' he took a step forward.

Delgado moved his right thumb very slightly and the weapon began to hum softly; the plasma orb attained a subtle luminescence.

Ormerod looked squarely at Delgado and began to walk slowly around the table between them. They maintained eye contact, their faces grim.

'You won't kill me, Delgado,' said Ormerod confidently. 'You've changed too much, lost all that made you what you once were, every trait, every strength. Look at you now. You're weak – like a lovesick adolescent, too wrapped up in your own emotions and obsessions to think clearly. Just what is it that you think you can achieve here? You're in the heart of the Supreme Headquarters of Military Intelligence, for God's sake. Say you manage to get upstairs to Myson; what do you intend to do then? Where do you think you can go?' Ormerod stopped walking; he was face to face with Delgado by this time, just centimetres from him. 'Don't throw it all away now, Alex,' he whispered. 'Not like this. Give me the gun. I promise I'll do my best for you. Trust me.'

Delgado shook his head very slightly, but his face was bitter, as if he was on the verge of a breakdown. The barrel of the small gun started to tremble; he gripped the weapon so tightly that his knuckles turned white.

Ormerod slowly raised one hand and reached out until he was holding the barrel of the gun. Not for one moment did he break eye-contact with Delgado. For a few seconds they faced each other, holding opposite ends of the small weapon. They were like a strangely distorted reflection. Bucky and Girl watched, immobilised by the bizarre scene being enacted before them.

Ormerod's grip on the gun barrel tightened. Delgado's mouth opened as if he were about to speak, to say some last redeeming word. Ormerod smiled, then raised his other hand and placed it on Delgado's elbow. 'Give me the gun, Al,' he said gently. 'You know you can't go on. Give in now and save yourself. Give me the gun.'

Delgado released his grip so that the weapon was hanging limply in his fingers. Ormerod smiled again and looked down to take the gun from him.

Delgado blinked. Saw Ormerod's lips moving. He knew that he was saying words of reassurance, telling him he had made the correct choice, that his decision had been wise. But Delgado was deafened by the anger in his blood and could not decipher the words: such cognisance was now beyond him.

In a moment of cold awakening he clawed his way back from the brink of defeat. He would not give in; such failure had never been acceptable to him, and never before had there been so much at stake. He re-established his grip, snatched the gun and smashed it into the side of Ormerod's skull before he had time to react.

Ormerod fell but was still half-conscious, making deep moaning sounds as he rolled on the floor, hands clutched to his bleeding temple. There was a knock at the door; and the emotional traces Delgado's nobics fed to him from the source confirmed his suspicions of Ormerod's betrayal.

His thought processes accelerated as his nobics calculated probabilities and projected outcomes to varying scenarios. There was another knock, louder, more insistent. He adjusted the weapon in his hand, then reached over to the bed and grabbed a pillow. He rolled the semi-conscious Ormerod on to his back, placed the pillow over his face and fired once. There was a short, dull sound. Ormerod stopped moving, his limbs suddenly limp. Blood seeped from beneath the pillow. The unmistakable odour of death filled the room.

A fist hammered at the door; a male voice shouted Ormerod's name.

'Get into the bathroom,' ordered Delgado. 'Quickly.'

'Don't you want us to—'

'Just get into the goddamn bathroom!'

There was prolonged pounding from the door, more than one voice calling. As Bucky and Girl went into the other room Delgado dragged Ormerod's body beneath the table, thankful both for the man's dark carpet, which should hide the blood-stain long enough, and for the fact that he could not see his dead colleague's face – or what was left of it. He stood, repositioned chairs, reached over to the door release then quickly stepped back into the shadowy corner by the bed.

Two young PPD officers strode into the room, weapons drawn. They motioned silently to each other, clearly tense, aware that something was amiss. They cast a cursory glance around the room, then the one nearest Delgado pointed at the bathroom door. They moved towards it slowly, one stepping to each side of it. When they were both facing away from him Delgado reset his weapon and primed it.

'Looking for a good time, boys?' he said.

The two men spun. Frowning hard in the spotlight's glare, they could not see him in the shadow. They looked for a few seconds. Only when one of the men finally spotted him did Delgado fire.

He released two bolts in rapid succession. One shot sliced

the nearest officer virtually clean in two; he collapsed immediately. The second shot was less effective and merely disabled the second man, taking a chunk out of the right side of his waist. He fell to the floor and drew his knees up to his chest, rolling on top of his already dead colleague. Blood leaked from his mouth, bubbled from his nostrils and seeped through his hands which were clutched to his side. He groaned and rolled, his legs kicking. He tried to stand but simply fell to the floor; huge amounts of blood surged from him with the impact. He writhed and moaned, a tormented coil spouting agony-induced gibberish.

Delgado watched for a few moments, a slightly confused expression on his face. These were his colleagues, and yet . . . He took two steps forward, raised the gun, and fired twice more.

Bucky and Girl emerged from the bathroom.

'Shit,' said Bucky. 'We thought you'd had it, man.'

Delgado looked up. He felt old, but also a more subtle, deep-rooted weariness that he could not pinpoint. He ran his right hand across his stubbled cheeks and chin.

'We'd better get out of here,' he said. 'If my thinking is correct, these are cohorts of Ormerod's. He would've wanted to keep any bounty for himself, so I doubt the alarm's been raised yet. But these guys will start to stink soon, so even if they're not missed from duty they'll be found. Come on. We've no time to waste now.'

He stepped over the bodies, opened the door and peered into the corridor. 'All clear,' he said. 'Let's get to the lift. Move.' He stepped back to let Bucky and Girl pass, waving them forward with urgent motions of the gun in his hand. Before he left the room himself he glanced at the three bodies on the floor, and felt deep sadness.

The lift doors opened. The corridor in front of them was long and narrow, with a huge circular window at the opposite end. Delgado checked his weapon then took a step forward, peering cautiously out; a few dimly glowing lights cast short creamy smears along small areas of wall, but everything else was trapped by the all-consuming blackness of shadow. There was no movement, little sound other than the rush of air passing through ventilation ducts. The occasional deep thud of heating vents opening and closing was sudden and irregular. Despite his familiarity with such scenes, Delgado found it eerie and somehow disturbing. It was as if the three of them had descended into the rusting bowels of some huge, decommissioned war vessel rather than risen to the residential level of one of the most powerful men in the galaxy.

They remained crouched at the back of the lift, watching, listening. The place seemed to be deserted: there were no cyborg guards, no automatics, no slug-dazed nymphs. Delgado wondered briefly whether they were on the wrong level. Or had Myson already left Earth and taken his whole bizarre entourage with him? But, despite the contradictory evidence, deep in his consciousness he sensed that Lycern was close: he could feel her and the child.

His heart beat a little faster.

They moved stealthily out of the lift into the corridor, and pressed themselves into the dark recess between two vertical buttresses.

'You recognise this place, man?' whispered Bucky, glancing around him. 'You know where we have to go from here?'

Delgado shook his head and peered along the corridor. 'Can't say that I do, Bucky. I always came in by flier. But most of what I saw last time I was here was like this – a little more lively, I'll admit, but much the same.'

'So what do we do now we're here?' asked Girl.

'Exactly what we came here to do: we find Myson.'

'What about your Seriatt friend?'

Delgado glanced up and down the corridor a few more times. 'Your weapons armed?' he said.

'Sure.'

'Of course.'

'Right. Follow me and keep your mouths shut.' Delgado stepped out of the shadows and began to stride confidently along the corridor.

It was longer than it had at first appeared, and the window at the far end – comprised of many triangular panes joined by thick bands of metal – was much larger and further away. At frequent intervals the corridor was intersected by other, smaller corridors; these seemed even darker than the main thoroughfare. The three intruders paused at each junction, but were confronted by no one; the place appeared to be deserted.

As they approached the window and the corridor running past it, Delgado heard a noise. He waved Bucky and Girl back against the wall and they pressed themselves into wedges of darkness, waiting silently. The sounds became more distinct moment by moment, until two nymphs walked past the window. They were chattering to each other in the strange, delicate tongue their kind used among themselves. The glare from the huge window distorted their fragile forms, their bodies looking grossly swollen, their flesh diffused by the harsh abrasive light, all definition lost. Delgado watched them laughing and playing together as they passed. He tried hard to lock onto the emotions or moods of either creature, but was unsuccessful. He was uncertain whether he was focusing incorrectly or whether they were simply unreachable.

When the two nymphs had disappeared, he turned to Bucky and Girl. 'Myson's chamber must be that way,' he whispered, indicating the direction the nymphs had taken with the barrel of his gun.

'What makes you so sure?'

'They must be going to see him. If they'd already been with him they wouldn't be laughing. Come on. We'll follow them.'

Delgado led them along the corridor, keeping the nymphs in sight but making sure they didn't get too close. They climbed a flight of stairs leading up to a wider, brighter corridor. The wall to one side of this stairway was made of glass and overlooked the city. Delgado walked across and gazed out.

He saw habitats, roadways, the russet expanse of the beginning of the Dead Zone and the grey mountains in the distance. He pressed his face against the glass and looked along the side of the building, spying a couple of small flier platforms and one much larger one a little further along. He turned and looked around him, trying to orient himself. The layout began to clarify in his mind: Myson's chamber was on the highest level, surrounded by corridors on three sides. Then there was another stairway parallel to this one on the opposite side of the building, running into a corresponding corridor. The huge window in Myson's personal chamber was on the fourth side, with his own flier platform attached to that. Delgado pressed his face against the glass again but was unable to see the platform; he simply had to hope the flier was there when they arrived.

He turned to the others. 'We're nearly there,' he said in a whisper. 'Myson's room is up around this corner. This place is considered virtually impregnable so security is lax, but Myson's particularly paranoid and has powerful cyborgs guarding the door to his chamber – so watch your ass, OK?' He looked at each of them for a long moment; they nodded solemnly. Then he turned and continued to climb the stairs.

When he had almost reached the corner, Delgado stopped and listened. He could no longer hear the nymphs laughing: they were probably already in Myson's chamber. He looked back at Bucky and Girl; they were both alert, weapons drawn and primed. Delgado lay on the floor against the wall, then peered very slowly around the corner into the adjoining corridor.

His viewpoint from the floor was oddly disorienting, but the scene was unchanged since his last virtual visit: two Hostility Class cyborgs guarding the door to Myson's suite; patrolling vee-cams. The cyborgs had sensitive scanners, so the three of them would be detected the moment they entered the corridor. It was only because such a small proportion of his body was in the corridor that Delgado had not already been spotted.

The vee-cams would almost certainly be linked to the cyborgs' detection systems, and fitted with some kind of small armament. When the cyborgs became aware of them, so would the vee-cams, and vice versa. When attacked, they would alert every guard between here and Olympus Mons.

Delgado drew back slowly. 'Two Hostility cyborgs and two vee-cams,' he whispered.

Bucky raised his eyebrows and pulled a face. 'That's it? No problem, man.'

'Don't underestimate the power of those cyborgs, Bucky. They're not like anything you've ever seen before, and I hope you don't see their kind again. The systems used by Hostility Class are tremendously advanced, and the nobic evolution they utilise can work *very* quickly. They're not easy to kill. Unless you can maintain a high volume of well-placed hits, they get rebuilt and repaired right before your eyes. It's impressive, but not something you want to have to face in combat if you can help it. The vee-cams will be armed too, but they only usually have small, limited capacity blasters or projectile units due to weight restrictions. They've got a pretty intense sting for their size, though.'

'So what are the tactics?'

'I'll go round to the other end of the corridor, draw their fire. When they respond, you two attack them from behind. Bucky takes the cyborg nearest to this end, while Girl concentrates on the vee-cams. I'll deal with the other cyborg. Remember, Bucky: you need to maintain an almost constant stream of hits. Even when they fall you'll have to keep firing until the body has virtually disintegrated and you've separated enough of the nobic components by a distance sufficient to prevent them reforming.' He looked at Girl. 'Vee-cams move quickly, so don't hang about or they'll catch you in crossfire. But because of the amount of energy regeneration involved, they can't manoeuvre and fire at the same time, so stay low by a wall and keep moving so they have to stay in front of you and need to keep repositioning, then you can pick them off individually. Be calm, take your time, and you should be OK. It's as simple as that. Any questions?'

'Just one,' said Bucky. 'I know we've implied this is death or glory for us, but when the alarm is raised and the place is crawling with cyborgs and vee-cams and God alone knows what else, is there any chance of us getting out alive once we're in there?'

'Myson's got a private flier on permanent stand-by, just in case there's some political crisis and he has to get away quickly. It's on a platform to which only he has access via the rear of the main chamber. We'll use that. Anything else?' Neither of them spoke. 'Right, stay low, keep your eyes on the end of the corridor. When I start firing you two let rip from this end. OK? Good.' Delgado checked his weapon briefly, then began jogging back down the stairs.

Delgado climbed the final few steps up to the corner slowly. He crouched, and very carefully eased his head around the wall. He could just see Bucky at the other end; he was lying on the steps, the side of his head a very slight silhouette against the brightness of the glass wall behind him. The cyborgs were utterly motionless, facing the wall opposite them; the vee-cams were bobbing very slightly in the air. Delgado smiled: he wondered if they had ever seen any combat.

He eased his way back round the corner, stood up and leaned against the wall. He closed his eyes, concentrating hard as he tried to access his weakening hyperconsciousness. Lycern and his son were very close to him now; their presence was stronger than ever.

He opened his eyes and licked his dry lips. He was both

excited and nervous; such emotions were sometimes dangerous in battle, but essential nonetheless. Once he stepped into that corridor they would have just a few minutes to deal with the cyborgs and vee-cams and get into Myson's suite before they were overrun. This would be his final assault, a last battle. But he had a driving force more powerful than at any other time now; he had to see it through.

He checked his weapon again, took several deep breaths, then turned into the corridor.

The cyborgs were turning to face him before he had taken even a single step. The autosighters at their temples flickered as they focused, gauged, assimilated. The plasma orbs on their weapons were already beginning to glow as they began taking strong, assured strides towards him; each footfall was resounding in the otherwise silent corridor.

Delgado raised his weapon at precisely the same moment the cyborgs raised theirs.

The corridor around him sparkled with dancing points of white heat as the vee-cams began to fire a rapid series of multi-burst rounds. Their tiny frames trembled and moved backward through the air with each frantic release of energy, but without the autosighters of their cyborg counterparts, their shots were poorly aimed. Delgado was hit twice in the upper left arm, but the wounds were minor and he continued to walk on with confidence. Girl would take care of the vee-cams; he had to concentrate on the cyborgs.

The first cyborg's shoulder exploded as he opened fire, but it continued to advance almost without pausing. Delgado kept firing, vaguely aware of shadows flickering at the other end of the corridor as Bucky and Girl attacked. Then the entire corridor was cut into brittle slices by the deafening sound and dazzling light of their combined weapons.

In the face of this new assault the vee-cams turned in the air and sped away from Delgado towards the other end of the corridor. He glanced past the cyborgs and saw Girl crouching against the wall, firing rapidly. *Keep moving, keep moving*, he thought.

The two cyborgs marched steadily towards him. The one to the right suddenly staggered forward a few steps, then fell to the ground; there was a large smoking hole in its back, from which protruded jags of shattered ribs, torn lungs exposed beneath.

Delgado continued to fire at the other cyborg. Half of its head was missing; he took several large chunks out of its abdomen. When he glanced across he saw the other cyborg already reforming, the immense wounds Bucky had caused rapidly being repaired. By the time he had taken six more steps the shattered cyborg, although still badly damaged, was back on its feet and heading along the corridor towards Bucky. The warped hole in its atomex backplate was the only indication it had been hit at all.

Delgado continued to fire a steady stream of pulses, but although they seemed to be hitting the cyborg successfully it continued unhindered; he wondered whether the nobic engines they utilised had been improved to the extent that they could repair and rebuild as quickly as their hosts were damaged.

An explosion and an intense flash of white light marked the destruction of one of the vee-cams. The second followed just a moment later, its brittle components scattering across the corridor floor. Delgado was vaguely aware of Girl standing up and making her way back down the corridor; she was limping slightly and had her left hand clutched to her right shoulder.

His target cyborg had taken several more hits to vital areas and was now little more than a walking half-torso: the head had been completely obliterated by some of Delgado's first shots, while the rest had turned the whole left side of the cyborg's body into a bloody tangle of fleshy ribbons. While it continued moving, all co-ordination seemed to have been lost;

it returned fire only occasionally, releasing apparently indiscriminate shots that were way off target, as if the cyborg was aiming by memory and guesswork.

Delgado stopped walking and crouched. He fired several times at the cyborg's legs until they collapsed beneath it. He continued to fire until it was little more than a squirming mass of biotechnical components and remnants of human muscle. Burning intestines spilled from what remained of the lower half of the body as the stubs of its shattered legs tried to continue walking; failing systems stank like rotting meat, merging with the smell of burning flesh.

Delgado stood again and fired ten high-powered, precisely-aimed shots. He stopped only when the cyborg was a smoking red–black carpet spread thickly across the dark floor. One or two areas of its remains squirmed as the biotechs and nobics tried to reform, but the distance was too great for them to cover, and soon they moved no more.

At the other end of the corridor Bucky and Girl continued to fire at the other cyborg. It danced as their shots hit it, the body jumping backwards with each impact. Large chunks flew from the torso and head, shattered pieces of armour exploding from it and sliding across the floor; it could not have long left. Delgado walked forward, released a few rounds, then stopped. He held up his left hand and the others also stopped.

'That's enough,' called Delgado, breathing heavily. 'Come on. Time to move.' He looked at Girl. She had been hit several times and looked pale, sweaty and tired. Her tunic was soaked with blood at the shoulder, but her leg wound seemed less serious. 'You OK?' he asked.

She nodded and glanced down at the dark patches on her tunic and trousers. 'Took a few hits, that's all. Scratches. Nothing I can't handle. Those vee–cams are quick little fuckers, though.'

'You sure you'll be OK?'

'Here, use some of this.' Bucky handed her a small canister of frozone. 'It'll stop the bleeding, speed the healing process.'

'Thanks.' She opened her tunic and sprayed the wound liberally. She glanced along the corridor; many rapid footsteps could be heard. She nodded towards the door. 'Let's get on with it, shall we?'

Delgado stepped up to the retscan panel. 'Alexander Delgado,' he said. 'Commander, Reactionary Forces.' The door remained closed. Had he spoken too quickly? Surely he hadn't been completely deleted from the system already. Had he? 'Come on, come on,' he hissed. He glanced to his right, towards the sound of the approaching footsteps. There was a click and a faint grinding sound, then, agonisingly slowly, the door began to slide open.

They were able to edge sideways into the chamber beyond just as the first discharged plasma shots began crackling along the corridor.

As soon as the door was closed Bucky turned and fired at the corresponding panel on the inside of the suite; with it destroyed, the door was sealed. It would now be extremely difficult for anyone to get in. Or out.

At the centre of the room, bathed in the thin grey light passing through the great domed window at the far end, was Lycern.

She was lying on a wide bed covered in *corniss* fur, surrounded by candles fixed into slender stalks; their faint light was reflected in the marble pillars and floor. Bowls of scented oils warmed by smaller candles were set on low tables, exuding a thin, aromatic smoke. Lycern herself looked pale, and was covered only in a sweat-soaked sheet. The *assissius* glands around her body were throbbing, seeping a thin white fluid which trickled down her sides, matting the fur beneath her. She appeared to be unconscious; her eyelids fluttered as if she were dreaming.

Delgado strode over to her, struggling against the surge of *muscein*, driven by paternal instincts equally alien yet entirely natural. The combination burned like acid. He found it difficult to remain rational or objective. His life had reached its zenith: this was the culmination of all he had been, or ever would be. He leaned over her.

'Lycern. Lycern,' he said gently. Nothing indicated that she was aware of his presence. He looked down at her body, swollen with the child she would soon deliver. It was his child; the life that they had created together. The sight of her parturient body aroused him sexually, and although nothing more than a natural reaction to the affirmation of his status as a man, he felt ashamed by it.

Bucky and Girl walked up behind him; they stood and looked down at Lycern. Girl touched Delgado's hand.

A vague flicker of movement caught Delgado's eye and he looked up. Behind the throne he saw two skulking figures – it was the nymphs they had earlier seen in the corridor.

Delgado walked around the bed and moved towards the two tiny creatures. They reacted immediately to his advance, using Myson's great seat as a protective barrier, edging around it to shield themselves. Delgado stopped, held out a hand. 'I won't hurt you,' he said, trying to keep his trembling voice soft. 'Just tell me how she is. What is her condition?' As he spoke, a series of loud, dull thuds echoed through the room. Delgado looked over his shoulder towards the door and saw it vibrating. He turned back towards the nymphs. 'You have to help me,' he said. 'I won't harm you. Just answer my questions. Please.'

One of the nymphs – the frailest, most delicate creature Delgado had ever encountered – peered around the arm of the great throne. 'Baby coming,' she said, her voice the consistency of angels' breath. 'Birth soon.' She ducked back behind the throne.

Delgado glanced at Bucky, Girl, Lycern; then looked at the flier on the platform outside. Another series of impacts shook the door to the chamber.

'Better hurry up if you want to get out of here, man,' said Bucky as he and Girl ran to opposite sides of the room, taking up defensive positions behind pillars. 'Those guys will be in here pretty soon. We don't have long.'

Lycern moaned and rolled onto her side. Delgado returned to her and touched her face; her skin was burning. Her *assissius* glands were very swollen, throbbing rapidly and secreting a thicker, creamier gel than before. It was like nothing he had ever seen from her. Delgado shouted at the trembling nymphs: 'How long until the birth?' The first creature flinched, glanced towards the door, back to Delgado. 'How long!' he yelled.

The nymph shook her head. Perfect tears began to run down her delicate face. The other nymph also began to cry. 'Baby here soon,' she sobbed. 'General coming to see.' Her words dissolved into choking sobs. Lycern wailed and shuddered. The door jarred violently, and its entire surface began to glow, radiating heat.

Delgado looked at Lycern; she was only minutes away from birth, he knew. This knowledge and all its implications came to him in a white heat. And so it was then that he relaxed completely, every tension in his body suddenly smoothed away. He had no choices now, no decisions to make, no options to consider; it was a relief.

He gently stroked Lycern's hair, then turned and walked purposefully across to Bucky. 'You two go without me,' he ordered. 'She can't be moved and I can't leave her here. Not now.'

'But—'

'She's about to give birth, Bucky. I can't leave her. Take Girl and go.' He turned and waved Girl over to them. 'You two are leaving,' he said to her. 'Take that flier to the Dead Zone or wherever it is you want to go. Escape, get away from the city.'

'But we can bring her,' said Girl, her eyes pleading. 'If you stay you'll be killed. All of you.'

'I might be killed,' said Delgado flatly, staring past Girl at Lycern, 'but Myson won't kill a child he thinks is his own, and he'll need that child's mother if he wants to maintain the relationship he so desperately seeks with Seriatt.' He looked into Girl's eyes and spoke softly. 'My son's about to be born. I have to see that, see the new life emerge, whatever the cost. What else have I got? It's all life is about. There is nothing else.'

Lycern moaned again, the sound deep and guttural. Sweat trickled from her forehead; she rolled onto her back, rested for a moment, then raised her knees, spread her legs wide and released an agonising wail. The door shuddered again; part of it fell into the chamber.

Delgado turned to Bucky. 'Take Girl and go, Bucky. There's nothing you can do here. Save yourselves. Let's call it a damage limitation exercise. Move!'

Bucky glanced around him, at Girl, at the disintegrating door, at the flier on the platform just beyond the thick glass. He looked back to Delgado and shook his head. 'I feel like I should say something poignant,' he said. 'But I can't think of anything. You have to do what you have to do, man.'

'There's nothing to say. Go.'

There was a brief pause, an awkward moment as their lives separated. Girl touched Delgado's hand and looked deep into his eyes. As another large piece fell from the door and part of the wall around it, Bucky grabbed Girl by the arm and dragged her towards the flier platform. They had no time to look back.

Delgado walked over to Lycern and looked at her distended belly. He thought of the child within and wondered what would happen to the boy, what he would become. Where would he go? What principles would he hold? There were a hundred thousand variables, every one of them vital. Since he had learned of the pregnancy they were the things Delgado had wanted to take part in: shaping a human being who, despite the odds, might somehow be able to make a difference. Someone who might do better than him. The knowledge that part of him would live on after his own death, that his genes would be carried on through infinity, was somehow comforting. It was the ultimate goal of every living creature.

He heard a loud, high-pitched whining and looked behind him, Myson's bulky flier was lifting from the platform, rising rapidly on thick columns of dense, dark vapour. The cumbersome craft turned on its axis, and the roar of its engines trembled the glass as it powered away across the city.

The door shuddered and more large pieces fell away. He could see the heads of several cyborgs on the other side, could hear Myson shouting hoarse instructions.

As Delgado calmly checked his weapon the nymphs scurried away to a corner by the huge glass window. He knew that, whatever happened next, his whole life had led to this; every microsecond that he had ever existed was a link in the chain leading to this moment. He could have changed nothing. He was at the cusp of his own existence.

Delgado took several deep breaths and, as if all the prerequisite actions had to be performed, walked across to one of the pillars, crouched behind it, and prepared for his last battle.

Lycern moaned and rolled and clutched at her belly. Pieces of glowing molten metal scattered across the shining glass floor as the door finally gave way and two huge cyborg guards strode into the room. The large and powerful weapons they carried hummed loudly. Multiple autosighters flashed into every dark corner. They walked further into the room, paused briefly, and within half a second both nymphs had been torn apart by a torrent of precisely-aimed plasma, the autosighters guiding several shots before realising no threat was posed. Many of the window's huge panes were turned to hot liquid by the immense heat, and slipped to the floor where they formed tiny transparent globes. A harsh and turbulent wind roared past the new openings, and the nymphs' scant remains were sucked through the window and into the sky beyond.

Delgado was crouching behind one of the marble pillars, watching Lycern intently. At least a dozen nymphs had crowded around her, trying to support her body, holding her hands, encouraging her. Even though her cries were becoming increasingly anguished and frequent, Delgado could sense her inner calm. The child – his son – would soon be born, and his delivery was as natural for her as eating or sleeping, just another facet of her being. Delgado also knew with certainty that the baby was healthy and strong. He knew because Lycern knew; as did the child.

Delgado turned at a noise behind him; with his body shielded by the dense stone pillar, the cyborgs' sighting units had not detected him. With the room apparently safe for their General to enter, they walked up to the window to look out across the city. In the bleak grey sky beyond, Delgado saw a flier silhouetted against gunmetal clouds, rising steeply. The craft looked like the one Bucky and Girl had taken, but he knew they would already be far away. As one of the cyborgs raised an arm to point at the craft, Delgado raised his weapon and fired.

The cyborg fell forward and out through the window. The other was hit less accurately and only stumbled a few steps. Delgado stood, cursing the time it took for his weapon to charge fresh plasma.

The cyborg's nanotech engines quickly repaired the unit sufficiently for it to function; it turned to face him at exactly the same moment the charge light on his weapon became illuminated. Delgado was briefly aware of the speckle of autosighters flashing across his body. The two weapons fired simultaneously.

The cyborg staggered backwards, slipped on the cooled glass marbles and cracked its head against the thin metal edge of the window frame. It immediately tried to stand but seemed unable to balance or co-ordinate itself. It flailed for a few moments, its weapon firing at random, before slipping on more of the tiny glass spheres and crashing through an unbroken part of the window.

Delgado saw none of this. He was lying on the floor, one cheek pressed against the cold marble pillar, the other compressed by his left arm, which was pushed up at an odd angle, so that his elbow was close to his face. The rest of his body was without much tangible sensation. An oddly painless feeling of roughness beneath him suggested that his chest was badly damaged; somewhere deep within he suspected that he was lying on his own shattered, exposed ribs. Each shallow breath was a sheet of pain. Out of the corner of one eye he could see a pool of dark liquid spreading across the smooth floor from beneath him; he was surprised by how warm it was when it touched his face.

His nobics quickly began to fade; reliant on equilibrium in the brain, using its fluid to carry their components, even the most advanced evolutions needed an optimum environment to function properly. Despite his relatively recent acquisition of them, the depth of emptiness Delgado now felt indicated the extent to which he had become reliant upon their existence. It was like losing a limb or sense. His head began to ache intensely, his spinal fluid leaking from him; but although great, this pain was distant, an aside.

Mere seconds passed.

Unable to move, the only normal faculty left to him was his hearing. Across the room, Vourniass Lycern cried out as she was encouraged through the final stages of labour by Myson's attending nymphs. She was close, so close.

The anxiety and tension in Lycern's cries increased, heightening with each new breath. The nymphs fell silent; Myson stopped moving; the whole universe seemed to focus on the Seriattic *conosq* who was about to give birth. The insidious spectres of eternal blackness clawed at Alexander

Delgado, and while their offers were tempting to accept, he resisted, willing himself to remain conscious until he knew there had been a successful beginning.

Distant and clouded, Delgado heard footsteps approaching, the sound of weapons arming, General William Myson barking orders.

Then his child was crying.

Seven

the legacy of antiope

Bucky struggled with the unfamiliar controls of Myson's luxury flier. It had been so long since he had flown any kind of machine that a complex and finely tuned state-of-the-art aircraft such as this was a baptism of fire. He found the lumbering vehicle large and unwieldy, unable as he was to utilise its full autopilot functions or link with its interneural interface. Its containment fields were particularly difficult to focus correctly at low speeds. As if this wasn't enough, Bucky was well aware that although their chances had never been brilliant, if he didn't manage to find greater manoeuvrability soon the probability of being blasted out of the sky by xip fighters was almost total.

Bucky tried to push the flier towards a sub-orbital arc that would – if his calculations were accurate and his piloting skills up to scratch – bring them back down on the other side of the mountains beyond the Dead Zone. There they would be safe in the foothills and forests on the shores of the poisoned ocean.

But even though he was distracted by the difficulties of flying the craft, something else nagged at him too; something indefinable. He glanced at Girl, who was sitting next to him. She was frowning hard, monitoring the status of the containment field generators. The flier dropped suddenly in a pocket of air. Bucky tensed, reacted, adjusted, coaxed the machine upward once again. Out of the corner of his eye he saw that Girl was looking at him.

'You OK?' she said.

He nodded. 'Sure. You think this thing's going to get us out of here?'

'What's wrong, Bucky? I can tell there's something bugging you.'

He looked out of the thick window to his left. 'I've just got this feeling of, you know, like we're abandoning Delgado. What altitude are we at?'

'Twelve thousand five hundred metres. I feel the same – but there was nothing else we could have done, Bucky. He wanted to stay. He *had* to stay. We would've stayed in his position.'

'We shouldn't have left him. What's our speed?'

'Twelve hundred. There was nothing we could do.'

'We didn't try very hard though, did we?'

'So what are you proposing we do about it? Go back and see if we can help him?'

Bucky looked across at Girl, his expression blank but nonetheless revealing.

She was silent for a moment. 'Oh fuck. You're right. Of course you're right. You'd better take us back,' she said resignedly. 'Before it's too late.'

Bucky turned the cumbersome craft as quickly as he could without letting it fall out of the sky, and they headed back towards the city.

As Bucky brought the flier rapidly down, struggling to maintain a balance between speed and manoeuvrability, flashes of brilliant light were visible within Myson's chamber. Bucky increased speed slightly.

As they closed on the building they saw that the huge domed window was shattered, but could make out no detail in the darkness of the room. Girl tried to find some form of enhancement device to enable them to see into the building, but the flier was too complex and its functions too many for her to do so quickly enough.

'What are we going to do?' she asked. 'You think you can control this thing enough to be able to land it back on the platform? That's a pretty small area – and you're not much of a pilot.'

'True, but it's our only chance,' Bucky said. He glanced between the actual view through the viewport in front of him and the highflyer display in the central console. 'If I can get below and approach from beneath, this thing'll shed speed naturally. Once we've landed we get out quick and rush in, all guns blazing.'

'We haven't got that many guns to blaze, Bucky.'

'We've got to give it a shot.'

'I know, I know. Shit. I wish Clunk was here.'

'And Lox. And Headman.'

Bucky coaxed the unwilling flier to sink below the level of Myson's landing platform, keeping as close to the building itself as he dared. He was surprised to hear the raucous, irregular wail of the aircraft's engines echoing back at them off the building, a huge, grey cliff-face adorned with glossy square windows. One slip, one lapse in concentration, and they would be spread thinly across its grimy surface. He closed his sweating hands tightly around the controls, easing the vessel up towards the platform. Speed and angle seemed exactly right. Although he did not feel happy, Bucky smiled.

Just then, an updraught of warm air emitted by some or other discharge pipe at a lower level suddenly caused the craft's speed to increase dramatically; the vehicle became more feisty, resistant to his will, and he was forced to pull away from the side of the building. The vessel rose sharply, passing the shattered window and platform at considerable speed. Bucky briefly glanced down; two large cyborgs were standing in the window looking out across the city. One of them looked directly at the flier and raised an arm, pointing.

Bucky looked away, adjusted his grip on the controls and

shouted at Girl to release the fields to their widest spread; the flier slowed and became noticeably quieter as she complied. Bucky turned as sharply as he dared.

The flier almost stalled but he managed to bring it around, and aimed it at the landing platform that had drifted into view from the top right corner of the viewport. The cyborgs seemed to have disappeared.

But the craft's speed was too great, its angle of descent too steep for a successful landing despite Bucky's efforts, and a few moments later the flier smacked hard against the platform.

It bounced once, then slid along the broad surface of the landing platform in an explosion of orange sparks. The vehicle turned slightly as it skidded along, then crashed through the already shattered window to become embedded deep in the room amid a landslide of debris and dust.

It was a couple of minutes before they came to. Bucky was the first to look out through the viewport. At first he was met with darkness, but as his eyes adjusted, through the dust he recognised Myson's chamber.

It bore no resemblance to the suite they had visited only a little while before. Many of the pillars had been demolished and several large areas of the ornate ceiling had collapsed. A few bodies were visible – part of them, at least – crushed and broken beneath large chunks of rubble.

'How's it look?' asked Girl wearily as she began to stir.

'Not good. I think we've fucked up big time. Come on.'

They disembarked and picked their way among the debris. The air was thick and gritty; fragments of glass and masonry crunched and crumbled underfoot. It was devastation, carnage.

As they carefully explored what remained of the chamber, Girl saw Delgado lying next to one of the few pillars that remained standing; at first glance he looked uninjured. As she knelt next to him she called to Bucky.

'We were too late, anyway,' he was saying a few moments

later. 'He was shot up pretty bad. Probably dead before we crashed in.'

Girl stood and looked around the room, hastily wiping a tunic cuff across her eyes. 'What about Myson? Or the Seriatt?'

Bucky shook his head, exhaled, coughed briefly in the dust. 'In here? I don't know. Let's have a quick look around.'

They climbed over the rubble, wary of nobics discreetly reforming cyborgs in dark corners.

They found Lycern lying on the floor next to the bed. Much of her head had been crushed by a large piece of fallen masonry; another piece rested across her naked, broken legs; blood-stained *corniss* fur was draped across her abdomen.

'We killed her,' said Girl, horrified. 'We came here to help her and we killed her. Oh my God, Bucky. What have we done?'

'We didn't kill her,' said Bucky. 'Look at her chest, her abdomen. Those burns are from a HiMag. They let her give birth then they killed her. Simple.' Girl closed her eyes, unwilling to allow herself to believe it. Bucky placed a hand on her shoulder. 'Come on. We shouldn't be shocked or surprised. We're dealing with Myson here, remember? He'd got his insurance, his guarantee that Earth and Seriatt would not go to war. That was all he wanted in the end.'

'But where's the child?'

'Probably taken away by Myson before we returned. God alone knows where it is now. We can't help it, wherever it is. All we can do is pity it.'

They looked down at Lycern's body for a few more moments. The heavy pendant she wore lay next to her ear, the chain lying limply across her shoulder. Girl reached down and gently unfastened and removed it.

'For Alex,' she said softly, and placed it in one of her pockets. Bucky then reached down and covered Lycern's head with the cloth in which she had been draped: it seemed the right thing to do, however inadequate.

Bucky turned and looked back at the flier; it seemed fairly

intact. 'Come on,' he said. 'We'd better see if we can get out of here. We might be able to pull that bird free with the fields if we're careful. Xips'll be here soon. Guards. Whole loads of shit. Let's go.'

They walked quickly back towards the craft. As they did so a slight movement caught Bucky's eye; he spun around, drawing and priming his blaster. The movement came from beneath a broad, fallen ceiling panel which was resting against one of the pillars. Bucky stared; Girl turned and gasped. Lying in the grit and the dust, protected from the devastation by the rigid triangle that had formed around it, was the baby.

They rushed to the child. Girl scooped him up in her arms and instinctively opened her tunic to place the cold, shocked infant next to her warm chest. The child opened his eyes briefly, then closed them again. He was perfect in every detail: his tongue, his lips, his eyes, the tiny nails of his fingers. Despite the odd, Seriattic aspect evident in his features, they both saw Alexander Delgado in the baby's tiny face.

'My God, Bucky,' breathed Girl. 'What does this mean?'

'I don't know. I guess Myson must be under this lot somewhere after all. Come on.' He looked at the child again. 'We have to leave now if we're going to save him. And we have to save him. We owe it to Delgado.'

Girl pulled Lycern's pendant from her pocket and placed it carefully around the child's neck. 'There,' she said. 'Now it is right.'

Bucky and Girl looked into each other's eyes for a moment then, and were joined by bonds stronger than any they had previously encountered. Perhaps this was also their beginning.

As they ran towards the flier with the child, the sound of approaching voices echoing behind them, both knew that their greatest challenge was yet to come.

The Planetary Council was called to emergency session. Assembled in the conference chamber, the ranks of dignitaries in the tiers of their miniature amphitheatre complained about the lack of consideration demonstrated by General Myson in calling them together at such an hour. While some had managed to put on their ceremonial garments, others had steadfastly refused in protest, remaining in their bed robes. Councillor Matheson, who was particularly annoyed at being dragged from his suite and notorious for his reluctance to comply with accepted Council conduct, had insisted on bringing his companion to the chamber with him. She was a voluptuous girl of no more than twenty years, who sat on his knee throughout the proceedings; her vitreous gown made it clear to all why he had been unwilling to leave her behind.

The Council sat waiting, increasingly frustrated in the cosseted confines of their ceremonial chamber. The heat of the room was intense, and their discontented murmurings were constant and many. Only when General William Myson entered the room did silence finally descend.

As he made his way into the chamber, Myson's face was endowed with a smile broader and more genuine than any of the councillors had ever seen. Behind him were four nymphs. In a break from normal custom, Myson did not position his chair behind the table at the head of the chamber, but instead moved it into the centre of the room. The wooden floor creaked as the heavy throne moved forward, its tiny containment field generators buzzing loudly, until Myson stopped in the semi-circle formed by the councillors. He gazed at the aged men who surrounded him, his eyes bright, his face glowing.

'Gentlemen, you are no doubt wondering why you have been summoned to this chamber at such an unusual hour,' he said. 'The reason is simple: I could not wait until morning to deliver the wonderful news to you.' Heads turned, questioning eyebrows raised. Myson looked back towards the chamber entrance and beckoned. A nymph clutching a small parcel of cloth moved shyly forward. She carefully handed the bundle to Myson before scurrying away.

He gazed down, his elation clear. Slowly, carefully, he turned the parcel around and tipped it up for those before him to see. The face of the sleeping newborn child was wrinkled, a rich pink in colour. The baby's eyes were tightly shut, its lips perfect lines, its hair a dark blur just visible beneath the cloth that wrapped it. The councillors in the chamber looked down upon the infant with eyes made dispassionate by years of cynicism. While all uttered noises of approval and congratulation, only one or two felt genuinely moved.

Myson raised a fat, swollen hand to quiet the gathered number. 'Gentlemen,' he said when silence had returned, 'it is my great pleasure to present you with my son, Michael, Structure's future Commander Supreme and *Monosiell* of Seriatt.' There were more murmurs of congratulation, a brief ripple of politically motivated applause.

And on the opposite side of the building, use of brute force extricated a damaged flier from the rubble of a demolished chamber. Once free, the machine turned rapidly, its engines belching plumes of black vapour as it climbed above the city, the three occupants seeking refuge near the shores of the poisoned sea.